The Mist and the Darkness

Charles S. Viar

CFIS PRESS
WASHINGTON, DC

This is a work of fiction. Most of the characters and events are fictitious, although some historical figures appear under their own names. All rights reserved.

Cover Art by: Gary Bloom
Copyright © 2014 Charles S. Viar

ISBN-13: 978-1502889416

ISBN-10: 1502889412

CFIS PRESS
WASHINGTON, DC

All rights reserved.

Dedicated to my daughter, Anastasia.

ACKNOWLEDGEMENTS

This book dates to 2008, when I had the pleasure of watching the film version of Stephanie Meyers' *Twilight*. Although far outside the target demographic, I've been a sucker for Vampire stories for as long as I can remember. So when I found myself at Union Station early one afternoon with my tasks for the day complete, I couldn't resist temptation when I walked past the theater then located in the lower level. After pausing to eye the display posters, I bought a ticket and went in.

Twilight had caused a sensation when it was published, attracting legions of fans – and not just teen aged girls. As I learned from the almost incessant media coverage, adolescent boys and even adults of both genders raved about the story. For that reason, I was both curious and hopeful as I took my seat in the darkened theater.

I wasn't disappointed. The director, Catherine Hardwick, had done a brilliant job of turning a supernatural teen romance into a film that was interesting, entertaining, and at times gripping. Although put off by Bella and unimpressed by Edward, I enjoyed it nonetheless. For me, at least, the outstanding performances of Rachelle Lefevre, as the shamelessly wicked Victoria, Ashley M. Greene as the delightful Alice, and the deadpan humor of Billy Burke as Chief Swan made the film worthwhile.

But after leaving the theater, I began wondering how the story might have played out if the central roles had been reversed. Instead of the lovesick Bella pursuing the remote and conflicted Edward, I wondered what might have happened if a hormone-driven 17-year-old male had deduced the secret of a gorgeous female Vampire under similar circumstances, and pursued her with all the enthusiasm – and dubious intentions – of a typical adolescent male.

After trying and failing to imagine myself in that position, I concluded that scenario was even more implausible than the one depicted in *Twilight*. First of all, the aspiring Casanova would have to have a working knowledge of Vampires, and Vampirism, and the ability to pick them out of a crowd. Not likely…

Second, he would have to be enormously confident and capable. Let's face it – trying to make time with a creature who could rip your throat out takes nerve. Lots of nerve…

Third, he'd have to be either bored with or disinterested in the young women who would populate his school. That implied a great deal more life experience than your average 17-year old male.

And finally, he'd have to have a solid grasp on tactics and strategy, and be a bit of a schemer. Let's face it – seducing a Vampire without getting killed in the process would be no easy feat. It would take a great deal of cunning and calculation to pull *that* off…

As I puzzled over the problem, the character of Andre Marchand slowly emerged from the mists of my mind. Born in France to a French father and an American mother, I imagined Andre to have grown up in two overlapping worlds, comfortable with the ambiguity of being both a stranger in, and an accepted member of, the society into which he had been born. Orphaned just before his 14th birthday, he'd become independent at an early age. And his restless sense of adventure – and a propensity for taking risks – encouraged him to strike out on his own, by running away from his court-appointed guardian and enlisting in the Foreign Legion with a fake ID.

During the twenty-six months that elapsed between his under-aged enlistment and eventual discovery, I imagined that Andre would have acquired an arsenal of deadly skills, a wealth of experience and – a bit later – a decidedly dim view of Vampires. That he would find himself attracted to one is ironic, but altogether in keeping with his free spirit.

A good kid, I thought. *But at 17, he's a loose cannon…*

Although experienced beyond his years, the wisdom that sometimes comes from worldly exposure had yet to catch up with him. Thus his inability to resist a challenge, and his fantastical scheme to seduce Elspeth McGuire. But despite Andre's habit of creating light-hearted chaos everywhere he goes, I couldn't help but like him. So with that settled, my mind turned to the object of his desire.

In *Twilight,* perfect and undying love were the norm, whether it be between Dr. Cullen and his wife, Esme; Alice and Jasper; Rosalie and Emmett; or, eventually, Bella and Edward. But having been around the romance block once or twice, that didn't strike me as especially common. If Vampires could love, it seemed to me that they would love in much the same way as humans – which meant rather haphazardly. Some might build an enduring romance, others would drift in and out of relationships, while others might spend decades or even centuries searching for "the one."

Since Vampires are relatively few and far between in the world that emerged from my mind, it seemed to me that more than a few Vampires would find the search for romantic fulfillment frustrating and littered with disappointments. It also seemed to me that a romantic attraction to humans would be inevitable – at least for those Vampires that chose to live otherwise ordinary lives – while at the same time posing special challenges, wrenching choices, and unimaginable heartbreak.

How a "civilized" Vampire coped with that dilemma, I thought, would shape their lives in important ways. As I pondered the problem, Elspeth McGuire gradually emerged. Elspeth is beautiful, playful, kind, and loving – and deeply frustrated. She longs for the deep and enduring love celebrated in *Twilight* and shared by her adoptive parents, but has yet to find it in her 70-some-odd years.

Enter Andre Marchand. Immediately attracted to him on the first day of school, she finds herself in a quandary. He's smart, handsome, charming, and playful – and a bit of a tease. He's popular with the athletes and the social aristocracy and unlike the other students, he's nice to her – he even flirts with her, sometimes, or at least she imagines he does.

He's also maddeningly enigmatic. In the fictional world taking form in my mind, humans harbor a deep, subconscious fear of the Vampires that pass amongst them, which reveals itself through the pheromones they unwittingly excrete. But Andre is different – the scent of fear is entirely absent with him, and Elspeth wonders why. And she wonders if, somehow, he's uncovered her secret…

For Andre, Elspeth is a challenge; for Elspeth, Andre is a mystery. The story that follows is this story of how this unlikely pair eventually get together.

I can't speak for other writers, but for me, at least, fictional characters emerge in response to specific problems. When I first conceive of a book, I start with the concluding scene and then begin asking myself questions: What would have had to have happened for the story to reach this point? What kind of character would find himself – or herself – in this sort of situation? What sort of setting would make it possible, or at least imaginable? How would they react? And who else would have done what to make the story turn out as it did?

It was through this process that the story and the other major characters took shape: Dr. McGuire and his wife, Elizabeth; Elspeth's adoptive siblings, Nathan, Daniel, and Lydia; Andre's uncle, Dr. Marchand; and of course, the bemused Headmaster Renfrowe.

When I first began writing this story, I wasn't sure if I would ever publish it. I wrote it more for my own amusement than anything else, and because of its rather whimsical nature, I thought I would probably print it out when finished and keep it for myself. But after the manuscript was read by several friends and enthusiastically endorsed, I decided to go ahead and share it with the interested public.

I would also like to take this opportunity to apologize to any readers offended by the occasional profanity found in the pages that follow. In a better world, perhaps people wouldn't swear. But human nature being what it is, they do – and I reluctantly concluded that any effort to sugarcoat that fact would detract from the story.

In closing, I would like to thank Stephanie Meyers for the story that inspired me to write *The Mist and the Darkness*; my friend Dietra Knight for reading and commenting on the draft manuscript, and for helping me with the proofreading. I'd also like to thank my sister, Jane, for reading and commenting on the draft despite her aversion to the supernatural.

I'd also like to thank you for picking up this book. I hope you enjoy reading it as much as I enjoyed writing it.

Charles S. Viar
Washington, DC
2014

The Mist and the Darkness

Charles S. Viar

INTRODUCTION

A French Foreign Legion Outpost,
Surobi District Afghanistan

After popping off three quick rounds, Corporal Andre d'Arton of the French Foreign Legion ducked behind the sandbagged wall and waited for the inevitable return fire. After a round slammed into the protective barrier, d'Arton began crawling along it. He'd moved three feet to the right last time; this time he decided to shift his position by eight feet to the left.

He was halfway to his destination when a heavy machine gun opened up behind him, providing cover fire for Sergeant Beauchene. A moment later, the sergeant dove behind the sandbags. Then after pushing himself up onto one knee, he cradled his rifle and looked over at d'Arton. "What the hell are you doing, Corporal?"

D'Arton looked over at him and grinned. "Keeping Jerkoff-Jamal busy until the airstrike gets here, Sergeant."

Puzzled, the sergeant asked him who'd called for air support. D'Arton grinned a second time, and said "Colonel Rochelle, Sergeant."

Sergeant Beauchene sighed and shook his head. "If Capitaine Marcell finds out your Evil Twin's been calling in airstrikes again, he's going to have your hide!"

D'Arton snickered. "So what's he going to do? Send me to some shithole in Afghanistan?" Then he popped up and fired on full automatic before ducking back behind the barrier.

A half-second later, another round of return fire slammed into the sandbags. This time, Sergeant Beauchene jumped up and fired a burst. After ducking back down, he told d'Arton that it seemed like the sniper was out to get him. "So what'd you do to Jamal? Have sex with his camel?"

D'Arton grinned, shook his head, and huffed. "Now that's a vicious rumor, Sergeant! It was his goat, if you must know..."

The Mist & the Darkness

Then after cocking his head to listen, d'Arton pointed through the barrier in the direction of the approaching high-pitched roar. "Here come the jets!" Then after turning and leaning back against the wall, he set his rifle aside and fished in his pocket for a battered pack of cigarettes. After shaking one free, he stuck the filtered end in his mouth and searched through his other pocket for his lighter. He'd just lit it when four 250-kilogram bombs exploded 300 meters beyond the perimeter. After the shockwave rolled over them, d'Arton peeked over the sandbags and chuckled, before turning to his sergeant. "Looks like Jamal just got his 72 virgins."

Glancing over the sandbags, Beauchene chortled. "With his luck, they'll be fat and ugly." Then he ordered d'Arton to report to the command bunker. "Capitaine Marcell wants to see you."

After swearing, d'Arton looked over at the sergeant. *"Now what???"*

Beauchene shrugged. "He didn't say, but you'd better get a move on."

D'Arton nodded, and lifted his weapon before taking off at a half-crouch. The jets may have sent Jerkoff-Jamal to the Promised Land, but his cousins were still out there…

D'Arton was halfway to the command bunker when he heard the hollow *Thunk!* of a mortar, then two more in quick succession. After glancing over his shoulder to see three shells arcing over the sandbagged perimeter, he sprinted for the nearest slit trench. The first shell landed ten feet from his shelter, the other two just beyond. *That better not be Jamal's wife*, d'Arton growled, as dirt and sand rained down upon him. *Because I just did her a favor…*

After waiting a minute or so to see if any more shells were coming his way, d'Arton hopped out of the trench, and trotted the remaining 20 meters to the command post. After slinging his weapon over his shoulder, he pushed through the opening and marched up to the folding table that served as the Capitaine's desk. Stopping three feet short, d'Arton came to attention and saluted. "Corporal d'Arton, reporting as ordered, Sir!"

The Capitaine looked up and returned his salute, but didn't tell d'Arton to stand at ease. He was in trouble again.

"So what's with the mortars, d'Arton?"

Still standing at attention, the corporal replied. "Retaliatory fire, Sir. A couple of jets took out that sniper who's been harassing us – and that apparently upset some of his friends."

The Capitaine leaned back in his chair, and gave the corporal an irritated look. "And I suppose those were the jets called in by a certain 'Colonel Rochelle'?"

With his back straight and shoulders squared, and his eyes fixed on the back wall of the bunker, d'Arton faked an innocent look and said he wouldn't know. "I'm just a corporal, Sir – no one ever tells me anything."

After glaring at him for a long moment, the Capitaine said "Uh, huh." Then he leaned forward and picked a sheet of paper up off the table. After glancing at it to get the name right, he looked up at d'Arton again. "So I don't suppose you'd know anything about a 16-year-old 'adventurer' by the name of Andre Marchand…"

Oh shit! thought the corporal. *Now I'm screwed…*

CHAPTER 1

After checking the rearview mirror, Dr. Neill McGuire slowed the Jeep Grand Cherokee and turned on the right flasher. Still slowing as he passed the sign welcoming visitors to Sanctuary Cove, he turned right onto the asphalt lane that led to the home he'd built for his family. Set a half-mile back from the county road that ran along the shoreline on four hundred acres of unspoiled wilderness, the six-bedroom Tudor had been built to specification. Although it had every modern amenity, it looked as though it had stood there for centuries. With the steeply pitched roof, the decorative half-timbering, the crossed gables, small windows and the half-dozen chimneys, it reminded him of the grand country estates he had admired in England so many centuries before.

After bearing to the right around the circular drive, he brought the vehicle to a halt some twenty feet from the main entry. As he turned off the engine, he looked over at his wife beside him and smiled. "Home again, my love."

Smiling back, Elizabeth McGuire unfastened her seatbelt before leaning over to kiss him. "Thank you, Neill…

"It was a wonderful vacation."

And it had been – three weeks hunting and camping in the Canadian wilderness, followed by a week in Montreal for a medical convention. While Neill had been absorbed in lectures and symposiums, she and the children had dodged the late afternoon sun to shop, take in movies and sightsee. The evenings had been filled with plays, operas, and concerts – the very best that Montreal had to offer.

Pleased by her lingering kiss, Dr. McGuire smiled before kissing her forehead. Then after withdrawing the keys from the ignition, he clambered out and walked around to the rear of the vehicle to wait for the kids. Although it was difficult to see through the heavily tinted glass of their Land Rover, the kids were apparently engaged in yet another argument. It was a minute or so before Daniel cut the

The Mist & the Darkness

engine and opened the door. As he climbed out, followed by his adoptive brother and two sisters, Neill called for their attention.

"OK, listen up gang!

"Let's get the gear unloaded and put away in the storage shed, and the bags up to their respective rooms…

"Family meeting in 15 minutes, so bring your books and your notes with you."

Suppressing a smile, he ignored their groans and opened up the back of his Grand Cherokee. Mindful of the early morning sun, he pulled Elizabeth's bags from the storage compartment and set them on the asphalt before retrieving his own. Suddenly aware of his wife's presence, he turned and smiled. "Let's leave the heavy lifting for the chain gang over there."

Nodding, she put her free arm around his waist and accompanied him to the waiting double doors.

After finding the right key, Dr. McGuire opened the one on the right ceremoniously. "After you, Madame."

Recoiling from the stale air that greeted them, Elizabeth waved her hand across her face and grimaced. "Dear God, this place smells like a crypt!"

"Why don't you open up the windows, while I make some coffee?"

After grimacing again, Mrs. McGuire nodded and made a run for the closest window.

After spending the past five centuries treating the sick, the injured, and the wounded, Dr. McGuire had become inured to even the most malodorous of structures, but he appreciated her discomfort nonetheless. An acute sense of smell was part of the price they paid for their indefinite existence.

After running the water in the kitchen for two or three minutes to clear the lines, he filled the decanter with water and poured it into the top of the coffee maker. Then after lining the basket with a paper filter, he measured eight scoops of ground coffee and deposited them one by one before snapping the unit shut. There was no cream in the refrigerator, of course, but he rarely used it anyway. Although he could tolerate fairly large amounts of fresh-brewed coffee, the fat content in cream made it problematical. On a good day, he could handle small amounts.

Leaning against the kitchen counter as the coffee brewed, he could hear the kids bickering as they hauled the bags upstairs. Daniel had apparently offended Elspeth again, and the kids had taken sides. Nathan was standing above the fray, aloof and disinterested as usual, but Lydia – rather surprisingly – was supporting Elle.

After the machine chimed, Dr. McGuire gathered an overlarge mug and a coaster from the cupboard, and retrieved the sugar from the refrigerator, where Elizabeth had put it before they'd left on vacation. It was summertime, and she had no intention of inviting unwanted insects into her house.

After stirring a half-teaspoon into his mug, Dr. McGuire carried it and the coaster into the dining room, which had been modeled on one of the Great Halls characteristic of Late Mediaeval architecture in England. After setting the coaster on the twelve-foot oaken table, and his mug on the coaster, he took his seat at the head and waited. Upstairs, he could hear his wife rounding up the kids.

After they tromped down the stairs that ended in the foyer, he waited expectantly as they filed in one by one. Sitting down in no particular order, they placed their books and their notepads on the table. Apparently, none of them wanted any coffee.

After Mrs. McGuire sat down adjacent to him, he asked if everyone was ready.

After they all nodded, Dr. McGuire suggested that Elizabeth begin.

Agreeing, she opened her notebook and glanced over a couple of pages before clearing her throat. "To be entirely honest, I was shocked – horrified might be a better word – when Elle came back to the hotel with *Twilight*...

"My first reaction was the writer – this Stephenie Meyer – had written about us." Then after pausing a moment to glance around, she continued. "But after reading it, it seems to me that the similarities between the Cullen family she presents and ourselves are superficial at best..."

Then after glancing down at her notes again, she pulled the ink pen she'd lodged in the spiral binding and clicked it. Placing it against the paper in front of her, she suggested they start with the similarities.

"To start with, the Cullens are a Vampire family living in a small town with the shore to one side and dense woods to another…"

"And as with our own family, the father is a medical doctor."

Then shifting in her seat, Mrs. McGuire noted the Cullens were also civilized. "And like us, they don't feed upon humans…"

"But at that point, the similarities break down and the differences emerge. The Cullens are on the West Coast and we're on the shore of Lake Champlain in Vermont…"

"Mrs. Cullen is a homemaker, and I'm an artist…"

"And the Cullen family has five adopted teens – three boys and two girls – where as we have two of each…"

"And an Indian tribe figures prominently in Mrs. Meyer's story, while the only Native American anywhere near us is Professor Greywolf out on South Point."

Then after clearing her throat again, Mrs. McGuire put down her pen and looked suddenly perplexed. "Excuse me for a moment," she said. "I think I'd like some coffee after all."

Returning to the table a minute or two later with a smaller sized cup, she resumed her seat.

"Now where was I…

"Ah, yes – the differences…"

"The physical descriptions diverge as well. Dr. Cullen is described as being 23 years of age, physically, and tall and thin and muscular, while Neil is 34 in human terms and stands six feet tall – which is not really unusual in this era – and is rather more powerfully built. Moreover, he has sandy hair and green eyes while Dr. Cullen has blonde hair and what she describes as golden eyes…"

"His wife Esme is described as having caramel-colored hair, slender, and having a heart shaped face with dimples. Her physical age is given as 26, and her eyes are golden as well – that apparently being a characteristic of Vampires in her story. In contrast, I'm five foot six inches, a bit more curvy I think, and have red hair and blue eyes."

Then after brushing a wayward strand of hair from her face, she grinned. "And I'm not even *close* to 26!"

As the boys snickered, Lydia laughed and challenged her. "Yeah right, Mom…

"And you're a big liar too!"

Mrs. McGuire grinned and denied it, before continuing. "And then Dr. Cullen was supposedly a Vampire hunter in 17th Century England, who was bitten in a chase – while your father was a 16th Century Scottish Magister who deliberately infected himself as part of a medical experiment…"

At which point Elspeth balled her hand into a fist and thrust it into the air.

"Yea, Dad!" she exclaimed. *"Way to go!"*

Chuckling, Elizabeth slipped her hand over her husband's. "Don't listen to her, Neill…

"Scientific curiosity is incredibly sexy…"

The two boys groaned, and Lydia rolled her eyes. "Get a room, for God's sake!"

As Mrs. McGuire gave her a withering look, Dr. McGuire looked down at the table. Then after a moment he looked up with a sheepish grin. "OK, so that wasn't the best idea I've ever had."

After smiling at her husband, Mrs. McGuire continued. "As with your Father and myself, the descriptions of the Cullen children and their histories are off as well.…

"She describes one daughter – Alice – as being tiny with short black hair and graceful as a ballerina…

"And the other as tall, statuesque, with wavy blonde hair, and writes that she's 'the most beautiful person in the world'…"

"True," Daniel interjected. "But Elle's every bit as whacked as that 'Alice' chick."

As Lydia giggled and Nathan chuckled, Dr. McGuire gave them a remonstrative look. "Don't make fun of your sister."

Ignoring her father's defense, Elle pointed across the table and gave Daniel an evil glare. "Just wait," she threatened.

After a stern look from her adoptive mother, she sat back in her chair and huffed. "He started it!"

Then after a long moment of silence, Mrs. McGuire cleared her throat again. "Finally, the author's depiction of Vampires is, uh…

"Rather unusual, shall we say."

Leaning forward, Lydia interjected. "Yeah, what's with that marble stuff?"

Where upon Elle thrust her arm out over the table, for all to see. "And that whole sparkly thing…

"Does this look sparkly to you?"

Before anyone had a chance to answer, Nathan spoke for the first time. "And the super human strength and speed…

"We've got an edge, certainly, but it's only fifteen or twenty per cent, and that's on a good day – many a Vampire has been killed by humans."

Dr. McGuire nodded. "Point well taken, Nathan…

"We have an edge, as you put it, in strength and speed, and also in the acuity of our senses. Our instincts and our intuition are generally superior, our wounds heal much faster, we don't scar, and we're unaffected by human diseases…

"But as you've just pointed out, we're far from invulnerable….

"Aside from the traditional methods of dispatching us – sustained sunlight, decapitation by sword or axe, fire, a wooden stake through the heart or drowning in Holy Water – we're vulnerable to many modern weapons as well. Bullets won't kill us, of course, but a couple of shots in the chest will lay us out flat for hours."

Nodding, Nathan agreed. "I took out a Vamp with a rifled musket in '81" – by which he meant 1781, near the close of the American Revolution.

"Yeah, but that didn't kill him – you still had to cut his head off," said Daniel in rebuttal.

Nodding matter-of-factly, Nathan explained it was more a matter of severing his spinal cord. "There wasn't enough left of his head to axe."

Shivering involuntarily, Mrs. McGuire informed the boys that was a great deal more detail than needed. Nodding in agreement, Dr. McGuire asked if anyone else had something to add.

Sticking up her hand, Elle said she really liked the story. "And 'Edward' is hot!"

Grinning, Lydia agreed. "But he's got some issues…

"That control thing of his is like, *way* over the top."

Smiling indulgently at the girls, Mrs. McGuire spoke again. "I think your Father had more pertinent things in mind."

Shifting in his seat, Daniel raised a finger. "I think someone ratted us out."

Nathan shook his head dismissively. "Nah, it's more like a second or third-hand story the author picked up somewhere along the way…

"Someone that knows us – or more likely, someone that knows *of* us – let a vague reference slip, and she turned it into a tale…

"And a rather good one, by the way."

Glancing over at his eldest son – Nathan being a month older than his brother, in human terms – Dr. McGuire nodded. "I'm inclined to agree…

"But just to make sure, I called our attorneys and they're going to have their private investigator run a background check on Mrs. Meyers…

"I don't really expect them to come up with anything, but I think due caution is in order."

Elspeth nodded, and tapped on the book in front of her. "Every girl in school has probably read this by now, so I think we should keep a low profile."

Lydia rolled her eyes, sighed, and shook her head. Then she pointed at the book in front of her. *"News flash!*

"This has been out for *years*…"

Looking rather embarrassed, Elspeth pursed her lips together. *"Oh*…

"So how come we hadn't heard about it?"

"Well, let's see," Daniel said rhetorically. "Because we've been living out in the sticks?"

Embarrassed, Elspeth pursed her lips together again and looked down at the table. "Well I still think we should keep a low profile."

By now sarcastic, Daniel asked her just exactly how low a profile she had in mind. "I can't even remember the last time someone said 'hi' to me in the hallway…

After looking down at the table, Elspeth pursed her lips sadly. "You're lucky," she said softly. "They're mean to me…"

CHAPTER 2

Mrs. McGuire looked at her youngest daughter sadly.

Life for civilized Vampires was hard, especially for the young. They couldn't stay in one place for any length of time – because people would notice they weren't aging – and they had to assume new identities and establish new credentials at regular intervals. That wasn't especially difficult for artists such as herself, or those that made their living as skilled craftsmen, but it had become increasingly hard for professionals such as her husband, and even harder for the kids. Dr. McGuire could still cycle through medical school every twenty-five years or so, but it was an entirely different story for them. The shelf life of their identities was no more than fifteen years at most, so they were forced to cycle through high schools and colleges at much shorter intervals.

It was difficult psychologically as well, because emotional maturation slowed to a glacial pace when one became a Vampire, and the children had to calibrate their behavior and alter their appearance to conform to their assumed ages. Isolation was another problem – forming bonds with humans was problematical at best, and generally heartbreaking, so they had little social interaction. Aside from their necessarily superficial interactions with the people around them, and the rare visits to or from other civilized Vampires scattered across North America, they had only themselves.

It was even harder for Elspeth, she knew. Elle was different – she could be quiet and shy at times, and some people thought her off-beat sense of humor made her a bit odd. But once you got to know her, she was a joy to be around.

If only they'd give her a chance, Mrs. McGuire thought sadly.

Convinced that the stress the children endured accounted for their bickering and occasionally irritating behavior, Mrs. McGuire tried to make up for the poverty of their social lives with an abundance of love. By then lost deep in thought, she was startled by her husband's voice.

"I think we've pretty much covered everything we need to, so unless someone has something else to add I'm going to call for an adjournment...

"Anyone?"

After a moment of silence, Dr. McGuire nodded. "All right, then, we're agreed the book poses no immediate danger. So let's continue on as before, keeping a low profile so as not to attract any unwanted attention...

"Everyone agreed?"

As his family nodded, Dr. McGuire stood up. "I'm going to run down to the clinic, and see how Dr. Sanders has been holding up without me...

"In the meantime, gang, school starts tomorrow – so make sure you're prepared for class."

As the kids groaned, he bent over to kiss his wife. Then after promising to be back in a couple of hours, he picked up his mug and his coaster, and carried them into the kitchen.

After depositing them in the sink, he exited through the kitchen door and stepped out on the flagstone path that led around the house. After glancing around to make sure the groundskeeper had taken good care of the four acres of clearing that passed for a backyard, he visually inspected the greenhouse and Elizabeth's studio that stood alongside his laboratory, situated just before the tree line. Satisfied to see they were all still standing, he strolled around the garage and onto the circular drive. Disguised as a stable and attached to the house by an enclosed connecting link, it could accommodate six cars with space to spare.

Climbing into his Grand Cherokee, he started the engine and eased the vehicle forward. Retracing the morning's path from the county road, he turned right again and followed it a half-mile through heavy woods before turning right again on Sanctuary Cove's main road. Formally named "The Lake Road," the locals referred to it as "The Strip."

The Cove had a long and generally unfortunate history. A lakeside convergence of six ancient trails, it had originally been a gathering place for the Abenaki tribe that had once inhabited the area. French traders later made their way down Lake Champlain, and put into The Cove to barter with the natives. A small trading post was eventually built there, which changed hands several times during the French and Indian War and again during the America Revolution. It remained disputed territory until the Jay Treaty of 1794 established a boundary commission, which finally mapped the U.S.-Canadian border. But the handful of trappers, traders and fishermen that lived there were apparently never informed they were residing on American territory. In all likelihood, they wouldn't have cared one way or another.

By the time the War of 1812 broke out, the Abenaki had long since retreated across the Canadian border. Trade that had run north from The Cove now took a more southern direction, connecting the tiny settlement to New York. Consisting mostly of animal pelts, moonshine and dried fish, it provided little more than a subsistence existence. But in the five decades that led up to the Civil War, some hundreds of farms had sprung up in the vicinity and the population had grown to almost 2000 souls. After the war, however, the entire area slipped into a slow, downward spiral. The once hopeful community had shrunk to a few hundred people that eked out a meager living farming, fishing, and smuggling. The downward slide reversed briefly during Prohibition, as The Cove provided an excellent staging area for running American cigarettes north, and Canadian whisky south. But when Prohibition was repealed in 1933, it resumed. Already staggered by the Great Depression, residents of The Cove sank once again into poverty.

But things turned up unexpectedly in 2003, when Winston DePew's life fell apart. Born in The Cove some 40 years before, Winston had been subjected to relentless teasing due to his excessive weight, thick glasses, and pronounced stammer. But his parents died just after his thirteenth birthday, and his maternal grandparents in Albany were appointed his legal guardians. Flourishing in the new environment, Winston soon demonstrated remarkable academic abilities. After winning a scholarship to MIT, and taking advanced degrees in computer science and mathematics, he spent almost a decade at IBM before signing on with a dot-com start up. In less than five years, he'd turned his stock options into a multibillion-dollar fortune.

Smart enough to sell before the dot-com bubble burst in 2000, he promptly made an even bigger fortune in real estate speculation.

And if he hadn't come home one night to find his beautiful wife entwined with another man, he probably would have retired and enjoyed the good life. But the divorce that followed was ugly and expensive, and Winston soon found himself gripped by dark depression. He haunted his 26-room mansion at night, playing video games and drinking until dawn – and when he awakened, usually late the next afternoon, he snorted enormous quantities of cocaine before staggering back to the in-house video arcade he'd built during happier times. He was headed for an early and tragic death, when one night he had a sudden epiphany – realizing that computer games were the only things he still cared about, he decided to create the greatest game company the world had ever seen. Two weeks later he reappeared in The Cove with a team of lawyers and architects, and began work on a corporate headquarters for Infinity Entertainment.

After buying the entire lakefront, he successfully lobbied the state government to incorporate The Cove as a town. Then after relocating the families that lived on his newly acquired property to temporary house trailers a couple of miles inland, he went to work. He built a modern road complete with curbs, gutters and sidewalks along the entire crescent formed by the lake, and set the architects and builders to work on rebuilding what had passed for a settlement. A three-mile long length of road was built 1500 feet behind the new Lake Road, conforming to its curvature, and a new business district was constructed. Although ultramodern in almost every sense, Winston had ordered the architects to employ classic New England designs and traditional building materials. Entirely new, the five-block stretch of shops and offices looked like they'd been there for centuries – as did the new, two-story lakeside hotel.

Then on either side, he built two new subdivisions of brick and stone for the townspeople he'd displaced, and his new employees.

A third road was constructed a mile from the second, with intervening woods remaining as a park, and three new buildings were built along it at half-mile intervals. The first was a combined elementary and middle school, the second a high school and the third the headquarters building for his new video game company. Although technically private institutions, the schools had negotiated a contract with the county to educate all the children living within the incorporated area.

The high school was unique in other ways as well. Dedicated to academic excellence, with particular emphasis upon science and technology, Winston had named it after Sir Isaac Newton. Intending to attract outstanding students from all over the country, it boasted a lavish scholarship fund, the largest secondary-school endowment in North America, two dormitories, and the best teaching staff in New England. All of the instructors had Master's degrees, and two-thirds had Ph.D.s.

But after having rebuilt The Cove from the ground up, Winston had vanished as suddenly as he'd appeared. According to the Harvard-trained CEO of Infinity Entertainment, he had gone on a "creative sabbatical" – which apparently was corporate-speak for detoxification in a Tibetan monastery. But since his company had staffed up by then, no one really cared.

Although Infinity Entertainment had saved The Cove from extinction, it was the clinic Neill McGuire built that put it on the map. A year and a half before moving his family from rural Michigan, he had negotiated a partnership with Dr. Dale Sanders. A refugee from Harvard Medical School, Sanders had given up teaching to practice hands-on medicine in a more tranquil venue. But as the county's only surgeon, he quickly realized he needed a partner. After receiving Neill McGuire's impressive resume and cover letter in response to the ad he'd placed in a medical journal, he'd called him on the phone. Even more impressed by his young colleague's knowledge – and his willingness to invest a small fortune in the practice – he quickly cut a deal.

As part of that agreement, Dr. McGuire financed a new clinic with state of the art equipment: in addition to a fully equipped medical laboratory, it boasted the latest in X-ray technology, and the only CAT scan and MRI units in thirty miles. It also had a ward capable of accommodating ten people, a fully equipped dental suite, an ambulance manned by certified EMTs, and a small restaurant.

Located dead center in the woods that separated the second and the third roads, it was probably the only building in the entire incorporated area that Winston hadn't built. Completed only eight months before – which was a day or two after the McGuire clan arrived in The Cove – its design was modern and functional.

But as Dr. McGuire pulled into his reserved parking space by the staff entrance, he wasn't thinking about the clinic. Lost in thought, he was sorting through an uneasy premonition instead.

Something told him his life was about to be turned on end.

CHAPTER 3

After turning off the ignition and climbing out of the vehicle, he passed through the sliding doors and strode into the rear east-west corridor of the rectangular building, where the physician's private offices were located. Turning right on the north-south corridor that centered the building, he was en route to the front desk to pick up his messages and mail when Dr. Sanders suddenly pushed through the double doors with a steaming cup of coffee in hand.

Smiling, Dr. McGuire greeted him and extended his hand. "Morning, Dale...

"How's business?"

Stopping a couple of feet in front of him, Dr. Sanders transferred his coffee from right to left and grasped Dr. McGuire's hand. "Glad you're back, Neill...

"And in answer to your question, remarkably slow – I haven't had a customer all morning."

Surprised, Dr. McGuire asked him how he'd gotten along during his month-long absence. After shrugging and taking a sip of his coffee, Dr. Sanders told him to come on back to his office and he'd tell him all about it. Reversing direction, Dr. McGuire walked alongside the older man and listened.

"Usual stuff...

"Aside from our regulars, I treated a couple of hikers for exposure after a Sheriff's Deputy brought them in, and a hunter who managed to shoot himself in the foot on the hotel's parking lot...

"And a couple of people injured in a car wreck up at the Junction."

Surprised again, Dr. McGuire asked him how they'd ended up in The Cove.

"Well, it seems our reputation has grown, because the county ambulance crew brought them here."

Having arrived at his office door, Dr. Sanders handed his cup to Dr. McGuire while he searched his pockets for his keys. Then after retrieving them, he opened the door and waved Dr. McGuire inside.

"But the big news," he said, "Is we've got a new doc in town."

Smiling broadly, Dr. McGuire asked if he'd signed him up.

Setting his coffee cup down on his desk before settling into his chair, Dr. Sanders shook his head. "I tried, but I couldn't talk him into it…

"Seems he has his hands full with an FDA approval process, a private research project and a wayward nephew."

Then grinning from ear to ear, he laughed. "You have *got* to hear this one!"

Settling back in his chair, Dr. McGuire smiled politely. "So tell me…"

Taking another swig of coffee, Dr. Sanders leaned forward and grinned again. "A young guy named Marchand, graduated from the Sorbonne a few years back and did his residency at Columbia…

"Board certifications in trauma surgery, internal medicine and geriatrics."

Impressed, Dr. McGuire leaned forward. "You're kidding!"

Shaking his head, Dr. Sander said no. "So I tried to hire him, but he begged off…

"Has some new process under review with the FDA, so he's going back and forth between here and Washington all the time…

"Lawyers won't let him talk about it, so I'm not quite sure what that's all about. But he did say he thinks it might change the way we do transfusions…"

"Anyway, after explaining our predicament he agreed to help out in an emergency if he's in town – so if we get into trouble, we've got a third pair of hands we can call on…

"Sometimes, at least…"

Then after searching around on his desk, Dr. Sanders pulled a manila file out of a stack and handed it across his desk to Dr. McGuire. "Here's his paperwork."

Impressed as he flipped through the folder, Dr. McGuire asked if there were any chance he'd change his mind downstream.

"Damned impressive credentials – and if the Canadians keep coming, we're going to need another doc full time."

By that, he meant the Canadians that had begun coming down from Montreal for the more expensive but readily available medical care in The Cove. "How many do we have now? Two, three hundred?"

"About 280 or so, the last time I checked," Dr. Sanders agreed. Then he cracked up laughing. "But I think getting Marchand onboard depends on that damn fool nephew of his."

Smiling quizzically, Dr. McGuire asked him to explain.

"Well, it seems his older brother married an American girl, and they had a vineyard someplace in southern France until they got killed in a car wreck…

"And as the closest living relative, Dr. Marchand was appointed legal guardian for their 13-year-old son…

"So he moved the kid to Paris while he finished up his last couple of weeks in medical school, and after he graduated he took the kid with him to New York so he could do his residency.

"He enrolled him in some fancy prep school, and it seemed like everything was going along OK until he woke up one morning and found the kid had swiped $5000, and left him a note saying he was off on an adventure…"

Pursing his lips and shaking his head in disapproval, Dr. McGuire asked what happened next.

"Well, Dr. Marchand went to the New York police and filed a missing persons report. He gave the cops a photo, and a day or so later they called him back and said the kid had boarded an Air France flight to Bordeaux, which is the closest international airport to his old home …

"So Marchand figures the kid just got homesick – so he hops a plane to Bordeaux, and drives down to the kid's village to see if he can find him.…

"And he runs into an old girlfriend who tells him the kid had come and gone – he'd stopped in for a day, before taking off in a rental car again."

"A rental? I thought he was 13?"

Nodding, Dr. Sanders continued. "He'd just turned 14, but he'd picked up a fake ID and a workable credit card somewhere along the way…

"So Dr. Marchand drives up to Paris, and files another police report, and hires a private investigator to track the kid down before he gets into serious trouble. Then he has to go back to New York for his residency…

"So a month or two passes, and no word on the kid…

"The only good news is his body hasn't turned up in a morgue someplace.

"Then a couple of weeks later, he gets a letter from the kid saying he'd enlisted in the Foreign Legion under a fake name, and he's having the time of his life!"

After his jaw dropped, Dr. McGuire asked Dr. Sanders if he was kidding.

Grinning from ear to ear, Dr. Sanders held his right palm up in the air and swore to God.

"Anyway, the kid includes an international money order for most of the cash he'd made off with …

"And a promise to send the rest later."

Laughing, Dr. McGuire expressed his sympathy for Dr. Marchand. "*Oh Jesus…*

"That poor guy…"

Still grinning, Dr. Sanders told him that was just the beginning.

"So Marchand takes another leave from his residency, flies to Marseilles and drives out to the Legion's headquarters – where he demands to see the commanding officer…

"They make him cool his heels for a couple of days before escorting him onto the base and showing him into the commander's office – where he introduces himself, tells the general his nephew enlisted with a fake ID, and demands he release the kid…"

Now laughing himself, Dr. Sanders continued. "The general listens politely, shrugs, and tells him he's sorry the kid's caused him so much trouble – but there's nothing he can do about it…

"Because when you enlist in the Legion, they legally seal your identity and give you an entirely new one – so as far as the law is concerned, the kid's of legal age."

Chuckling, Dr. McGuire shook his head again.

"So anyway, Dr. Marchand flies up to Paris, and meets with an old friend of the family who's a member of their parliament – I think they call them 'deputies' over there – and asks him to help spring the kid...

"The deputy's known his nephew since he was in diapers, so he promises to help – but he warns Marchand it won't be easy...

"Then he tells him to go back to the States, while he comes up with a plan.

"So Marchand flies back to New York, where he gets another letter a month or two later – the kid's just graduated from parachute school, and he's enclosed another money order to pay off his tab..."

Incredulous, Dr. McGuire gasped. "Parachute school?"

Dr. Sanders nodded and grinned. "Yup...Parachute school!"

"But that actually helped, because the Foreign Legion only has one parachute regiment – so he finally has a rough idea where the kid is...

"The downside, though, is the paratroops have been sent to some Godforsaken place in Africa to help put down an insurrection."

Shaking his head again, Dr. McGuire tried to suppress a laugh. "This gets worse by the minute."

Grinning, Dr. Sanders agreed.

"So a couple of weeks later, Marchand gets a call from his Deputy-friend, who says he's going to put an amendment in the next appropriations bill requiring the French military to give parliament the names and photos of everyone in uniform that enlisted over the past twenty-four months...

"And once he has those, Marchand can come back and ID the kid. After that, he thinks they've got a shot at prying him loose...

"But the bad news is the bill won't come up for a vote until June at the earliest, so he's going to have to be patient."

Shaking his head again, Dr. McGuire chuckled.

"So June finally rolls around, the bill gets passed and Marchand's Deputy-friend demands the military fork over the stuff...

"But it turns out some reporter had been sniffing around, and ran a story about how the Parliament is investigating the military for using 'child soldiers' – and then all hell breaks loose...

"The Leftists start climbing all over the military and the Rightwing types start accusing the Lefties of undermining national security...

"And in all the shouting and shoving, the kid gets lost in the shuffle.

"It's not about him anymore, but about the 'Honor of France' or some such crap."

Incredulous, Dr. McGuire asked if Dr. Marchand ever got his nephew out of the Legion.

"Yeah, eventually – and the kid was none too happy about it...

"The French military had been dragging its heels, and it didn't turn over the names and photos until last February...

"By which time the kid's in Afghanistan with his regiment, chasing bin Laden through the mountains."

"You're kidding!" said Dr. McGuire.

Dr. Sanders grinned, shook his head, and said no. "So now the fun starts...

"Since the Legion still maintains his nephew is legally 18, they won't let him go – so Marchand calls a press conference and lets it all hang out...

"Instant chaos – parliament goes nuts again, everyone is slinging mud back and forth, and it mushrooms into a national scandal...

"So after a couple of weeks of that, the President decides enough is enough and orders the Legion to transfer the kid to Paris, and have him report to his office...

"So the kid gets off the plane, and guess what? Turns out he's been promoted to corporal, and won a couple of medals...

"And he tells the press he *likes* the Legion!"

Covering his face with his hand, Dr. McGuire looked down and shook his head again. *"Oh God,"* he muttered.

Laughing harder, Dr. Sanders told him the best part was the meeting with President Chirac.

"Marchand said he'd been summoned to the Presidential Palace, and was shaking hands with the President when the kid marches in and salutes...

"So after they all sit down, the President tells the kid he's caused a major political crisis – and that as the President of the Republic, he's going to resolve it right then and there...

"Suddenly realizing he's in a world of trouble, the kid gulps and says 'Yes, Sir.'"

"So the President asks the kid what the hell he thought he was doing enlisting in the Legion, and the kid says he was just having a little adventure...

"So the President comes unglued, and starts screaming about how his 'little adventure' is about to cost his party 50 seats in parliament – and he's *royally* pissed.

"So the kid says he's really sorry, and the President tells him sorry doesn't cut it in politics...

"And threatens to ship his butt off to Devil's Island, and make him spend the rest of his enlistment marching up and down guarding the ruins of the old prison...

"So after making the kid squirm a bit, the President gives him a choice – if he's willing to cooperate, he'll order him transferred to the Inactive Reserves instead, and send him back to the States with his uncle so he can finish high school...

"And just to make sure the kid doesn't cause any more trouble, he's willing to sweeten the deal by promoting him to Sergeant."

Laughing harder, Dr. Sanders continued. "So after giving the kid a moment to think it over, President Chirac asks him what it's going to be...

"Guarding rocks at Devil's Island, or sergeant in the Inactive Reserve..."

By now laughing hysterically, Dr. Sanders could barely continue. "So the kid looks the President right in the eye, and says 'First Lieutenant works for me.'"

Doubled over his desk howling, Dr. Sanders began pounding the surface with the palm of his hand.

"Can you believe it? The little bastard blackmailed the President of France!"

Laughing almost as hard as Dr. Sanders, Dr. McGuire pressed his hands against his stomach and bent over. When he could finally get the words out, he looked up again and wiped the tears from his eyes.

"And he ended up here?"

Still laughing hysterically, Dr. Sanders shook his head up and down.

"After they got back to New York, Marchand sent the kid to a shrink – who promptly called in a psychologist, who called in an educational psychologist…

"And they all agreed the kid has three problems…

"First of all, his IQ is off the charts – he's a bona fide genius…

"Second, he has a thing about adventure – and that's just not going to go away…

"And third, he absolutely, positively hates cities…

"So their unanimous recommendation was that Marchand move the kid out to the country, buy him a horse and some dogs, and let him hunt and camp and commune with nature."

Still chuckling, Dr. McGuire nodded. "Makes sense…

"So he's going to enroll at Newton?"

Grinning, Dr. Sanders said yes. "He's 17 now, and he's going to be a junior…

"But for God's sake, Neill, don't tell anyone…

"Because after that little adventure of his, the Headmaster's worried he may be a bad influence on the other kids so he's on probation…

"And if they find out about the Legion, he's gone…"

Suddenly serious, Dr. McGuire nodded. "Not a word…"

CHAPTER 4

At precisely ten minutes to nine the next morning, First Lieutenant Andre Marchand of the French Foreign Legion (Inactive Reserve) turned his perfectly restored 1963 Corvette Stingray into the student parking lot located on the south side of the main building of Newton Academy. Painted metal-flake blue and equipped with chrome wheels, a 396 cubic inch engine, and a completely restored interior that included an AM-FM radio and a CD player, it was far too nice a vehicle to park just anywhere. Steering it into a distant spot away from the other cars, he cut the engine. But as he engaged the brake, his attention was suddenly drawn toward a muddy Land Rover that had just pulled onto the lot.

Holy crap, he thought. *Vampires!*

For most humans, it's almost impossible to identify a Vampire by sight. They survive by passing unnoticed among their prey, and to casual observers they're indistinguishable from the humans they hunt. But after a late night back-alley brawl with three of the freaks in New York, Andre had become far more attentive.

There were quite a few of them around – about five for every million people, by Andre's estimate – but the fact that four of them had just pulled into a rural high school parking lot came as a surprise.

Especially since they hardly ever hang out together...

Pretending to be busy with the ragtop's interior clamps as they climbed out of the Land Rover, Andre averted his gaze until they'd begun walking toward the main entrance. It was only after their backs were safely turned to him that he looked back.

Two guys, and two girls...

About 17 or 18, in human terms.

Then suddenly struck by the massive incongruity, he broke up laughing. *And the Headmaster thinks I might be a bad influence???*

Shaking his head in wonder, he climbed out of the Vette. Then after retrieving his briefcase from behind the driver's seat, he closed the door and locked it. After setting the case on the ground, he straightened his tie and smoothed his trench coat. The skies were overcast, and the weather report on America Online had predicted an early afternoon rain.

Taking another discreet look at the fang gang, his eyes were drawn to the girls as they made their way up the short flight of exterior stairs that led into the main building.

Damn! A couple of Eight-Point-Five's on the Derriere Scale...

Then after a moment's reflection, he upped their score. *More like Nine-Point-0, when I think about it...*

After pursing his lips together and shaking his head, he sighed. Then after one last admiring glance, he picked up his case and set off for the school's Administrative Office.

It wasn't hard to find – he'd been there three weeks before, when his uncle had talked Headmaster Stephen Renfrowe into giving him a chance. Possessed of remarkably acute hearing, Andre had overheard their intense conversation while seated in the Headmaster's outer office. After almost an hour of the muted back and forth exchange – and a telephone conference with the French Ambassador in Washington – his Uncle had finally come to the doorway and summoned him inside.

Standing at attention in front of the Headmaster's desk with his eyes front and his shoulders squared, Andre relaxed only slightly after Dr. Renfrowe told him to stand at ease. The Headmaster was concerned, he said, that Andre's unusual background might exert an undesirable influence on the other students, and he questioned whether Andre would be able to fit into a civilian high school…

But he was going to give him a chance, on one condition – his twenty-six months in the Legion would have to be kept secret. If word leaked out, the Headmaster was going to bounce him out of Newton so fast it would make his head spin.

Although Andre was fluent in English – it was actually his first language, as his mother had been an American – he still had trouble puzzling out the colloquialisms. But he caught the drift from the Headmaster's body language and facial expression, so he nodded and agreed to the terms, and thanked him for his indulgence.

Surprised by the smile that had begun creeping across the man's face, he listened as Dr. Renfrowe confessed that he'd had a few youthful adventures of his own – he'd enlisted in the U.S. Army at seventeen, and spent four years in the 101st Airborne Division.

"So as one paratroop to another, I'm warning you to meticulously observe this agreement of ours. If you screw up, you're gone…

"That clear, Marchand?"

After Andre came to attention again and nodded, Dr. Renfrowe chuckled. "Good – now get the hell out of my office!"

Smiling softly at the recollection, Andre entered the building and traversed the enormous foyer. After making his way through the mass of students heading in different directions, he pushed open the door to the Admin Office. As he approached the counter, an attractive young woman of perhaps 20 or 21 glanced up from the other side, did a double take, and began to flush. Toying with her, Andre smiled.

"Bonjour, Mademoiselle…

"My name is Andre Marchand, and I was instructed to report here on the first day of class."

Blushing badly, she smiled. "Oh, yes – the new student."

Then after searching through a pile of papers stacked to the side, she handed him a stapled sheaf that had his name written across the top in red.

"On the top of the page here is your schedule and room numbers, with the names of your instructors, and a map of the school just below…

"And on the second there's another map, showing the location of your locker and its number…

"The rest of the stuff is an introductory packet which I think you've already received, a parking sticker that goes on the windshield of your car if you drive, and some other information about the cafeteria, the school store, and the student lounge."

Having already discovered that American women were complete suckers for the French language, Andre smiled engagingly and thanked her in French.

"Merci, Mademoiselle…"

Then after letting his gaze linger provocatively, he turned on his heel and marched toward the door. Just as he reached it, the girl called out.

"Andre?"

Turning about, he looked at her quizzically.

Flushing again, she smiled shyly. "I know it's hard fitting into a new school, so if you need any help with anything come see me." Then she smiled again, and after brushing back her hair with her fingers she pointed at the nametag pinned to her blouse. "My name's Patti."

"Merci, Pah-ti," he said, employing the French pronunciation. And then with practiced elegance, he told her she'd been most kind.

Andre managed to find his locker, stow his trench coat, and make it to his first class just as the bell rang. After introducing himself to Mrs. Morgan – his new English Lit instructor, who'd insisted that he greet the other students and tell them about himself – he spent the rest of the fifty-minute academic hour alternately examining the text Mrs. Morgan had issued him, and thinking about the Vamps he'd spotted on the parking lot.

Probably just recycling their identities, so they're not immediately dangerous…

The Mist & the Darkness

Given the circumstances, it was a reasonable assumption – because broadly speaking, Vampires came in three categories – Feral, Predators, and Civilized.

Feral Vamps were the most vicious and unpredictable of the lot. Most often the victims of botched attacks, they became Vampires without really understanding what had befallen them. Experiencing the surge of power that accompanies the change from human to Vamp, but not yet aware of their limitations, they were prone to reckless and often fatal behavior. Andre had heard about one who supposed sunscreen would protect him from the noonday sun, and very foolishly went to the beach. Another he'd heard about decided to take down the leader of a rival gang, on the theory that guns couldn't kill Vampires. That was true insofar as it went, but after his intended victim put six 9mm rounds in his chest and another through his head, he found himself sprawled in an alley – probably unconscious, and definitely unable to move. Twenty minutes after the sun arose, he burst into flames.

The Predators made it through the transition, and successfully adapted – either through a stroke of luck, or with the assistance of the Vamp that turned them. Conscious of their vulnerabilities, and fully aware of what would happen if the authorities were forced to acknowledge their existence, they gravitated to poorly-policed places and preyed upon people who would never be missed – for the most part pimps, prostitutes, drug dealers and petty criminals in the inner cities, but occasionally individual hunters or campers in the wilderness. Smart enough to cover their tracks, they stashed the bodies in abandoned buildings or heavy underbrush, where they wouldn't be found until it was too late to perform an autopsy, or destroyed the evidence in other and often creative ways. One Vamp in New York had gained a measure of fame – or notoriety – by carrying around a sawed-off shotgun, which he fired into his victims' necks to erase the bite marks.

Civilized Vamps were a good deal more complex. For the most part Vampires who had for some reason remained attached to their previous lives, they preferred to live among humans. They maintained a quiet and low-key existence, surviving off willing donors or blood sold from the backdoors of hospitals and blood banks – and more than a few actually owned the facilities they fed from.

Given the phenomenon of compound interest, Civilized Vamps were almost always well-heeled. One human lifetime was sufficient to amass a substantial investment portfolio, two enough to become a millionaire, and three often enough to break into the Billionaire's Club. Their biggest problem was avoiding an IRS audit, the next was keeping their names out of Forbes. Investors for the most part, they typically lived in expensive penthouse suites, supported Liberal causes, and gave generously to charities. Aside from the fact that they weren't, technically, human, they were model citizens.

But they could be dangerous as well – they valued their privacy and protected their secrets jealously. They could – and often did – react violently to blackmail. Many a fool had suffered a gruesome death after threatening to expose them.

Suddenly jerked back to reality by the bell, Andre scribbled his reading assignment in his notebook and packed up his gear. Withdrawing his schedule from his shirt pocket, he noted the room number and set off down the hall.

Because his next class was located in the North Wing, Andre cut through the huge open area that housed the cafeteria, the student lounge, and the school store. Unable to resist the temptation, he stopped at the lounge and bought a Café au lait from the refreshment bar and spent the next seven minutes savoring the surprisingly good brew. Unlike most schools, Newton ran on a fifty-minute hour, giving the students ample time to visit the restrooms, retrieve books from their lockers, or grab a cup of coffee.

Misjudging the time, he arrived just as Dr. Marigold was welcoming the assembled students to The History of Late Antiquity. Noticing him standing at the door, she gestured for him to come in. A short and rather plump woman in her mid-thirties, she was friendly, cheerful, and astonishingly bright. She was also lustful, and deeply frustrated by the The Cove's lack of single men her age.

Andre greeted her, as he handed her his schedule. *"Bonjour, Madame Professeur…*

"My name is Andre Marchand."

After glancing over his document, she handed it back and smiled. *"Bonjour, Monsieur Marchand…*

"And since it seems you already know who I am, I'd like you to introduce yourself to the class."

As he turned, he noticed the two Vamp girls sitting together in the back of the class.

Fils de pute!

If their presence wasn't disconcerting enough, the taller Vamp with the long, light brown hair compounded his unease by leaning over to the other one and whispering "Check out the hottie."

That apparently flew right past Dr. Marigold, but not the students seated in the back. Several of the girls giggled and a couple of the guys rolled their eyes – and one of them sarcastically remarked upon his dress. Wearing a navy-blue double-breasted blazer, with a regimental tie off-setting his starched button-down shirt, khaki wool slacks with a razor crease and spit shined loafers, he looked more like a teacher than a student.

Ignoring the whispered comments, he made a determined effort to avoid eye contact with the Vamps as he introduced himself. "Good morning…

"My name is Andre Marchand, and this is my first day at Newton…

"I was born and raised in the Gascony region of France, but I moved to Paris after my parents died when I was thirteen, and I've lived with my Uncle – Dr. Philippe Marchand – ever since…

"First in Paris, while he completed medical school at the Sorbonne, then in New York while he was doing his medical residency, and now here in The Cove."

Not exactly the truth, of course, but the abbreviated biography managed to sidestep his 26-month adventure in the Legion.

Dr. Marigold smiled sympathetically. "I'm so sorry for your loss, Andre…

"But I trust your uncle has taken good care of you?"

Andre nodded. "I've been very fortunate in that regard."

Smiling sweetly, Dr. Marigold spoke again. "Just out of curiosity, Andre, how old is your Uncle?"

After pausing for just a moment to recall his uncle's cover story, Andre informed her that Philippe was 28.

Trying hard to hide her disappointment, Dr. Marigold forced a smile. "I presume he will be practicing medicine here?"

Andre shook his head. "No, Madame, he is conducting medical research – the early explorers claimed that the local pine bark had amazing healing properties, and he's investigating those claims in order to determine if they have merit…

"With any luck, he may discover a new drug."

After telling the class how wonderful that was, she asked Andre to share his outside interests.

Not entirely comfortable disclosing that sort of information in front of the Vamps, he hesitated a moment. Then deciding to turn the situation to his advantage, he explained that he enjoyed Mediaeval history, athletics, and the outdoors.

"For relaxation, I enjoy camping, swimming, and horseback riding…

"And in terms of sports, fencing, kayaking, running and soccer." Mindful of the both the Headmaster's warning and the Vampires unwelcome presence, he'd left out skydiving, martial arts and combat arms. Andre had a black belt in karate, and his skills with the broadsword and the Katana were good and getting better with practice. He was even more adept with bows and crossbows, and was an expert with automatic weapons, handguns, and explosives.

But they can find that out the hard way…

Clearly impressed, Dr. Marigold smiled and remarked on his wide range of interests. Then suddenly changing the subject, she complimented Andre on his English.

Smiling modestly, he explained that he'd learned it from his American mother.

"Well good," said Dr. Marigold as she switched into French. "You probably won't have any trouble keeping up then, but if you do I'm quite fluent *en francais*."

Smiling again, she switched back to English and apologized for not having an extra text. Promising to have one for him the following day, she pointed in the direction of the dark-haired Vamp and asked him to take the last unoccupied desk next to her. "I'm sure Elspeth McGuire will be happy to share with you."

Merde!

But since that was definitely not the time or place to make a potentially fatal slip, Andre nodded and walked to the back of the class. Summoning his most charming smile, he greeted her softly before setting his case on the desktop and sitting down.

"Bonjour, Mademoiselle."

The Vamp returned his greeting with a demure smile, before scooting her desk over a few inches at a time. While she was preoccupied, Andre checked her out.

Her chestnut hair was piled atop her head in an almost haphazard way, creating something of a windswept look that – somehow – accented her milk chocolate eyes. Her makeup, eye shadow, and lipstick seemed almost professionally done, and she was wearing a pair of designer jeans and a white blouse with pearls, covered by an open, flimsy beige linen jacket that fell beneath her waist.

Having a finely developed appreciation for fashionable women, Andre had to admit he liked the look. Then as he moved his desk over to meet her in the middle of the aisle, he glimpsed the better part of a finely curved breast nestled in an exquisite lace bra.

Swearing silently in French, and then in English, Andre was wondering what he'd done to deserve that particular torment when she opened her text. Turning half in her seat, she pushed the book over so he could read the print before leaning toward him – and as she did, her blouse fell open again. He was desperately trying to remind himself that she was a blood sucking Creature of the Night when the fragrance of her perfume waft across the half-foot or so that separated them, and completely trashed his concentration.

Oh Lord, he thought. *This ain't gonna be easy…*

CHAPTER 5

Andre enjoyed the class. Dr. Marigold was a good lecturer, and clearly a master of the subject matter. She'd spent the fifty minutes providing the class with a broad overview of Late Antiquity – from the dissolution of the Western Roman Empire in 476 AD to the fragmentation of the Carolingian Empire some four hundred years later – and Andre had found the *tour d'horizon* immensely interesting.

Charles S. Viar

Disappointed when the bell rang, he had nodded politely toward Elspeth and thanked her for sharing her book. Then as she closed the text, Andre scooted his desk back into place. After securing his notebook and pen in his briefcase, he snapped it shut and stood. Intensely preoccupied with the school map, he was surprised by a female voice behind him.

"What do you have next?"

It was Elspeth – now standing behind her desk, with the taller Vamp beside her.

"Calculus," he said. "South Building, Room 204." Then after glancing at the taller Vamp, he summoned forth a practice smile and greeted her. "Bonjour, Mademoiselle…

"I'm Andre Marchand."

Returning his smile, the girl nodded. "Nice to meet you, Andre…

"I'm Lydia McGuire, Elle's sister."

Still smiling, he looked her in the eye. "*Enchante*, Mademoiselle."

Looking suddenly ill at ease, Elspeth said they had to go. Then pointing in the direction of the South Building, she informed him that his class was on the Second Floor.

Picking up his case, Andre nodded. "Right." Then after thanking her for the directions, he marched out the door.

The girls followed him through the doorway, before stopping at Elspeth's locker so she could deposit her history text. As she manipulated the combination lock, Lydia whispered and grinned.

"I think he likes you."

Taken aback, Elspeth glanced up at her sister, half-hidden by the locker door. Then after giving her an irritated look, she curtly informed Lydia that Andre had seemed very nice – and then after glancing around to make sure no one could hear her, she reminded her that he was a human.

Ignoring the clear implication that Andre was out of bounds, Lydia played upon her words instead.

"Well, obviously, Sherlock…

"Those pheromones of his stunk up the entire room!"

Slamming her locker shut and spinning the combination, Elspeth glared at her sister before taking another furtive glance

35

around. "Oh for God's sake," she whispered. "He's a seventeen year old guy...

"They get turned on by anything that moves!"

After leaning over to take an exaggerated sniff of Elspeth's neck, Lydia grinned. "Yeah? And what about 71-year old Vampires?"

Huffing, Elspeth pushed past her sister and headed down the hall. Catching up with her a few steps later, Lydia waited for a group of students to pass before leaning over and whispering again.

"So are you gonna taste him?"

Furious, Elspeth wheeled around to confront her. *"Absolutely NOT!"*

Then after glaring at Lydia, she glanced around again. *"In case you've forgotten, WE DON'T DO THAT,"* she hissed.

Smiling triumphantly, Lydia shrugged. "A pity," she said. "He smells delicious!"

After staring at her sister for a long moment, Elspeth shook her head in disgust. "You're pathetic." Then she wheeled and marched off to her biology class.

After waiting for a moment to make sure her little sister wouldn't turn back, Lydia grinned as the outlines of a wondrously wicked plan emerged from the shadows of her mind. More perceptive than she liked to let on, she'd seen the sparks fly between Andre and Elspeth – and if she played her cards right, there was a better than even chance they'd give her the opening she'd been looking for...

Hook those two up and Neill and Elizabeth will be so worried about Elle that I'll fall off their radar screen...

And then it's play time for Moi...

Having turned in the other direction after history, Andre was completely unaware of the plot Lydia was hatching as he climbed the steps in the South Building. But he was concerned, nonetheless – Elspeth's sudden discomfort when he'd introduced himself to Lydia suggested she was the more aggressive of the two. A generally desirable trait for high school girls, it was far less appealing when it came to Vamps.

Gonna have to watch that one, he thought, as he walked through the door of his next class.

After introducing himself to the teacher and receiving his book, Andre took his assigned seat. Once the bell rang, the roll was called and the rest of the books handed out, Dr. Martin made him stand and introduce himself again. After a smattering of applause and a couple of catcalls, he resumed his seat and focused on the teacher's introduction.

Although he'd signed up for all Advanced Placement courses, Calculus was the only one that struck him as potentially difficult. Catching up on the courses he'd missed during his twenty-six month adventure hadn't been especially difficult because most of them could be learned at home. But mathematics was a whole different story – weak in that area from the beginning, he'd sweat blood all summer mastering algebra and geometry. Fortunately, his uncle was a mathematical wizard.

Still, he knew he was going to have to concentrate in this class – which made the absence of Vampires all the more welcome.

Especially that little dark-haired one…

Trying hard to focus on Dr. Martin's *tour d'horizon* of AP Calculus, he kept drifting back to the class before. The scent of Elspeth's perfume had been sublime, and her close physical presence provocative. Trying hard to avoid the memory of her perfectly formed breasts, he had to keep reminding himself that the little freak was supposed to be six feet under.

Not easy, as he was forced to admit, because Elspeth was just plain hot. Not as pretty as her sister, to be sure – but endowed with a strangely intangible quality that drew him to her.

Bloody hell…

I've got to stop thinking about her!

CHAPTER 6

Relieved when the bell finally rang, Andre jotted down the night's homework assignment and tossed his notebook and his Calculus text into his briefcase alongside his English book. Then after standing, he consulted his schedule again before heading to the gym.

The Mist & the Darkness

The only building on the entire campus that looked even remotely modern, the gym was an enormous structure behind and to the south of the cafeteria. Connected to the South Building by a long, covered walkway, it stood beside the athletic field and the rows of bleachers that lined it. After pushing through the double doors that opened into a long hallway that ran the length of the structure, Andre paused to orient himself. Seeing the sign extending out over a doorway marked "Coach," he walked the twenty feet or so before knocking. As he waited for a reply, a male student walked over.

"Looking for Coach Jordan?"

Andre nodded. "I have gym this hour…"

The other boy gestured with his head. "Locker room's this way."

Tall and muscular, he led Andre through a door into a small entryway formed by a metal partition, and then to the left. After they emerged into a humid room filled with rows of lockers and benches, the other student asked if he had his gear.

Not quite certain what he'd meant, Andre said he's just arrived at Newton that morning. Nodding, the other boy told him he could pick up his gym uniform at the School Store. It was located next to the Student Lounge, both of which were accessible from the Cafeteria, and it was open all day and for an hour or so after the last class. In the meantime, he should report to Coach Jordan out on the gym floor. "But take those shoes off first – if he catches you wearing leather soles on his wooden floor, he'll have you for lunch!"

Thanking him for the advice, Andre slipped off his shoes and went in search of the teacher.

Finding him standing in the middle of the basketball court with a half-dozen students around him, Andre waited until the instructor noticed him. After checking to make sure he was in his socks, the Coach marched over and asked him who he was and what he wanted.

By now used to the drill, he handed the man his schedule and explained he was a new student.

The Coach glanced over his schedule, and handed it back. "No gear, huh…"

Then after rattling off the list of things he'd need for class, and instructing Andre to pick them up at the school store, he pointed toward the concrete cinder block wall that separated the basketball courts and exercise areas from the locker room. "Go stand over there with McGuire."

Son-of-a bitch!

Another damn Vampire...

Shaking his head in disbelief, he walked over and stood next to the bloodsucker. "Mr. Jordan instructed me to wait with you." Dressed in gym clothes, the Vamp wasn't especially tall but he was powerfully built. Glancing over, he gave Andre a disinterested nod.

After the Coach called the class to order and took the roll, he announced the weatherman had been lying again so they were going outside for calisthenics and wind sprints. Then he pointed at the Vamp, and yelled across the floor. "Sun's still out, McGuire, so I want you and the new guy to take the dust mops to the floor – got it?"

After the Vamp nodded, the Coach blew his whistle and the class raced for the exterior doors.

The Vamp jerked his head in the direction of a closet. "Come on."

Opening the closet door, he pulled two of the three-foot wide dust mops from inside and handed one to Andre. After taking it from him, Andre asked the freak his name.

"Daniel," said the Vamp. "Daniel McGuire."

Following along behind him, Andre decided to press his luck. With his blonde hair and blue eyes and his laid-back manner, he looked a lot more like a Surfer left over from the 1960's than a serious threat. Relaxing a bit, Andre asked him if he was any relation to Elspeth and Lydia McGuire.

Turning slightly, the Vamp nodded. "My sisters."

Filing that for future reference, Andre decided to press a bit farther. "So how come you're not outside with the rest of the class?"

Frowning, Daniel explained he had a medical condition. "Solar urticaria – it's kind of like being allergic to sunlight...

"Makes me break out in hives."

Since that was the usual cover story for Vamps, Andre had been expecting it. Masking the wheels that were turning in his head, he pretended to commiserate. "That sucks."

The Mist & the Darkness

As he stopped at the edge of the B-Ball court, the Vamp nodded. Then after pointing at the court, he informed Andre that he usually did the basketball area first, and then the rest of the Gym. "Coach Jordan is a complete fanatic when it comes to the court, but he usually doesn't check the rest of the floor very carefully…

"So focus on getting this area right."

They spent the rest of the hour pushing the mops up and down the court, before expanding their sweep to cover the rest of the gym. Finishing up just as the bell rang, they stowed their mops and headed for the door.

Daniel hadn't said much, but he seemed decent enough. He'd answered Andre's questions politely, and more or less honestly, and he'd even smiled occasionally. He and his family had moved to The Cove last December so his father could pursue a promising opportunity at the Clinic, the entire family shared his problem with sunlight, and that he and his siblings were adopted…

Surprised by the Vampire's unexpected openness, Andre was still reflecting on what he'd shared as he made his way to the Cafeteria after gym. Surprised to hear someone shouting his name in the hallway, he turned in time to see the big fellow who had helped him find Coach Jordan running towards him. Coming to a halt alongside Andre, he introduced himself as John Wilkinson, and explained the Coach had told him to look after him. "I'm Assistant Captain of the football team, and he's hoping you're into sports."

After shaking Wilkinson's outstretched hand, Andre rattled off his list of physical pursuits as they entered the cafeteria. Surprised by that fact that someone that big was also intelligent, Andre explained he was going to have to bust his ass to make grades because he was thinking about following his uncle into medicine. "Getting into a good school is really tough these days."

Wilkinson nodded. "No problem, we've filled out the team for this season but some of our best guys are graduating in June…

"So maybe think about it for next year, OK?"

They continued talking as they moved along the serving line. Then after paying for his lunch – meatloaf, corn, mashed potatoes, a salad and a Coke – Andre accompanied him to the "Jock Table" – which was actually four medium-sized tables which had been pushed together to accommodate Newton's athletes and the cheerleading squad. After sitting down at a proffered seat, Andre listened as Wilkinson introduced him to the football team's captain, and then the captains of the B-Ball, track, hockey and baseball teams.

"Coach is hoping Marchand will come out next year, so he wants us to make him feel welcome."

That apparently included some good-natured teasing, because after he was introduced around the table he caught a ration of light-hearted grief for being a "foreigner."

"I thought all you French guys were fags," said one.

"Man are you misinformed," said another. "They get all the hot chicks!"

At that point – which was roughly halfway through his meatloaf – Wilkinson leaned over and asked him if it was true that French girls were really easy. "I heard they're something else..."

Laughing, Andre explained that the French didn't look at sex in the same way that the Anglo-Saxons did. "It's all about love, my friend...

"But unlike the English-speaking countries, the French think love is something to be joyously experienced...

"It doesn't have to last forever..."

He was about to elaborate on that point when one of the guys interrupted. "Speaking of love, Marchand, the McGuire girls are checking you out."

Oh Christ!

Tensing, he asked the guy where they were located and how far away they were.

"Off to the left, sitting in the shadows along the north wall," he said.

Relaxing a bit, Andre muttered a bit too loudly. "Figures...."

"The freaks are probably hungry."

Mistaking his muted sarcasm for sexual innuendo, the First String cracked up. But after they stopped laughing, one of the players told him to forget it. "They're cold as ice, man."

Thinking that was only a slight exaggeration, Andre watched as Wilkinson nodded. "Jimmy asked Elspeth to go out once, and she shot him down...

"Some crap about how her parents are really strict, and don't let them date."

One of the guys nodded. "Yeah, and her sister blew me off with the same horse shit…"

"But it's complete crap – they're just stuck up rich kids that think they're too good for us peons."

After the other guys nodded in agreement, Wilkinson pointed at a gorgeous blonde strutting over to the table. "Now Kathy, on the other hand, knows how to show a guy a good time."

Then rising halfway out of his seat, Wilkinson bellowed. "Hey, Norse! Get your cute little bootie over here, and meet our new man!"

Smiling at the summons, Newton's head cheerleader put her tray down at an empty place before sauntering over and wrapping her arms around Wilkinson's neck. Then as she dropped her hands down to his chest, she leaned over Wilkinson's shoulder and fixed her eyes on Andre. She smiled invitingly, as her V-neck top fell open to reveal her admirable wares.

"Hi there," she said in a husky voice.

Watching the spectacle from across the cafeteria, Elspeth McGuire frowned and made a face. Thoroughly irritated, she rammed her fork into the garden salad before her. Ignoring the fact that she'd split the bowl in two, she pursed her lips and shook her head.

"That girl is disgusting!"

Glancing over at her sister, Lydia agreed. "A complete slut," she said. "But you'd better watch it, Elle – she's after your boyfriend!"

After glaring at her sister, Elspeth told her to knock it off. "He's not my boyfriend, and you know it!"

Grinning, Lydia leaned over and sniffed her neck. *"Оиииииииииииии…*

"Jealous, aren't we?"

After glaring at her sister again, Elspeth stuck her nose up in the air. "*Am NOT!*"

Then without another word she stood, picked up her tray, and marched off.

Bemused, Nathan glanced over at his brother and asked what was up with the girls.

Shrugging, Daniel forced down a forkful of salad before draining his water glass. "New guy from France…"

CHAPTER 7

After he finished eating, Wilkinson took Andre to the school store so he could buy his gym gear.

With the entrance located twenty feet to the left of the cafeteria's serving line, it balanced the student lounge at the other end. Resembling an upscale department store, it was packed with merchandise. In addition to the usual school supplies – paper, notebooks, pens, pencils, erasers and so on – it had a book section with hardcover and paperbacks; a music section with all the latest CDs and CD players; a DVD section, an electronics section that sold laptops and printers and their associated paraphernalia, a section for grooming and personal hygiene items, and a clothing section that featured gym clothes and school-oriented casuals.

After finding the right sizes, Andre grabbed an athletic uniform and a selection of Newton sweatshirts, a gym bag, a combination lock and a backpack. Having paid for it with his credit card, he thanked Wilkinson for his help and set off for his locker. He'd just finished cramming his gear into it when the bell rang, issuing the ten-minute warning for his next class.

Aside from all the other differences, Newton operated on a unique schedule as well. Class kicked off at 9:00 AM, and ran through 5:00 pm. With an hour off for lunch, that made for a schedule of five solids – not including gym, which met three days a week, interspersed with a personal hour that could be spent in the Lounge or off campus if one were an Upper Classman – and a study hall. Or if one were a nerd, a geek, or a masochist, one could take five solids, an elective, and study hall.

Having had little experience with structured education – he'd been home-schooled in France, and only attended the preparatory school in New York for a few weeks – Andre had opted for the five solids and study hall. That meant he had another hour to go in the cafeteria.

Fortunately, the study hall supervisor wasn't especially strict. As long as the students were quiet and cleaned up after themselves, they were free to go to the lounge for a coffee or a soft drink, and could munch on the brownies or doughnuts they sold there. Being full from lunch, Andre opted for another *Café au lait* before reporting to the supervisor. Since there wasn't a fixed seating arrangement, he picked a small table along the exterior glass curtain wall and cracked his calculus book.

Intrigued by the day's assignment, he was lost in thought when the bell rang. Surprised, he threw his stuff in his case and took off in search of physics.

After locating it on the first floor of the South Building, Andre checked in with the instructor. After Dr. Bergen took the roll and assigned seats, Andre had to get up and go through the introductory drill again. Seated next to Wilkinson at the end of the third row, he was congratulating himself on having pulled a Vamp-free hour when the fourth member of the Fang Gang walked in. After banging his head on his briefcase so hard he almost knocked himself out, Andre started swearing under his breath in French.

After the Vamp apologized to Dr. Bergen and offered a plausible excuse, he took the last remaining seat at the back of the first row. Muscular like his brother, he was taller and had brown hair and blue eyes. But unlike Daniel, who looked like the laid back surfer he'd once been, Nathan – if Andre had heard his name correctly – wore his rather long hair pulled back in a style that probably dated from the late 1700's. Erect and proud, he carried himself like a soldier. Curious, Andre wondered which army he had served in, and when.

Physics passed quickly. Intrigued by Dr. Bergen's overview of the course – which would include excursions into the theoretical realms of black holes, alternative universes, and time travel – Andre was looking forward to examining his text in detail when he got home that night. Disappointed again when the bell rang, he said goodbye to Wilkinson and started the trek back to the North Building for his last class.

French hadn't been Andre's first language, but he'd spoken more French than English for most of his 17 years. Although it was bound to be an easy "A," there was a reason he'd selected it –

grammar and spelling had bored him to tears, and he needed to work on both. It was a safe bet his French language skills would be tested eventually, and given his background a poor score would make him look like a fool.

Surprised by the fact that he was only the third student to arrive, he presented his papers to Monsieur Parshall and picked up his book. Then after being informed he could pick whatever seat he wanted, he claimed the last seat in the center row.

The room filled up quickly, and Monsieur Parshall was waiting for the bell when Elspeth McGuire slipped through the door. As surprised to see him as he was to see her, she smiled shyly as she took the only remaining seat next to him. Then glancing over, she grinned. "Padding your GPA, huh?

Attempting to look innocent, Andre cocked his head. "Hey, I hear French is a tough language…

"You'll probably have to tutor me."

Smiling and frowning at the same time, Elspeth pursed her lips together and looked down at her desk. "You're teasing," she said softly.

Surprised by her response – shocked would be a better word, actually – Andre hesitated for a moment. Recovering, he forced a polite smile. "Maybe a little."

Theoretically, at least, Vamps have the same range of emotions as humans. But practice was another matter – most of them bought into the myth that Vampires are immortal, despite all evidence to the contrary, and firmly believed they were a superior species. But because Civilized Vamps interacted with humans on a routine basis, they usually tried to tone down their arrogance for PR purposes. Most of the time, though, it was there, lurking just below the surface.

But Elspeth, for some reason, seemed surprisingly unaffected.

Andre was puzzling through that particular paradox when the bell rang. After clearing his throat and calling for attention, Monsieur Parshall introduced himself. A French-speaking native of Quebec, he'd taken his undergraduate degree in journalism before being hired by a major newspaper. After spending ten years as a reporter in Paris, he'd enrolled at the Sorbonne and taken a masters degree in French Language. Then after knocking around the Third World as a UPI stringer, he'd finally met and married an American girl in Australia and they'd eventually settled in Vermont. Impressed by the teacher's Parisian accent, Andre made a mental note to watch his own – lest the snobbish instructor dismiss him as mere *paysan*.

But unfortunately, the class went downhill from there – and despite his recent dose of caffeine, Andre had to fight to stay awake. On the bright side, though, he managed to avoid the temptation posed by Elspeth's blouse. After congratulating himself when the bell rang, he gathered up his gear and bolted for the door.

Slipping into the stream of students that filled the hallway, he made his way back to his locker in the North Building – which was located twenty feet or so from his second period history class. He was in the process of pulling his gym stuff free when he heard a crash a few feet to the left, followed by a muted exclamation. Turning slightly to see what had caused the commotion, he was surprised to find Elspeth down on one knee, picking up the books she'd dropped. Given the geometry involved it was impossible to overlook her breasts, now suddenly displayed in all their glory. Transfixed by the extraordinary sight, his jaw dropped and his eyes widened.

Wow...

That was an entirely normal reaction for a 17-year old male – but unfortunately, Lydia had caught him in the act. Approaching from an unexpected angle, she was grinning from ear to ear.

Oh Christ! he swore. *Talk about busted...*

Quickly turning back to his locker, Andre finished retrieving his gear. Embarrassed, he slammed the door shut and banged his head against it.

Idiot!

Not quite sure how to extricate himself from that one, he took a deep breath before turning on his heel. Nodding at the sisters – who were now standing next to Elspeth's open locker conversing – Andre wished them a good evening, and brushed past them in a hasty retreat.

CHAPTER 8

He was still wondering what kind of moron fixates on a Vampire's breasts when he wheeled the Vette into his uncle's driveway ten minutes later. After gathering up his stuff, he marched up to the front door and punched in the access code before pushing it open with his shoulder. Then after stepping inside, he pushed it shut with his heel and made his way up the steps to his bedroom. Tossing his gear on his bed, he stripped off his clothes and changed into jeans, boots, a wool shirt, and a light vest. Then after putting on his Stetson, he picked up the map he'd been working with – along with the yellow crayon he was using to mark it – and stuffed them both into his shirt pocket, before strapping his Legion combat knife around his thigh and heading downstairs.

Serious business, he thought as he unlocked the gun cabinet hidden in the hallway closet.

There's at least six of the freaks around here, and probably more...

And the fact that they were well behaved in public didn't mean jack.

Pulling a 9mm semi-automatic nestled in a shoulder holster from its peg, he strapped it on and reached into the top drawer for magazines and hollow points. After filling four, he drew his weapon and checked the action. Satisfied, he slipped a magazine into place and chambered a round. Then after pushing the safety to the on position, he slipped it back in the holster and pulled two thirty-round AK-47 magazines from the drawer. Loading them with hollow points as well, he laid one on the end table against the wall beside the closet door before pulling his AK-47 from its perch. After checking the action, he popped the second magazine into place, flipped the safety on and slung it over his shoulder. Then after placing the extra mag in his vest pocket, he pulled his Katana from its resting place before closing the cabinet and spinning the combination dial to secure it. Then he headed out to the stable.

Exiting through the rear kitchen door, Andre was surprised to see the Plexiglas dome over the pool had apparently been completed. Pleased to see the basin filling, he made a mental note to start swimming laps as soon as the pool filled and the water temperature stabilized.

Probably a couple of days…

After passing by the pool, he was even more surprised to see the stable door still open. Puzzled that the new hand was still there, he checked his watch. "Hey, Ben!

"Working late?"

"Hey Andre," came the reply. "Come on in."

After swinging wide so he could see what was inside before actually entering, he strolled through the large double doors. Finding Ben Watson saddling up Josephine – the mare – he stopped, and asked him what was up.

As he turned around to reply, the older man's mouth fell open and his eyes widened. "You plan on starting a war?"

Shaking his head, Andre said no. "But after getting chased by that damn bear, I decided I'd better pack a little firepower on the trails."

Eyeing Andre's hardware skeptically, he shook his head. "Not exactly what I'd recommend for bear."

Andre shrugged. "A burst of hollow points ought to do the job."

After a moment's consideration, Ben shrugged. "You know, that whole thing was weird…

"Black bears hardly ever attack anyone – he must have already been spooked when you ran into him."

Then after tightening the saddle, Ben asked if Andre wanted to take Josephine. "I took Bonaparte out this morning, but between the pool contractor, the roofer, and the repairs I'm making on the stable I didn't get around to Josephine…

"I was going to take her out myself, and see if I could find the dogs – they chased a rabbit into the woods a half hour ago, by the way."

Nodding, Andre said Josephine would do fine – and told him not to worry about the dogs, because they'd come home when they got hungry. Then after changing the subject back, Andre asked Ben what might have panicked the bear that had chased him and Bonaparte the week before.

Perplexed, Ben ran his hands through his long gray hair. "Hell, I don't know...

"But I've lived around these parts long enough to know how dangerous the woods are."

Then after pausing for a moment, he shrugged and guessed a pack of wolves might have been harassing the creature. "The state claims there aren't any wolves around here anymore, but that's a BS story if there ever was one...

"They're out there, because I've seen 'em myself."

Shifting on his feet, Andre nodded. "Makes sense," he said. "They ever kill anyone?"

Ben turned around again. "Not that I know of...

"But you wouldn't believe how many hunters and campers disappear around here every year...

"Couple a three hundred in the woods, maybe half that many on the Lake."

Alarmed – and now suddenly suspicious – Andre asked him how he knew that.

Turning around again and leaning against the horse, Ben shrugged. "Oldest boy – my stepson – works for the State Police task force on organized crime, and he's their liaison officer with the Royal Canadian Mounted Police across the border...

"He tells me about three hundred American cars and vans turn up in Montreal's chop-shops every summer, and maybe a hundred boats...

"But the funny thing is all owners have vanished without a trace...

"No stolen vehicle report, no missing persons report, no bodies."

Puzzled, Andre asked him how the hell that could be. Ben shrugged, and said the reporting system was screwed up. "Think about it...

"Some camper drives up here from New York, parks his car or van and heads off into the woods...

"Then the vehicle disappears, and so does the owner and all his gear. There's no physical evidence a crime was committed...

The Mist & the Darkness

"Hell, there's not even any evidence they were here unless they happened to use a credit card in-state…

"But Vermont just isn't that big, so the odds are they didn't even stop for gas."

Thinking that made sense, Andre nodded. "And the state government's covering it up?"

Ben shook his head to the contrary. "Given the way the system works, there's nothing to cover up – just a lot of American vehicles turning up on the Montreal black market. The fact that the owners are missing makes it a mystery, not a crime."

Then Ben laughed sadly. "Not that anyone in government actually cares…"

"That's par for the course," Andre replied. Because he'd already figured out governments were big tax machines that didn't really care about the people they ruled. If they did, they would have done something about Vampires a long time ago.

As Andre took Josephine's reins from Ben's outstretched hand, he asked if there were any other nasties in the woods he should know about.

After staring at him for a long moment, Ben turned away. "Trust me, Andre…

"You *don't* want to know."

Not quite an admission, but for Andre it was close enough. *There's Vamps in the woods, and Ben's seen them…*

Probably out on the Lake, too…

Nodding to himself as Ben walked away, Andre led the horse out of the stable before securing his Katana's scabbard and climbing into the saddle. Cantering Josephine past the little memorial that marked the spot where a previous owner of the house had died, he turned the horse onto the nearest of the three north-south trails that ran past The Cove.

Taking the southerly direction, Andre focused on the terrain. He wasn't looking for Vamps that day, or even evidence of their presence – he was looking for observation posts and ambush sites instead. Having already covered the trail north to the Canadian border, he wanted to chart the southern part before moving deeper into the trees. As far as he had been able to determine, no one had been killed in either The Cove or its immediate vicinity in over forty years – but the woods were apparently a whole 'nother story...

After pulling the AK-47 off his shoulder and releasing the safety, he chambered a round before cradling it in his right arm. Based on what Ben had said, Andre surmised that one or more groups of Vamps were feeding in the woods, and fencing their victims' vehicles, boats, and camping gear across the border.

Probably follow the tourists...

That season had just wound down, and the hunting season was about to begin. Thinking the Vamps were probably less inclined to attack heavily armed hunters than campers, Andre was reasonably convinced that most of them had already cleared out. But given the way his luck had been running that day, he wasn't going to take any chances.

Some of the freaks are probably still hanging around...

With that very much in mind, Andre brought Josephine to a halt a half hour later and climbed down in front of a natural rock formation. After scaling it and finding a crevice that provided excellent cover, he pulled his map out of his shirt pocket and marked it with the crayon. From where he crouched, he could see three hundred yards south, down the trail, and a bit more than half that up the trail to the north. Noting that it also provided an excellent view of the southern portion of The Cove, he congratulated himself on finding a perfect observation post.

Which in fact it was – because if he'd brought his binoculars, he might have glimpsed the McGuire sisters through their kitchen window. Gathered around the table with their adoptive mother, Lydia was teasing Elspeth again.

CHAPTER 9

After climbing down from the rocks, Andre had re-mounted Josephine and followed the trail the remaining two miles or so until it began running parallel to the old county road that ran along the lake.

The Mist & the Darkness

With the sun settling low on the horizon, he decided to take the road back into The Cove, and then follow the state road home.

It took more than an hour, but it was a pleasant ride. So after removing the bridle, saddle and blanket, and brushing down the horse, Andre checked to make sure that she and Bonaparte had oats and water. Then after gathering up his gear, he closed up the stable and went back inside the house. He cleared the AK, wiped it down and secured it in the gun locker. But even with Ben out back in the cottage allocated to the stable hand, the two superbly well-trained guard dogs that had finally found their way home, and a state of the art alarm system, he kept his sidearm in the shoulder holster and the Katana hung on his back.

He didn't really think they'd get hit that night, but the fact that there were at least six Vamps in town and probably more in the woods was disconcerting. Although they couldn't actually enter the house without an invitation, there was nothing to keep them from tossing a Molotov cocktail through his window – and Civilized Vamps, at least, had been known to hire humans to do their dirty work. So after uncorking a fresh bottle of wine and knocking out his homework at his bedroom desk, he started working his way through the various possibilities that might confront him in The Cove.

As far as the McGuires went, Andre was more convinced than ever that his initial take was right: they were Civilized Vamps, recycling their identities in The Cove. Unless he threatened them, he had nothing to worry about. The only real issue was what they would consider a threat.

An unprovoked confrontation, certainly – especially one that threatened to blow their cover. But even then, Andre was almost certain they wouldn't attack him in public or semi-public places. The three north-south trails that ran by The Cove were more problematical – the father away from town, the more potentially dangerous they were.

The Vamps in the woods posed a more complicated threat. From what he'd learned from Ben, they were probably a group of Predators engaged in grand theft. In that case they were motivated by profit as well as blood, and that made them more or less predictable. Given the fact that no one from The Cove had been murdered in the last 40 years or so, or even vanished mysteriously, they'd probably made a calculated decision to leave the locals in peace. As long as they didn't wander too far into the woods, they didn't have anything to worry about.

That left the Feral types, who posed a far more serious danger. Given the fact that Vamps in general are a fairly territorial lot, Andre suspected the Fang Gang that was jacking the cars and boats wouldn't tolerate the Feral types on their turf during the summer months. So the real question was whether they moved into the area after the thieves cleared out in the fall.

Leaning back in his chair as he finished off his glass, he had to admit he didn't know. Aside from his late night encounter with three of the fanged freaks in New York, he didn't have a whole lot to go on. Given their lower body temperatures, it seemed reasonable to suppose they went south for the winter. But since Feral Vamps were an unpredictable bunch, that analysis was entirely conjectural. Making a mental note to research it on the Net the next day, he decided he should discuss it with his uncle, too – when he eventually got back from Washington.

Convinced he'd taken things as far as the facts would permit, he placed his Katana on the floor by his bed and hung the shoulder holster on the back of his chair. After withdrawing his weapon from it and inspecting the safety, he placed it under his pillow before bolting the door from the inside.

As he turned, *Buffy the Vampire Slayer* suddenly came to mind. *Freaking place is like Sunnydale*, he thought...

Probably even got a Hellmouth buried underneath the damn school...

CHAPTER 10

Andre was still chuckling about that when he wheeled the Vette into the student parking lot the next morning. After finding a distant parking space, he climbed out and retrieved his backpack from behind the driver's seat. Having overdressed the day before, he'd toned things down a bit. He was still wearing summer weight khakis,

The Mist & the Darkness

a tie, and spit-shined loafers, but he'd substituted a lightweight hooded jacket for the blazer and the backpack for the briefcase.

Having arrived almost a half hour before start of business, he made his way to the cafeteria. Because Newton had almost 200 dorm rats, it served three meals a day – except for Sunday, when it served brunch and dinner. But the student lounge was open from 8am through 10 pm Monday through Friday, and on Sundays, and until midnight on Saturdays.

Half tempted by the breakfast line – scrambled eggs, bacon, sausage, toast, hash browns, juice and coffee – he hesitated for a moment before heading into the Lounge instead. He'd already eaten a standard continental breakfast that morning, so he just wasn't that hungry.

As he approached the open double doors, he was surprised to see the Fang Gang exiting with coffees in hand. Thinking that was something you don't see every day, he forced a smile and greeted them in French.

"Bonjour Mesdames, Messieurs."

Lydia gave him a "Gotcha Grin," Elspeth tried to frown but half-smiled anyway, and the guys snickered and said "Hey!"

Given their reaction, there was only one possible conclusion. *Big Sis ratted me out...*

Temporarily forgetting the fact that Lydia was a Vampire, he made a mental note to even up with her the first chance he got. Then after spending a couple of minutes in line at the coffee bar, he passed two dollars over the counter and headed out the door with a *Café au lait* in hand.

The McGuires were sitting at the same table as the day before, along the northwest interior wall. Sheltered from the morning sun that poured through the exterior glass curtain wall, Lydia and Elspeth were apparently surfing the net on their laptops while the guys talked. Thinking he might as well catch up on the news, Andre found an empty table and took off his backpack. After swinging it around and resting it on the tabletop, he retrieved his computer and sat down. After firing it up, he began reading the international section of *Yahoo News*.

Same stuff different day, he thought. *A major terrorist attack in Iraq, inconclusive fighting in Afghanistan...*

And more BS out of North Korea.

Bored, he closed out *Yahoo* and clicked on the bookmark for *le Monde*.

Finding nothing of interest in the French newspaper, he closed the laptop and shoved it back into the padded carrying compartment in his backpack. Then he grabbed his gear, got up and headed for the "Upper Class Smoking Lounge" – in reality, a corner beneath the steps outside where the Juniors and Seniors could sneak a smoke.

Newton officially banned smoking on campus, but as long as students were out of sight the faculty and staff pretended not to notice the Upper Classmen – and women – that huddled in the shadow of the steps. In fact, the janitorial staff had even put a canister ashtray out there so they wouldn't litter the concrete with cigarette butts.

Thinking hypocrisy was the grease that lubricated the gears of society, Andre shook a *Gauloises* free as he rounded the steps outside. An American variant manufactured in the United States, it was made with light tobaccos and was barely half as strong as the traditional variety sold in France.

Surprised to see one of the Jocks leaning back against the corner formed by the intersection of the retaining wall and the steps, Andre nodded and said "Hi" before pulling a lighter out of his jacket and lighting up. Not really knowing any of the other students, he smoked it in silence.

Back in the cafeteria, Elspeth frowned. She'd seen Andre make his way outside, and guessed where he was going. Aside from the fact that she didn't like cigarette smoke in the first place, the odor of tobacco overwhelmed the human scent. That was important to Vampires, because every human emotion generated a faint but specific smell – and once a Vampire learned to interpret them, it was fairly simple to infer what was going on in human heads.

Andre had puzzled her the day before. Because Vampires appeared to be human in almost every way, they were rarely recognized – at least not at the level of waking consciousness. But deep down inside, people often sensed a dangerous presence, and the subconscious fear they experienced found expression in a number of subtle ways. One was a sense of generalized anxiety; another was the mix of smells they emitted.

But as they sat together in History class the day before, Elspeth had been confused. Andre had been a bit nervous, of course, but that was to be expected from someone on their first day in a new school. And while there had been a surge of adrenalin and testosterone when he'd sat down, the smell of fear had been entirely absent. But what had surprised her were the mingled scents of mastery and control – and that, eventually, had made her wonder if Andre somehow knew what she was.

For a Vampire, that would normally be an unsettling, fearful prospect – but for some inexplicable reason, she found it exciting. Then thinking back to the surge of pheromones that had overwhelmed the other scents after Andre had sat down beside her, Elle smiled to herself.

I may be a monster, she thought. *But I'm still pretty!*

With that, she collected her purse and her books. Ignoring Lydia altogether, she told her brothers she was going to class early.

Elspeth was still angry at her adoptive sister. Lydia had teased her unmercifully about Andre, but she was even more upset by the fact that Lydia had accused her of deliberately flashing him in the hallway. That had been entirely accidental, and if Lydia thought she'd done it on purpose she should think again.

And it was totally unfair – because compared to Lydia, she was a paragon of virtue.

Lydia had been orphaned in 1922 at the age of twelve. Taken in by her maternal aunt in Chicago, she'd dropped out of school when she turned 16 and taken a job singing in a speakeasy. She had a beautiful voice, and might have become famous if she hadn't been so careless – she'd gotten mixed up with a gang of bootleggers, and when she wasn't entertaining them at the club, she was drinking and dancing with them until all hours of the night, and doing God knows what else.

Given her lifestyle, the decent people who knew her figured her days were numbered, and they were right. Walking home late one night, she was attacked by a Vampire who'd almost killed her. If an off-duty police officer hadn't chanced upon them and emptied his service revolver into the perp, it would have been the end of the road. But Lydia got lucky twice that night, because Dr. McGuire was then living only two or three doors down. Awakened by the gunfire, he'd grabbed his medical satchel and raced to the scene. And so by an astonishing coincidence, the only Vampire physician then practicing in North America stemmed the bleeding and saved her life.

But even after five centuries of research there was nothing Dr. McGuire could do about the virus that had invaded her body, except help her through the transition. After she recovered, he and his family had taken her in.

Although the McGuire household had provided her with a far better environment than anything she'd experienced in her 17-and-a-half years, she'd never fully subdued her wild inclinations. She still drank, she still smoked occasionally, and she still slept around – and not just with other Vampires. She'd left a string of broken hearts from one end of the country to the other, and most of them had been human.

In contrast, Elspeth had only a minor indiscretion to her name – the daughter of a Baptist preacher, she'd made the mistake of sneaking off one night in the fall of 1956 and going to a drive-in movie with a handsome young man she'd met the day before. As they were huddling under a blanket watching the movie, he'd nicked her with his fangs. Mistaking the Vampire's bloodlust for a sexual come-on, she'd slugged him before jumping out of the car and racing to the concession stand. The sympathetic manager had driven her home, and all might have been well if the infection hadn't overwhelmed her immune system. When she finally realized what had happened, she'd packed her suitcase and fled into the woods that surrounded her small Alabama town.

Somehow managing to resist the temptation to feed off of humans, she'd moved into an abandoned shack located deep in the forest and survived by hunting and trapping animals. It was during one of her hunts that she stumbled across the McGuires, who had been living in a nearby town for almost a decade. Jumping at the opportunity to join them, she accompanied them to their new home in Colorado a few weeks later.

It wasn't like she hadn't had any boyfriends in the fifty some odd years that had passed since then. She'd gone out with several Vampires, but she'd always broken it off when things started getting physical. It wasn't that she was a prude – far from it. But she wanted more than most Vampires were willing to offer: a loving relationship, like the one her adoptive parents had.

Of course Lydia teased her about that, too, so throughout her first period Trig class Elspeth alternately fumed at her sister and puzzled over Andre. When the bell finally rang, she was happy and relieved.

Arriving at their shared history class just after he did, she returned his muted greeting with a soft smile and took her place. Then quite unexpectedly, she turned in her seat and addressed him. "Smoking, huh?

"That's really bad for you, you know!"

Surprised, Andre looked over at her incredulously. *And sitting next to a Vampire is healthy?*

Then suddenly amused by the irony, he chuckled. "Well, I don't do that very often."

After cocking her head and giving him a probing look, she stuck her nose up in the air and said "Good."

Then she turned back to face Dr. Marigold, as the teacher took the roll.

Wondering what the hell that had been about, Andre stole a look at Elspeth. She had her hair down this time, and was wearing a dark blue skirt and a white silk blouse, a brightly colored scarf around her neck, pearl earrings, sheer stockings and two-inch heels. Impressed, Andre gave her credit.

Not bad for a chick who's stone-cold dead…

Then after sneaking a glance at Lydia, he was forced to admit the Big Sis wasn't bad either.

Less distracted than the day before, Andre spent most of the class absorbed in Dr. Marigold's lecture about the dissolution of the Western Roman Empire. Far more interesting than English Lit the hour before, he was scribbling furiously in his spiral notebook as Elspeth discreetly sniffed the air. Unable to extract anything of use from the odor that still hung heavy on his clothes, she realized her attempt at intelligence gathering would have to wait until French that afternoon.

But having forgotten all about her plan, she was taken aback when Andre joked as she took her seat next to him in sixth period.

Hoping the presence of Vampires at school was more farce than drama, Andre looked over at her and feigned surprise.

"Mademoiselle," he exclaimed in an absurdly exaggerated French accent. *"We cannot keep meeting zees way."*

Then after throwing up his hands, he shook his head. *"Zee people weel talk!"*

After a moment of stunned incredulity, Elspeth broke up laughing.

But unfortunately for her, the instructor had just started calling the role. Irritated by her merriment, Monsieur Parshall looked down at the seating chart to ascertain the name of the miscreant. Then after looking back up, he gave Elspeth a withering glare.

"Mademoiselle McGuire," he demanded to know. "Is there something you'd like to share with the class?"

Whereupon Andre whispered out of the side of his mouth, "Told ya…"

With that, Elspeth completely lost it. Bent over her desk howling, she shook her head back and forth.

After fuming for a long moment, the imperious instructor glared at Elspeth again and informed her in an icy voice that she could ponder that in detention.

Uh oh…

Aghast that Elspeth was being unfairly punished for his jest, Andre leaped to his feet. "Monsieur Professeur, please do not blame Mademoiselle…

"The fault is mine."

Now glaring at Andre, Monsieur Parshall paused for a moment. "How very chivalrous, Monsieur!"

Than after looking down and scribbling a note on his roster, he continued in a voice that reeked of sarcasm. "I'm sure the Headmaster will be pleased by your gallantry."

Oh crap…

CHAPTER 11

He wasn't.

But on the bright side, Headmaster Renfrowe was a great deal less upset than Andre had feared. After listening to his slightly edited explanation of the incident and accepting his emphatic assumption of responsibility, Dr. Renfrowe had pointed at the floor and demanded 250 pushups. After Andre knocked them out, the Headmaster tore up their detention slips, and told him to get lost.

Still sitting in a chair outside the Headmaster's door, Elspeth had been relieved to learn their sentences had been commuted.

So rather than return to French class – from which they'd been banished for the day – the two jailbirds spent the rest of sixth period hanging out in the student lounge, swapping lies over *Café au laits*. Andre had listened attentively to Elspeth's cover story, and pretended to believe it. Then after she'd finished, he'd told her his.

Considerably more credible than the one Elspeth had pitched, Andre felt confident that she believed it. But all things considered – sipping coffee with a Vamp in the Student Lounge topped out at 11.5 on his 10-Point Weirdness Scale. Had it actually been possible, her off-beat sense of humor and corny jokes would have pushed it even higher.

Fortunately, there hadn't been a great deal of fall-out. Although sharing a coffee with Elspeth had raised a few eyebrows, he'd been able to explain it away in terms of professional courtesy. Physicians were thick as thieves, he told the Jocks and Cheerleaders over lunch the next day, and if he weren't nice to the McGuires his uncle would raise hell about it. Then in order to quell the fast spreading rumors – and keep his romantic options open – he'd pulled out a picture of his second cousin. Three years older and stunningly beautiful, she'd inscribed the photo in a manner that could be mistranslated as sensual. Informing the football team she was college sophomore in Montreal, he scored extra points for having an older girlfriend.

Andre was still chuckling about that as he pounded down the pavement of the State Road a week later. Slowing slightly as he approached the lane that led to the house he shared with his uncle, he congratulated himself on a good run – eight miles up to the junction with the Interstate, and eight miles back on the state road. He was sweating of course, but nowhere close to tired. Barely aware of the rucksack strapped to his back containing forty pounds of sand, he slowed again as he made the right turn onto the asphalt that led to the Chalet.

The place was enormous. Built by a railroad baron at the turn of the twentieth century, it had served as a luxury-hunting lodge until the man's death in 1920. Passed along to his eldest son, it had remained in the family until the late 1960's when it had been put up for sale. Bought by a retired steel magnate as a country retreat, it remained a hideaway for the New York's rich and powerful until a new investor purchased it in 1989. That owner had operated it profitably until stricken by a heart attack four years later.

He had been a better businessman than financial planner, and when the staff found his lifeless body aside the closest of the old Indian trails that crossed the far eastern edge of the property, the lodge had promptly closed. With no will, the Chalet and the rest of the man's estate had been thrown into probate court. When the tax and inheritance issues where finally resolved three years later, a millionaire from Silicon Valley had bought the place and promptly remodeled it. The original sixteen bedrooms on the second story of the main portion of the Chalet had been reduced to six, the ground floor kitchen had been completely remodeled and modernized, and the interior finishes replaced along with the all of the wiring and plumbing. The enormous dining room to the left of the entry foyer had been left almost unchanged, but the equally spacious living room to the right had been completely re-done, as had the combination bar and recreation room that extended from it.

The aging Olympic-sized pool behind the Chalet had been torn out and replaced, along with the tennis courts that stood off to the right, and the stable that lay beyond had been rebuilt from the ground up. But after the golf course had been turned into a pasture, the only reminders that the Chalet had once been a commercial property were the cottages that lay a half-mile beyond at the edge of the woods. One had been left as residence for the stable master, and another for the groundskeeper, and the last for a combination cook and maid.

After spending the better part of four million remodeling the Chalet to suit his tastes, the new owner had taken a major hit with the dot-com implosion and was almost forced into bankruptcy.

He'd managed to hang onto it until 2006, when an improved real estate market had persuaded him to sell. Andre's uncle had chanced upon it in an Internet ad, and after virtual tour of the 1500-acre property, he'd bought it as an investment. But after finally managing to pry André out of the Legion in 2008, Dr. Marchand had accepted the counsel of the psychiatrist and the psychologists, and moved there.

Having lived in The Cove for more than a month, Andre had begun to think of the Chalet as home. Slowing his pace again as he emerged from the wooded lane onto the manicured grass, he pushed his sweatband higher on his forehead before coming to a halt before the double doors of the entranceway. Surprised to see his uncle's car in the driveway, he ran in place for another minute before pushing the right one open.

After calling out in French to announce his return, Andre closed the door behind him. Hearing the pop of a wine cork, he made his way through the dining room into the kitchen. "You're back early," he said.

Half turning as he poured a glass, Dr. Marchand nodded. "My meetings went surprisingly well, for once."

Nodding, Andre said "good."

"Does that mean you're going into clinical trials?"

Chuckling as he sipped from his glass, Dr. Marchand shook his head. "Not yet, but the FDA's given it 'fast-track status' so they may start any day now."

Finishing the glass, he poured another. "Would you care to join me in the den?"

Andre nodded. "Yeah, we need to talk…

"But give me a couple of minutes to shower first."

As his uncle nodded, he turned and retraced his steps before bounding up the over-wide staircase to his room. Then after dropping his pack and pulling off his clothes and tossing them in the general direction of the wicker hamper, he strode into his bathroom to shower.

Much refreshed, he strolled into the den some seven or eight minutes later. Looking up from the journal he'd been perusing, Dr. Marchand pointed at the glass of wine on the small table that separated his leather-bound chair from the other, and asked him to take a seat.

"You said we needed to talk. I presume it has to do with your school?"

After sniffing the wine, Andre took a sip. "The school's fine, Uncle…

"But I have some, *uh*…

"Interesting classmates, if you will…"

Raising his eyebrows, Dr. Marchand repeated his statement. "Interesting?"

Cradling his glass in his lap, Andre nodded. "Four Vamps – two girls, two guys, posing as family and passing as juniors."

Taken aback, Dr. Marchand looked at him incredulously. "You jest!"

Shaking his head to the contrary, Andre said no.

"They are civilized, I presume?"

After taking another drink, Andre shrugged. "I think so…

"They moved here last January, and so far at least there haven't been any problems. I've checked around, and there haven't been any killings within miles of The Cove as far back as anyone can remember."

Dr. Marchand nodded thoughtfully. "The four passing as students…

"I presume they have 'parents'?"

Andre nodded. "Dr. and Mrs. McGuire."

Stunned, it took a moment for Dr. Marchand to react. *"Mon Dieu!*

"From the clinic?"

Andre nodded again before draining his glass. "Yes, Sir."

Then after standing, he asked his uncle if he'd like another glass. After Dr. Marchand said no, Andre excused himself to refill his own. Then after returning and settling back into his seat, he asked if his uncle had met Dr. McGuire.

Dr. Marchand shook his head. "No, he was on vacation when I visited. But the senior physician – Dr. Sanders – was there, and he spoke very highly of Dr. McGuire…

"He described him as an exceptionally able surgeon."

Andre shifted in his seat and nodded. "That makes sense – his so-called kids are smart as hell. They took the top four places in academic achievement last year."

After fumbling in his suit coat, Dr. Marchand pulled a Gauloises from a crumpled pack, and lit it. "I presume you've met them by now?"

Andre nodded, and reached for the pack his uncle had tossed on the end table. Ignoring Dr. Marchand's scathing look, he shook a cigarette free and lit it. Deciding it would be better to let the hour he'd spent with Elspeth in the student lounge slide, he told his uncle they were well mannered and polite, but a bit distant.

"They stick to themselves, and as far as I'm aware they're not involved in any social activities."

Then after taking another sip of wine, he continued. "Most of the other students think they're clannish and stuck-up, but I've spoken to them all and they've been quite nice…

"So I think they're just recycling their identities."

Dr. Marchand nodded. "Do you have any classes with them?"

Andre nodded. "At least one class with each, and I sit next to one of the girls in History and French."

Dr. Marchand gave him a weary look. "And she is pretty, no doubt?"

Andre grinned and nodded, before draining his glass. "Yes."

Dr. Marchand sighed. "And I suppose you intend to seduce this creature?"

Andre hesitated for a long moment. Then sloshing his wine around in his glass, he 'fessed up. "Well, the thought's occurred to me…

"But for now, at least, I'm just kind of getting to know her."

After shaking his head in silent disapproval, Dr. Marchand shifted in his chair and pointed his finger at Andre for emphasis. "You're an idiot, you know."

Having heard that before, Andre chuckled and took another sip of wine. He was about to reply when Dr. Marchand continued. "Had

I known your mother would give birth to a fool, I might not have been so pleased when she married your father."

Making a face, Andre glanced over. "You can't blame it all on her, Philippe – and besides, I thought you liked my mom."

Dr. Marchand drew on his cigarette again, before correcting him. "I loved your mother – she was a saint, you know…

"But I cannot believe you inherited your rebellious streak from the Marchand side of the family."

"Need I remind you that twelve hundred years ago our common ancestor rode with Charlemagne? Or that our family has stood as a pillar of civilization for more than a millennium?

"Aside from the noble blood that runs in our veins, we have given France six marshals, eleven generals and five admirals – not to mention a president, distantly related – and three prime ministers…

"As well as scores of ambassadors, government ministers, philosophers, clerics, scholars, jurists, scientists and physicians of renown."

Then Dr. Marchand chuckled, and took another drink of his wine. "And now a corporal of the *Légion éntrangere!*"

Thinking that was a bit unfair, Andre retorted that he would have made sergeant in another year. "Except a certain uncle – who-shall-remain-nameless – pulled strings in Paris, and got me booted!"

"And besides," he added in mock churlishness, "I'm technically a First Lieutenant these days."

Smiling at his nephew's defense, Dr. Marchand retorted. "Yes, and if you're a First Lieutenant, then I'm Joan of Arc…"

Then after chuckling again, Dr. Marchand looked at Andre, and raised his glass. "But you have proved yourself in battle and you have shed your blood for France – and for that I must commend you."

Although Andre appreciated his uncle's recognition, he decided to press him a bit harder by reminding the elder Marchand that he'd had an adventure or two of his own. "I seem to remember Father telling me about a certain swordsman who got caught *in flagrante* with the Persian Emperor's favorite wife, and slaughtered half the palace guard fighting his way out of the harem…

"And then, *let's see*…

"Who could forget about Countess Nicole?

"Or that little incident with the Madame de Pompadour…

Dr. Marchand shrugged, as the slightest hint of a smile crept across his face. "I warned your father not to tell you those things, for fear you'd repeat my indiscretions."

Incredulous, Andre turned in his chair. "Indiscretions? You call seducing the King's favorite mistress 'an indiscretion'???"

After sighing, Dr. Marchand shook his head dismissively. "That was blown far out of proportion."

Astonished by his uncle's cavalier response, Andre stared at his uncle in disbelief. "Out of proportion???

"For God's sake, Philippe! You made a fool of the King!"

Dr Marchand chuckled, and shook his head to the contrary. "Andre, I can assure you that His Majesty was not the least bit embarrassed that I seduced Madame…

"On the contrary – he was *impressed!*"

Figuring that was probably true, Andre lit another cigarette and shook his head again. *The man shacked with every beautiful aristocrat from Dublin to Tokyo, and he's upset that I'm crushin' on one little Vamp girl???*

With his nephew momentarily stilled, Dr. Marchand shifted in his chair and became suddenly serious again. "Andre, you're far too headstrong for me to dissuade you from pursuing this affair, but I must warn you that romantic relationships between humans and Vampires rarely end well."

Thinking there was no point in debating that particular fact, Andre stubbed his cigarette out in the ashtray and drained his glass.

Yeah, well – you oughta know…

CHAPTER 12

After a long moment of silence, Dr. Marchand continued. "I'm sure I've mentioned this before, but under the circumstances it bears repeating…

"With the Vampire, the sex drive and the killer instinct are closely connected – in a moment of passion, she could rip your throat out without even realizing what she's done."

Fully aware of that fact, Andre nodded before reassuring his uncle. "I barely know the girl, Philippe...

"We say 'hello' in the hallways, but little more than that. She and her supposed siblings keep to themselves, and in any event they're not especially popular with the friends I've made..."

That was true, insofar as it went. But since he knew there was no way his uncle would ever approve of his intentions toward Elspeth, Andre changed the subject instead. "But aside from the McGuires, there's something else I wanted to discuss with you...

"According to Ben – the stable hand you hired just before you left – vacationers have been disappearing around here for decades...

"Campers in the back woods, and boaters out on the Lake."

After leaning back in his chair and staring at the ceiling for a long moment, Dr. Marchand shook his head. *"Son-of-a-bitch!"* he swore in French. "I should have known..."

After informing his uncle he was going to retrieve his map, Andre got up and walked into the dining area. Opening the closet door that hid the gun cabinet, he entered the combination and pulled the door open. Then after retrieving the folded up map he'd stashed there, he closed the doors and passed back through the living room into the den.

Opening the map on the six-sided gaming table, he gestured for his uncle.

After pinning the corners down with an ashtray and some other odds and ends, he gave Dr. Marchand a quick overview of his explorations, with particular emphasis on the first and second set of north-south trails.

"I've explored the first one very carefully, and marked the best observation posts and ambush sites with yellow crayon...

"The first trail in seems fairly safe – as I said earlier, no one has been murdered around here for decades and as far as I can tell there haven't been any unexplained disappearances among the townspeople, or animal attacks either...

"That said, vacationers have been disappearing by the hundreds every summer and their cars and boats are turning up on the Montreal black market. According to Ben's stepson – the state police officer – their owners are vanishing without a trace...

"Absolutely nothing to link their disappearances to this area."

The Mist & the Darkness

Dr. Marchand nodded thoughtfully. "So we have a highly professional gang of Predators operating in the vicinity. Did he mention anything else?"

Andre nodded. "First of all, he says there are wolves in the woods. And since the state claims they were wiped out decades ago, that may be significant…

"It suggests the government is hiding something from the public. But more important than that, Ben saw something out there that scared him so bad he won't even talk about it."

Dr. Marchand looked up and raised his eyebrows. "The Predators?"

Andre said he wasn't sure what Ben had seen, but he was inclined to think that Ben had chanced upon a group of Vamps feeding. "But I think you're probably right about the Predators – they're operating in the deep woods during the camping season…

"Killing the campers, stashing their bodies and fencing their stuff in Montreal…

"But whatever it was that scared Ben, it happened last winter – *after* the camping season, and about the same time the McGuires moved here."

After nodding thoughtfully, Dr. Marchand asked Andre if perhaps Ben had seen them hunting in the woods.

Andre nodded. "That had been my first thought. But the more I think about it, the less persuaded I am…

"So the question that's been troubling me is whether the criminal Vamps are hanging around in the winter, or if we have a more complicated problem."

Dr. Marchand stared at the map for an interminable moment before he replied. Choosing his words carefully, he said he was inclined to think there were at least two groups of Vamps in the area. "The Predators will be following the most vulnerable targets north in the summer and south in the winter, and carefully covering their tracks as they go…

"So the fact that Ben survived whatever it was he encountered suggests that he may have stumbled across one or more of the Feral variety."

Andre nodded. "But why would they remain in the north during winter? Especially during the hunting season?"

Dr. Marchand shrugged. "As I've explained, the process of becoming a Vampire can be physically and emotionally traumatic, and many who make it through the transformation suffer from severe neurological and psychological damage…

"Given that defining characteristic, feral Vampires are entirely unpredictable. There's often no rhyme or reason to their behavior…

"But having survived the change with a diminished level of functionality, we shouldn't be surprised that some lack the wit to migrate."

Nodding, Andre traced a line across the map with his finger. "I propose we define the second trail inland as our outer perimeter…

"And consider anything between that and the first inland trail as a free-fire zone."

Dr. Marchand nodded, and then looked at Andre. "But you are excepting the McGuires?"

After hesitating just for a moment, Andre nodded – unless they were hunting humans.

Nodding again, Dr. Marchand concurred. Then after pointing to a spot inland, he said they should mount a long-range patrol. "This valley – it looks to be about ten miles from here – it forms a natural convergence point…

"It seems a likely place for Feral Vampires to winter."

Andre nodded. "I've already planned a patrol for the weekend, so I'll swing through there."

Dr. Marchand shook his head emphatically. "No – wait until I get back," he said. "If my suspicions are correct, it will be far too dangerous to go alone."

After studying the map again and reflecting on his uncle's warning, Andre nodded. Then suddenly curious, Andre asked him where he'd put the scent-killer. Perplexed and clearly irritated, Dr. Marchand asked if he'd been patrolling without it.

"Well I've been on horseback, so it wouldn't have made any difference."

Nodding, his uncle told him there was a gallon in the upstairs closet, and then asked him what he'd been doing about his scent at school.

"Well I forgot where you put the stuff – and in any event, I don't think it's a good idea to give away a tactical advantage like that until I'm sure the McGuires can be trusted…

"So I've been covering my scent with cigarettes."

After granting the logic, Dr. Marchand glared at his nephew anyway. "Andre, you have to quit those damned things…

"You have no idea how much harm smoking inflicts upon the human body!"

Catching the look that flickered across his young ward's face, Dr. Marchand stiffened. "Don't start on me, Andre…

"You know damn well my circumstances are different!"

Suppressing the smile that had attempted to creep across his face, Andre nodded.

Then after glaring at his nephew again to emphasize the point, Dr. Marchand changed the subject. "Now tell me about the wolves…

"I find it curious the state denies their presence, even though they've been spotted by local citizens."

Andre shrugged. "Well I don't think Ben reported the sighting. He's more than a bit cynical when it comes to government."

Dr. Marchand said that was to be expected, given his unfortunate experience in the military. "You know he was wounded and left behind to die in El Salvadore."

After Andre nodded and said he'd overheard their conversation, Dr Marchand asked if Ben had described the animals in any way.

"Their size, their color?"

Andre shrugged. "I didn't think to ask him, but I will tomorrow." Then suddenly curious, he asked his uncle why it mattered.

Dr. Marchand thought about it for a moment. "It's just a hunch, at this point. But it occurs to me that the situation here may be even more complex than you've imagined."

It took a moment for that to sink in. "*Oh Christ!*" Andre exclaimed. *"Werewolves?"*

Dr. Marchand shrugged. "It's no more than a suspicion for now, but I suggest you get on the Internet tonight and do a thorough search regarding local legends and, especially, the ancient native legends."

Wondering why he hadn't thought of that, Andre shook his head and sighed before looking up at his uncle. "This damn place is like Sunnydale!"

Chuckling at the reference, Dr. Marchand nodded. "So it seems – but I'm afraid we'll have to make do without The Slayer."

Then changing the subject, he told Andre to get into his padding. "Given the threat-environment, we need to work on your Katana."

Dr. Marchand had once been the finest swordsman in Europe, and he probably still was. But with the Samurai sword, Andre was slowly but surely gaining on him – and one of these days, he was going to be even better.

Pleased by the thought, Andre rolled up his map and told his uncle he'd meet him out on the side yard in five minutes.

CHAPTER 13

After training with his uncle, Andre completed his homework before searching the Net. The Abenaki Indians had originally inhabited the area, and as far as he could tell none of their myths and legends mentioned werewolves. In fact, they didn't even seem to have a word to describe them.

But strangely enough, several accounts written by the early European settlers referred to the beasts – so if there were werewolves in the woods, he concluded, they'd probably come across the Atlantic by boat. Then after typing up a short summary for his uncle and taping it to the refrigerator, he'd gone to bed. By now far more relaxed than the week before, he slept with his Legion combat knife. But as a precaution, he'd transferred his firearms and his sword upstairs to the gun rack he'd installed in his room.

Now in his second week at Newton, Andre had fallen into a routine. He got up at 6:00 each morning, exercised, showered, and ate before leaving for school at 8:10. Arriving around 8:20, he made his way to the Student Lounge where he bought a *Café au lait* before perusing the news online. He ate lunch with the Jocks, used the story about his imaginary girlfriend to hold Kathy Norse and the rest of the Cheerleading Squad at bay, and smiled and said hello whenever he encountered the McGuires.

And for the most part, he successfully resisted the temptation to flirt with Elspeth.

By that time he'd become so used to the McGuires he'd all but forgotten they were Vampires. So as Elspeth turned into the hallway some twenty feet ahead of him the following Thursday, his attention was focused on her swaying hips rather than her fangs. Lost in the sort of fantasy only a teenaged Frenchman could have, it took two loudmouthed Geeks to bring him back to reality.

"There goes Weird Elspeth," said taller one with thick glasses, as she walked past. Whereupon the shorter one with the spiked hair laughed. "She's not just *weird*," he said. "She's *UGGGGLY!*"

Offended by the gratuitous attack, Andre maintained his pace as they approached. And then when they were within range, he dropped his books before reaching out and grabbing them by their collars. Pivoting, he slammed them back against the lockers that lined the hallway. Then after tightening his grip on the two terrified freshmen, he glared at one and then the other.

"Do you know who I am?" he demanded.

Scared out of their wits, the two quaking Geeks shook their heads back and forth. So after glaring at them again, Andre introduced himself. "I'm Andre Marchand, and I'm an Upper Classman – which makes me a *Very Important Person* around here."

Then after pausing for a moment to let that sink in, he continued. "As a matter of fact – I'm so important that Headmaster Renfrowe doesn't even hand out detention slips until he's cleared them with me!"

As their eyes bulged, the smaller geek gasped "Detention?"

Andre glared at him before roaring in his best drill-instructor voice. *"YOU HEARD ME, FOOL!"*

By now so frightened Andre thought they might wet their pants, he glared at them again. One was still shaking, the other had sweat beading on his forehead. Both of them had a look of abject terror in their eyes.

"Now I heard what you said about Elspeth McGuire…

"And if it were any of your business, I would tell you that Ms. McGuire is a perfectly lovely young woman – she is bright, personable, well-mannered, and polite…

"And she's neither weird nor ugly!"

Then after pulling the Geeks close, he glared at them again before bellowing. *"IS THAT CLEAR?"*

Nodding in unison, they managed to squeak. "Yes, Sir!"

Then after glaring at them for another long moment, he dropped his voice before warning them that Upper Class Women were off limits to freshmen and sophomores. "So don't even *think* about criticizing them…

"In fact – don't even *look* at 'em!"

Nodding, the two Geeks swore up and down they'd never, EVER do it again.

Justly skeptical, Andre tightened his grip on their collars. Then after another long silence, he demanded to know if this was their first offense.

Lying through their chattering teeth, the two delinquents swore they'd never been in trouble before. But even though they were obviously blowing smoke up his butt, Andre told the two miscreants he was going to let them off easy this time.

"But if you so much as *look* at an Upper Class Woman again, you're going to spend the rest of your *lives* in detention…

"Is that clear?"

Horrified, the smaller geek squeaked. *"Lifetime detention???"*

After a harsh glare, Andre nodded. *"You heard me, fool…*

"You're gonna be cashing your social security checks in the cafeteria!"

As the knees of the smaller geek buckled, the other one pleaded. "Please Mr. Marchand, we didn't mean any harm…

"We were just joking around!"

After halting the smaller one's slide and lifting him back up on his feet, Andre glared at them again.

"All right," he finally said. "Since this is your first offense, I'm going to let you go."

Then after slamming them back against the lockers again, he released them. "But I'm warning you…

"If you ever mess with an Upper Class Woman again, you're going to get *Life-Time-Detention!*"

Then he gestured with his head, and roared. *"NOW GET OUT OF HERE!"*

As the two terrified Geeks ran for their lives, the crowd that had gathered behind Andre in the hallway began applauding. Wilkinson clapped him on the shoulder, and said "Way to go!" while Kathy Norse declared it was about time someone put the little snerts in their place.

Another Cheerleader, standing farther back, expressed her outrage. "Can you imagine? Geeks criticizing us???"

Grinning, Andre gave the crowd a thumbs-up sign. And then to the accompaniment of more cheers and whistles, he picked up his books and set off for class.

By the beginning of fourth period, the whole school had heard about the incident – including, unfortunately, Headmaster Renfrowe. Summoned to his office from gym class, Andre reported in his athletic clothes.

Standing at attention in front of the Headmaster's desk, Andre waited as he finished scribbling something on a legal pad. After completing whatever it was he had been writing, Dr. Renfrowe looked up and scowled. "I understand you manhandled two freshmen in the hallway this morning."

In an effort to persuade the Headmaster that the incident had been wildly exaggerated, Andre explained he had merely advised them on proper hallway etiquette.

But Dr. Renfrowe didn't buy it. After giving him an exasperated look, the Headmaster told him to knock off the BS. "I heard all about it, Marchand."

Thinking his goose was cooked, Andre locked his eyes on the wall above the Headmaster and wondered what guard duty at Devil's Island was going to be like.

After a long and uncomfortable silence, Dr. Renfrowe said he understood the two freshmen had been mouthing off about Elspeth McGuire.

Still standing at attention, Andre nodded. "Yes, Sir."

Then after an even longer silence, the Headmaster sighed. "This is your lucky day, Marchand…

"Because less than 15 minutes ago, Dr. Purcell informed me he'd caught the little bastards hacking the school's computers, in some sort of grade-changing scam...

"They were changing less-than-satisfactory grades to A's for a hundred bucks a pop."

Astonished, Andre glanced at the Headmaster incredulously.

Leaning back in his chair, Dr. Renfrowe sighed. "The little pricks have been in trouble since preschool."

Then after glaring at Andre again, the Headmaster informed him that under any other circumstances he would have given him a week's suspension for banging them around. "But since you put the fear of God in 'em, you may have done me a favor."

Realizing he'd just caught the break of a lifetime, Andre tried hard to suppress the smile that was attempting to steal across his face.

There was another long pause as Dr. Renfrowe weighed his options. Then at long last, he picked up his pen, turned the page of his yellow pad, and scribbled a note. After he finished, he signed it, tore the page free and folded it over before handing it across his desk.

"You lucked out of the suspension, Marchand, but that doesn't mean you're off the hook. Report to Coach Jordan and give him this."

Taking the folded sheet of paper from the Headmaster, Andre asked if there would be anything else. When Dr. Renfrowe shook his head and said no, Andre did a crisp about-face and started for the door. But just as he reached it, the Headmaster called after him.

After Andre turned around to face him, Dr. Renfrowe leaned back in his chair and looked at him quizzically. "You got something going with Elspeth McGuire?"

Surprised, Andre hesitated a moment before shaking his head. "Not really..."

After staring at Andre for a long moment, Dr. Renfrowe pursed his lips and nodded. "Trust me, Marchand...

"You could do a *lot* worse!"

CHAPTER 14

It was just after 5:30 that evening when Andre finished up his sentence – 1000 push-ups and 100 laps around the 440-yard track. By Legion standards that was a joke, and he was still chuckling about it when he hit the showers. Emerging from the gym fifteen minutes later, he stopped off at his locker.

After passing through the North Building, he made his way through the Center Building that housed the Administrative offices, the cafeteria, the Student Lounge and the Bookstore. Turning right into the cavernous foyer and transiting the marble floor, he pushed open a set of double doors and started down the steps. Much to his surprise, Elspeth McGuire was walking along the sidewalk at the base of the steps, with a load of books cradled in her arms. She'd apparently gone to the Library after classes and, for some inexplicable reason, decided to take the long way around to the parking lot.

Thinking she looked cute carrying the load of books, Andre grinned before letting out a low wolf whistle. But since she either ignored it or thought it was for someone else, Andre launched into an old Roy Orbison song as he reached the bottom of the steps.

Pretty woman, walking down the street
Pretty woman, the kind I'd like to meet…

Andre not only had a beautiful singing voice but a powerful one as well – so Elspeth wasn't the only one who heard him. The moment he began singing, the twenty or thirty students hanging out by their rides in the student parking lot turned to look. Realizing the song was for her, Elspeth stiffened as the other students stared.

Following along behind her into the parking lot, Andre was still singing as he turned off at an angle toward his car. Trying hard to ignore him, Elspeth had lowered her head and picked up her pace.

From the corner of his eye, he could see her siblings lounging against their Land Rover as he started the last and final verse.

Having reached his car, Andre let the song fade from the air as he reached for his keys. Still pretending the song hadn't been addressed to anyone in particular, he opened the door. Then as he pulled off his backpack and tossed it into the passenger seat, he used the motion to steal a glance at the McGuires' Rover. As they backed out of their spot, he could see Elspeth leaning over and covering her face in her hands, as Lydia and the guys sang. Apparently, they'd picked up where he'd left off.

Chuckling, Andre grinned at the students who had witnessed his impromptu concert and climbed into his car. After starting the engine, he followed the McGuires out of the parking lot and down to the first intersection at a respectful distance.

Sitting in the backseat of the Rover with her face still buried in her hands, Elspeth demanded to know if Andre was behind them as they accelerated through the intersection. Grinning in the rearview mirror, Nathan informed the Pretty Woman that he'd turned off. "But we can drop you off at his place if you want."

Dodging Elspeth's lightning-fast retaliation, Nathan slipped into a deliberately exaggerated version of his native South Carolina drawl. "What's the matter, Darlin'…

"Embarrassed by a little attention?"

As Daniel and Lydia laughed, Elspeth growled. "Just drive, you jerk!"

When they reached the McGuires' Tudor five minutes later, Elspeth jumped out of the car the moment it stopped moving and stormed into the house. Ignoring her adoptive mother's greeting from the kitchen, she raced up the steps for the safety of her room. After slamming the door shut, she banged her head against it for good measure.

Surprised and concerned, Mrs. McGuire picked up the flower arrangement she'd just completed and carried it into the dining room, where Lydia and the boys had gathered around the table. Setting the flowers in the center, she looked around before asking them what was going on with Elle. "Was someone mean to her again?"

As the others laughed, Daniel grinned. "You should have seen it, Elizabeth!

"Elle was walking down the hall and a couple of Freshman Geeks made a crack about her being weird and ugly weird…

"And Andre Marchand heard it – you know, the new guy from France?"

After pausing for a moment, Mrs. McGuire nodded. "Oh, yes, Dr. Marchand's nephew."

After nodding, Daniel told her that Andre had grabbed the two little twerps and slammed them up against the lockers. "And he *really* chewed their butts!"

Suddenly concerned at the mention of physical force Mrs. McGuire gasped. "He didn't hurt them, did he?"

Grinning, Lydia interjected. "Nah, he just scared the pants off 'em…"

Then she cracked up laughing. Having a hard time getting the words out, Lydia pointed at Nathan. "You tell her," she squeaked.

By now laughing himself – at both the incident, and his sister – Nathan haltingly recounted how Andre had told the little creeps he was Headmaster Renfrowe's main man, and they were going to get *LIFE-TIME-DETENTION* if they ever made fun of an Upper Class Woman again.

Chuckling, Mrs. McGuire reached across the table to push a wayward flower back into place. "Surely they didn't believe that, did they?"

By now howling along with Daniel and Lydia, Nathan nodded. "And he said if he caught them doing it again, they were going to be cashing their social security checks in the cafeteria!"

Laughing at the absurdity, Mrs. McGuire sat down at the table with her children. "And that's why Elle is upset?"

Shaking his head back and forth, Daniel said no. "Headmaster Renfrowe heard about it and sent Andre to the gym as punishment…

"Made him do a thousand pushups and run a hundred laps."

Aghast, Mrs. McGuire looked up. "Oh my God!" she exclaimed. "A thousand push-ups and 100 laps?

"Dear Lord, that's what – 20 miles???"

Daniel laughed and nodded again. "Yeah, but that's not even the best part...

"Because Elle had to go to the Library after school to get some books, so she was walking around the building to the parking lot when Marchand came out the main doors...

"And he saw her walking by, and whistled at her...

"So she was really embarrassed, and ignored him – so he started singing that old 60's song, *Pretty Woman*...

"And Elizabeth, you should have seen it – Elle's face turned *bright* red!"

Finding that hard to believe, Mrs. McGuire stared at him for a long moment. "But how could that be?" she finally asked. "Vampires don't blush!"

Still laughing, Lydia nodded. "Yeah, well that's the theory...

"But trust me on this one – Elle turned red as a beet!"

After a moment of shocked silence, Mrs. McGuire stared at the tabletop before finally shaking her head. "She couldn't be sick, could she?"

As the boys grinned, Lydia giggled.

After a moment of suspicious silence, Elizabeth McGuire leaned back in her chair. Then after eyeing each of the kids in turn, she demanded an explanation.

"OK, guys – what's going on?"

CHAPTER 15

Elizabeth McGuire did everything possible to make life as normal as possible for her family – and that included a family dinner every evening. It wasn't much by human standards – a glass of blood supplied by McGuire Medical Research, Ltd., poured into elegant cut-crystal glasses and accompanied by a small center-plate of expensive imported crackers and cheese, followed by coffee and after-dinner chocolates. But the evening ritual helped keep them connected to their human lives, and if they only nibbled on the crackers and cheese and chocolates, that was OK.

Given the importance she attached to the family dinners, Mrs. McGuire had become concerned when Elspeth had refused to come down and join them. So after asking her husband to supervise the after-dinner clean up, she went upstairs and softly knocked on her bedroom door. "Elle, may I come in?"

After hearing something that might have been a "yes," Mrs. McGuire pushed open the door and went inside. Finding her youngest daughter sprawled on her bed with her face buried in her pillow, she sat down beside her and placed her hand upon her shoulder.

"Want to talk?"

After glancing up, Elle shrugged. "They told you, huh?"

Nodding, Mrs. McGuire said yes. "They said a couple of the younger students had been mean in the hallway – and that Andre Marchand had spoken up for you."

Elspeth nodded into the pillow, before sitting up to face her mother. "But it was more than that, Elizabeth…

"He grabbed them by the collar, and banged them up against the lockers!"

Mrs. McGuire smiled softly. "Well as an adult, I can't really approve of that sort of behavior," she said. "But speaking as your mother – I think they had it coming."

Scrunching up her nose, Elspeth nodded emphatically. "Yeah, me too!

"But Headmaster Renfrowe found out about it, and Andre got into a lot of trouble."

Nodding sympathetically, Mrs. McGuire sat there in silence for a long moment. Then after brushing Elspeth's hair out of her eyes, she smiled softly. "I understand he whistled at you after school."

Flushing, she looked down and tried to frown. "Yeah."

After pausing for a moment, Mrs. McGuire smiled again. "And then he sang you a song?"

Still looking down, Elspeth nodded. Then as her red cheeks turned to crimson, she smiled. "That old 60's song, *Pretty Woman*."

Chuckling, Mrs. McGuire expressed her approval. "Well, that was very sweet of him, you know."

After Elspeth nodded, her mother asked if he had a good singing voice. Elspeth's eyes widened as a look of astonishment stole across her face. "Amazing!" she said. "He sings as well as Lydia!"

Smiling, Mrs. McGuire said she'd heard he was really handsome as well.

Grinning, Elspeth nodded. "You wouldn't believe it!

"He's more handsome than the law allows – he's got chestnut hair, and these amazingly bright green eyes…

"And this little tiny waist and these huge shoulders!"

Cocking her head and raising her eyebrows, Mrs. McGuire said he sounded like a movie star.

"Definitely!" said Elspeth. "Imagine a 17-year-old version of Brad Pitt – only better looking!"

Placing her hand on her chest, Mrs. McGuire inhaled. *"Oh my!"*

Grinning, Elspeth said he reminded her of her adopted father. "You know," she said. "Outrageously handsome and smart and *really* nice!"

Smiling softly, Mrs. McGuire nodded. "That's your Dad!"

Then Elspeth pursed her lips together and looked down again. "But here's the thing, Elizabeth…

"Andre's the only person in that whole school who isn't mean to me…"

Then after pausing for a moment, her face contorted as she burst into tears. Throwing her arms around her mother's neck, she sobbed. "But if he ever finds out what I am – he'll *hate* me!"

Not knowing what to say, Elizabeth McGuire pulled her daughter close against her, and stroked her hair. With tears welling in her eyes, she thought about what the kids had to endure. It was heartbreaking – but since there was nothing she could do about it, she hid the pain she felt for them and tried to make their lives as happy as possible.

After several minutes, there was a soft knock on the door. "It's your father, dear…

"May he come in?"

Pulling back a bit, Elspeth nodded as she wiped the tears from her eyes. Then as her mother got up to open the door, she pulled a tissue from the box on her nightstand, and gently blew her nose.

Without saying a word, Dr. McGuire took his wife's place on Elspeth's bed. Then after she finished dabbing at her eyes, he listened as she apologized. "I'm sorry," she said. "I didn't mean to make a scene."

Smiling softly, Dr. McGuire nodded. "I understand you had a pretty tough day."

After looking down, Elspeth nodded silently. As she did, her father put his arm around her shoulders. "This life we lead can be hard…"

Still looking down, Elspeth laughed bitterly. "Except we're not really alive, you know."

Chuckling at the jest, Dr. McGuire shrugged. "Maybe not in the strictest sense of the term," he said. "But I think we're close enough to qualify."

Elspeth returned his smile with a soft, sad smile of her own. "Yeah, I guess being un-dead beats being dead-dead…

"But sometimes I wish I were still human."

After nodding, Dr. McGuire agreed. "There's hardly been a day in last 500 years that I haven't wished the same thing, and wondered what my life would have been like…"

Sniffling, Elspeth nodded. Then very suddenly, she looked up. "Neill," she said. "Is it ever possible for a Vampire to be friends with a human?"

Then after looking down, Dr. McGuire hesitated for a long moment. Finally, he nodded.

"Sometimes, Elspeth…

"It's difficult, and it doesn't happen very often – but on rare occasions, yes, it's possible."

Cocking her head, Elspeth asked if he'd ever had a human friend. After Dr. McGuire hesitated for a moment, Mrs. McGuire said it was OK.

"I think she should know, Neill."

Immediately curious, Elspeth asked him what it was she should know.

After pulling back a bit, Dr. McGuire looked into Elspeth's eyes and smiled a soft, sad smile. "I haven't told you before, because I didn't want to encourage false hopes…

"But I've had several human friends over the centuries."

Puzzled, Elspeth cocked her head. "Really?"

Dr. McGuire nodded. "One was a colleague during my teaching days in Amsterdam, and another was my partner in a clinic we ran back in the 1830's."

Suddenly curious, Elspeth asked him if he'd ever had a human girlfriend. "I mean, after you messed up that experiment and turned yourself into a Vampire."

Chuckling, Dr. McGuire dodged the question. "Maybe one or two," he said with a smile.

Still standing a few feet away, Elizabeth McGuire's jaw dropped. Feigning outrage, she told her daughter not to listen to him. "You should have seen him in Philadelphia!" she said.

Then after raising her eyebrows and lowering her head in mock disapproval, she told Elspeth that her father had been "Quite the squire" in those days.

Grinning, Elspeth turned to back her father. "So you got around, huh?"

Shaking his head in denial, Dr. McGuire accused his wife of exaggerating. But after finally admitting he'd occasionally danced with human girls at socials, he turned suddenly serious. "But it's very difficult, Elle…

"Friendship with humans carries a high price – at some point they'll either deduce the truth, or you'll have to tell them…

"And some of them will disappoint you, and turn against you…

"But it's even more painful if they remain faithful – because then you'll have to watch them grow old, and you'll have to watch them die."

All of which was true, of course.

But he didn't tell his daughter that he'd loved a human woman once – and stayed by her side for more than a half-century, until her enfeebled heart finally gave out.

CHAPTER 16

Bright and early the next morning, the McGuires piled into their cars and headed for Burlington. Having an excused absence, the three-day weekend was a lark for the kids and a welcome diversion for Mrs. McGuire. But for Dr. McGuire, it was purely business.

Six months before moving to Vermont, Dr. McGuire had set up a private blood bank in that city. With a population of less than 40,000 Burlington isn't a very large town – but it was less than an hour from the new house he was building, and it held three colleges. The students were young and healthy and often broke, so Dr. McGuire saw a chance to fulfill four good purposes through a single act. By paying twice the going rate for blood, he could help a lot of kids through school while ensuring an adequate supply for his family, his research, and the local hospitals.

With his wife beside him in the passenger seat of his Grand Cherokee, he took the lead as they turned onto the State Road that led to I-89. Nathan and Daniel followed behind in the Land Rover, while the girls took up the rear in Elspeth's bright pink VW Bug.

The Cove had been fogged in again, so Dr. McGuire proceeded cautiously. He could see through it, of course, but for human drivers the fog was far more problematical. But by the time they reached the Junction and turned south on I-89 the mist had lifted enough to pick up the pace. Having never fully adjusted to the automotive age, he stayed in the right lane and kept his speed a bit below 55.

It wasn't that Dr. McGuire was a bad driver. But having spent four of his five centuries on horseback, there was something unnatural about the glass and steel vehicles. They were far more comfortable than riding a horse or traveling in a buggy or a wagon, and he appreciated both the climate control and music provided by the radio and the CD player. But he missed the magnificent animals that had once provided humanity with transportation, and deep down inside he remained firmly convinced that God had never intended Man – or Vampires, for that matter – to travel more than 20 miles a day.

Reaching over to turn down the CD player a bit, Mrs. McGuire broke the silence by saying she was worried about Elspeth. After taking a deep breath and exhaling, her husband nodded. "I know she's lonely, and I'm sure Andre Marchand is a good kid...

"But I'm concerned she might jeopardize our situation here." Then after a long moment, he continued. "Most of all, I'm worried she'll be hurt."

Nodding, Mrs. McGuire agreed. "Me too, Neill…

"I don't want her to have to go through what you did."

She was referring to the Countess Gabrielle, the human he had loved in Paris so many centuries before. A devout Catholic, she had refused his offer to become a Vampire – but even after her refusal, his love for her had been so great that he'd remained with her until the day she died. Watching her change from a beautiful and vivacious young lady into a woman so worn by time that he could barely recognize her face had been a heart-breaking experience. The memory had haunted him, and it was more than a century before he could bear to return to the city they'd shared.

Dr. McGuire nodded gravely. "She's too young to really understand the full implications of human friendships."

After a moment's silence, Mrs. McGuire sighed and spoke again. "I know, Neill…

"But I'm so pleased that someone at the school is nice to her."

Dr. McGuire nodded, before glancing over and smiling. "Do you think the Marchand boy likes her?"

Mrs. McGuire's face lit up, and she chuckled. "Lydia tells me he always smiles when he sees Elle – and she claims he even flirts with her a bit."

Then leaning back in her seat, she pursed her lips together. "Oh dear God – this is *complicated*!"

Chuckling, Dr. McGuire wondered what his wife would say if she knew about Andre's little adventure in the Foreign Legion. Then thinking that she'd probably drag Elspeth off to the nearest convent, he laughed out loud.

Glancing over suspiciously, Mrs. McGuire asked him what that had been about. But having promised Dr. Sanders that he would

The Mist & the Darkness

guard Andre's secret, he couldn't tell his wife the truth. So rather than lie, he dodged the issue.

"You're right," he said. "It *IS* complicated."

Then suddenly serious, he looked over. "And it *could* end badly."

Mrs. McGuire didn't say anything. Worried, she balled up her fist and pressed it against her mouth instead. Then after a long silence, she changed the subject. "Think we'll see the ghost?"

Relieved by the change of subject, Dr. McGuire glanced over and grinned. "Well, we have reservations at the Ethan Allen."

That was actually one of the newest hotels in Burlington, and certainly the most luxurious. But it had been built on the site of a much older inn, and more than a few of the guests had reported seeing the ghostly outline of a man dressed in Victorian clothing sitting in one of the upholstered chairs, reading a newspaper and smoking a cigar. The odor of cigar smoke in the Lobby had offended many of the guests, so in an effort to quiet their complaints the quick-thinking manager had roped off the apparition's chair and placed a rather elegant sign beside it explaining the smell and boasting of the ghost. The first patron who caught him on camera would win a week's stay, compliments of the establishment.

The manager's dodge had turned out to be an enormously successful advertising gimmick, as people flocked to the hotel in the hope of catching sight of the ghostly figure. Whether the hotel Lobby was actually haunted or not remained an open question for Dr. McGuire – but he'd spent enough time on ancient premises to be firmly convinced that ghosts exist. If he hadn't been a Vampire during his last visit to Balmoral Castle, he probably would have had a heart attack...

Chuckling at the memory of the apparition that had scared the hell out of him in a darkened hallway during the dead of night, he told his wife to make sure she kept her cell phone at the ready. "Maybe we can win the prize."

After that, they slipped into a comfortable silence. As was so often the case when he and Elizabeth were alone, the time passed without any conscious recognition. For in what seemed like less than a moment, they reached the hotel.

After unloading their bags and checking in, Dr. McGuire glanced at his watch. "I've got a full day ahead inspecting the blood bank, so let's meet in the dining room at 7:00." Then after distributing keys to their rooms, he kissed his wife on her forehead and turned back to his car.

The boys spent the day working out at the hotel's gym and lounging around the indoor pool, while Elizabeth and the girls walked to Burlington's quaint little shopping district. Dodging the mid-morning sun by hugging the buildings, they stopped to get their hair and nails done before checking out the dozens of little shops and stores that made up the commercial district.

Vampires generally avoid mirrors and other reflective surfaces, as it takes an act of will to project their image upon them. It was a difficult trick to learn, and it was often tiring, so the McGuire women generally cut and styled each other's hair. But every once in a while, they gave into temptation and visited a salon.

The same applied to shopping. For the most part they ordered their clothes from catalogues or online retailers, or made them at home, but every now and then they ventured into stores as well.

They repeated their journey the following morning, with the boys accompanying them part of the way. Peeling off at combination comic book shop/arcade, they disappeared until dinner.

Having finally finished inspecting the blood bank and the series of meetings he'd scheduled with the manager and the nurse practitioner that supervised the EMTs, Dr. McGuire took his family out for a movie. After a ferocious fight, the guys gave in to the girls and agreed to sit through the celluloid version of *Twilight* – which was playing again in Burlington, as part of the PR buildup before the second film of the series was released.

The irony of a family of Vampires going to see a film about a family of Vampires had amused Dr. McGuire – especially when a row broke out in the theater lobby, where they were selling the second and third books of the *Twilight* series and franchise-related mementos. Having really gotten into the preview for *New Moon*, Nathan and Daniel bought hooded sweatshirts embossed with "Team Jacob" – which Lydia promptly condemned as stupid. In reprisal, she'd bought "Team Edward" pullovers for herself and Elspeth.

Still arguing as they exited onto the street, Daniel slammed Lydia. "That whole Human-Vampire love thing is *sooooooooo* yesterday!"

"Oh yeah?" she shot back. "And I suppose big furry mutts are cool???"

"Hey!" Nathan retorted. "Werewolves are *way* cool!"

"You're gross," retorted Lydia.

"Yeah, well I hear Werewolves are better lovers."

"Oh sure," Lydia scoffed. "If you like having your leg humped by a big smelly mutt!"

Having been born in a far more genteel time, Mrs. McGuire was shocked. "Lydia!" she exclaimed. "Mind your manners – please!"

Grinning, the elder daughter looked over and offered her mother an apology of dubious sincerity. "Sorry Elizabeth…

"I keep forgetting about that Victorian thing of yours."

Having been born in 16th Century Scotland – a time of shocking ribaldry, even by modern standards – Dr. McGuire chuckled. But in deference to his wife's sensibilities, he didn't say anything. Instead, he took her hand and walked along with her in silence.

After they'd reached a more or less deserted section of sidewalk, Lydia suddenly looked over at her father. "Have you ever seen a Werewolf?"

After glancing around to make sure there weren't any humans in earshot, Dr. McGuire smiled softly and nodded. "They used to be fairly common…

"But they're nearly extinct these days."

Glancing over, Nathan asked him why that was.

"Gunpowder," Dr. McGuire explained. "Back in my day they were so hard to kill that only the bravest warriors would even attempt it. Given their speed and agility, it was almost impossible to hit them with a silver tipped arrow…

"And even then a bow would rarely kill them. You had to move in close with a lance or a sword, and that was extremely dangerous…

"But once muskets became commonplace, the advantage shifted to the humans. I haven't heard much about them since the mass slaughter in the Scottish Highlands about 1680 or so."

"A pity," said Nathan. "A Werewolf would look good hanging on my wall."

Confused, Lydia looked over at him. "I thought you liked Werewolves?"

"*No,*" said Nathan. "I didn't say I *liked* them – I said they were *cool.*"

After they reached their hotel, the McGuires split up. Still bickering about Vampires and Werewolves, the kids went to the hotel's game room while Dr. and Mrs. McGuire retired to the bedroom of their suite. Sipping a glass of wine she'd ordered from room service, Elizabeth McGuire asked her husband how he'd liked the film.

"Rather ironic, all things considered…

"And a bit close to home, after that incident with Andre Marchand."

Mrs. McGuire nodded. "But it was a fun story, don't you think?"

Dr. McGuire agreed. "Actually, it was…

"It's the first Vampire film I've ever enjoyed." Then after kissing his wife, he suggested they get some sleep. "I want to enjoy the hunt tomorrow."

Awakening early the next morning, the McGuires swung by the blood bank to pick up a fresh supply packed in ice. Then after securing it in the back of the Grand Cherokee, they formed up their convoy and headed for Overlook Park on the shores of the Lake. Built during the Great Depression as a public works project, the Overlook was a small federal park just off the road that ran along the shore. In addition to a magnificent view, it featured public restrooms, stone barbeque pits and picnic tables. After coming to a halt in the empty parking lot, Dr. McGuire got out and called to the kids. "Let's get the gear out and suit up."

By that he meant the nets they'd brought with them, and bright orange hunting vests and hats.

By human standards, Vampires are fast – but unlike the film version they'd seen the night before, they weren't fast enough to run down animals. They were ambush predators, and while that worked well enough with humans it was a whole different story with other warm-blooded animals. Most of the creatures in the woods could smell them a mile away, and the prey animals would flee – although

The Mist & the Darkness

the larger predators occasionally stood their ground, and challenged their right to the territory.

In order to catch the prey animals, the McGuires had developed a system based upon the Mediaeval hunt: they set up nets before backtracking and spreading out to drive the animals into them.

Although the human blood Dr. McGuire obtained through the blood bank was more than sufficient to sustain them, the taste of stored blood left a lot to be desired. It didn't produce the exhilaration – some called it frenzy – of fresh, warm blood. Nor did it provide the thrill of the hunt, which was so important to their sense of well-being.

That said, Vampires could and occasionally did use firearms – which accounted for the fact that Nathan was busily engaged in loading his musket. After he finished ramming the ball into place, he slung it over his shoulder and pulled on his coonskin hat.

After looking at him incredulously, Daniel shook his head. "You look like an idiot in that hat, Bro."

Scowling at his brother, Nathan told him to back off. "This is my lucky hat – bagged my first bear wearing this thing."

Then after adjusting it, he grinned. "First Redcoat, too."

Mrs. McGuire was appalled by the reference, and so was Elspeth. Nathan was the only McGuire that had ever deliberately taken a human life – but given the circumstances, it was all too easy to understand.

When Nathan was fifteen, he'd left his South Carolina village one morning to hunt deer. When he returned late that evening, he found the charred bodies of his family and the other villagers in the smoldering ruins of the church. Patriots all, they'd provisioned the county militia and provided them with intelligence. Having wearied of the relentless harassment and mounting casualties inflicted upon them by American irregulars, British cavalry under the command of the infamous Colonel Tarleton had brutally retaliated by herding the villagers into the church and burning it to the ground.

After finding the charred remains of his family and burying them in a shallow grave, Nathan had loaded up a wagon with all the shot and powder and food he could find, and headed for the swamp where Francis Marion and his band of guerillas had holed up. Although he was still too young to enlist, the Swamp Fox was a distant relation on his mother's side and Nathan hoped he could use his familial connection to join up.

He'd spent more than a year in the swamp tending the horses and helping with the cooking before he was finally given the chance to exact revenge. He had taken his place on the American line at the Battle of Camden, and had later fought at Ft. Watson and at Ft. Motte, and then at the Battle of Eutaw Springs before marching north to Yorktown. On a foraging expedition after the British surrendered, he'd been jumped by a Feral Vampire deep in the woods. He'd eventually killed his attacker with his knife, but not before it had bitten him. That the Vamp had been wearing a tattered British uniform had only added to his seething hatred.

But if his mother and sister were absorbed in his past, Nathan was focused on the immediate future. After slinging his powder horn and his shot bag over his shoulder, he looked around. "Everyone ready?"

After seeing his family was prepared, Nathan led them into the woods. Having spent the better part of forty years on the frontier, he was the natural leader for their expeditions.

With the exception of Dr. McGuire, Nathan was the only one who really understood how dangerous the backwoods could be. So even though his brother and sisters carped about it, he enforced strict discipline on their hunting trips. In order to prevent distractions, talking was strictly forbidden; and he insisted they maintain ten-foot intervals, and continuously scan the woods around them. The Black Bears native to the region were far less aggressive than their Brown cousins to the west, but they'd been known to occasionally attack humans – and being predators themselves, they weren't especially intimidated by Vampires. But even more worrisome were the mountain lions that had found their way back into New England a decade or so before. Even though he didn't have a shred of scientific evidence to back it up, Nathan was firmly convinced the big cats bore some kind of grudge against his kind. He'd been attacked by the beasts twice before, and he'd barely survived the encounters.

After forty-five minutes of silent progress through the woods, he raised his hand and brought the column to a halt outside a little clearing just short of the second north-south trail.

"Son-of-a-bitch!"

Hanging from the low-lying branches of a solitary tree close to the center were a dozen plastic bags of fresh, hospital quality human blood. Below and slightly off to the side someone had driven a post into the ground and nailed a sign to it, with neatly painted red letters and a big red arrow pointing up at an angle:

FREE BLOOD!
(HELP YOURSELF)

"I don't believe it," muttered Daniel. "It's a trap!" hissed Lydia. "Well duh-uh," whispered Nathan.

Then after gesturing for his family to fall back, he turned and addressed them in a low voice. "Stay low, keep quiet, maintain your intervals, and watch out for an ambush." After they nodded, Nathan slipped into the bush. Moving quickly but silently, he led them back to their cars at the Overlook.

As they emerged from the trees a half hour later, Elspeth shook her head. "Who'd be stupid enough to fall for a dumb trick like that?"

A muffled explosion in the woods answered her question an instant later.

Uh oh...

As the column of oily-black soot from immolated Vampires billowed above the distant treetops, Daniel gave her an exasperated look. "Some of our intellectually-challenged cousins?"

As her eyes crossed involuntarily, Elspeth nodded. "Right."

Then she took off for her VW at a dead run. "Last one home's a ninny!"

CHAPTER 17

If Elspeth was nervous when she arrived at school the next day, Andre was sweating bullets. He'd been dressed in a sniper's creep suit when the McGuires approached his kill zone, and his face and hands had been expertly covered in camouflage paint. But he'd never tested his uncle's scent killer under field conditions, so he had no way of knowing if the McGuires had picked up on his smell. Given the fact that he'd almost sent them to the Promised Land, that had become an important consideration.

Having noticed movement in the woods, he'd picked up the remote control detonator for the improvised explosive devices he'd planted around the clearing. Lying beside a large boulder on a heavily vegetated hill two hundred feet away, he'd placed his thumb on the button that served as a trigger. Unable to believe anyone would be dumb enough to actually help themselves to the bags of blood he'd hung from the tree, he hadn't booby-trapped them. They were a lure, intended to encourage Feral Vamps to enter the clearing for a closer look – and the sign, to divert their attention away from the trap.

All in all, it was a clever ambush. But unfortunately for Andre, he'd failed to take into account the possibility that the McGuires might be the ones who walked into it. So when Nathan appeared at the edge of the clearing, his eyes bulged and his heart skipped a beat.

Oh shit!

The IED's were remote controlled, but since they were altogether illegal he'd fabricated them himself. Given the weather – and the static electricity that had begun building up in anticipation of the storm that was coming down from Canada – there was a better than even chance they might detonate on their own. So as beads of sweat formed on his forehead, he closed his eyes, grimaced, and gently pushed the power switch to the "Off" position.

With the silence unbroken by an explosion, Andre let out a deep sigh.

The Mist & the Darkness

Relieved to see the McGuires backing into the woods, he whispered a prayer of thanks to St. Martin. Not being especially religious, the patron saint of French soldiers was the only one he'd ever bothered to learn.

Thinking the near-disaster had been way too close for comfort, Andre mulled over the implications. The bad news was the McGuires knew there was a Vampire Hunter in the vicinity. The good news – he hoped – was they didn't know it was him.

After spending another motionless half hour by the boulder, Andre calculated the McGuires were long gone. Deciding to call it a day, he'd risen on one knee and was shaking a cigarette free from a nearly crushed pack when three Vamps strolled into the clearing. Freezing in place, he slowly reached for the remote control.

"Hey, check it out!" yelled the first Vamp. "Free blood!"

"Cool!" exclaimed the second. "Grab it!" yelled the third.

Andre waited until they'd rushed into the center of the kill zone before pushing the detonator. An instant later, the Vamps were engulfed in an enormous fireball.

The shock wave from the massive explosion swept Andre off the ground and hurled him back five or ten feet. After slamming into a tree and sliding down the trunk, he made a mental note to himself:

Dear Dumbass, it said. *Lighten up on the plastic explosives next time...*

With his ears ringing and his lungs filled with acrid smoke, Andre stared at the black, sooty cloud billowing upward in stunned silence. Then after realizing an explosion that big was bound to attract unwelcome attention from the authorities, he ripped open his pack and pulled his orange hunting vest and hat from inside. After putting them on, he stuffed the detonator into the side pocket and grabbed his AK-47. Coughing and gagging, with the weapon in one hand and the pack in the other, he took off at a dead run.

On the way home, Andre had been wondering how he was going to deal with the McGuires at school the next day. But after only a couple of miles, he realized he had a whole 'nother problem to worry about. Less than ten minutes after he'd nailed the Vamps, the first helicopter appeared in the sky over the woods – joined by others at two or three minute intervals.

By the time he pushed open the front doors of the Chalet a half hour later, there were at least 20 of them circling the still smoldering site. Most of them bore American markings, but three or four had the Canadian Maple Leaf painted on their sides.

Way to go, fool. You just created an international incident!

According to the satellite TV news, an unknown number of terrorists had apparently infiltrated across the Canadian border and had – for reasons that were still unclear – detonated a massive explosive device in the woods just south of The Cove. State police were already on the scene assisting the county sheriff's department, and a battalion of U.S. Army Rangers had just lifted off from Ft. Bragg. Elements of the Canadian special forces were standing by to assist, while agents from the FBI, the Border Patrol, and the Bureau of Alcohol, Firearms, and Tobacco were flooding into the area. According to a spokesman for the Department of Homeland Security, the threat level had been raised to Condition Red for the entire coastline of Lake Champlain and residents were asked to report any suspicious activity.

Hoping that didn't include people with singed eyebrows and a barely discernible French accent, Andre gulped as the live coverage shifted to the White House. With a grim look fixed upon his face, President Obama informed the nation that a terrorist "event" had apparently occurred in the Vermont woods approximately 16 miles south of the Canadian border. After informing the American people that he'd just spoken with the Prime Minister of Canada, he stated a joint contingency plan was in effect and working smoothly. Although it was still unclear why the terrorists had blown up an uninhabited woodland, he promised the American people that he would not rest until they were captured or killed.

Uh oh...

Thinking that just couldn't be good, Andre watched in disbelief as the coverage switched to Ottawa. After strolling up to a microphone, the Prime Minister recited the few known facts about the incident before informing the Canadian people that helicopters of the Canadian Air Command had crossed the border to assist the U.S. Air Force, and the 5 Canadian Mechanized Brigade Group and elements the Primary Reserve were taking up blocking positions along the frontier to prevent the terrorists from escaping back into Canada.

Andre's jaw dropped as the coverage switched to Paris. According to the French Ministry of Defense, reconnaissance aircraft had just been launched from the decks of the aircraft carrier *Charles De Gaulle* – which had been on joint maneuvers with the Americans and the Canadians off the coast of Maine – and the French jets were expected to reach The Cove any minute.

Thinking his goose was cooked better than a Thanksgiving turkey, Andre buried his head in his hands and wondered if it wouldn't be a good time to call the French Ambassador and tell him the deal was off. But a quick calculation told him it would take a couple of weeks for the paperwork to go through, and by that time he'd probably be in the slammer.

But unfortunately, Plan B – which consisted of hanging tight, and hoping the G-Men didn't find any DNA evidence – wasn't much better. So as he pushed through the school's double doors the next morning, he was a lot more worried about the Feds than the McGuires.

Newton had been ringed by heavily armed troops from the Vermont National Guard when he'd arrived, and agents from a Joint Federal Task Force were inside setting up interviews with the students to see if they had seen or heard anything suspicious the previous day. Relieved to learn they were still focused on terrorists, he'd carefully printed his name and homeroom, and then his address and telephone number, on the form attached to a clipboard an FBI agent had thrust into his hands. Then after signing it, he made his way into the lounge for his pre-class coffee.

Sitting down at the Jock table, he pulled out his laptop and pretended to read the news as he worked on his cover story.

Why yes, officers, I was out in the woods hunting Vampires when I heard the explosion...

Thinking that probably wouldn't fly, he decided to bluff his way through the interview by claiming he'd been at home working on his Calculus.

Although considerably less plausible than the truth, he was hoping they'd believe a crock like that as he closed his laptop and pulled his calculus book out of his pack. Turning to the section following the one they were working on, he memorized as much as possible in order to provide his interrogators with a credible level of detail.

But that turned out to be unnecessary. After he'd been pulled out of his first period class for an interview in an empty classroom, he'd answered a couple of routine questions and explained he'd been home working on his math the day before. Aside from the thunder from the storm that had passed over, he hadn't heard anything. Fortunately, they hadn't noticed his singed eyebrows, or his hint of an accent.

Ten minutes later, he was back in class listening to Mrs. Morgan drone on and on about Beowulf. Finding it difficult to believe that a fool wearing a helmet with horns sticking out the sides merited the adulation she was heaping upon him, he was relieved when the bell finally rang.

Suddenly reminded of his little problem with the McGuires, Andre had winced when Elspeth walked into history class. But as she walked down the aisle and took her seat, he didn't detect fear or hostility. She seemed a bit more nervous than the other students – but not, as far as he could tell, about him.

Thanking the Lord for small favors – or in this case, a rather large one – he let out a sigh of relief. Then after composing himself, he smiled and said good morning.

After returning his greeting, Elspeth leaned over and asked him if he'd had his interview. Nodding, Andre told her it was no big deal – they'd just asked him a couple of questions, and given him a number to call if anything suspicious came up. Obviously relieved to learn the Feds wouldn't delve into her background, Elspeth closed her eyes for a moment before taking a deep breath and nodding. Then after a moment, she shook her head. "Can you believe it?

"Terrorists in The Cove!"

Thinking that wasn't half as weird as Vampires, Andre fought hard to suppress his laughter. But fortunately for him, the bell rang and Dr. Marigold began taking the roll. After accounting for everyone, she started to give the class a pep talk. Terrorism had been around in one form or another since the beginning of time, she said, and it was something they just had to learn to deal with. Then she advised the class to stay calm, trust the authorities, and support one another. "We'll get through this," she promised.

She was about to say something else when the intercom speaker high on the wall suddenly came to life. After asking for everyone's attention, Headmaster Renfrowe paused for a moment before informing the students and faculty that he had an important announcement. Then after clearing his throat, he continued:

"The White House has just announced a rental van bearing Canadian license plates was pulled over by the New York State Police a few minutes ago, and four Islamic terrorists taken into custody. According to the police, the van was packed with plastic explosives similar to the type detonated in the woods just south of here yesterday…

"According to the White House spokesmen, the New York State Police were responding to an Alert issued by the Federal Bureau of Investigation based upon a tip from a local resident, who had seen the van and four suspicious characters at the Overlook yesterday morning."

Then after a brief pause, he informed them the terrorist alert had been rescinded, and they could all relax.

Thinking he was on the roll of a lifetime, Andre decided it was time to initiate Phase I of *Operation Elspeth*. So as soon as Dr. Marigold looked the other way, he leaned over and whispered.

"Hey Elle…

"You know that project we have to do for Dr. Marigold?"

After she nodded, Andre suggested they do it together.

Suddenly excited, Elspeth's face lit up as she smiled. "That would be fun!"

CHAPTER 18

Thinking that her scheme to divert her parent's attention away from her lusty plan had just received an unexpected boost, Lydia was trying hard to suppress a triumphant grin as Andre and Elspeth held a brief hallway conference after class. After comparing schedules, they decided the week was a write off so they'd have to get together after school the next Monday or Tuesday.

After the G-men and the National Guard departed that afternoon, things had settled back into a routine. Then for some inexplicable reason, time seemed to accelerate and Friday rolled around before Andre knew it. Finding himself standing in line behind Elspeth at the salad bar, he teased her about the absurdly small salad she was preparing for herself.

"Going on a diet?"

Apparently surprised to find Andre in line behind her, she'd frozen in place for a moment. But after she gathered her wits, she turned and frowned before ruefully admitting it. "I'm trying to lose five pounds."

Thinking she'd be better off cutting back on blood than salad, he pretended to commiserate. "Must be tough being a girl."

Turning to face him, Elspeth pursed her lips together and nodded emphatically. "It *really* is!"

In the process of filling his bowl, Andre looked up suddenly and gazed through the curtain glass at the rain outside. Depressed by the relentless downpour, he muttered the hope that the weather would improve before Sunday.

Overhearing him, Elspeth asked why. "Have big plans for the weekend?"

Which translated from Girl-Speak meant, "Are you going to see your girlfriend in Montreal?"

As he ladled bacon ranch dressing on his salad, Andre shook his head. Then rather absent-mindedly, he said he was just "hoping to get in a couple of jumps Sunday afternoon."

Having mistaken his explanation for a sexual allusion, Elspeth stepped away from the salad bar and scowled.

"*Jumps?*" She repeated with icy sarcasm. "Is that what they call it in France?"

Realizing he'd just been caught in the linguistic equivalent of a drive-by, Andre quickly shook his head. "That's *not* what I meant."

Then after glancing around to see if anyone else had overheard him, he jerked his head toward an empty table in a deserted section by the wall. "Over there."

Puzzled, Elspeth followed him the twenty or so feet. After Andre stopped just in front of the table and turned to see if she was with him, she asked what he'd meant in a low whisper.

After glancing around again, he whispered back. "Parachute jumps." Then he gestured for her to take a seat.

Since that didn't quite compute, it took Elspeth a moment to respond. "You mean skydiving?"

Andre shrugged. "I guess that's what you call it here."

After they'd sat down at the unoccupied table, Elspeth leaned over and asked him where he'd learned how to skydive. And then after glancing around again to make sure no one was listening in, she asked him what was so secret about a hobby.

Leaning over, Andre whispered again. "Well, see, that's the thing…

"I learned how to jump in the military, but the Headmaster said he'd boot me out of here if anyone found out."

Incredulous, Elspeth scrunched up her nose. *"You were in the military?"*

After glancing around again, Andre grinned. "Yeah, after my parents died the court ordered me to live with my uncle. But I hated Paris, and New York was even worse…

"So I got a fake ID, skipped out for France, and enlisted in the Legion."

It took a moment for that to sink in. *"The Legion…"*

Then it hit her. As her jaw dropped and her eyes bulged, she thrust her hands down on the table and sat bolt upright in her chair. "The *Foreign* Legion?"

Clenching his teeth together, Andre hissed for her to be quiet. Then after glancing around again, Andre leaned over and asked her why she didn't just announce it over the intercom.

Cringing, Elspeth raised her shoulders and made an embarrassed face before apologizing. Then suddenly curious, she asked him if he'd been sent overseas.

Andre nodded. "I was with the *2e Régiment Étranger de Parachutistes* – the Second Parachute Regiment – so I spent a little over a year in Africa, and then about six months in Afghanistan."

"Afghanistan?" Elspeth gasped. *'Isn't that where all the fighting is?"*

Andre laughed. "Yeah, well you could have fooled me...
"Because the terrorists always took off and ran when they saw us coming."

Surprised, Elspeth leaned forward and whispered again. "Really?"

Suddenly serious, Andre nodded, then glanced around before whispering back. "The Legion has a reputation, you know...

"They didn't want to fight us."

Amazed and astonished – and not quite sure she should believe him – Elspeth said, "Wow!"

Then after nibbling on her salad, she leaned forward again, and asked Andre what his uncle had done. Rolling his eyes, he told Elspeth she wouldn't have believed it. "Uncle Philippe went completely postal, and raised all kinds of hell with the Government."

Grinning, Elspeth asked him if that's how he got out.

Nodding sadly, Andre said his uncle had caused the French Government so much embarrassment that they'd cut him loose.

After studying his face for a long moment, Elspeth looked up at him incredulously. "You wanted to *stay* in *Afghanistan?*"

Andre shrugged, and said not really. But he liked the Legion and he'd wanted to stay with his regiment.

Dumbfounded, Elspeth stared at him for a long moment. "Andre," she finally said. "*Are you stupid?*"

Andre laughed, and said people asked him that all the time. "So I guess so."

Laughing, Elspeth pressed her face in her hands. "I *don't* believe you!"

Then after looking up, she told Andre to be careful. "Jumping out of airplanes is dangerous, you know."

Andre laughed, and denied it. But after she insisted, he said he'd exercise due caution.

"You promise?"

Surprised by the apparently genuine look of concern on her face, Andre nodded. "I promise."

Seemingly pleased, Elspeth smiled. Then suddenly aware of all the talk going on behind her in the cafeteria, she stiffened in her seat. "Are people staring at us?"

Andre glanced around and grinned. "Yeah, I think we've just caused another scandal."

As her eyes crossed, Elspeth buried her face in her hands. *Oh God*, she thought. *I'm never going to hear the end of it…*

Which turned out to be more or less the case – because Kathy Norse had been bragging she'd have Andre wrapped around her finger in less than a month, and word of her boast had gotten around. So the fact that Andre had blown off the Jocks and the Cheerleaders to have lunch with a social outcast like Elspeth McGuire caused people to sit up and take notice.

By the time fifth period had rolled around, the female population at Newton had split into warring camps. The Cheerleading Squad, the Student Council and the rest of the socially acceptable girls lined up behind Kathy. As far as they were concerned, Elspeth McGuire was a shameless Jezebel, clearly intent upon victimizing poor, sweet Andre Marchand.

But the Nerds, Geeks and other social outcasts – who were by far the largest percent of the feminine population at Newton – had lined up solidly behind Elspeth. As a straight "A" student with no social life, they claimed her as one of their own. And for what it was worth, they were firmly convinced that Andre had demonstrated refined taste and excellent judgment in choosing Elspeth over Kathy.

With the female population of Newton poised on the brink of civil war, Elspeth had been stunned when girls who'd never even spoken to her suddenly smiled and said hello in the hallway after lunch – and positively shocked when Mary Sue Poindexter stopped her after sixth period, and invited her to a pajama party. Barely able to mumble an excuse, she thanked Mary Sue for the invitation before fleeing down the concourse to Lydia's locker. Tugging her sister's arm, she told her they had to make a run for it.

"Come on, girl – we gotta get outta Dodge!"

An exaggeration, but not by much – insults were flying back and forth between the In Crowd and the Outcast Alliance, and it was only a matter of time before an ill-considered bitch-slap ignited an all-out war. Vampire or not, Elspeth knew better than to get involved in a catfight – especially one that involved her.

Grinning as another group of misfits passed by and enthusiastically greeted her more diminutive sister, Lydia laughed and said she hadn't had this much fun since the Purple Gang shot up the Showboat Lounge.

Exasperated by her sister's cavalier attitude, Elspeth rolled her eyes. "You're an idiot!"

Although not entirely unjustified given the circumstances, it was certainly ill-advised – because Lydia had driven her own car that day, and she beat Elspeth home by three minutes or more. After parking her perfectly restored Trans Am in her usual spot in the garage, Lydia hurried through the connecting link. Elle had handed her the perfect opportunity to set her con in motion – and exact a bit of revenge in the process.

Finding her adoptive mother making another flower arrangement in the dining room, she smiled triumphantly. "Elizabeth," she said. "You won't *believe* what happened at school today!"

Puzzled, Mrs. McGuire looked up. "Pray tell?"

Grinning, Lydia haughtily informed her that Elspeth had caused another scandal. "And it was *positively* delicious!"

Horrified, Mrs. McGuire gasped as Elspeth came storming through the door. Then after warning her mother not to listen to the big floozy, she glared at Lydia and demanded she stop exaggerating.

Then turning to her mother, she insisted it was no big deal.

Incredulous, Lydia's jaw dropped. *"Like hell!"* she exclaimed. "You almost got lynched for sitting with Andre Marchand at lunch…

"And if the Cheerleaders knew you're a Vampire – they would have staked you on the spot!"

CHAPTER 19

Having grown up in a culture where religion was deeply ingrained, Dr. McGuire had never been comfortable about working on Sundays. Physicians were excepted from the prohibition against laboring on the Sabbath, of course, and the accident-prone made that all but inevitable. Even so, he had never been able to overcome the tinge of guilt he experienced when attending to less than life-threatening emergencies on Sundays.

Having finished with his last patient just after 4:00, Dr. McGuire was reasonably confident he'd be able to leave when Chief Petty Officer Albert Gomez came in at 5:00. A recently retired Navy Corpsman with 28 years experience in both field and hospital medicine, the Chief was one of the best trauma guys in the business. He and another former corpsman pulled the night shift at the clinic, alternating four nights on and four nights off.

After telling the receptionist he'd be in his private office if she needed him, he started down the hall for the back of the building. After reaching his hideaway, he unlocked the door before making his way around his desk and sitting down. Although he had a ton of reading to catch up on, there were other more pressing matters on his mind. One was the terrorist attack, the other was his youngest daughter.

Although inherently implausible, the weight of the evidence had forced him to reluctantly accept the official explanation for the explosion. He had seen the bags of blood with his own eyes, and the sign as well – but even so, the government's account was beyond dispute: a local resident had seen the van and its four passengers pulling away from the Overlook about 15 minutes or so before he and his family had arrived, the van had been driven by known terrorists, and it was packed with the same type of home-made plastic explosives that had detonated in the woods. So for Dr. McGuire, there appeared to be only two possibilities: either the terrorists were also Vampire Hunters, which seemed unlikely at best; or they had set the trap in the woods as a diversion. Whatever the actual case, he and his family were safe – and that's what really mattered.

The other problem was less threatening but far more vexing. Elspeth clearly liked the Marchand kid, and from what he'd gathered from his other children, Andre seemed to reciprocate. The problem, of course, was that Elle was a Vampire and Andre was human – and that spelled trouble. His greatest concern was that his daughter would have her heart broken. But he was also worried that she might accidentally reveal his family's secret.

He knew Elle would never deliberately do anything to expose them, but hiding her condition from a human boyfriend was problematic at best. Although Elle insisted they weren't an item – and the testimony of her siblings had so far substantiated her claim – things were clearly moving in that direction, and neither he nor his wife had the slightest clue how to handle it. Had it been Lydia, he would have been far less concerned.

His eldest daughter was a free spirit, easily content with a casual rendezvous. But aside from her penchant for sleeping with humans – a habit he'd been forced to ban after an unfortunate incident in California – he wasn't worried about her. Elspeth, however, was an entirely different story – she wanted to love and to be loved.

As he rested his chin on his folded hands, it occurred to him that Dr. Marchand was a complicating factor. As a colleague in a small town – and a prospective partner in the clinic – social contacts were inevitable. Professional courtesy had obliged him to invite Marchand to dinner, and it was only a matter of time before his busy schedule permitted him to accept. One of these days, Dr. Marchand would turn up at their door – in all likelihood, with his nephew in tow...

Dr. McGuire was still pondering that when the phone on his desk buzzed. "Got a customer in Exam Room One, Doc."

After telling the receptionist he'd be right up, he stood, straightened his tie, and headed for the front. Stopping outside the door of the examination room, he pulled the paperwork from the plastic file holder attached to the wall and examined it. Then chuckling at the irony, he strode into the room.

"*Andre Marchand,*" he grinned. "How's our Legionnaire today?"

After flushing, the 17-year-old sitting on the exam table grinned sheepishly. "I guess the word's out, huh?"

Smiling, Dr. McGuire told him that his uncle had mentioned it to Dr. Sanders. "But don't worry, we'll keep your secret!"

Yeah, you keep my secret, Fool – and I'll keep yours...

But rather than actually say that, Andre suppressed a laugh and thanked him politely instead.

As he did, Dr. McGuire extended his hand and introduced himself, before asking Andre how he was.

After smiling sheepishly, the younger Marchand pointed at his right foot and said he'd been better.

"Messed up my ankle, Sir."

With the military jump suit and boots he was wearing, and the helmet and the half-open parachute pack resting against the corner of the room, it didn't take a rocket scientist to figure out what happened. But Dr. McGuire asked him anyway.

"Nothing serious, Sir…

"Lines tangled on my third jump, and it took me a while to get them straightened out – so I was a bit closer to the ground than intended when my chute opened."

Raising his eyebrows, Dr. McGuire gave Andre a serious look. "Sounds to me like you had a close call."

Shaking his head, Andre denied it. "It happens now and then. But it's not really serious if you know what you're doing."

Then he grinned from ear to ear. "But it's a good thing I wore dark trousers!"

Laughing at the jest, Dr. McGuire pulled up a stool and sat down beside the exam table. Looking up, he asked Andre if his uncle had examined his ankle.

"No, Sir. He's in Washington again, so I called him on his cell phone. He said I should come in and have you or Dr. Sanders take a look."

Nodding, Dr. McGuire reached out and examined his booted foot. "Think anything's broken?"

Andre shook his head. "I don't think so…

"I probably just sprained it."

Nodding, Dr. McGuire said he wanted to take an x-ray. "Your boot is going to have to come off…

"How bad does it hurt?"

Andre dodged the question. "I can hack it, Sir."

Nodding again, Dr. McGuire began gently unlacing his jump boot. After taking the laces all the way down, he grasped the back of his patient's leg with one hand and teased the boot off with the other. Andre stiffened, but didn't make a sound. Surprised by the lack of response, Dr. McGuire looked up.

Andre was looking straight forward, his eyes locked on the wall in front of him. His face had drained of color, his eyes were dilated, and there was sweat pouring down his forehead.

Damn, he thought. *The kid's hardcore...*

Knowing it must have hurt like hell, Dr. McGuire set the boot down beside the exam table before getting up to retrieve a pair of surgical scissors from a drawer. Then he began gently cutting the sock away.

After he finished, he looked up again. Andre's gaze was still fixed on the wall, his hair was matted and wet, and his face white as a sheet and covered in sweat.

Looking down without saying anything, Dr. McGuire examined his ankle. All but certain no bones had been broken, he told Andre that it looked like a Grade 2 Sprain. "But let's get you into X-ray just to make sure."

Then after telling him to wait while he got a wheelchair, he walked out in the hallway and retrieved one from an alcove. After helping Andre into it, he pushed him down to the x-ray room for some pics.

Back in the exam room ten minutes later, Dr. McGuire pulled the x-rays up on the oversized monitor mounted on the wall and studied them for just a minute. Then after nodding, he told Andre that he'd been fortunate. "It's just sprained," he said, but warned him that it remained potentially serious.

"If you don't take good care of yourself for the next couple-a-three weeks, it may not heal properly...

"And then you could end up with a painful and persistent problem downstream."

Then after turning away from the monitor, he told Andre he was going to put it in an Aircast. "You normally need to wear the cast for two weeks to ensure proper healing, but I'd suggest your uncle take a look at it every couple of days after he gets home...

"In any event, you'll need crutches for the duration and possibly a cane for another week or so after that."

Then after picking up the phone and buzzing the receptionist for an Aircast, he gave Andre a very serious look. "No strenuous exercise for 90 days, and no parachuting until you're cleared by a qualified physician."

After frowning and nodding, Andre suddenly looked up and grinned. "I'd better come back and see you then, because Uncle Philippe is still fuming about that whole paratroop thing."

Chuckling at Andre's description, Dr. McGuire crossed his arms and grinned. "Andre, I *have* to ask…

"What the *hell* were you thinking when you joined the Foreign Legion?"

After flushing, Andre shrugged. "Well, Sir" he said sheepishly, "It seemed like a good idea at the time."

Laughing at the absurdity of it all, Dr. McGuire informed him that he'd put his uncle through a lot of grief. Nodding sheepishly, Andre looked down at the floor again and said he was really sorry about that. Then after looking up suddenly, a huge grin spread across his face. "But I've gotta tell ya…

"It was one *HELL* of an adventure!"

Laughing in disbelief, Dr. McGuire shook his head back and forth. *The kid's trouble*, he thought.

But even so, he couldn't help but like him.

CHAPTER 20

Ben had picked Andre up from the clinic, and he drove him to school the next day. After pulling his battered Ford pickup truck up to the front steps, he told Andre he'd be back at 6:00 and then waited as he struggled out the door. After righting himself on his crutches and struggling into his backpack one shoulder at a time, Andre thanked him and closed the door. Half hobbling and half hopping, he turned around to see the McGuires standing together at the bottom of the steps.

The guys grinned and said "Hi," Lydia looked away, and Elspeth glared. Wondering what was up with that, Andre hobbled over and bade them a cheery good morning.

After giving him a withering look, Elspeth demanded to know what happened to his leg. Surprised that Dr. McGuire hadn't told her, he shrugged. "Sprained my ankle on my third jump yesterday…

"No big deal."

That was entirely true from his perspective, but it clearly wasn't what Elspeth wanted to hear. After an icy and interminable stare, she huffed. "You *promised* you'd be careful!"

Confused by her reaction, Andre said he had been.

After tilting her head over and glaring at him again, Elspeth turned to her sister. "Come on, Lydia, let's go."

Thinking there had been some sort of massive communications breakdown, Andre started to explain he'd had a minor glitch with his chute and it was no big deal. But before he could get the words out, Elspeth had wheeled around and silenced him.

"I am *NOT* speaking to you, Andre Marchand!" Then she stuck her nose up in the air, and marched up the stairs with her sister in tow.

By now completely puzzled, he turned to Elspeth's brothers. "What just happened here?"

Grinning, Daniel informed him he'd just experienced The Wrath of Elspeth.

"Yeah, I got that part," Andre said. "But why?"

Grinning, Nathan asked if he'd promised her he'd be careful. Nodding in the affirmative, Andre said "yeah" – and insisted he had. "Minor problem with the chute, that's all."

Still grinning, Nathan shook his head. "You're screwed, Bro…

"Because as far as she's concerned, you broke your promise."

Looking at Nathan incredulously, Andre said, "Oh, give me a damn break."

Laughing, Daniel said they would – but there was no way Elspeth was going to cut him any slack.

"You're on her Bad List, Dude."

Leaning over his crutches, Andre pondered that for a moment. Then after looking up, he asked Daniel how long that was going to last. After glancing over at Nathan, Daniel said that depends. "If you apologize and really suck up to her, she'll probably start talking to you in a couple of days…"

Startled, Andre stared at them. "A couple of days?"

Nathan and Daniel nodded in unison. Then after chuckling, Nathan told him there was always Plan B.

Looking over quizzically, Andre asked him what that was.

Nathan laughed. "Plan B consists of an apology, a considerable amount of groveling, and a dozen roses."

Wondering where the hell he was supposed to get roses in The Cove, Andre mulled it over for a long moment. Then he told Nathan an apology and roses were doable – assuming he could find any – but not the groveling. "That's out of the question."

Grinning, Daniel shrugged. "Well, then there's Plan C – just ignore her for a week or two, and she'll lighten up."

After thinking it over, Andre decided he liked that option the best. "Plan C it shall be, gentlemen!" Then he started hobbling up the steps of the school.

Surprised by the fact that the McGuire guys had walked alongside him, he turned when he reached the top. "Just out of curiosity…

"Does she do this to you?"

"All the time," said Daniel.

Nodding as he walked alongside, Nathan glanced over and grinned, before explaining the silent treatment was Elspeth's version of hard time. "She thinks it's some sort of heavy-duty punishment – but if you live in a house with three women, it's more like a blessing."

Laughing, Daniel agreed. "Ain't that the truth!"

"OK," said Andre. "So I just ignore her?"

After they nodded and said "Yup," Andre gave them a thumbs-up sign and hobbled off to his locker.

Most people would think being ignored by a Vampire was a good thing, but on that particular morning Andre was frosted. First of all, Elspeth was being totally unfair – because he really had been careful. Second, it was none of her damned business – if he got his jollies jumping out of perfectly good aircraft, so what? And third, he didn't appreciate the fact that he'd suddenly become the center of attention.

From a physical standpoint, Newton was a large school. But with a student body of just under 400, news traveled fast. Word of his contretemps with Elspeth had spread like wildfire, and rumors were flying all over the place. According to one, Elspeth had broken his leg after he'd gotten fresh with her over the weekend. According to another, they'd been sleeping together for months, and she'd broken it after Andre refused to make an honest woman out of her. But the one that had gained the most traction was the claim they were secretly married, and Elspeth had caught him fooling around.

It was all totally absurd, of course – but since he had clearly committed *Lese majeste* against the newly anointed Queen of the Nerds, Geeks, and Other Misfits, her minions were out for blood. As he hobbled into English Lit, the hallway was filled with hateful stares and muttered invectives.

After fuming through English Lit, Andre hobbled into History three minutes late. As he made his way down the aisle to his seat, Elspeth ignored him. Not in the mood for female games, he returned the favor.

But by the time lunch rolled around, he was furious. Aided by one of the Jocks – and ably assisted by one of the Cheerleaders – he managed to get his tray to the athlete's table. But after one of the Nerd Girls confronted him in mid-course and assailed him as a "low-life cheater," he'd had enough. Asking Wilkinson and one of the other football players to help him up on his chair, he told them he had an announcement to make. Grinning, they hoisted him up.

Steadying himself by placing his left hand on Wilkinson's shoulder, he drew himself up and bellowed in his best command voice. *"GARDE-A-VOUS!"*

Having mistakenly spoken in French, he followed up with a hurried and roughly accurate translation. *"THAT MEANS LISTEN UP, PEOPLE!"*

As a shocked hush fell over the cafeteria, Andre continued. *"A LOT OF RUMORS ARE FLYING AROUND, AND NONE OF THEM ARE TRUE – SO I'M GOING TO SET THE RECORD STRAIGHT...*

"ELSPETH MCGUIRE DID NOT BREAK MY DAMN LEG! I SPRAINED MY ANKLE PARACHUTING YESTERDAY...

"AND FOR YOUR INFORMATION, I DIDN'T EVEN SEE ELSPETH THIS WEEKEND – AND WE'RE NOT DATING, WE'RE NOT SLEEPING TOGETHER, AND WE'RE SURE AS HELL NOT MARRIED!!!

Then after pausing for a moment to look around, Andre continued. *"WE'RE JUST FRIENDS – OR AT LEAST WE WERE UNTIL SHE STARTED RAGGING ON ME ABOUT JUMPING!*

"SO FOR YOUR INFORMATION, LADIES…

"GUYS ARE INTO SPORTS, AND IF WE HAPPEN TO BE INTO EXTREME SPORTS IT'S NONE OF YOUR DAMN BUSINESS!"

Then after sweeping the cafeteria with his eyes and glaring at the female population, he finished. *"YOU GOT THAT, GIRLS?"*

Absolute pandemonium ensued – the Jocks and most of the other guys jumped to their feet, cheering, whistling, and applauding, while the girls made faces and booed. After dodging a Ho Ho one of the Geek Girls had launched in his direction, he asked Wilkinson to help him down. But before Wilkinson could grab his belt and shoulder, Elspeth climbed up on her chair and demanded silence.

"FINE!" she screeched.

"IF YOU STUPID GUYS WANT TO BASH YOUR BRAINS IN PLAYING FOOTBALL OR HOCKEY, OR ANY OF YOUR OTHER STUPID GAMES…

"OR SPLATTER YOURSELVES ALL OVER THE GROUND SKYDIVING, YOU JUST GO RIGHT AHEAD!

"BECAUSE WE DON'T CARE!!!"

Then she stuck her nose up in the air, hopped down off her chair, and marched out of the cafeteria – followed by her sister, Lydia, and most of the other Newton women. Aside from the Cheerleaders, who had lined up behind Andre and the guys, and a couple of the girls from the Student Council who'd thrown in their lot with them as well, the Fair Sex had vanished from view.

Now more frosted than ever, Andre was struggling down from his chair when the intercom speaker roared to life.

"MARCHAND!" the Headmaster bellowed. *"MY OFFICE – RIGHT NOW!"*

So after fighting back the temptation to give the speaker a one-finger salute, Andre scarfed down half a burrito before hoisting his backpack and hobbling off to Dr. Renfrowe's office. Propped up by his crutches, he stood at attention as the Headmaster slammed his door shut.

Marching over, he shoved his face within millimeters of Andre's. *"What the hell was that all about, Marchand?"*

After scrunching up his face, Andre informed the Headmaster he had merely been correcting a misconception or two.

After glaring at him for less than an instant, the Headmaster yelled. *"BULLSHIT!*

"I could hear you and Elspeth McGuire screaming all the way from the cafeteria!"

Then after glaring at him for an uncomfortably long moment, he stepped back. "Now what's going on with you two?" he demanded to know.

Exasperated, Andre said he didn't have a clue. "She took one look at me this morning, Sir, and jumped all over my case...

"Then she told me to get lost, because she wasn't talking to me – and then all the rumors and innuendo started flying, and I've been taking flack ever since."

After tilting his head over and crossing his arms across his chest, Dr. Renfrowe glared at him again. Then after looking down at Andre's air cast, the corners of his mouth began turning up.

"So she's mad at you for screwing up a jump?"

As Andre's face began to flush, he nodded. "Last Friday – after I told her I was going to make a couple this weekend – she made me promise I'd be careful."

Then very hurriedly, Andre explained he had been. "Stuff happens, you know?"

Grinning, Dr. Renfrowe nodded his head. "So you promised her you'd be careful, and then you went out and busted your ass?"

Scrunching up his face again, Andre bounced his head back and forth. "That's how she sees it, Sir."

By now chuckling, Dr. Renfrowe made his way around his desk and sat down in his chair. "Way to go, *Dumbass!*"

Then after closing his eyes and shaking his head back and forth again, Dr. Renfrowe looked up. "Didn't they teach you how to pack a 'chute in the Legion?"

Flushing badly, Andre assured him they did. "But it was humid, and misting pretty bad, and some of the lines apparently stuck together and tangled a bit on my third jump."

Pushing himself back from his desk, the Headmaster chuckled before telling him he should have used his reserve.

Still standing at attention, Andre nodded ruefully. "Yes, Sir."

There was a long moment of silence before Dr. Renfrowe spoke again. "All right," he said...

"Now I don't give a tinker's damn what kind of language you use when we're speaking in private, but public profanity is strictly prohibited by the school code…

"And you're an adult, Marchand – regardless of what your driver's license says – so I expect you act like one…

"Got it?"

Nodding, Andre said he did.

After staring at him for another, deliberately long moment, Dr. Renfrowe passed sentence. "You owe me 1000 pushups and two hundred laps when that ankle of yours heals."

Acknowledging him with a nod, Andre said it would be two or three weeks. Then after Dr. Renfrowe informed him he didn't give a damn *when*, Andre asked if there would be anything else.

After pausing for a long moment, the Headmaster leaned back in his chair again and placed his hands together.

"A word of advice, Marchand…

"Good women are hard to find – so if you let Elspeth McGuire get away, you're a bigger fool than I thought!"

CHAPTER 21

A chill fell over Newton. If the long dormant tensions between the socially acceptable and the outcasts had threatened to explode into outright warfare, Andre's outburst in the cafeteria had cut across the battle lines and confused the issue. Not entirely sure as to where they stood, most of the students at Newton hesitated.

The Cold War between Elspeth and Andre continued as Monday turned into Tuesday, and Tuesday into Wednesday. After it became apparent she was still ignoring him Thursday morning, Andre shrugged it off and concentrated on the business at hand – which included a stunningly beautiful coed he'd met in an online chat room.

A 20-year old sophomore from the University of Vermont with flaming red hair, she'd mentioned she was struggling with French. After checking the photo on her profile, and glancing over her bio,

Andre had introduced himself and offered to help her. Explaining he'd been born and raised in France, he told her he'd moved to the States after a stint in the military in order to attend an American university. Although a dual citizen, he had to spend a year in state with his uncle in order to establish residence.

Not exactly true, of course – but then it wasn't entirely false, either.

After thanking him profusely, the girl had introduced herself. Her name was Tiffany, she was from Baltimore, and majoring in biology. Good with science and math but terrible with foreign languages, she was scared to death she was going to flunk her introductory course. After a couple minutes of commiseration, Andre gave her his number and told her to call him.

She had a beautiful voice, and a good sense of humor, so Andre had spent the rest of the night drilling her in basic phrases and correcting her pronunciation. In the process he found out she'd just broken up with her boyfriend, hated her roommate, didn't have a car and was perennially short on cash – which was perfect, because she spent as little time as possible in the dorm, and she didn't have the means to check up on him.

Adding icing to the cake, she thought skydiving was totally cool.

They'd spent an hour or so on French every night since, and another hour or so flirting. Although they hadn't decided on getting together in person, Andre was in no hurry. He couldn't drive the Vette until he got out of the Aircast, and in any event his instincts told him to take it slow. He was sure she'd already decided to sleep with him, but she hadn't yet decided on when.

So as it happened, he was thinking about Tiffany when he wheeled Ben's pickup truck into the parking lot by the drugstore Thursday evening. Not exactly a great piece of machinery, but it had an automatic transmission so he could at least drive it. After parking it in the almost deserted lot, he clambered out. Pulling his crutches from behind the seat, he steadied himself before hobbling into the store.

He was in the process of putting a half-dozen boxes of herbal digestive aids into the wire basket he'd picked up by the door when he heard a familiar voice behind him. "Hi, Andre!"

After shifting his weight and making a difficult half-turn, he was surprised – actually, shocked – to see Elspeth standing there smiling. Incredulous, he asked if she was speaking to him again.

After pursing her lips together and laying her head over to one side, she smiled. "I was upset with you because you hurt yourself after promising me you wouldn't, but then I realized it's not really your fault…

"Because you're a guy, and guys can't help being stupid."

Not quite sure how to take that, Andre pursed his lips together and nodded.

Right…

Then after a moment, he shrugged and asked what she was doing there.

"Oh!" she said. "Make up and lipstick are on sale, so I thought I should stock up."

Smiling happily, she bounced up on her toes and held out her basket. "See?"

Not quite sure why a Vampire needed 20 different shades of lipstick and eye shadow – let alone moisturizers, foundation, blush, and all the other implements of deception girls liked to lug around in their bags – Andre tried to feign interest by asking her how much they were taking off.

Big mistake – because Elspeth promptly starting pulling one item after another out of her basket. "See this eyeshadow?

"*Fifty percent off – can you believe it?* And the lipstick – it's *sixty* percent off!"

"And the blush is *half off*, and the eyeliner pencils are *30 per cent off* and…"

Wishing he'd kept his mouth shut, Andre made a mental note to bang his head against something really hard when he got home.

Having finally finished, Elspeth smiled happily. "I love buying stuff on sale!"

Thinking that was somehow hardwired into the female psyche, Andre briefly wondered if it had carried over into her Vamp life or if she was faking it as part of her cover. But since he was desperate to change the subject, he put the question aside and asked her if she'd had dinner yet. After she said no, Andre told her he was going to get something at The Fort. "We still have to talk about our class project, so why don't you join me?"

After hesitating for the briefest of moments, she smiled. "I'm not really hungry," she said. "But I'll come with you."

So after hobbling up to the checkout counter and paying for his stuff, Andre waited at the door while the clerk scanned the massive inventory Elspeth had dumped on the counter. Thinking she'd bought enough makeup to last well into the next century, he shrugged. *At least she shops the sales…*

Which was rather ironic, given the fact the McGuires were probably as rich as his uncle.

The Fort was a popular restaurant, which had supposedly been built on the exact spot where the first European explorers had constructed a stockade way back in the 1600's. Although archeologists hadn't found a shred of evidence to support that particular legend, the owner thought it made for a good motif so he named his restaurant after the mythical outpost anyway. Like everything else in The Cove, it was quaint.

It was also nearly deserted when they arrived, so they were able to get a small table by the large storefront window. After taking her hooded rain jacket and hanging it on one of the pegs that lined the rough-hewn walls, Andre hung his field jacket up beside it before hobbling back to the table and taking his seat. Smiling across the table as the waitress gave them their menus, he waited as Elspeth ordered a Diet Pepsi before ordering a Coke for himself.

Ignoring his menu, he asked her if she'd given any thought to their project. After Elspeth frowned and said no, he told her he had an idea. "According to the book, armored knights began to arise in the century after Charlemagne…

"But since they had a hard time telling friend from foe in all that armor, they put identifying pennants on their lances and family crests on their shields. So I was thinking we could pick out a famous knight, and you could sew a pennant with the knight's symbol on it and I could make a shield with his crest, and we could give a report on his life and explain what the designs on his pennant and shield meant."

Staring across the candle burning in the center of the table, Elspeth suddenly became enthusiastic. "Cool idea!"

Then she asked him if he had any particular knight in mind.

Andre shook his head. "But my uncle is an amateur Mediaevalist, and he has hundreds of books about that period and thousands of illustrations."

After thinking about it for a moment, Elspeth agreed with Andre's suggestion that they try to find a knight in one of his uncle's books. Then she paused for a moment, and asked if it would be OK to include Lydia. "She's an incredible seamstress, and she's already decided on making a Mediaeval dress for herself…

"But if we asked her really nice, I bet she'd make us costumes from that era too, and then we could give our report on the guy dressed up like Lords and Ladies!"

It was a fantastic idea, but Andre didn't think there was any way in hell Lydia was going to make clothes for all three of them. But Elspeth shook her head. "Are you kidding? She loves to sew – in fact, she makes almost all her own clothes at home."

Surprised – shocked would be a better word, because he'd thought the McGuires wore strictly designer brands – Andre told Elspeth he was game. Reaching into her purse for her cell phone, she said she'd call her right then. Seeing a chance to sneak a smoke, Andre nodded, got up, grabbed his crutches, and told her he'd be right back. Frowning as he made for the door, she punched in the number for Lydia's cell.

Settling back in his seat five minutes later, he ignored the frosty look on Elspeth's face. "So what did she say?"

Elspeth told him she loved the idea, and couldn't wait to get started. Nodding, Andre had just picked up his menu and begun looking it over when Elspeth curtly informed him he was ruining his health.

"And you know what? Kissing a guy that smokes is like making out with an ashtray!"

Chuckling, Andre asked her if she did that often.

After trying to force a frown, Elspeth told him he was a jerk as she picked up her menu. After pretending to study it for a moment, she put it aside. "I'm just not hungry," she said.

Ignoring her comment, Andre reached down for the bag that held the digestive aids he'd just bought and pulled out one of the packages. As he unwrapped it he said, "Let me guess…

"When you were about three or four, you came down with a flu-like illness that made you really sick for a couple of days. And then when you recovered, food no longer smelled or tasted good, and you've had digestive problems ever since."

Taken by surprise, Elspeth sat back in her seat. Shocked – or more accurately, scared out of her wits – she inhaled sharply. Frightened and confused, she didn't know what to say. Thinking her only chance was to fake it, she took a deep breath and asked Andre how he knew that.

Andre had just finished popping two capsules free, so he raised his index finger before putting them in his mouth and washing them down with water. "Well aside from the pale complexion and slightly depressed body temperature, I've watched you in the cafeteria…

"Nothing but salads."

Then he grinned, and handed her the package. "I've got the same problem, but these work wonders."

Still so scared she could barely move, she forced herself to accept the package he handed across the table. "What are they?" she whispered.

Andre shrugged. "Just some ordinary garden herbs, some amino acids, and some probiotic stuff."

After turning the package over in her hands, Elspeth read the label. Trying to pretend interest, she asked if it really worked.

"Yeah," he said. "I really got hammered when I was about three or so, but 'Gascon Flu' is common where I grew up. So the pediatrician put me on a local variation of this stuff, and I haven't had any problems since…"

Then he looked over, and urged her to try them.

Frowning, Elspeth studied the ingredients again. Thinking there was no way a Vampire could die of poison, or even get sick from something like that – unless it contained Holy Water or garlic, of course – she decided she'd better play along. Andre had clearly mistaken her condition for a more human ailment, and she didn't want to correct him.

So after popping two of the capsules out of the tin foil, she said a quick little prayer and downed them. "Thanks," she said as she handed the package back.

Then after pausing for a moment, she asked him if he was going to bring his uncle's books to the school so they could look them over together.

Pretending to be horrified by the thought, Andre pushed himself back in his seat. "Are you kidding? Those books of his are from the Middle Ages, and he'd skin me alive if anything happened to them!"

Elspeth frowned. "So what do we do?"

Andre shrugged. "Come on over Saturday or Sunday, and we can go through them in Uncle Philippe's library."

Elspeth frowned, and looked down at the table. Entering a human's house was tricky – Vampires needed an explicit invitation at the door – and she knew her parents weren't going to like it. Seeing her discomfort, Andre suggested she bring Lydia and her brothers.

Grinning, he told her he'd feel safer that way. "Because you won't try to seduce me with them around."

Flushing, Elspeth did that half-smile, half-frown thing of hers, and said she'd ask. "But my parents are really strict, and they don't like the idea of us taking time away from our studies…

"You know, grades and all."

By that time The Fort had filled up, and the smell of expertly cooked food had begun to filter through the dining section. As the waitress walked by carrying a tray of burgers, Elspeth suddenly sat bolt upright in her seat and placed a hand across her stomach. "Oh my God!" she exclaimed. "I thought I wasn't hungry!"

Seriously hoping she was referring to human food, Andre watched as she snatched up her menu and studied it with bulging eyes. "What's good?" she breathlessly demanded to know.

Relieved, Andre forced a smile. "Personally, I like the Bacon Cheeseburgers with lettuce, tomatoes, onions, and mayonnaise, and the French fries…

"But I've heard just about everything else is good too."

Trying hard to control herself, Elspeth asked if he could call for the waitress. After turning in his chair and raising a finger to summon her, Andre turned back to Elspeth. Confused and frustrated, she asked him how she was supposed to choose. "Everything looks so good!"

Then after putting the menus aside when the waitress arrived, she told Andre she couldn't make up her mind. "Order for me!"

Grinning, Andre told the waitress they'd like two Bacon Cheeseburgers with lettuce, tomatoes, onions, and mayonnaise with large orders of fries on the side – and another round of drinks, please...

Fortunately, service at The Fort was fast. So when the waitress placed their plates on the table five or six minutes later, Andre relaxed. Given the starved look that had appeared on Elspeth's face, he'd been worried she might jump up and snatch someone's burger right out of their hands.

As he watched her demolish her plate, he chuckled to himself. *Humans one, Vampires zero...*

Obviously still hungry after she'd finished off the last of her fries, Andre asked her if she'd like dessert. "I'm gonna have the Brownie Sundae...

"Three scoops of vanilla ice cream served on a steaming hot brownie and covered with whipped cream, nuts and chocolate sauce."

As Elspeth's eyes bulged and her mouth dropped open, Andre told her they could just split one if that sounded like too much. Apparently unable to speak, she shook her head back and forth plaintively.

Grinning, Andre flagged down the waitress and ordered two of the mountainous desserts.

CHAPTER 22

An hour later, Elspeth screeched to a halt in front of the Tudor's main entrance. After pulling eight plastic bags filled with groceries from the back seat of her VW, she raced up to the front door. Pushing it open and then slamming it shut with her foot, she tore through the foyer and then through the dining room into the kitchen. Ignoring the surprised looks and uncertain greetings from her adoptive mother and siblings at the dining room table, she threw the bags up on the preparation island and started ripping them open.

"Damn! Where the hell are the microwave plates?"

After finding one in the cabinets, she rummaged through the cartons of ice cream, soft drinks, potato chips, microwave popcorn, cans of nuts and bottles of toppings until she found the brownies. Ripping the plastic box open, she sliced the contents into four very large pieces, put one on the microwave plate and popped it in the machine. Guessing 30 seconds should do it, she pulled a bowl from one of the shelves and began rooting around in the drawer for the ice cream scoop. It had to be there, because she'd bought it herself.

It wasn't, so she grabbed a large spoon and attacked one of the vanilla ice cream cartons. After forcing almost half the carton in the bowl, she popped open a bottle of nut toppings and poured it over the small white mountain she'd made. Knowing that probably wasn't the right sequence, she grabbed a can of whipped cream and covered the whole mess. Then after ripping open the freezer and scooping a handful of ice into a glass, she grabbed a smaller spoon, the bowl, a glass, and a two-liter bottle of Diet Pepsi and raced for the table.

Ignoring the stunned looks of her mother and siblings, she threw herself into a chair and attacked the dessert. Then suddenly aware she'd left the brownie in the microwave, she rammed her spoon into the ice cream and bolted for the kitchen. Reappearing a moment later – juggling the steaming treat from one hand to the other – she sat down again before dropping it into the pile of whipped cream that topped the vanilla scoops. Then after grabbing her spoon again, she started shoveling the contents of the bowl into her mouth.

As Daniel, Nathan and Lydia looked on in disbelief, Mrs. McGuire slipped away from the table to find her husband. Worried by Elle's bizarre behavior, she pushed her head through the door of his study and asked him to join her in the dining room. "I think there's something wrong with Elle…"

Alarmed, Dr. McGuire jumped up and followed his wife into the dining room. As he stood in the open entryway, his jaw dropped.

Vampires could eat human food, of course, and Civilized Vampires often did to maintain their covers. But no matter how well prepared it was, the smell was unappetizing, the taste ranged from poor to disgusting, and it wreaked havoc on their digestive systems. But there was Elspeth, shoveling spoonful after spoonful of ice cream, toppings and brownie into her mouth with obvious relish.

"Elle?" he finally asked.

Looking up briefly, she acknowledged him. "Oh, hi, Neill!" Then she pointed with her spoon at her nearly empty bowl. "You've *got* to try some of this...

"It's *really* good!"

Deeply worried, Dr. McGuire walked over. "Ice Cream Sundae?" Having never actually had one, he wasn't sure.

After spooning the last bit of brownie into her mouth, she nodded. "And you know what? You can put the stuff in the bowl in any order, and it still tastes the same!"

Then she sat bolt upright. "Oh damn! I forgot to put the ice cream away!"

Jumping up, she raced for the kitchen. After hearing the freezer compartment door open and shut a half-dozen times, Dr. McGuire heard the microwave come to life. Following Elspeth into the kitchen, he asked her what she was doing.

"Making microwave popcorn," she said. "It's supposed to be really good!"

By now completely confused, Dr. McGuire asked Elspeth if she could explain what was going on.

Staring through the glass window as the popcorn bag began to expand, Elspeth told him she'd run into Andre Marchand at the drugstore. "And he asked me have dinner with him at The Fort, so we could talk about our History project..."

Then as the popcorn began to pop, she turned around and searched through the stuff she'd piled on the preparation island behind her. Finding the 20 boxes of the herbal digestive aids she bought in a bag with some other groceries, she tossed him a pack. "So anyway, Andre told me he'd had this 'Gascon Flu' thing as a kid and after that food didn't smell good or taste good and he'd had digestive problems until he started that stuff...

"And he was thinking I'd had it too because I hardly ever eat anything at school – so he suggested I try some."

After the microwave went "bing," she pulled the bag of popcorn out and sniffed it. Smiling happily, she poured it into a big bowl. "So anyway, I took a couple – and man, do they ever work!

"After a couple of minutes, food started smelling good and when the waitress brought our order it was *fantastic!*" Then she looked up and grinned. "And no problems in the bathroom, either…"

Mystified, Dr. McGuire followed his daughter back into the dining room. After taking a seat beside his wife, he studied the label on the box of digestive aids intently. Seeing the capsules contained nothing that could harm a human – let alone a Vampire – he looked over at his wife and shook his head. "I don't understand…"

Daniel had overhead their conversation while they were talking in the kitchen, and out of curiosity he'd gone in to find the supplements. He'd taken two, and they kicked in as Elle neared the bottom of her bowl. Reaching across the table, he'd tried to grab some popcorn – but Elspeth was just too fast. After slamming her fist down on the back of his outstretched hand, she bared her fangs and hissed.

"Get your own damn popcorn!"

Shocked, Mrs. McGuire remonstrated her. "*Elspeth McGuire!* We do *NOT* bare fangs at family!"

As Daniel swore at her from across the table, Elspeth shoveled another fistful of popcorn into her mouth before firing back. "*Hey!*" she said. "We're talking *popcorn* here!

Then after shoveling some more into her mouth, she glared at her mother. "Serious business, Elizabeth…"

After giving her daughter an icy stare, Mrs. McGuire huffed. "Take care of this, Neill."

Then she turned on her heel and marched into the kitchen.

After surveying the wreckage, she shook her head sadly before picking up a box of "Ultra-Triple Butter" popcorn and studying the directions. Then after prying it open she ripped off the plastic wrap surrounding one of the folded up packages and placed it in the microwave. Then after punching in the recommended three minutes and 45 seconds, she started the machine.

As it began popping, she searched through the bags of chips and containers of dip, and the bags of miniature candy bars, until she found some of the supplements. Then after hesitating for a moment, she pried one of the boxes open and extracted two capsules. After washing them down with a sip of water, she leaned back against the counter and tried to sort things through.

But before she could make sense of that night, Elspeth bounded through the doorway carrying her empty bowl. Hearing the popcorn popping, she smiled excitedly. "Making more?"

Still irritated by Elle's behavior, Mrs. McGuire gave her a stern look. "That's for Daniel!"

Elspeth was disappointed, but she grinned when she saw the opened box of supplements. "Gonna try it, huh?"

Mrs. McGuire nodded. Then she raised a finger and pointed it at her daughter. "But if I gain a single ounce," she warned, "You're going to be grounded for a century!"

CHAPTER 23

In 500 years of medical practice, Dr. McGuire had seen less than a handful of sick Vampires. Although they occasionally came down with head colds or the sniffles, Vampires were immune to almost all human illnesses, and disease was entirely unknown. Nonetheless, Elspeth and Daniel had managed to make themselves deathly ill by stuffing themselves with ice cream and junk food. But aside from helping his wife clean up the bathroom where they'd disgorged, there was very little he could do.

Still nauseous when she went to bed that night, Elspeth had sworn off human food for all eternity. But that only lasted until lunch the following day. Unable to resist the dessert section, Elspeth had grabbed the last piece of chocolate cake from cafeteria line, and a vanilla and orange Bomb Pop from the ice cream freezer.

After sneaking a look at her from across the way, Andre congratulated himself on Phase I of *Operation Elspeth*, and reviewed the details of Phase II.

The big problem with Civilized Vamps was getting close to them without provoking a fight/flight reaction. Most of them lived in fear of discovery, and there was no telling how they'd react if they thought their secret identity had been compromised. That being the case, Andre had concluded the only realistic option was to first gain the McGuires' confidence and then let them gradually realize he knew the truth.

The Mist & the Darkness

Thinking that was easier said than done, he started working on a scenario for the next day.

Although his uncle was still out of town and not expected back until the next evening, Dr. and Mrs. McGuire had reluctantly approved Andre's proposed mid-day project meeting – provided, of course, Elspeth took her siblings along. Knowing she was attracted to Andre, and painfully aware of the fact that she had no experience with human boys, they were concerned by what might happen if the two of them were alone together. Although they didn't have to contend with the prospect of an unplanned pregnancy, they both knew a make-out session could easily end in an accidental homicide.

Elspeth was concerned, too, but by the time she knocked on Andre's door just after noon the next day she was more excited than fearful. It had been decades since she'd had any real interactions with humans – especially the male variety – so the prospect of spending time with Andre was almost thrilling.

Andre had spent most of the morning preparing. After promising to pay the maid double-time for coming in on a weekend morning to clean up the mess he'd made in his uncle's absence, he'd stashed anything that might cause problems or arouse the McGuires' suspicions. After taking his Uncle's crucifixes down from the walls, he'd hidden his Katana in his closet and locked the doors to his uncle's private office, bedroom, and chapel. Then after making a complete walk-through to make sure he hadn't missed anything incriminating or embarrassing – or hobble through, since he was still in the cast – he poured a cup of coffee, and took the dogs out on the back porch. Having turned in his crutches for a cane, he leaned it against the handrail before sitting down on the steps and firing up a cigarette. Then he draped his arm around Louie – short for King Louis – and warned him to behave. "Some Vamps are coming by in a few minutes, and I want you and Marie Antoinette to be on your best behavior."

After the dog licked him on the face, he very sternly instructed him to make sure his mate behaved as well.

Having finished his smoke, Andre picked up his cup and made his way back through the kitchen door. He was in the process of rinsing it out in the sink when the doorbell rang.

After he opened the door, Elspeth smiled. "May we come in?"

Knowing she'd ask for a formal invitation, Andre smiled and invited them across the threshold. Hoping they wouldn't get stuck in the doorway by supernatural forces like his uncle's last girlfriend, Andre stepped aside so they could enter.

Glancing around after entering the vestibule, Daniel said "Wow – I thought we had a big house!"

Grinning, Andre explained his uncle had bought it as an investment. Then after taking their coats and hanging them on the coat tree beside the door, he offered to give them the nickel tour.

Escorting them through the living room – which had once been a lobby – Andre showed them the den, and the combined ground floor bar and recreation room that extended from it. After assuring them the juke box was in working order, he took them back the way they had come and through the dining room and kitchen to show them the pool and the stables. Pausing at the kitchen door, Andre warned them about the dogs.

"Let me slip through the door, and grab their collars – they're really very nice, but I'll have to introduce you."

Then as the McGuires exchanged nervous glances, Andre slid through the barely opened door to grab Louie and Marie. Pulling them back to the edge of the porch, he called for Elspeth and her siblings to join him. "Just make a fist and hold it out for them to sniff, and they'll be fine."

Wondering if that was really a good idea, Elspeth hesitated for the briefest moment. Dogs were a territorial lot, and perceptive to boot. No matter how well disguised a Vampire might be, she knew there was no way they could fool a canine. Descended from wolves, most of them retained at least some of their predatory instincts – and more than a few were willing to fight for their turf. A bit frightened, she had to struggle to keep her fangs from extending.

But as she slipped through the door, she was surprised to see the dogs relax and start wagging their tails. Whatever it was Andre had said to them had a calming effect, so she balled her fist and stepped forward. After each of the dogs sniffed it in turn, she waved for her siblings to join her. Then after turning back to Andre, she asked him what their names were.

Pulling up on the larger dog's collar, he identified the animal as "King Louie." Then repeating the process with the slightly smaller animal, he identified her as "Marie Antoinette – but we just call her Marie."

Grinning, Elspeth knelt down beside Marie and patted her on the head. Then after looking up as her brothers and sister introduced themselves to the animals, she smiled. "We should get a dog!"

Laughing, Nathan told her she was dreaming. "There's no way Elizabeth is going to let a mutt in the house!"

Grinning, Andre told them to follow him down the steps. After hobbling to the bottom, he pointed at the domed enclosure fifty feet back and identified it as the pool. "Heated and enclosed, so we can swim all winter." Then hoping they'd pick up on the hint, he told them he loved to swim at night.

Fantasizing about Elspeth in a bikini, he headed past the pool for the stables.

Ben wasn't there – which was probably a good thing, given his mysterious encounter in the woods – but the doors were open. Flipping on the lights, he picked up a plastic bag filled with sugar cubes as he made his way to the first stall. Turning around, he handed one to each of the McGuires before introducing them to his horses.

Bonaparte was the biggest horse Elspeth had ever seen. Unlike most of the horses in America, he was a *destrier* – a European warhorse, as Andre explained. Bred for speed, endurance, and aggression, they'd carried armored knights into battle for centuries.

More frightened of Bonaparte than she had been of the dogs, Elspeth pursed her lips together to hide her fangs and tentatively extended her hand. Relieved when the horse licked the sugar cube off her palm, she stepped back quickly. "He's nice," she said in a doubtful voice.

Picking up on her unease, Andre suggested she might like Josephine better. Handing her another sugar cube, he watched as Elspeth edged forward to the next stall. Then after pursing her lips together again, she held out her hand for the mare. After Josephine licked the sugar cube into her mouth, Elspeth edged forward a bit more. "Will she mind if I pet her?"

Andre smiled and shook his head. "No, I think she likes you."

So after pausing for just a moment, Elspeth took another step forward and stroked the side of Josephine's head. "She's beautiful."

Watching as she warmed to the animal, it occurred to Andre that there was some sort of weird feminine bonding thing going on. Curious, he asked Elspeth if she rode.

Smiling sadly, she said no. "But when I was five, I had a pony ride for my birthday!" Clearly enjoying the memory, she turned around and smiled. "It was my best birthday party ever!"

By that time Lydia had strolled over. "No way in hell you'll get me on one of those things," she said. "But Neill – our father – and Nathan are really good horsemen."

Thinking she'd just given away an important piece of information, Andre called over to Nathan. "Hey, I hear you and your dad like to ride."

Nathan nodded. "Yeah, Neill and I are country boys – as opposed to the City Slickers that make up the rest of the family."

Chuckling at the barb, Andre suggested they do a trail ride sometime. "Somebody around here has to have a couple of extra horses, and we've got spare saddles."

As Elspeth's eyes lit up, Andre glanced at his watch.

"Damn...it's almost 1 o'clock. We'd better hit the books." So after leading them back into the house, he told Daniel and Nathan there was a game room downstairs with a pool table, a big screen TV, and some pinball machines.

Grinning, the two guys said they were on it – just as soon as they finished checking out the suits of armor standing guard in the entryway, and the Mediaeval weapons displayed on the walls. Curious, Lydia asked him if all that stuff was real.

Nodding, Andre informed them that Uncle Philippe was a huge Mediaevalist. "He collects anything he can lay his hands on from that era, including the books we're going to go through."

As he turned back to the others, Lydia reached for the blade of one of the broadswords mounted on the wall. Shouting *"STOP!"* he lunged for her wrist. Then after seizing it in mid air, he apologized and explained it was sharp as a razor.

Andre's action had been well intended, but almost fatal. Out of the corner of his eye, he had seen Daniel's fangs extend and Nathan lunge to restrain his brother. Struggling to maintain a calm demeanor, he carefully released Lydia's wrist. Ignoring her clenched jaw and the terrified expression upon Elspeth's face, he made a mental note to himself:

Dear Dummy, it said. *Lunging at Vampires is NOT a good idea!*

Andre's heart had leapt into his throat when Lydia had reached for the sword, and he knew the McGuires could hear it pounding. So after breathing a deliberate sigh of relief to divert their attention, he warned them to be careful before leading them through the living room into the study. Then after pointing out the Mediaeval flags and banners that hung from the walls, he pulled a half-dozen ancient manuscripts from the built in shelves and then two more modern volumes. Carrying them over to the large oaken table in the center of the room, he set them down before handing the first of the modern books to Lydia and explaining it had hundreds of photographs and drawings of period dress. Then after gesturing for Elspeth, he opened the second.

"This one has reproductions of thousands of 'coats of arms' – sometimes called 'heralds' – and probably as many pennants…

"So after we pick the design, we can look up the knight or noble family that used them – or if you wish, we can reverse the order and pick the knight or family first."

By that time Lydia had already pulled out a chair and was engrossed in the clothing of the era. Following her example, Elspeth sat down and opened the book Andre had given her, and began slowly thumbing through it. "Man," she said after a couple of pages. "These are amazing!"

Glancing over, Lydia said she should check out the dresses. Pushing her book over a bit, she grinned. "Can you imagine yourself in that?"

It was a color photograph of a model in a floor length red silk dress, with an inverted pleat in front and a form-fitting top that pressed her breasts together and pushed them up. As Elspeth's eyes opened wide, she gasped. "Oh my God, it's gorgeous!"

Hoping like hell that Elspeth would pick something similarly revealing for her presentation, Andre grinned as he opened one of the older manuscripts and began thumbing through the listings of noble families. Preferring the game room to musty old manuscripts,

Daniel and Nathan excused themselves and headed downstairs. Realizing it was going to take a while to find what they were looking for, Andre hoped the guys liked pool and pinball.

After distributing Cokes an hour or so later – including the two he'd carried downstairs, with difficulty – Andre returned to his seat and started on the third of the ancient texts. Although any nobleman would do for the report, he was hoping to find one with an especially dramatic history that would make for an interesting presentation. Most of the stuff in the volumes seemed pretty mundane, but his grasp of Mediaeval French was so poor he couldn't be entirely sure. Another half hour into his research, he came across a guy that had supposedly killed 100 Saracens in a single battle. Thinking that had to be a crock, he was about to sneak out for a smoke when he heard the front door suddenly open.

After his uncle called out "Bonjour," Andre called back in French. Telling Philippe the McGuires were visiting, he asked him to come back and meet them. After a moment's pause, his uncle called back and said in a minute. Satisfied, Andre told the girls Philippe was back.

Looking up from her text, Lydia gasped when Dr. Marchand strolled through the door. He was tall, standing at least 6'2" – and even though he was dressed in an elegant three-piece business suit, she could see the muscles rippling beneath the fabric as he strode into the study. More importantly, from Lydia's point of view, he was also gorgeous beyond belief. He had reddish blonde hair, a neatly trimmed beard and moustache, and sparkling blue eyes. Thinking her heart might actually start beating again, she placed her hand on her chest.

Oh my…

She was exaggerating, of course – for contrary to popular opinion, Vampires actually have a heartbeat. But it's so slow and so weak that it's barely perceptible.

Smiling, Dr. Marchand greeted them with a cheery "Bonjour!" Then after switching to English, he made a point of welcoming them to his home. "I'm so pleased to finally meet you…"

"Andre has told me so much about you."

Dr. Marchand's subtle reiteration of Andre's initial invitation to their home flew right past the girls. So after mumbling an incoherent greeting, Lydia glanced over at Elspeth with eyes the size of saucers. Equally surprised but a bit better mannered, Elspeth returned his smile with one of her own. "It's our pleasure, Dr. Marchand."

Then after exchanging polite chitchat for several minutes, Dr. Marchand asked them how the project was going. Frowning, Elspeth said not very well. "We're trying to come up with an interesting Lord who had a really cool herald as well – but so far we haven't made much progress."

After listening carefully, Dr. Marchand turned and walked over to the bookshelves. After studying the titles for a moment, he pulled out a volume and began thumbing through it. Then suddenly smiling, he announced he'd found what he was looking for. "Why don't you use Lord Montaigne?"

Handing Elspeth the open book, he told her that Hugh Montaigne had been an exemplary knight in the Kingdom of Jerusalem during the Crusades. "And his shield was quite expressive – a winged dragon with outstretched talons."

After glancing at the book, Elspeth pushed it over in front of Andre. *"Look!"* she exclaimed. *"It's perfect!"*

After studying the images of the knight and his colors, Andre had to agree. Then looking up at his uncle, he asked him who Lord Montaigne had been. Smiling softly, Dr. Marchand reminded him that Montaigne had been Lord Baylin's closest friend and companion. "They died together at Salifed Pass…"

Taken aback, Andre paused for a moment. *"Right,"* he said slowly. *"That Lord Montaigne..."*

Smiling sadly, Dr. Marchand nodded. "He was the best and bravest knight of all Christendom."

After consulting with Elspeth to make sure she was satisfied with the choice, Andre thanked his uncle for his help. Nodding graciously, Dr. Marchand said he'd missed lunch and was going to make something to eat.

Tempted, Andre asked him what he was going to fix.

After pondering the question for a moment, Dr. Marchand grinned. "I think I'll make a batch of Crusaders' Stew…

"Shall I make some for you and your friends as well?"

Thinking there was no way in hell he was going to eat that crap again, Andre glared at his uncle before shaking his head.

"*Uh...*"

"*No, thanks!*" he said emphatically. "We'll order a couple of pizzas instead."

CHAPTER 24

Lucky for Andre, Uncle Philippe's reference to Crusader's Stew had flown past Lydia and Elspeth. So after thanking the Lord for small favors, he'd had gone downstairs to find out what kind of pizza Daniel and Nathan wanted while his uncle busied himself in the kitchen.

Finding Nathan holding a scimitar, Andre grinned and warned him to exercise due caution. "You're gonna be singing falsetto if you're not careful!"

Wincing at the thought, Nathan put it back in its scabbard and replaced it on the wall. Then after conferring with his brother, he told Andre they'd split a large sausage, pepperoni, and onion pizza.

After calling The Fort and placing their order from the rec room phone, Andre hobbled back up the stairs and returned to the study. Elspeth had just excused herself to visit the ladies room – which gave Lydia an opening. After standing up and rummaging through her purse until she found a tape measure and a small note pad, she told him she needed to take his measurements. Given the fact that Lydia was going to make him a suit of clothes, Andre obliged her. Standing still, he waited until she'd measured his neck, arms, chest and waist. But it wasn't until she knelt down before him that he realized she was jerking his chain.

After telling him to open his legs a bit, she spent an inordinate amount of time measuring his inseam. Both amused and aroused by her presumption, he looked down and playfully challenged her. "You wouldn't dare!"

Grinning wickedly, Lydia reached up and grabbed the top of his jeans with her left hand. Shoving her fingers inside, she held the top of the tape in place with her thumb while slowly brushing the cloth measure down his front with her right hand in a deliberately provocative manner. Pretending to measure his drop, she lingered as Andre cursed her with a whisper. Then after fighting a losing battle with his physiology, he took a deep breath, and silently cursed her again.

Bitch!

Having finally finished, Lydia wiggled her fingers inside his waistband before releasing him and standing up. Still grinning from ear to ear, she winked at him before turning to her notepad and writing down the numbers.

Muttering under his breath, Andre dove for his chair – which turned out to be a good thing, because Elspeth bounded into the room an instant later. Lucky for him, the smell of his uncle's cooking had filled the house by then so she didn't pick up on the pheromones provoked by Lydia's tease.

Trying hard to avoid Elspeth's gaze, Andre spent the next half hour scanning the dozen or so Medieaval suits and dresses Lydia had picked out onto a flash drive, and then a chapter about Lord Montaigne. Just as he finished, the guys came up the stairs carrying a Season I DVD of *Buffy the Vampire Slayer*. Explaining they'd never seen it because they'd been stuck in the wilds of Michigan's Upper Peninsula – with a satellite TV antenna that worked only occasionally, and dial up computer connection that barely worked at all – they asked if they could watch it.

Suppressing an ironic grin, Andre led them back through the living room and into the ground floor bar before putting Disc One into the DVD player attached to the wide screen TV mounted on the wall. Once the pizzas and soft drinks arrived, Andre pushed the play button and told everyone to take a seat. Joined by Dr. Marchand, they watched the first three episodes together.

CHAPTER 25

Watching the McGuires cheering on The Slayer had bordered on hysterical, and Andre was still chuckling about it a week later as he saddled up Josephine.

Having finished with her saddle, he hoisted up the saddle bags and fixed them to the back of it. Once he'd finished, he picked up the 10 x 12 envelope he'd laid on the barrel top behind him, and stuffed it in the left bag. Satisfied it wouldn't get wet if it rained, Andre took Josephine by the bridle and led her outside. Then after telling Bonaparte to behave, he closed the door and swung up on the horse.

The McGuires had left for New York the day after the project meeting, to accompany Mrs. McGuire to an art show. An accomplished artist, she was offering a dozen or so paintings at an upscale gallery and she'd taken the kids along for a week's excused absence. Surprised to find Newton positively weird without the Fang Gang, he'd taken notes for Lydia and Elspeth in history, Nathan in Physics, and Elspeth again for French. Not sure whether they were back yet, and uncertain as to whether Dr. McGuire had gone with them, Andre was going to leave the big envelope that contained them at the front door if they weren't home.

After taking the AK-47 off his back, he chambered a round before checking the safety and slipping it into the scabbard. Then he settled into the saddle for the ride over to the McGuires'.

Andre's ankle had more or less healed by then. After sending the McGuire kids home the week before with a note and two bottles of expensive French wine for Dr. and Mrs. McGuire, his uncle had carefully examined the injury. Satisfied that it was doing well, he'd decided the Aircast was no longer necessary. So after wrapping his nephew's ankle in an elastic bandage, he'd repeated Dr. McGuire's warning and told him to take it easy for the next couple of months. Given the risk of re-injury, parachuting was out of the question until after the turn of the year – by which time it would be too cold, anyway.

By now the first week of October, the days were still warm. And despite the heavy cloud cover, the sun still peeked out occasionally. Basking in the warmth of the Indian Summer, Andre guided Josephine down the state road and into town. Turning left on The Strip, he followed it to the county road before turning onto the narrow asphalt lane that led to the McGuires' residence, a mile or so later. Although he'd never been there before, he'd Googled it on his computer for directions and distance.

An eighth of a mile down the lane – about halfway to the house – he was surprised to hear a convoy of vehicles approaching from behind. Guiding Josephine to the right, he glanced over his left shoulder as a Grand Cherokee passed, followed by the familiar Land Rover and then Elspeth's VW. Congratulating himself on perfect timing, he adjusted his Stetson and guided the horse back onto the road.

The lane was narrow and overhung by trees, a fact that made Andre a bit nervous. The McGuires might be Civilized, but they were situated too close to the innermost trail for comfort. Since it seemed entirely plausible that some of their less amiable cousins might be lurking about, he scanned the tree line carefully until he finally emerged into the clearing where the McGuires had built their home.

Invading a Civilized Vampire's turf was always a tricky proposition, but given the circumstances Andre had decided it was a reasonable risk. But he'd made that calculation five days ago in the safety of history class, and as the clouds closed in again he was beginning to have second thoughts.

The McGuire convoy had parked in front of the house, with Dr. McGuire's Grand Cherokee in the lead, the Land Rover about ten feet behind it, and Elspeth's VW in the rear. Having already unloaded their baggage, the McGuires were standing there waiting for him as he approached. Smiling, he brought Josephine to a halt about five feet from where Elspeth and Lydia were standing. Wearing tight jeans and an even more revealing knit top, Lydia was dressed to kill.

Thinking that wasn't necessarily a good omen when it comes to Vampires, he suppressed his nervousness and smiled again before stealing a glance at Elspeth. Dressed in jeans and boots, a pink sweater, a brown leather jacket and a really cute floppish hat that matched, she looked incredible. Under any other circumstances he would have complimented her on the outfit, but mindful of the circumstances – and her parents' watchful gaze – he smiled at her instead.

Elspeth smiled back, and said "Hi" before rushing forward to grab a hold of Josephine's neck. Looking up expectantly, she asked Andre if he'd brought any sugar. So after greeting the rest of the

McGuire clan, he pulled a small plastic bag from the pocket of his field jacket and handed it to her.

After taking the sugar cubes from Andre's outstretched hand, Elspeth turned around to her parents. With a huge smile dancing on her face, she called out to them. "Elizabeth! Neill! Come meet Josephine!"

Then she took a sugar cube from the bag, and held it up for the horse.

Smiling politely, Dr. McGuire and his wife strolled over, apparently unconcerned by Andre's unexpected visit. As he climbed down from the horse, Mrs. McGuire extended her hand and introduced herself. "You must be Andre," she said. "I'm so pleased to finally meet you."

After nodding at Dr. McGuire and smiling at his wife, Andre took Elizabeth McGuire's hand and assured her that the pleasure was his. Then after a brief exchange, Mrs. McGuire turned to Elspeth and the horse. After stroking Josephine's neck, Mrs. McGuire turned back toward Andre and smiled. "She's beautiful."

After acknowledging her compliment, Andre shook hands with Dr. McGuire. Admiring the horse, Dr. McGuire asked if she was a *destrier*. Nodding, Andre explained Uncle Philippe was a huge fan of the Middle Ages, and had bought Josephine and Bonaparte so he could compete in tournaments. "He likes to joust."

Surprised – and genuinely impressed – Dr. McGuire arched his eyebrows. "That's a rough sport," he said.

Suddenly curious – and hopeful that Dr. McGuire's remark had given him an opening – Andre laughed. "Yeah, and he complains about my parachuting!"

Then without giving Dr. McGuire a chance to reply, he asked him if he'd ever ridden in a tournament.

Chuckling, Dr. McGuire said no. "But I've watched a few, and the jousting matches are really impressive." Then in an effort to change the subject, he asked Andre what had brought him into their neck of the woods.

After glancing around at Lydia, Nathan and Daniel, Andre grinned. "Bad tidings, I'm afraid...

"Exams tomorrow in history and physics, and a major quiz in French." Laughing as the kids groaned, he turned and stepped back

The Mist & the Darkness

to the saddlebags. Extracting the 10 x 12 envelope, he opened it and pulled out three clipped bundles. "I know you all had excused absences, but I brought you copies of my notes and the homework assignments just in case."

Impressed by his thoughtfulness, Mrs. McGuire beamed. "How nice of you, Andre!"

As he handed out the sheaves, Daniel and Lydia began cursing under their breath. Ignoring them, Elspeth turned to her father. "Neill," she said emphatically. "I want a horse!"

Smiling softly, Dr. McGuire nodded. "You know I was just thinking we should add a stable." Then he looked over at his wife. "Liz?"

Mrs. McGuire walked over to her husband, and after wrapping her arm around his waist and pulling him close, she looked up and said it was a wonderful idea. "I used to ride when I was a girl, you know."

Smiling at the way his wife had just covered her tracks, Dr. McGuire nodded. She'd been born in Philadelphia in 1861, and had grown up long before the automotive age. So after glancing around at the rest of the family, he said it was settled. Turning back to his wife, he suggested she draw up a sketch and fax it to their architect.

As she promised to do it the next day, Josephine turned ever so slightly. Glimpsing the stock of the AK-47 protruding from Andre's scabbard, Nathan grinned and asked if he planned on hunting with an assault rifle. "I'm pretty sure that's illegal, Bro."

Suddenly concerned, Dr. McGuire glanced over at Andre.

"Nah, I'm just trying to stay out of jail," he said. Then he grinned, and told the McGuires that Chief Beauregard had threatened to lock him up if he had any more bear problems.

Puzzled, Dr. McGuire repeated the last part of his statement. "Bear problems?"

Grinning again, Andre explained that he'd taken Bonaparte out the day after they'd arrived in The Cove. Since the poor horses had been stuck in a trailer for almost 20 hours en route to their new home, he'd decided to race the animals up the Inner Trail. But less than a mile from the stable, he and Bonaparte had come face to face with the biggest bear he'd ever seen. "We have a few of them in

Gascony, but they're not as big and most of them are afraid of people...

"But this one – he was not only huge, but mad as hell...

"So Bonaparte took one look at the fur ball, reared up, wheeled around, and took off as fast as he could run – which is about 40 miles an hour, so I was hanging onto the saddle for dear life...

"Anyway, after a half-mile or so I looked back over my shoulder and there was that stupid bear chasing after us...

"So Bonaparte was running for the stable, and as soon as we got there I jumped off and slammed the doors shut. I was thinking the bear would just nose around for a couple of minutes and then go back in the woods, so I'd taken Bonaparte's saddle off and started brushing him down when I heard the bear roaring outside...

"And then he started banging against the doors, like he was going to knock them in. So I didn't know what to do, because all the guns were in the house and the bear was just outside...

"Then I remembered animals are afraid of fire, so I broke off a mop handle and wrapped the mopping end up in wire and dunked it in kerosene."

"Anyway by this time the bear was pawing at the windows, and I had to do something. So I fired up the torch with my lighter, and went out through the small door and around the side of the stable...

"I'd just turned the corner when I ran right into the bear – so I shoved the torch at his face, and he took off and ran. So I figured fair is fair – he chased me, so I'll chase him!"

As Dr. McGuire chuckled and Elspeth giggled, Andre continued the story. "So the bear ran 500 feet or so, then stopped and turned around to see if I was still behind him. Then he took off and ran another 500 feet, and did it again...

"So I chased the stupid fur ball down to the State Road, and I was running after him, yelling and screaming at the big wuss to come back and fight when Chief Beauregard pulled up in a squad car. So after he rolled down the passenger side window and leaned over, he looked me up and down and asked if I was on my way to the Olympics...

"So I said 'No Sir,' and pointed down the road. "Just chasing that bear."

The Mist & the Darkness

"So the Chief looked at me like I was a complete idiot, and asked me where I'm from. So I told him France, and he rolled his eyes and said, 'Well, I guess that explains it.'"

As the McGuires cracked up laughing, Andre grinned. "Then he told me if he ever caught me chasing a bear again, he was gonna lock us both up in the same cell!"

Still grinning, Andre shrugged. "So I figured I'd better bring my rifle with me."

CHAPTER 26

The McGuires thought the story was hilarious, so by the time Andre remounted Josephine a few minutes later he was congratulating himself on the success of his plan. Despite the fact that he'd invaded their turf with an automatic weapon, Elspeth had been happy to see him, and so were her siblings – at least until he'd announced the exams, and handed out his notes – and Dr. McGuire had accepted his presence without apparent alarm. As icing on the cake, Mrs. McGuire had been warm and friendly, and Andre was convinced she'd been pleased by his visit as well.

She'd invited him in and even asked if he would join them for dinner. Thinking an invitation like that could be interpreted in more ways than one, Andre had cautiously begged off. Explaining that he still had to take Bonaparte out, and then cram for the next day's exams, he'd thanked her anyway. So after promising to give Uncle Philippe their thanks for the wine he'd sent them, Andre turned Josephine around and headed home. But given the number of hunters in the woods – and the statistical certainty that at least half of them were trigger happy – Andre decided to take the roads rather than chance the Inner Trail.

Phase III *Operation Elspeth* involved backing off, to see what developed. The key to getting close to her lay in making her family comfortable with his presence – and that was going to take time. But that turned out to be fortuitous, because his life suddenly accelerated.

Charles S. Viar

Although technically a private institution, Newton Academy's charter obliged it to function as a public school as well. Neither fish nor fowl in the eyes of the Vermont high school athletic association – and less than five years old, to boot – it had taken The Powers That Be four years to figure out how Newton fit into the grand scheme of things. But after scratching their heads, juggling schedules, and studying maps, they finally worked Newton into a conference. So after four long years of playing exhibition games against anyone that would take them up on a challenge, the Newton Apples were finally playing for real.

Due to scheduling weirdness, they'd played their first three games away. But now at long last, they were going to finally play on their own turf, and as a member of Newton's aristocracy Andre had to be there. So the following Saturday, he'd turned up at 1:00 pm to cheer them on. Held under leaden skies, the game quickly degenerated into a massacre.

Although Newton's team wasn't especially good, the others in their conference ranged from poor to miserable, and the team they played that day was the worst of the lot. By the time the mist had turned to drizzle at half time, the score was 47-0.

Andre wasn't especially interested in American football. Having grown up on the European version – known in the States as soccer – he thought the American version was too slow and too long, especially since it involved freezing his butt off in a windswept bleacher. But as a Jock in Good Standing, he feigned interest and cheered the team on. Having had the foresight to bring a poncho, a blanket and a flask of brandy, he stayed at his post in the bleachers until the sound of the buzzer finally filtered through the rain and the howling winds that had come up in the final quarter.

After congratulating Wilkinson and the rest of the team in the locker room, Andre headed home. There was a post-game victory party at Kathy Norse's house at 7 pm, and he had to put in an appearance. But since he had scheduled a late date with Tiffany in Burlington, he made a token appearance and slipped out early.

The rain had stopped almost as suddenly as it had started that afternoon, and by the time he wheeled the Vette into the parking lot of the hotel just before 9 pm the skies had cleared. The stars were out, the moon was full, and Andre was feeling lucky.

Having spent the past three weeks alternately tutoring her in French and flirting, he'd been waiting for her to invite him up. When she finally did, the tone of her voice said it all.

Andre had driven up to Burlington a couple of times, but he hadn't stayed over. A quick check on the Internet convinced him the Ethan Allen was the place to stay. So after making a reservation, he'd sent Tiffany an e-mail asking her to meet him in the lobby at 9. She'd fired back an e-mail saying she'd be there, and asking him what she should wear. Feeling mischievous, Andre decided to push his luck. "Something sexy," he replied.

After pulling his bag from the trunk and handing the valet his keys, he slung his gear over his shoulder and strode into the lobby. Not seeing anyone who resembled her pic, he shrugged and marched over to the desk. Handing the clerk his fake ID and a genuine American Express card, he stated his name.

After entering his name and credit card number into the computer, the clerk smiled. "Why yes, Mr. Marchand. We have you in room 214."

As Andre was replacing his ID and credit card in his wallet, he heard a familiar feminine voice behind him. "Andre?"

As he turned around, his eyes bulged.

Andre had known Tiffany was a beauty, but when he sent his last e-mail he hadn't thought there was a snowball's chance in hell she'd actually dress to specification. But she had...

Her hair was piled on top of her head, her makeup was perfect, and she was dressed in heels, a dark blue mini skirt, a sheer white blouse pinned daringly low – *sans brazier* – and covered by a lightweight jacket that fell to her hips.

Holy crap...

Trying desperately not to let his eyes wander, Andre forced a smile and acknowledged her greeting. Almost as tall as he was in her heels, she had stunningly beautiful green eyes. Unable to resist the temptation, a sly glance a bit further south threatened to reduce him to a blithering idiot.

It was a close call. But after recovering his wits, he asked the desk clerk to have his bag delivered to his room. Then he smiled, and escorted Tiffany into the restaurant.

The Ethan Allen billed itself as a non-smoking hotel, and for the most part that was true. But the restaurant had a small, well-ventilated section behind a partition in the rear that the Maitre d' reserved for special guests. So after listening patiently to Andre's request – and discreetly palming the $50 bill Andre had slipped him – he led them to a quiet table behind a freestanding partition along the glass curtain wall. After thanking the man for his indulgence, Andre seated Tiffany at the table before walking back to check his field jacket. Then after returning and taking his seat, he shook a cigarette free and lit it before telling her what a pleasure it was to finally meet her. Smiling, she slowly and – Andre hoped – deliberately, leaned over to retrieve a pack of cigarettes from her purse on the floor beside her chair.

It was a stunning view...

Having caught him in the act as she straightened, Tiffany smiled demurely and pretended to ignore his less than artful glance as Andre leaned across the table to light her cigarette. "So you were in the Foreign Legion?"

Now certain that Tiffany's erotic display had been intentional, Andre grinned and nodded. "The Second Parachute Regiment."

Clearly intrigued, she smiled as the steward handed Andre the wine list and insisted he tell her all about it. Glancing up as he ordered a $150 bottle, he said he would – provided she told him about American universities. "That's why I moved to the States, you know."

Much to Andre's surprise, the steward took his order without asking either of them for an ID. Thinking underage American drinkers probably ordered beer rather than expensive wines, Andre was about to ask her to explain how American colleges worked when she looked at him in astonishment. "Do you know how much that wine costs?"

Andre smiled and nodded. "A bit more than they charge in France, but it's from my family's vineyard – and it's an excellent year."

Stunned, Tiffany looked at him with eyes the size of saucers. "Your family's vineyard?"

After Andre nodded, Tiffany sat there for a moment taking it all in. "You must be really rich," she finally said.

The Mist & the Darkness

Andre shrugged. "I have a pretty decent draw from my trust fund, but everything else is controlled by my uncle." Then not wanting to go into detail, he changed the subject.

After shaking her head and refusing to tell him about university life, she pretended to pout before accusing him of not being fair. "Tell you what," she said. "We can trade questions, one at a time."

Thinking that wasn't a bad idea as the steward stepped forward to pour their wine, Andre agreed. Then after sniffing the cork and taking a tiny sip, he told the steward it was fine.

They spent the next four hours drinking wine, eating dinner and trading questions that became ever more personal. Then finally, somewhat after 1:00 AM the lights went from dim to bright. Taking the hint, Andre drained the last of his glass and asked Tiffany if she'd like to come up to his room for a nightcap. A stupid question by then, but as a gentleman in doubtful standing, it was one he thought he should ask. So after she gave him a naughty smile, he called for the check and asked the waiter to have another bottle sent to his room.

When Andre woke up the next morning, Tiffany had already dressed and was writing him a note. Seeing him stir, she came over and sat down on the edge of the bed. She had to leave for a study group at the library, but she wanted him to know what a wonderful time she'd had. Then after making him promise to call her that night, she leaned over and kissed him goodbye.

Only half-awake, Andre rolled over and went back to sleep – which turned out to be a good thing, because one floor down and around the corner, Lydia and Elspeth had just finished packing up. Satisfied they hadn't forgotten anything, they picked up their bags and headed for the restaurant.

Strolling through the open doors a few minutes later, they waited by the freestanding sign for the hostess. Having driven up to Burlington in search of fabric for their history project costumes, they were talking about the special orders they'd made at the fabric shop when Elspeth suddenly stiffened.

Thinking there was just no way, she sniffed the air a couple of times to make sure her senses weren't deceiving her. Then she turned to Lydia, and whispered incredulously. "That's Andre's scent!"

Trying not to be as obvious as her sister, Lydia sniffed discreetly. Then as her eyes widened and her jaw dropped, she gasped. *"Oh my God..."*

Then she pointed at the rather disheveled redhead, paying for a large cup of coffee at the carryout stand. *"It's that girl..."*

CHAPTER 27

When Andre wheeled the Vette into a parking spot Monday morning, he was still basking in the glow of a terrific weekend. Aside from her beauty and physical passion – both of which ranked high on his list of desirable feminine traits – Tiffany was also bright, personable, and riotously funny. And if he felt a tinge of guilt about having spent the night with her, he'd quickly dismissed it. Thus far at least, there was nothing going on between him and Elspeth – so he was a free man.

And in any event, there was no way she'd ever find out...

As Andre climbed out of the car and hoisted his backpack, he saw the McGuires' Land Rover rolling past a couple of rows beyond. For some reason excited to see Elspeth, he trotted through two lanes of cars to greet them as they emerged.

By the time he'd reached them, Daniel, Elspeth and Lydia had climbed out and gathered together as Nathan locked the driver's side door. Calling out a cheery greeting, he expected them to respond in kind.

Wrong, Kimosabe...

The guys looked at him skeptically, Lydia ignored him, and when Elspeth finally spoke, her icy tone dropped the temperature a good 20 degrees. "Good morning, Andre," she said. Then she stuck her nose up in the air and marched off with Lydia in tow.

Coming to a halt some five feet from Nathan and Daniel, Andre looked at them quizzically. "Now what?" he demanded to know.

As Daniel grinned from ear to ear, Nathan chuckled. "You are *soooooooo* busted!"

Huh?

Then they both cracked up laughing.

Wondering what was going on, Andre demanded to know what was so funny. Still laughing, Nathan had to take a minute to regain control. "Well," he drawled. "Let's just say you weren't the only one at the Ethan Allen Saturday night."

Oh crap…

Wincing, Andre exhaled sharply. "She saw me???"

Daniel grinned, and shrugged. "I'm not sure about that part, Bro – but she knows about the hot-looking redhead."

Andre winced again. *"Ouch."*

Thinking that was the understatement of the century, Nathan looked at him incredulously. "Ouch don't begin to cover it, my man…

"You're gonna pay for that!"

After staring down at the asphalt, Andre shook his head. Then suddenly angry, he protested.

"That's not fair," he said. "We're not going together – hell, we're not even dating!"

Daniel chuckled. "A minor technicality, Bro." Then he stepped forward and threw his arm around Andre's shoulders.

"But don't feel bad – been there, done that."

Not entirely comfortable with a Vamp that close to his throat, Andre turned toward him and asked how long it was going to take for Elspeth to get over it. After pursing his lips and rocking his head back and forth a couple of times, Daniel looked at Andre quizzically. "Believe in reincarnation?"

Puzzled, Andre shrugged and said he wasn't sure.

"Well, I'm thinking that's your best bet."

After Andre looked over at Nathan, the taller Vamp chuckled. "Nah…

"Graduation at the latest. Let's see – that's what, 18 months or so?"

After looking down at the asphalt again, Andre shook his head back and forth before looking up again. "Man, this sucks!"

Nodding, Daniel said "Big time."

Realizing he'd really put his foot in it, Andre thanked them for cluing him in. Then he turned and headed for the school.

Needless to say, the day did not go well. Somehow or another, word had gotten out about his liaison in Burlington, and the Outcast Alliance was all over his case. He'd found a death threat taped to his locker, written in purple ink by an anonymous female hand on flowery notepaper – with a big smiley face incongruously placed at the bottom – and at least a dozen post-it-notes proclaiming various sentiments, among them being "Andre's a Rat!" and "Elspeth Forever!"

But on the bright side, the fact that he'd been shacked up in the most expensive hotel in Burlington with an older woman had won him massive numbers of points with the Jocks. Mistaking Tiffany for his imaginary girlfriend from Montreal, members of Newton's various athletic teams shook his hand or slapped him on the back, while most of the Cheerleaders sighed in envy.

The one prominent exception to that was Marianne Wilson, who had apparently seen through his subterfuge. Stopping him in the hallway after gym, she discreetly let him know that she was available. It was a tempting offer, and under any other circumstances Andre might have taken her up on it. Marianne was bright and pretty, and she had a reputation as a Goldilocks Girl – not too hot, and not too cold.

But even then, the day seemed to drag on forever – so much so that Andre had found it difficult to contain his impatience. When the bell finally rang at 5:00 pm, he was out of there like a shot.

Arriving home less than 10 minutes later, he dumped his gear on his bed and changed into riding clothes. From a technical standpoint at least, Ben was supposed to take both horses out each day but since Andre liked to ride they'd worked out an alternating schedule. On even numbered calendar days Ben took Bonaparte out in the mornings and Andre took Josephine out in the evenings, and on odd days it was reversed. Being an even day, Andre was looking forward to an hour or so of quality time with the colt.

Hoping for some quiet time for himself, he rode Bonaparte into town, and along The Strip before heading back. He spent the ride into The Cove relaxing, but on the way back he began assessing the damage. Surely, there had to be some way to salvage the situation with Elspeth.

The Mist & the Darkness

From any reasonable point of view, he thought, she was being totally unfair. He had been hitting on her, to be sure – but they weren't dating, and he certainly hadn't made any commitments.

But there was some sort of weird chemistry at work there, and he had to admit he liked her. He liked her gorgeous face, her beautiful milk-chocolatey eyes, her awe-inspiring figure, the sound of her voice, the way she laughed, the way she blushed, that funny half-smile half-frown she made when he teased her – hell, he even liked her whacked-out sense of humor.

As he thought about it, he realized he liked everything about her. *Well, except for that Vampire thing...*

Thinking Headmaster Renfrowe had been right when he'd said Andre would be a damned fool if he let her get away, he made a mental note to bang his head on the next boulder he encountered. Fortunately, there weren't any between The Cove and the stable.

Having brushed down Bonaparte and made sure the horses had food and water for the night, Andre went back inside the Chalet and poured a glass of wine before heading upstairs to do his homework. Disinterested and a bit dispirited when he finally sat down at his desk, he considered blowing it off. Since he had perfect marks so far, and was in tight with most of his teachers, he was pretty sure they would accept a need for down-time as an excuse. He was still weighing the possibility when his cell phone sprang to life, and began playing *La Marseillaise.*

Glancing at the caller ID, he was surprised to see Tiffany's cell number on the display. Having told him she'd be at the library until late that night cramming for an exam, he hadn't expected to hear from her. Picking it up, he answered in French.

Tiffany replied in English, and by the tone of her voice he could tell something was up. Concerned, he listened intently – until she got to the part about how she and her ex-boyfriend had had a long talk, and decided to get back together. Realizing that she had called to dump him, he rolled his eyes and said "Uh huh, I understand" a couple of times before telling her he'd see her around. Irritated beyond belief, he ended the call, stood up, and marched over to the window.

Wondering if the concept of break-up sex had somehow failed to make it across the Atlantic, he stared out into the woods. Then

after the better part of five minutes, he looked up at the Heavens and remonstrated the Creator. *You could have just given us sports and booze, but noooooooooooooooooooo...*
You just had to make women, and screw it all up!
He'd just added a *"Way to go, God!"* when the lights dimmed for a split-second as the exterior floodlights kicked in. As the dogs barked and the barely audible alarm sounded, adrenalin surged through his system. Racing back to his desk, he rolled the mouse on his laptop and clicked on the Chalet's security page.
Damn!
Three intruders had triggered the perimeter alarm. Rolling the mouse again, he clicked on the button for the infrared sensors.
Son-of-a-bitch!
There were three Vamps cutting across the far north edge of cleared property, and two of them were carrying something big.
Wheeling around, Andre raced over to the far wall and grabbed his Katana. Then after slinging it over his shoulder, he grabbed his AK-47 from its perch and two fresh magazines. After slamming one into position and shoving the other into his belt, he raced down the steps. Charging through the dining room and into the kitchen, he careened to a halt by the rear door and doused the lights. Then he pushed it open, and rolled through it onto the porch.
Ignoring the frenzied dogs in the kennel, he bounded to his feet and jumped over the porch railing. Rolling when he hit the ground, he came up in a half-crouch and began advancing toward the pool's Plexiglas dome.
Peering around the edge, he could see Ben standing out in the open with a pump shotgun at the ready. After whistling to alert him to his presence, Andre stood up and called out. "What's going on?"
Ben turned around and started walking toward him. "Beats the hell out of me," he yelled back. "The dogs went nuts, the flood lights came on, and the alarm sounded."
Worried for more reasons than one, Andre asked him if he'd seen anything. Ben shook his head and explained it had taken him a couple of seconds to load up. By that time whoever or whatever it was that had intruded had made it to the woods. Silently noting that Ben had emphasized the word "whatever," Andre closed the

remaining ten feet and pointed at the far north end. "I think they crossed over there."

Nodding, Ben reached into his pocket and pulled out a miniature flashlight. Not quite sure why he needed a penlight when the entire area was illuminated, Andre walked alongside the older man until they reached the area the Vamps had cut across. Noting the barely discernible tracks, Ben knelt down and examined them carefully. "Three of them," said the former Green Beret. "One in the lead, and two behind – the two in the rear were carrying something heavy."

Andre already knew that from the monitor. But since he didn't want to disclose the fact that the alarm system had infrared sensors as well as video cams, he knelt down and pretended to study the tracks himself. He'd just finished running his finger around one of the footprints when he heard the sound of gunfire.

Wheeling in the direction it came from, he could see a half-dozen muzzles flashing on a hillside a half-mile distant. *"Jesus Christ!"* he whispered.

"They're firing on full auto..."

CHAPTER 28

The Cove was in an uproar. There hadn't been a serious crime in the hamlet in more than forty years, so the fact that burglars had broken into Henry Rohbards's mansion had everyone talking.

As the CEO of Infinity Entertainment, Rohbard had been in New York negotiating with financial backers at the time of the break-in. Having taken his wife along with him, the house had been deserted when the burglars cut the electrical feeds – thereby shutting off the alarm system – before smashing in the back door.

The *modus operandi* was crude, and it had amateur written all over it. But Rohbard had accidentally left a laptop open and on, and the built in camera had revealed something else altogether – for while the thieves had made a point of stealing the jewelry Mrs. Rohbard had carelessly left about, and their brand new 80-inch digital TV, they'd also opened the safe in her husband's office, removed the documents contained within, and carefully photographed each one in turn before putting them back in the safe and closing it again. The fact that they'd left almost $40,000 in cash undisturbed clearly pointed to the fact that the burglars were highly skilled professionals covering their tracks by making it look like an amateur job.

When the maid discovered the break-in early the next morning, she'd called Chief Beauregard. Shocked by her report, he'd rushed to the scene with both his full time police officers. Realizing he was in way over his head, he called Infinity's chief of security before appealing to the county sheriff's department for assistance.

Informed of the news fifteen or twenty minutes later, Henry Rohbard cancelled the meetings he'd scheduled for the day and raced to the airport. Boarding the corporate jet, he flew back to Burlington and took a helicopter from there. Arriving at The Cove just two and a half hours after learning of the break-in, he surveyed the wreckage before picking up the phone. After spending the better part of fifteen minutes in a hushed and worried conversation with the head of the Securities and Exchange Commission in Washington, he called the FBI's regional office.

After Winston DePew hired him as Infinity Entertainment's CEO in a fleeting moment of sobriety, Rohbard had led the company to greatness. In less than five years, it had become the single largest digital game maker in the world, and Rohbard had spent most of the last twelve months working out a plan to take the company public. The initial stock offering of ten million common shares would have put trillions in the company's coffers – and billions in his pocket.

The break-in was clearly an act of corporate espionage, and it didn't take long to prove it. After an alert FBI Agent noticed the still open laptop and realized the webcam had been left on, he'd run the images back. Having watched the safecracker pop the safe open on the first try, he'd come to the obvious conclusion that it had been an inside job. The only real question was who had provided the thieves with the combination.

That appeared to be answered when Henry Rohbard's secretary failed to show up for work the next morning. After dispatching two agents to her house and finding it deserted, the FBI obtained a search warrant and smashed in the door. It later turned out that Rohbard had a key to her place – but that wasn't something he wanted anyone to know.

Especially his wife…

The FBI was close to wrapping up the case when the *New York Times* ran what was, by their restrained standards, a lurid piece on Henry's secret life. It turned out that Henry had something going with the girl that involved whips and chains and a number of other things the *Times'* editors thought best not to print. Although no one was quite sure what those other things might be, the smart money in The Cove was on dungeons, Nazi uniforms and – possibly – a goat. But since a substantial minority of the local citizenry was convinced it involved chickens instead, no one was entirely sure.

But despite the scandal, Henry's job was secure: Infinity's stock was still privately owned, and his latest game had shattered all previous records in sales and profitability. Entitled *Master of the Universe*, it was the first online game that racked up more than a million subscribers in the first week of release.

For a $10 monthly fee, anyone with a decent computer could sign up and play against all the other gamers in real time. Assigned a planet with a specified resource base in one of the thousands of cyber galaxies, the players had to choose among various investment strategies to build up their economic and technical resources in order to defend their planet and conquer others.

Each player started with the same economic, scientific, and military base, but with the right investments and research and development strategies they could increase their capabilities from crude, chemically powered rockets all the way up to starships powered by warp drives and armed with an array of exotic weapons.

Players were allowed to engage in diplomacy with anyone they chose, and to enter into alliances wherever they saw fit. They were also allowed to engage in espionage, covert operations, and to dispense with legal formalities such as declarations of war.

Nathan and Daniel had signed up for the game the day it hit the market, and after eight days of almost continuous play they'd moved up the galactic food chain to become "Sector Lords" – meaning they'd conquered all the inhabited planets in their vicinities. Having found themselves on opposite sides of their cyber galaxy, their plan was to fight their way across it and link up in the middle. Then after conquering the rest – and figuring out which set of strategies would reward them with an advanced warp drive – they'd attack the next closest galaxy.

The problem was they were still using a primitive type of space travel that required them to fly their fleets through wormholes in order to travel any significant distance. But since there was no apparent relationship between where you entered and where you popped out, their conquests looked more like a bizarre four-dimensional archipelago than an empire. And to make matters worse, they had run into ferocious opposition from a 12-year-old girl in China. Skilled and incredibly aggressive, she'd figured out they were acting in concert and organized an alliance of her own. Locked in a life and death struggle with "Ming the Merciless," Nathan and Daniel had ignored the scandal swirling around Infinity's CEO.

But having witnessed the gunfire in the hills, that was a luxury Andre could ill-afford. Unlike The Cove's police, the country sheriff's department, and the FBI, Andre knew there was a gang of Vamps operating in the woods – and given the detailed press reports, it didn't take a great deal of imagination to figure out what had come down. Someone with a great deal of experience in manipulating the stock market had planned on making a killing off Infinity's public offering – and the fact they'd hired a group of Vamp safecrackers to steal the insider information they needed to run the scam suggested a Civilized Vamp was behind it.

After putting the various bits and pieces together, Andre concluded the mastermind that planned the break-in had arranged for a meeting in the hills to exchange cash for the digitally photographed documents – and double-crossed them with a deadly ambush, to make sure they told no tales...

Probably hired mercenaries to do the dirty work...

Andre had waited until well after dark the following evening to make his way into the woods and up the hill to where he'd seen the muzzle flashes. Concerned by the prospect of hired soldiers and wary of the hunters that had flooded into The Cove for the Black Bears, turkeys and deer then in season, he'd taken his AK-47, his 9mm, night vision gear, two stun grenades from Uncle Philippe's arsenal, and a battery operated ultraviolet light unit to check for blood. After spending forty-five minutes creeping silently through the woods, he'd finally emerged in the small clearing where he guessed the Vamp burglars got whacked. Then after adjusting the filters on his flashlight, he'd methodically searched the place.

As he expected, the ground was littered with shell casings, and his ultraviolet light turned up blood all over the place. After carefully scraping a sample into a test tube, he ran his hands along the forest floor until he came across the sooty residue of an immolated Vamp. *Figures*, he thought. *They shredded the freaks with gunfire, then cut their heads off while they were down...*

Then very carefully, he followed the trail of boot prints and broken branches the assassins had left until they finally faded out deep in the woods. Realizing he'd tracked them as far as possible, he turned around and began the long trek home.

Since he'd stopped, backtracked, and set up an ambush a half-dozen times to make sure no one had followed him, Andre didn't get back to the Chalet until just before dawn. Trudging across the cleared section of the back area, he encountered Ben as he emerged from his cottage. After staring at Andre for an interminable minute, the stablehand started swearing.

"Goddamnit, Andre – what the hell were you doing in the woods?"

But before Andre could respond, Ben unleashed another torrent of invectives. "You don't have the goddamn experience to be out there alone!"

Then after striding over and shoving his finger in Andre's chest, he continued. "I don't give a goddamn if you *were* in the Legion!" Then he pointed at the hills behind them, and began screaming. "That's Bad Guy country, boy – and it *crawls*!"

By now livid, Ben jabbed his finger in Andre's chest again. "If I catch you out there again, I'm going to tell your goddamn uncle – you got that?"

After frowning and nodding, Andre said "Yes, Sir."

After glaring at him for a long moment, Ben turned on his heel and began marching away. But after a moment's hesitation, Andre called after him. "It would help if you'd let me know what's going on out there."

Ben stopped, and slowly turned around. After eyeing Andre for a long minute, he shook his head. "It's not your problem, Andre...
"Let it go!"
Then he did an about-face, and marched into the stable.

Although most people would have been exhausted by the trek through the woods, that sort of exertion didn't even qualify as chump change in the Legion. During his twenty-six months in the military, he'd marched for 36 hours straight at least a half-dozen times, carrying his weapon and a 120-lb. pack. So after showering, shaving, and changing his clothes, he headed off for class.

He had been looking forward to a tedious day, but after Mrs. Morgan handed out a school flyer announcing Newton's Halloween festivities, Andre perked up.

Halloween hadn't been especially well known in France when he was growing up, but his mother had thrown a party every year to introduce their village to the custom. The parents had grumbled about *Les Anglo-Saxons,* but the kids had loved it – and they weren't alone, because even though the French regarded Halloween as an American holiday, it was slowly but surely catching on. A couple of upscale bars in Paris that catered to expatriate Americans had started throwing Halloween parties in the early 1990's, and sensing a whole new market, French candy makers had promoted it heavily. By the time Andre had left France for the U.S., at least a third of the bars in Paris had adopted the custom and many of the retail establishments, too. But rather than trick-or-treat from door to door, the kids in Paris went from storefront table to storefront table, collecting candies, popcorn balls, and other goodies.

Being so widely scattered geographically, The Cove had adopted a similar approach: parents were invited to bring their little ghosts and ghouls to The Strip, where the merchants and anyone else who wanted to set up a table could hand out candy to the little monsters. There were only two rules: kids under 12 had to be accompanied by an adult, and they had to wear a costume to collect their loot.

But in addition to the festivities in town, Newton was going to throw a bash of its own. Students were encouraged to wear costumes to school, and the afternoon classes were cancelled so the students could assemble in the cafeteria area for an after-school party, complete with a popular band that was being brought in from

Burlington. The party would wrap up at 6 pm, and students could stay on for a special Halloween Dinner, or head into town if they liked.

The last two school parties had been enormously successful – someone had managed to spike the punch bowl with vodka without getting caught – and so the classrooms and hallways were abuzz with anticipation. Still two weeks away, most of the students were trying to decide what they'd wear.

The Jocks and the Cheerleaders had created a scandal the year before, by turning up dressed as pimps and streetwalkers – and since some of the girls had been sent home for indecency, and the rest of the In Crowd had been served with detention slips, they were trying to come up with something new and original that wouldn't get them hard time. As Andre listened to them debate the merits of various possibilities over lunch, the germ of an idea took root. Glancing over at Elspeth – seated at the "McGuire Table" in the shadows along the far wall, Andre grinned to himself.

Time to jerk that girl's chain, he thought.

So as Kathy Norse droned on and on about how sexist the Renfrowe Regime was for not permitting the girls to dress up like street sluts, Andre reached into his backpack to retrieve a pen and a notepad. *Let's see,* he thought. *I'll need an old fashioned tux…*

A white tie, a cummerbund, dress shoes, a red sash and some fake medals…

A cape, a top hat, and a walking stick…

Some of that really heavy white makeup like they use in the Theater Department, and some dark red lipstick…

And a set of fake fangs.

CHAPTER 29

Even though Elspeth kept up her Ice Princess act, speaking to him only when absolutely necessary, the next two weeks passed quickly. Although clearly sympathetic, Lydia had maintained her distance while Nathan and Daniel had been quietly supportive. But far more important from a morale standpoint, payback time was fast approaching.

Andre had ordered all the stuff he needed off the internet, and UPS had faithfully delivered it. Even though The Cove lay at the edge of the known world, Infinity Entertainment and the Clinic had made their thrice-weekly runs from Burlington worthwhile.

It had taken a lot of effort, but Andre had eventually figured out how to apply the white stage makeup properly. The blood red lipstick had been a stretch though, and he'd run through almost all of it before he'd finally figured out how to put it on without looking like an idiot.

Satisfied as he stood before the mirror on the morning of Newton's Halloween party, he congratulated himself. Dressed in an old-fashioned tux, with a white tie and a red sash adorned with reproductions of various European medals, he'd slicked his dyed hair straight back and artfully covered his face with makeup. After inserting the fake fangs in his mouth and applying the lipstick, he looked like a Vampire straight from Central Casting. Grinning, he placed his velvet cape over his shoulders and turned up the collar before reaching for his top hat and walking stick. Then after taking a few minutes to practice his deliberately absurd accent, he headed for school.

Since Andre had underestimated the time it would take him to dye his hair and dress, the McGuires were already seated at their table in the cafeteria, enjoying their annual jest when he pulled into the parking lot ten minutes later.

For the McGuire Clan, Halloween was a special holiday – it was the one day of the year when they could dress as they had when they were human. Dr. McGuire wore 16th Century Scottish regalia, including a traditional kilt, knee socks with a protruding dagger, a ruffled shirt, a rough leather vest and a beret. The only thing missing was the Claymore Sword his father had given him when he'd turned twelve. It was far too valuable to take out in public, and in any event it would probably get him arrested.

Elizabeth McGuire dressed as a proper Philadelphia lady, with a whalebone corset, an ankle length low-neck dress complete with a bustle, a choker necklace and, inevitably, a hat with an ostrich plume. Outdoors she carried a gaily colored parasol, which she liked to twirl

The Mist & the Darkness

over her shoulder. Nathan dressed in a deliberately frayed and soiled Continental Army uniform, with a bloody bandage wrapped around his head, while Lydia wore a flapper dress with a hat and fox stole. Elspeth dressed as a 1950's teen, with her hair back in a ponytail, bright red lipstick, a full skirt that fell beneath her knees, an overly tight sweater, and bobby socks and saddle shoes. Daniel wore the baggies and cut-off sweatshirt of a 1960's Surfer Dude, and carried a short foam board everywhere he went.

Having finished their morning coffee, the McGuire kids were getting up to leave when Andre strolled through the door. Taken aback, Nathan halted in place, Lydia's eyes bulged and Elspeth swore under her breath. Daniel laughed out loud, before calling out. "Hey, Drac!"

Suppressing a grin, Andre twirled his walking stick as he strolled over. "That ees Count Dracula to you, *paysan!*" he said in a deliberately absurd imitation of Bela Lugosi. Then after eyeing Lydia and Elspeth up and down, he demanded to know the names of the lovely ladies.

Chortling, Daniel complimented him on his costume. But Elspeth seemed far less impressed – because after frowning and shaking her head, she told him he looked ridiculous. Feigning anger and insult, Andre jerked back before wagging his finger at her. "Eet ees very dangerous to insult a Vham-pier, you know…

"I vill bite you on zee neck and make you my love slave!"

Then after a furtive glance around to make sure no one could overhear him, Andre continued in a hushed voice. "That ees what we Vham-piers do, you know…"

As Daniel laughed and Nathan chuckled, Lydia grinned lecherously and laid her head over to expose her neck. "Promise?" she asked in a hopeful voice.

After giving her sister a disgusted look, Elspeth glared at Andre. Then in voice dripping with sarcasm, she made a veiled reference to his tryst with Tiffany, by asking how many "love slaves" he had. Ignoring her none-too-subtle jibe, Andre looked down at the floor and shook his head sadly.

"Only one, Mademoiselle. But she ran away with zee Wolfman…

"It was a tragedy," he intoned. "A terrible tragedy…."

After glaring at him for a long moment, the corners of Elspeth's mouth began to creep up. *"Uh huh,"* she said. *"A tragedy."*

Then she huffed and rolled her eyes, before marching off.

Grinning, Andre called after her. "But Mademoiselle…"

"Zee position is open if you weesh to apply!"

Elspeth ignored him, but Lydia didn't. After pressing her body against his and straightening his tie, she stood up on her toes and brushed her tongue against his throat in a long, slow lick. "Elle won't," she said in a sultry whisper, "But I might." Then after stepping back, she grinned wickedly and winked, before sauntering off.

Holy crap…

After glaring at Lydia, Daniel turned back to Andre. "She's jerking your chain, Bro. The girl's a tease."

Still in a state of shock, Andre swallowed hard before nodding. *"Right…"*

Then after taking a long moment to compose himself, he thanked Daniel for the warning and wished the two brothers a Happy Halloween, before heading to the lounge to pick up his morning *Café au lait*.

After getting his coffee, he strolled back into the cafeteria and headed for the Jock table. Finding it strangely deserted, Andre glanced around before pulling out a chair and sitting down. He was wondering where everyone was when the Jocks and Cheerleaders began streaming through the open double doors – dressed implausibly as Nerds and Geeks.

Not quite sure he could believe his eyes, Andre did a double take before breaking up laughing: the guys were dressed in garish plaid shirts with pocket protectors, high-water khakis with white socks, high-top tennis shoes, and big thick glasses they'd taped in the center with white surgical tape. A few of them were wearing suspenders that clashed with their shirts, and all of them had greased their hair back.

But the girls were even worse – in addition to their puffed-up hair, lacquered in place with massive amounts of hairspray, they were wearing big thick glasses, garish lipstick, ill-fitting sweaters that didn't match their below-the-knee A-line skirts, and white socks and patent

The Mist & the Darkness

leather shoes. And as a final touch, they'd all made a mess out of their makeup.

It was funny as hell, but it was also cruel. More than a few of the social outcasts actually dressed like that, and not by design. They simply lacked the social skills to make themselves presentable. Realizing that nothing good was going to come from the In Crowd's deliberately insulting jest, Andre wondered what they'd been thinking.

After Wilkinson and Bob Johnson – the captain of the football team – sat down beside him, Andre shook his head. Then in a moment that later proved prophetic, he warned them that there was bound to be payback downstream.

Laughing, Johnson asked Andre what the Nerds were going to do about it – paint differential equations on their lockers? Then suddenly serious, he asked what was up with the Dracula thing. "Didn't you get the word on costumes?"

Andre shook his head, and Wilkinson winced. "Oh crap," he said. "I forgot!"

Turning to Andre, he apologized. "I thought I called everyone last Friday."

Andre shrugged and said it was no big deal, and then went on to cover for Wilkinson by saying he'd ordered his costume weeks before anyway. Then he grinned, and bared his fake fangs. "And chicks have a thing about Vampires, you know."

Which was apparently the case, because no sooner had the words left his mouth than Mary Ellen Roberts sauntered up behind him and wrapped her arms around his upper chest. Leaning over, she asked him when he was going to show her his crypt.

Turning in his seat, Andre peered over the breasts she'd thrust against his cheek and promised she could stop by just as soon as the contractor finished the renovations. "It vill be lovely, you know...A new bar, a high def TV, all new torture equipment, and zee finest rack zat money can buy!"

Puzzled, Mary Ellen asked him what he needed a bed for. "I thought Vampires slept in coffins?"

After sighing and shaking his head, Andre looked at her like the idiot she was. He was promising to show her how the guillotine worked when the bell suddenly rang. Relieved, he opened his jaws and playfully bit the breast Mary Ellen had shoved in his face, before disentangling himself from her arms and draining his coffee. Ignoring her suddenly protruding nipples, he pushed himself away from the table. "Another day," he proclaimed, "Another drachma!"

Then after putting his top hat in place and twirling his walking stick, he headed for his locker to collect his books.

First Period was more boring than usual. Having finally finished with the Beowulf Saga, Mrs. Morgan had moved on to the Arthurian Legends. As he listened to her drone on and on about Tristan and Isolde – an even older myth that contained the core elements of the later tales – Andre's mind drifted back to the McGuires. Unless he was wildly mistaken, their choice of costumes conveyed a wealth of information. In all probability, Nathan had served in the American Revolution, which made him somewhere around 250 years old. Lydia had apparently grown up during the 1920's, which made her close to 100, while Elspeth was probably in her 70's. That left Daniel, who was probably a decade or so younger.

Thinking Elspeth was old enough to be his grandmother, Andre grinned. *Hey! Older women are hot!*

Then after spending the better part of fifteen minutes engrossed in an erotic fantasy that involved Elspeth, a black bustier, fishnet stockings, five inch heels, handcuffs and a four-posted bed, Andre began drifting back to reality. Entirely oblivious to whatever it was Mrs. Morgan was explaining, he was wondering what Elspeth had been like as a human when the bell finally rang. So after making a mental note to follow up on that at a later date, he slammed his notebook shut and took off for history.

Arriving a few minutes after the McGuire girls, he pretended to ignore them. But after Elspeth began digging in her purse for a pen, Andre leaned over and raised up his arms, extended his fingers like claws, and bared his fangs. Startled by the dark shadow that fell across her desk, Elspeth shrieked, threw up her hands to protect herself, and fell out of her desk. Landing unceremoniously in the aisle, she began swearing under her breath. Lydia howled, the rest of the class clapped and cheered, and Dr. Marigold turned around from the blackboard to demand an explanation.

After clapping her left hand over her mouth to hide the fangs that had reflexively extended, Elspeth scowled, pointed at Andre

The Mist & the Darkness

with her right, and complained that "Dracula" had tried to bite her. Then after picking herself up and dusting off her skirt before resuming her seat, she looked over at Andre and hissed. "You scared me, you jerk!"

Andre was about to tell her "That ees what we Vham-piers do" when Dr. Marigold demanded order. Dressed as a witch, she picked a wand up off her desk and pointed it at Andre. "Listen up, Count...

"The next time you try to bite someone in my class, I'm going to turn your Transylvanian tush into a frog!"

As the class broke up laughing, Elspeth slammed her hand down on her desk and yelled, *"Do it! Do it!"*

Grinning, Dr. Marigold explained that "union rules" required witches to give their victims fair warning. "But the next time Count Dracula gets out of line, he's going to find himself on a dissection table in the biology lab."

After acknowledging the riotous applause from the class by standing and taking a ceremonious bow, Andre sat down and glared at the teacher in mock anger. "Thanks, Doc."

Then after the class quieted down and Dr. Marigold turned to the blackboard, Andre leaned over and whispered. "You deserved that for being mean!"

Whipping around in her chair, Elspeth fired back in a voice a bit too loud. *"Did NOT!"*

Having heard her, Dr. Marigold turned back to the class, and pointed her wand at Elspeth.

"You too, Bobby Socks..."

CHAPTER 30

Aside from the fact that the Ice Princess had sulked all the way through History class, the day had been fun. Since Halloween actually fell on the following day – that being Saturday, in 2009 – the abbreviated school day had fast degenerated into farce as the students looked forward to a long, homework-free weekend of partying.

Despite the fact that his ankle had long since healed, the school nurse had insisted he remain on the injured list for another two weeks. So rather than join the class in outdoor calisthenics, Andre had spent fourth period dust-mopping the gym floor with Daniel again. It was easy work, and it gave him a chance to gather some more intel.

After offering a lame excuse about having friends in California, Daniel admitted he really liked to surf. As far as he was concerned, riding a wave was like nothing else in the world – difficult and challenging, it offered a kind of high you couldn't get anywhere else. Thinking that was the way he felt about parachuting, Andre told him he could relate. He'd been hooked on his first jump.

So after spending the hour comparing notes and discussing the finer points of their preferred sports as they pushed their industrial-sized dust mops up and down the floor, Andre headed for the cafeteria. Due to the scheduling weirdness associated with Halloween, lunch was being served an hour late, which meant he had a study hall and nothing to study. So after checking in with the supervisor, he headed into the lounge for another cup of coffee. He managed to blow off the hour by reading the online news and surfing the net. Stumbling across *The Darwin Awards* – the posthumous honor annually bestowed upon on the fool that managed to kill himself in the stupidest possible way – he was thinking the little joke he'd played on Elspeth had probably made him a contender. He was still chuckling about that when the bell rang, and the serving line opened.

After stuffing his notebook into his backpack, he hoisted it over his shoulder and got into line. Having run late because of the inordinate amount of time it had taken to get dressed and made up, Andre was hungry. But when he arrived at the entrée section, he paused. The food in the cafeteria was usually pretty good, but the Monster Meat in green gravy looked decidedly unappetizing. But since it couldn't possibly be as bad as his uncle's Crusaders Stew, he reluctantly handed his plate across and told the server to load it up. Then after grabbing a dessert and a Coke, he made his way over to the Jock Table.

Sitting down next to Wilkinson, he asked about the drill. After managing to swallow a piece of greenish looking meat, Wilkinson grimaced before wiping his mouth with a napkin. "Man, they weren't kidding about this Monster Meat stuff!" Then turning to Andre, he told him the dance would kick off after lunch, and they'd probably stick around for a while.

"But my place at 7 – everyone's gonna be there." Meaning the Jocks and the Cheerleaders, and the handful of other students deemed socially acceptable by the In Crowd.

"By the way – you got the beer, right?"

Andre nodded. "I've got 20 cases of Sam Adams iced up in the stable, but I'll need someone with a truck to get them over to your place."

Wilkinson nodded. "Not a problem. Jimmy and I will be by around 6:30."

Still suspicious of the entrée on his plate, Andre was nibbling at the Putrid Potatoes the server had dumped alongside them. "That works," he said. Then after noticing the McGuires heading for the door, he asked Wilkinson what was up with them.

Wilkinson shrugged. "They usually blow off school functions," he said. "And since the City decided to coordinate with the school and have Trick or Treat tonight rather than tomorrow, they're probably going down to The Strip to set up the booth for the Clinic."

Thinking that might be worth his while, Andre told Wilkinson he wanted to check it out. "After we get the beer loaded up, I'm going to swing by there before I hit your place." Nodding, Wilkinson told him to take his time. "My parents aren't going to be back until late Sunday, so we're going to party all night." Then after taking a deep drink from his Coke, he looked over and grinned. "You still trying to make it with Elspeth?"

Andre shrugged, then lied through his teeth. "Well, I've still got that thing going on in Montreal, so I'm not exactly a free agent…"

Then after a long pause, he grinned. "But if that doesn't work out, I might give her a shot."

Wilkinson laughed. "She's definitely hot – but aside from being a couple of fries short of a Happy Meal, she's stuck up and her parents won't let her date anyway."

After glancing over his shoulder to make sure the McGuires had cleared the cafeteria, Andre laughed and defended her. "Everyone thinks she's weird and snobbish," he said, "But she's really not – she's just got a whacked-out sense of humor, and she's kind of shy."

After finishing off his Coke, Wilkinson shrugged. "Maybe so," he said. "But you might want to look a bit closer to home – Mary Ellen just broke up with that Frat guy from UV she's been dating, and she's ready to play."

Then he grinned, and looked over at Andre again "The girl's dumb as a post – but *definitely* a good time!"

After laughing and rating Mary Ellen as a "Maybe," Andre spent the rest of the lunch hour shooting the breeze with the athletes and flirting with the Cheerleaders. Then after the band arrived, he stuck around with Wilkinson until almost six, making a point to dance with Kathy Norse, Mary Ellen, and the other more or less single girls that graced the Jock Table. But even though he had a good time, his mind was elsewhere – quite specifically, with Elspeth McGuire, who had by then arrived at The Strip with her family.

Despite the misadventure in history class, Elspeth was in a buoyant mood that evening. She loved kids, and she couldn't wait to see their excited faces as they stocked up on Halloween loot.

During her first cycle through an assumed human identity, she'd taken a degree in elementary education with the intention of becoming a kindergarten teacher. And after graduating from the University of Colorado, she'd actually taught at a private school for almost a year. But after a near disaster on the playground, she'd reluctantly resigned – one of her kids had fallen off the jungle gym and torn a gash in her knee. Horrified by the blood lust that had nearly overpowered her, Elspeth realized it that it just wasn't safe for her to be around accident-prone tykes.

But Halloween was an exception. With her family there to provide support and encouragement – and if necessary, physical restraint – she was looking forward to handing out candy and complimenting the kids on their costumes. But as she pushed the last prefabricated plastic column into place for the Clinic's Halloween castle, she suddenly wondered how her adoptive father could handle being around blood all the time. As a puzzled look crept across her face, she turned to him and asked in a low whisper.

Vampires have an extraordinary range of auditory perception, and they are more than capable of conducting a conversation far

The Mist & the Darkness

below the level of human awareness. Although the McGuires generally refrained from speaking like that in public – there was always the chance that someone adept at lip reading might eavesdrop – it was already dark, and in any event they had their backs turned to the sidewalk.

Being perhaps the only Vampire in history who was utterly indifferent to human blood, Dr. McGuire smiled softly at her query. "After 500 years of surgical practice, it's lost its allure – when I see human blood, I automatically revert to the medical mode. My mind's focused on what's caused the bleeding, and how to stop it." Then he chuckled and whispered again. "I wouldn't even drink the damn stuff if I didn't have to."

Smiling, Mrs. McGuire stepped over and put her arm around her husband's waist. "Your dad's a Superhero!"

As she snapped an exterior panel into place, Lydia laughed. "Yeah, and his youngest daughter is a Super Klutz – you should have seen her in history class today!"

After giving Lydia a look that registered somewhere between consternation and resignation, Mrs. McGuire sighed. "Now what?"

Ignoring Elspeth's demand to "Hush!" Lydia grinned from ear to ear. "Andre Marchand came to school today dressed up like Count Dracula," she said.

"Really cool costume, too – tux, sash, cape, makeup, dark red lipstick and even a fake set of fangs..."

Ignoring her sister's now vehement objections, Lydia told their mother about Andre's prank in second period. After imitating his pose with her hands up and fingers extended like claws, Lydia broke up laughing.

"You should have seen it," she finally managed to say. "Elle wasn't paying attention, so she totally freaked – she threw up her hands and screeched, and then she fell out of her desk and landed on her butt!"

Mrs. McGuire closed her eyes for a moment and sighed, before asking Elspeth if she'd gotten into trouble again.

"*No!*" Elspeth fired back. "But Your-Daughter-The-Floozie should have – because Andre was showing off his fangs in the cafeteria, and Flapper Girl here exposed her neck so he could bite her!"

Having finished popping an interior panel into place, Dr. McGuire looked over at his wife as Daniel cracked up laughing. Standing on a six-foot ladder to secure the fastenings for the roof, he looked down and interjected. "Yeah, and that was just for starters…

"Elle was giving him grief about his costume, so Marchand said if she wasn't nice he'd bite her and turn her into his 'love slave'…

"So Elle stomped off, and Lydia grabbed Andre – and then she stood up on her tiptoes, and licked his throat!"

Elspeth's jaw dropped, Mrs. McGuire gasped, and Dr. McGuire began a slow count to ten. Seeing their reaction, Lydia waved her hand dismissively. "Oh for God's sake, people – I was just teasing!"

Then she turned to Elspeth, and assured her diminutive sister in an oh-so-condescending voice that she wasn't hitting on her boyfriend. Turning back to the rest of the family, she laughed and grinned. "But he is cute, you know!"

After growling, Elspeth looked around furiously. "Anybody got a stake? I'm gonna dust that trollop!"

Interposing himself between the girls, Dr. McGuire curtly informed them "That's enough!" Then he ordered Elspeth to the rental van to get the treats, Lydia to finish up the last couple of exterior panels, and Daniel to finish the roof so Nathan could spray the fake spider webs and put up the plastic skeletons.

Still fuming, Elspeth stomped off for the candy while Lydia gave the rest of the family an exasperated glare. "Come on, people, it was just a joke!"

Deeply upset, Mrs. McGuire whispered angrily. "Lydia, aside from your reputation – which you take *far* too lightly – a jest like that could expose us!

"Suppose he'd cut himself shaving this morning, and you smelled the blood? You might have lost control and *bit* him!

"And even if you managed to restrain yourself, he might have seen your fangs!"

The moment of silence that followed was broken when Elspeth slammed a dozen grocery bags filled with candy, popcorn balls, and other treats down on the table that faced the sidewalk. "It's not her fangs she wants to show him!"

Dr. McGuire closed his eyes and shook his head, before looking over at his wife. "I think you should handle this," he said. Looking back, Mrs. McGuire nodded curtly. "Thank you, Neill – I intend to!"

But before Dr. McGuire could make his retreat, Nathan stepped forward and raised his hands. "Wait a minute," he demanded. Then after glancing around to make sure he had their attention, he asked in a low and authoritative voice: "What makes you think Marchand hasn't figured it out?"

Dr. and Mrs. McGuire exchanged shocked glances, Daniel muttered, "Oh shit," Lydia's eyes bulged, and Elspeth gasped.

Folding her hands together over her mouth, she whispered. *"Oh my God…*

"What if he has?"

CHAPTER 31

Andre had turned up at the Clinic's booth a half-hour later, and in exchange for a popcorn ball he'd sung *La Marseillaise* in what he claimed to be Transylvanian. Bordering on hilarious, his performance had relieved a great deal of tension. But eight days later, the question of whether or not he'd uncovered their secret remained unanswered.

Having finished with his last patient of the day, Dr. McGuire had strolled over to the Clinic's tiny restaurant for a cup of coffee. As he waited for Chief Gomez to arrive and relieve him for the night, his mind drifted back to Halloween.

The evening had been a pleasant success. He'd enjoyed the parade of ghosts and goblins, princesses, pirates, comic book superheroes and even the occasional monster. Elspeth had been wonderful with the kids, gently cajoling them to sing a song, tell a joke, or perform a trick for their treats. As he sipped on the coffee that had grown lukewarm in his cup, he felt a twinge of sadness. Had she not been bitten, she would have been a wonderful mother.

He was about to finish off the last of his brew when the intercom came suddenly to life. "Dr. McGuire, report to Emergency Intake, Dr. McGuire to Emergency Intake!"

Jumping up from the table, Dr. McGuire covered the distance to the receptionist in seconds. Seeing him approach, she held up her finger and signaled for him to wait until she'd finished. Then after nodding, and telling whoever was on the other end of the line to make it quick, she hung up the phone and turned to face him. "County Sheriff's office just called, we've got four trauma cases en route."

Nodding, Dr. McGuire asked if they'd told her what had happened. "Some sort of accident, Sir. One victim is bleeding badly, the other three sustained minor injuries."

Nodding again, he asked her if Chief Gomez had arrived. "That was him on the phone. He'll be here in a minute."

Thanking her, Dr. McGuire turned into the hallway and strode down to the emergency intake. Located halfway down the building and opening to the east exterior, it was large, airy and fully equipped. Nurse Jackson was already there, laying out surgical instruments. As she looked up and informed Dr. McGuire they were ready, he heard the faint sound of sirens.

Two ambulances roared into the parking lot less than a minute later. The first did a half-circle, backed up to the automatic double doors and stopped, while the other backed in a few feet farther down. Jumping from their vehicles, the EMT crews opened up the back doors. As they extricated a blood-soaked girl lashed to a gurney from the first vehicle, three dazed and frightened young men climbed out of the second.

Striding out to meet the crews, Dr. McGuire and Nurse Jackson helped guide the gurney into the emergency area. Looking down at the terrified and trembling girl, he promised her she'd be all right.

With practiced precision, the four of them undid the restraints that held the girl to the dolly and lifted her onto the north operating table. Then after instructing Nurse Jackson to attend to the three boys, he pulled on a pair of surgical gloves. Having already noted that her airway was clear and unobstructed, and that she was breathing, he checked her pulse as he leaned over to listen to the external sound of her breath. Noting that the bandage the EMT's had applied to her upper forehead had apparently stopped the bleeding, he strode over to a cabinet for a blanket. Her skin was icy cold and he was afraid she might slip into shock. As he was laying

The Mist & the Darkness

the blanket over her, Chief Gomez strode into the room. Needing no instruction, he marched over and picked up the blood pressure instrument from the table Nurse Jackson had laid out. After gently wrapping the cuff around her arm, he began inflating it.

After warning the girl it might hurt a bit, Dr. McGuire began carefully teasing the bandage off her forehead. Beneath it lay a bloody gash that began just below her hairline and ran some two inches higher. Having finished checking her blood pressure, Chief Gomez stepped back out of the patient's line of sight and rocked his extended hand back and forth a bit to indicate the result was iffy. After Dr. McGuire acknowledged his signal with a silent nod, the Chief pulled a bag of whole blood from the refrigerated locker along the wall and began prepping an IV unit.

After taking a quick glance over his shoulder to see how Nurse Jackson was doing with the guys, he leaned over the girl as the Chief inserted the IV needle in her arm. "You've got a nasty gash on your forehead, and I'm going to sew it up…

"But you'll be OK, I promise."

Still trembling, the girl didn't respond. Her eyes were locked on a point somewhere on the ceiling, and filled with terror. Wondering what could have frightened her that badly, he began disinfecting her wound. As he finished, he glanced over at Nurse Jackson again. Having wrapped the three young men in blankets, she was escorting them up to the regular exam rooms. As the last one passed through the doorway, a County Sheriff's Deputy stuck his head through the portal to let him know he was there. Nodding to acknowledge the Deputy's presence, Dr. McGuire injected Novocain around the girl's wound. Then after waiting for it to take effect, he began stitching it closed.

After finishing five minutes later, he told the Chief he was going out in the hallway to consult with Nurse Jackson and confer with the Deputy. After Chief Gomez nodded, he strolled through the door and into the hallway. Encountering the nurse on her way back from the exam rooms, he asked her how the others were. After she ran through their vital stats and explained that none of them had been seriously injured, she apologized and said she couldn't make heads or tails out of their story. But in addition to being covered in scrapes and bruises, they were cold and badly frightened, and she thought

Dr. McGuire should take a closer look. After nodding and thanking her, he turned to the Deputy.

As Nurse Jackson returned to the emergency room to check on the Chief, the Deputy inhaled and shrugged. "I was patrolling the Lake Road about 10 miles south of here when the four of them came charging out of the woods yelling and screaming something about monsters...

"I could see the girl was covered with blood so I called for backup and an ambulance, and drew my weapon. One of the guys was carrying a geologist's hammer, and the other two had large rocks in their hands. After ordering them to drop 'em, I demanded to know what the hell was going on...

"The girl was hysterical, and couldn't speak, but the older male – he's a teaching assistant at the university – said they'd been on a field trip gathering rock samples when three guys stepped out of the woods and confronted them."

Then after inhaling again and resting his hands on his gun belt, the Deputy shook his head. "This is where it gets crazy, Doc...

"He claimed they were Vampires – I'm not kidding you – and they bared their fangs, and said they were going to kill them."

Trying hard to suppress his consternation, Dr. McGuire nodded. "And then what happened?"

"Well," the Deputy said. "It gets even weirder – because at that point they claim a Ninja with a samurai sword dropped out of an overhanging tree, and lopped the Vampires heads off."

Feigning amusement, Dr. McGuire asked the Deputy if he was jerking his chain.

The Deputy shook his head. "No, Sir! The girl was still too freaked to talk, but all three of the males told me the exact same thing – a Ninja suddenly dropped from a tree and cut their heads off, and then their bodies burst into flames."

Dr. McGuire forced himself to chuckle. "And the girl that suffered the wound?"

"Well Sir, they said they were terrified – so they took off for the road at a dead run, and the girl tripped and hit her head on a rock."

Dr. McGuire pursed his lips together again, and nodded. "That's consistent with my observation..."

Then after a moment's pause, he asked the Deputy if they had been doing drugs.

The Deputy shrugged. "Sure as hell sounds like it, Doc, but given the way the girl was bleeding I thought it was more important to get them here than it was to test them."

Dr. McGuire nodded, and told the Deputy he'd done the right thing. "But it sounds to me like they were smoking dope."

Nodding, the Deputy handed him a business card and explained his office would contact him if they needed anything else. After first examining the card and then pocketing it, Dr. McGuire paused for a moment and forced a quizzical look upon his face. "Just out of curiosity, Deputy, did they describe the 'Ninja'?"

The Deputy chuckled. "They said he was dressed from head-to-toe in one of those camouflage Ninja suits with a mask, and wielding a Samurai sword."

Dr. McGuire forced himself to smile. "Probably Bruce Lee again."

Then after the Deputy laughed at the joke, he excused himself. "I have to get the girl into radiology for a MRI, and take a look at her companions."

Tipping his hat, the Deputy thanked him for his assistance and strode away.

CHAPTER 32

The MRI results had been ambiguous, so Dr. McGuire decided to keep the girl overnight for observation. After telling the Chief and Nurse Jackson to move her into the Clinic's tiny overnight ward, he'd examined her three companions one by one. By the time he got to them, they had begun to question their own sanity. "I know what I saw, Doctor," said the teaching assistant. "But I also know that's impossible...

"There aren't any Vampires, I've never heard of ninjas in Vermont, and decapitated bodies just don't burst into flames..."

Dr. McGuire nodded, and began to gently misdirect him. "That's true," he said. "But if the local lore is to be believed, the woods are full of psychoactive substances." Then he asked if they had been handling any plant life with their bare hands.

After thinking about it for a moment, the TA nodded. "Yeah, just before we saw the 'Vampires' we'd dug an interesting rock out of the ground – and the bottom was covered with an unusual moss. Since it was so out of the ordinary, I passed it around and made sure everyone took a good look."

Now confident that his ruse would work, Dr. McGuire nodded. "I'm not a toxicologist, but it sounds to me like a case of inadvertent poisoning."

Thinking that was a logical explanation, the TA nodded emphatically. "That makes sense, Doctor…"

"But why would we all have the same hallucination?"

Dr. McGuire acknowledged that was a good question. "But I suspect you didn't, at least not at first. As you slipped into an altered state of consciousness, you probably talked about what was going on in your heads – and as you shared your subjective experiences with one another, they grew into a group hallucination." Then before the student could respond, he threw him another curve by asking if he'd checked his watch.

Desperately wanting to believe the doctor's hypothesis, the TA shook his head. "No Sir, I have no idea how much time might have elapsed between the time we found the rock and the onset of the hallucinations."

Dr. McGuire nodded sympathetically. "You know if I recall correctly, there have been similar outbreaks in Europe caused by molds that had grown upon rye grains. I'm fairly well convinced something along those lines happened to you and your undergraduate students – but fortunately, the reported effects were short lived. In a couple of hours, I think you'll be just fine."

Then after scribbling the hypothesis on the patient's chart, he warned him not to attempt to drive or operate equipment for 24 hours – just to make sure the toxin had worn off – before signing the release form and telling the kid he was free to go. "Just make sure someone comes to pick you up."

The Mist & the Darkness

Fortunately for Dr. McGuire, the two undergraduate students were as desperate as their TA for a logical explanation. So after making sure they'd bought into his tale of psychotoxins, he finished up the paperwork and turned the shift over to Chief Gomez before heading home. But as he cleared the parking lot, he called his wife and told her to organize a family meeting.

Finding them assembled around the dining room table when he arrived, he asked Mrs. McGuire if she would mind making a pot of coffee. "Something very serious happened at the Clinic today, and I think I may need a cup or two to calm my nerves."

With a worried look on her face, Mrs. McGuire got up and headed into the kitchen.

Still standing by his seat, Dr. McGuire thanked the kids for their presence. "This is important, so I think everyone should be here. I'm going to go help your mother in the kitchen, but I'll be right back."

Returning with an overly large mug three or four minutes later, Dr. McGuire waited for his wife to sit down before taking his seat. Then after taking a sip, he carefully explained what had happened and how he'd handled it.

After a moment of uncomfortable silence, Daniel laid his head over on his arm and groaned. "Are we going to have to move again?"

Dr. McGuire shrugged. "That's something we have to discuss – but first, I want to make sure everyone has their 'bug-out kit' assembled and ready to go." Having been forced to flee several times in the past, each of the McGuires kept a backpack stuffed and ready, along with $100,000 in cash, a driver's license, a passport, a cell phone, and functioning credit cards, all under fictitious but fully functional identities.

After each member of the family nodded, Dr. McGuire reminded them of their escape plan. "We have three extra cars garaged in or around The Cove. Once the signal is given, we split up into teams, pick up our assigned vehicles and head for the Canadian border using our new identities. Make sure you have thoroughly destroyed your old driver's licenses, passport, and credit cards…

"We rendezvous in 48 hours at the lake house in Ontario, but if that proves impossible we meet at the cabin in West Virginia within a week. But if it really hits the fan, we meet at the ranch in Patagonia within six weeks. Everyone understand?"

After Mrs. McGuire and the kids nodded grimly, Elspeth stuck up her hand. "So are we really going to have to move? I like it here…"

Dr. McGuire nodded. "That's what we have to talk about, Elle." Then he nodded at Nathan. "You're the soldier, Nate – what's your assessment?"

Nathan shifted in his seat, and looked down at the table for a long moment. "Well, Sir," he said. "If I understood correctly, the students report they encountered the Vamps about ten miles to the south…

"And that a 'Ninja' decapitated them…

"If true, there won't be any physical evidence the authorities will recognize, so I think we can rule out any problems from the state or county governments."

Then after looking up and gazing at his friend and adoptive father, Nathan said that leaves the Vampire Hunter. "Frankly," he said, "I've never heard of a single Hunter taking on three Vamps before, so I'm inclined to think it's an overly-bold amateur."

Dr. McGuire nodded. "Point well taken," he said. "So what kind of threat are we confronting?"

Nathan shrugged. "I think that depends on several factors. First and foremost, does he know we're here? If so, the threat level depends upon whether he discriminates between Predators, such as the ones he took out in the woods, and Civilized Vampires such as ourselves…

"If he makes that distinction, I think we're OK whether he knows we're here or not. But if he doesn't discriminate between good Vamps and bad, it comes down to how much he knows or how much he may discover."

Still stretched out on the table, Daniel agreed. Then after straightening himself, he said it was weird that a Hunter would be operating in northwest Vermont. "This is like the end of the known universe, you know?"

Lydia chuckled. "Ain't that the truth," she said. Then suddenly curious, she wondered aloud what the Vamps were doing in the woods in the first place. "We've been here almost a year now, and despite all the time we've spent out there we haven't encountered a soul…

The Mist & the Darkness

"Well, except for those knuckleheads that got blown up – but since we didn't actually *see* them get blown up, we don't really know what happened. Maybe it was just some kind of weird prank."

Mrs. McGuire said it was a good point, but thought there were other possibilities as well. Reaching over and placing her hand on her husband's, she asked him to assume for a moment that Vampires had actually been killed in the explosion. Wasn't it possible a Hunter had tracked them from someplace else? "Perhaps they came south from Montreal, or north from Albany or New York City?"

Dr. McGuire nodded, and said that seemed plausible. "I've never understood the government's explanation – I simply can't imagine why terrorists would detonate an explosion here, when they were supposedly on their way to New York to blow up Times Square…."

Nathan nodded. "I'm inclined to think the explosion in the woods and the terrorists were coincidental – which means a Hunter followed them here from someplace else, as Elizabeth suggested, or there's a Hunter living in the immediate vicinity that knows the woods a great deal better than we do."

Incredulous, Elspeth jerked upright. "A Hunter here in The Cove? You've got to be kidding!"

Nathan shook his head. "Not at all," he said. "I think it's a reasonable deduction."

Lydia, who was a great deal smarter than she liked to let on, looked at him skeptically. "OK, so we grant the logic and assume there's a Hunter in The Cove…

"What the hell is he doing *here*? And why hasn't he discovered *us*?"

Not wanting to answer the question directly, Nathan looked down at the table for a long moment before finally looking back up. "Think about the *modus operandi*," he said.

"The first attack employed an IED – that's an 'Improvised Explosive Device,' for those of you that haven't been paying attention to what's going on in Iraq and Afghanistan – and the second was carried out by someone who seemed to appear out of nowhere, and decapitated three Vamps with a sword…

"So how many people do we know who's familiar with the type of explosive ambush employed in the Mid East…

"Who's been trained to use camouflage, cover, and concealment...

"Has a whole house full of swords...

"And isn't afraid of multiple Vampires?"

As Mrs. McGuire gasped, Daniel sat bolt upright. *"Holy shit,"* he whispered. *"It's Marchand..."*

As a horrified look spread across Elspeth's face, she pushed herself away from the table. After looking around the table with desperate eyes, she shook her head in emphatic denial. *"No!"* she exclaimed. *"It can't be..."*

CHAPTER 33

The family meeting was very much on Elizabeth McGuire's mind the next evening as she struggled into her heavy winter coat. Having spent less than a year in The Cove, she wasn't sure when the fall ended and winter set in. But if the locals were to be believed, the cold had come early this year. The temperature had dropped below thirty in the late afternoon and it had begun snowing during dinner. Although the frozen droplets were coming down slowly, she was concerned they might become stranded in town if they didn't hurry. So after dispatching the boys to the kitchen to wash the dinner dishes, she called for the girls. A moment later, Lydia and Elspeth came pounding down the stairs.

Dinner had always been an important family affair for the McGuires, but after Elle had brought home Andre's herbal supplements, it had become far more enjoyable. Food tasted good again, and despite the fact that it contributed nothing at all to their physical well-being, Elizabeth loved cooking for her family. Having been raised in a deeply traditional home, it made her feel more like a wife and mother.

Almost as important was the fact that the girls had come to enjoy cooking as well, and that meant a great deal of quality time together in the kitchen. So as she led them through the enclosed walkway to her husband's four-wheel drive Grand Cherokee in the garage, she checked her pocket to make sure she hadn't forgotten the shopping list she'd so carefully prepared. Finding it there next to one of her gloves, she reached into her purse for her keys. But when Elizabeth pushed through the door into the garage, she was pleasantly surprised to find that her husband had already opened the large exterior door and started the vehicle for her.

As she climbed into the toasty warm cabin, she smiled to herself. *And they say chivalry is dead...*

Elspeth had climbed into the front passenger seat, and Lydia the rear. So after they finished fastening their seatbelts, she put the car into reverse and backed out onto the drive. Then after reaching above the visor and clicking the remote control that closed the garage door, she put the vehicle in drive and started around the circle to the lane. When she reached the tree line, she stomped on the gas.

Bounced back in her seat by the unexpected acceleration, Elspeth looked over at her mother. "Taking this security thing seriously, aren't you?"

Nodding, Mrs. McGuire said yes. "Nathan's right about this being the perfect spot for an ambush." Then after sighing sadly, she continued. "And after fighting the British from the swamps and the Indians on the frontier, he's an expert."

Elle nodded. "So are you going to have the contractor cut back the tree line like he suggested?" Mrs. McGuire nodded, and said she was going to call him first thing in the morning. "Frankly, it will be a relief...

"This road gives me the creeps."

Laughing from behind, Lydia teased her. "What's the matter, Elizabeth? Still afraid of the Headless Horseman?"

Irritated, Mrs. McGuire frowned and glanced over her shoulder. "Go ahead and laugh," she said. "But my father read me that story when I was a little girl, and I'm still having nightmares!"

Then after an involuntary shiver, she warned the girls they were bound to encounter some pretty strange things over the course of their indefinite lifespans.

Elspeth grinned. "Like the Ghost that almost gave Neill a heart attack back in Scotland?"

Slowing as she came to the end of the lane, Mrs. McGuire guided the vehicle through the turn before looking over to smile.

"That's a funny story now, but it wasn't then. It scared the living daylights out of the poor guy – and believe me, that's not easy to do. Your Father has more courage than any ten men I've ever met."

Lydia leaned forward. "So are all those stories about Scottish Highlanders really true?"

Mrs. McGuire bit her lip and nodded. "The Highlands were a pretty tough place when your father was growing up. Life was hard, and when the clans weren't at war with the English or the Irish they were fighting one another…

"It was a constant struggle just to survive."

Having already passed the county road that led west to the Junction, Mrs. McGuire let her voice trail off as she slowed for the stop sign at Trader's Road. After coming to a complete stop and carefully studying the three-way intersection, she turned right before turning left two blocks later onto Market Street. Passing the first two blocks of shops – most of which had closed at 5 pm, since it was Sunday – she turned right into the disproportionately large parking lot of the grocery store. Noting the slight but steady snowfall, she warned the girls they had to get in and out as quickly as possible. The last thing she wanted to do was get stuck in another snowdrift, and have to call her husband to come shovel her out.

Like Dr. McGuire, Elizabeth regarded modern transportation as unnatural. But unlike her husband, she had never fully mastered the art of driving, and had a long history of minor mishaps. Although running out of gas in the middle of nowhere was her specialty, plowing into snow banks ran a close second. Flat tires came in third – and try as she might, she could never figure out how the tiny little jack that came with the spare tire worked.

Mrs. McGuire parked in a deserted section in the far northeast corner to make sure a careless driver didn't ding her husband's car. So after turning off the engine and climbing out, she and Lydia waited for Elspeth to untangle her seat belt. After the youngest of the McGuire women finally hopped out and closed the door, they began making their way across the parking lot to the store. They'd just passed a new Ford pickup when the sound of a male voice wafted from somewhere behind them. He was singing, just loud enough for human ears to hear.

The Mist & the Darkness

Does she love me, with all her heart
Should I worry, when we're apart...

Lydia looked over at her sister and grinned. "That's your Boy Toy, Elle!"

Glaring at her taller sibling, Elspeth hissed at her to "Hush!" Then after an exasperated glance at her mother, she told Elizabeth McGuire to ignore him. "He's embarrassing me!"

During the course of the long family meeting the night before, Mrs. McGuire had eventually concluded the kids were probably right about Andre. He might be the Hunter, they agreed – although that was far from settled – but if he was, he meant them no harm. Andre clearly liked them, and if Elle wasn't being such a "bitch," as Daniel put it, they might be friends.

That said, she'd taken Nathan's caution to heart. Although her eldest son was more convinced than the others that Andre had uncovered their secret, Nathan didn't believe he was hostile. But he was well-armed and well-trained, and the scent of subconscious fear that humans typically exude in the presence of Vampires was altogether absent. "And that makes Marchand dangerous, regardless of his intentions."

With that thought lodged in the back of her mind, the possibility that Andre was hunting their kind made Mrs. McGuire nervous. So after glancing over her shoulder to make sure he wasn't armed, she suppressed her anxiety and forced a smile upon her face as he launched into the second verse.

As the sliding double doors automatically opened for them, Lydia grinned again and whispered. "So what's the answer, Elle? Enquiring minds want to know..."

Thoroughly irritated, Elspeth slammed her elbow into her sister's rib cage, and hissed that it was none of her damn business. Having dodged the heaviest part of the blow, Lydia laughed as she jerked a shopping cart free from the line inside the door. After pushing it toward her mother, she jerked another one free for herself and asked what she was supposed to get.

Mrs. McGuire had just finished teasing the second page of the grocery list free from the staple that bound it, when Andre strolled through the door. Still deeply conflicted, the sight of him dressed in a military field jacket with a green Foreign Legion beret perched atop his head made her sigh.

Hunter or not, she thought, *he's adorable...*

Pretending to notice the McGuire women for the first time, Andre stopped singing long enough to greet them with a mischievous smile. "Bonsoir, Mesdames!"

Then as he grabbed one of the much smaller shopping baskets from a stack, Andre gave Mrs. McGuire a sly wink before marching into the store. By now completely disarmed by his adolescent charm, Mrs. McGuire looked over at Elspeth and smiled. Still struggling with the cart Lydia had pushed in her direction, she was trying to ignore the whole thing.

Once inside the store, the McGuires split up – Mrs. McGuire headed over to the meat section while the girls took off in search of canned goods, household supplies, and treats. Then after spending the better part of ten minutes picking out the best cuts of beef, pork and poultry, she headed over to the fresh vegetable section before loading up her cart with premixed gravies and spices. After finding what she was looking for and crossing the items off her list, she headed for the next aisle to pick up coffee and tea. Vaguely aware of the music playing in the background, she pushed her cart around the corner and down two more aisles. Turning halfway round the next corner, she stopped at the end-display to examine the supposed bargains stacked there. From the corner of her eye she could see her daughters standing in front of a freezer case arguing over what kind of ice cream they should buy, when Andre suddenly bopped around the corner. Seeing the girls, he started singing along with the piped in music:

Sweets for my sweet, sugar for my honey
I'll never ever, let you go...

Peering down the aisle, she chuckled as Andre dumped his basket in Lydia's cart and grabbed her hands. Singing along to the music, they began dancing in the aisle. It was cute, but the glowering look on Elspeth's face suddenly concerned her. She was about to finish turning her cart into the aisle to intervene when Andre spun Lydia and reached her for her sister. Trying to feign rejection,

The Mist & the Darkness

Elspeth put her hands up to resist but Andre grabbed them anyway. Smiling and laughing, he coaxed her into a dance.

Deeply relieved that her daughters' rivalry hadn't ended in bloodshed, Mrs. McGuire had just finished backing her cart away from the frozen desserts section when Andre bounded around the corner. Still singing along to the piped in music, he didn't notice her until they almost collided. Momentarily surprised, he screeched to a halt before smiling and greeting her. "Hi, Mrs. McGuire!" Then before she could reply, he zoomed past her toward the dairy section.

Chuckling at his antics, she turned her cart back into the freezer aisle to rendezvous with the girls. After conferring with them briefly – and urging them to hurry up because of the snow – Mrs. McGuire set off in search of the remaining items on her list. Although Andre's scent still hung heavy in the air, he had apparently left by the time they met at the checkout counter. As they waited in line, Mrs. McGuire looked over at Elspeth and whispered. "He's darling."

Elspeth's face flushed, and she looked down at the floor before looking back up at her mother. "I know," she whispered back.

Then after a long moment of silence, Mrs. McGuire whispered again. "Maybe it's time to forgive him…"

Elspeth frowned, and shifted on her feet. "I'm not really mad at him, Elizabeth. I just want him to make up his mind – me or that other girl."

Then Elspeth looked up at her mother. "You know, 'values clarification' and all that…"

Mrs. McGuire nodded knowingly, and whispered back. "I understand, Elle – but I'm pretty sure he already has…

"Just give him some time."

Elspeth nodded, before looking up at her adoptive mother with a pained expression. "But then what?

"He'll find out what I am, and then he'll hate me!

In an effort to hide the tears welling in the corners of her eyes, Elspeth turned away before Elizabeth could answer. Then after pushing her cart into place behind Lydia's, she began unloading it onto the black rubber conveyor belt, as Lydia finished with hers. Thinking silence was probably for the best, Mrs. McGuire turned and began pulling items out of hers, to add to the massive pile on the slowly moving conveyor. Ten minutes and $381.97 later, they put the plastic bags back into their carts and headed for the exit. Shaking her head in disbelief at the bill, Mrs. McGuire glanced around to make sure no one could hear her. "When I was a growing up, working people were lucky to make $20 a *month*...

"And my father – who was the most respected surgeon in Philadelphia, you know – he never made more than $2000 a year in his *entire* life!"

Grinning, Lydia teased her. "And you walked ten miles to school every day, and it was uphill both ways!"

As they pushed their carts out into the cold winter night, Mrs. McGuire chuckled. "That's right," she said. "Barefoot, in knee deep snow!"

Glancing over her shoulder, Elspeth laughed and told her mother she was a nut. But an instant later, the back wheel of her cart locked up, bringing the contraption to a shrieking halt. "Damn it!" she swore. "This always happens!" Then after frowning, Elspeth told them she knew how to fix it. "You two go on, and I'll catch up with you."

After nodding, Mrs. McGuire pushed her cart around her and followed Lydia to their car. They were in the process of putting the groceries in the back when they heard Elspeth swearing again. She'd gotten the cart going and had made it to the edge of the parking lot when it had locked up again – this time after dropping into a two or three inch hole in the asphalt. After Elspeth refused their offer of help, saying she'd have the stupid cart unstuck in a minute, Andre suddenly emerged from the drugstore across the street.

After jerking the cart out of the rut, Elspeth tried to push it forward but the back wheel refused to budge. Swearing under her breath, she leaned over the handle and threw her hips into it just as Andre strode up behind her. Apparently oblivious to the fact that Lydia and Mrs. McGuire were waiting in the shadows less than 50 feet away, Andre glanced over at her rear end and grinned. Dropping his voice a couple of octaves he said, "Shake it, Momma!" in a playfully lecherous voice.

He hadn't spoken loudly, and he certainly hadn't intended his tease to be heard by others – but in the cold crisp air, even humans could have heard him. Lydia howled, Mrs. McGuire's jaw dropped in shocked amusement, and Elspeth lashed out with the back of her balled up fist. "Pervert!"

Andre dodged the blow, but the realization that Mrs. McGuire and Lydia had overheard his unmistakably suggestive tease brought him to a sudden halt. As his face flushed, he forced an embarrassed smile as he peered at them through the darkness. *"Ooops!"*

Then turning on his heel, he marched away. As he disappeared into the night, they could hear him berating himself under his breath. *"Way to go, Dumbass!"*

By now laughing so hard that tears were streaming down their faces, Mrs. McGuire and Lydia helped Elspeth carry her bags from the locked-up cart to the rear hatch of the car. Having tried and failed to ignore their hilarity, Elspeth glared at her mother and sister. "Yeah, real funny, guys – go ahead and laugh!"

CHAPTER 34

Still chuckling at Andre's *faux pas* when she wheeled the vehicle into the garage around 9:00 pm, Mrs. McGuire told the girls she was going out to the lab to speak with their father. "So put up the groceries, and I'll be back in a bit."

After traipsing across the backyard and knocking on the laboratory door, Mrs. McGuire pushed it open and asked if she could come in. Looking up from his computer, Dr. McGuire smiled and said, "Sure – I'm just trying to figure out how those supplements Elle brought home work."

"Making any progress?"

Dr. McGuire nodded. "Quite a bit," he said. "It's fascinating, as well, because it sheds new light on the virus."

Impressed, Mrs. McGuire glanced over her shoulder to judge the distance across the backyard to the kitchen. Pushing the door shut, she asked if her husband was any closer to a cure.

Dr. McGuire shook his head. "Well, it's one more piece of the puzzle. But I have to say, the ability to enjoy human food again is definitely a plus."

Mrs. McGuire chuckled, and dropped her voice to make sure the kids didn't overhear her from the house. "Speaking of human food," she said in a hushed whisper, "I wish you'd been at the grocery store tonight – you missed the cutest thing!"

Leaning back in his chair, Dr. McGuire looked up at his wife skeptically. "And I suppose it had something to do with a certain Andre Marchand – right?"

As her eyes sparkled, Elizabeth smiled. "Yes, Neill, it did – and it was *absolutely* adorable!"

After picking up a pen and grasping each end with his hands, Dr. McGuire sighed and leaned back in his chair. "That kid's going to drive me crazy," he said.

Grinning from ear to ear, Mrs. McGuire scurried over and climbed up on a lab stool. Then as she unzipped her parka, she asked her husband if he remembered that old Clyde McPhatter song *A Lover's Question*.

Smiling in sudden recognition, Dr. McGuire nodded. "Great song!" he said.

Smiling from ear to ear, Mrs. McGuire nodded excitedly. "Well we'd parked your car and were walking across the lot when Andre suddenly appeared behind us, and started singing that song just loud enough to hear…"

Dr. McGuire chuckled. "So what did Elle do?"

As her eyes sparkled, Mrs. McGuire explained that she'd been a little embarrassed but definitely pleased. "And then a little later in the store, they were playing *Sweets for My Sweet, Sugar for My Honey* – remember that one? – while Elle and Lydia were picking out ice cream…

"So Andre came strolling up the aisle, singing along with the music – and he reached out and grabbed Lydia, and they started dancing right there in the middle of the frozen dessert section!"

Dr. McGuire rolled his eyes, and sighed. "So much for keeping a low profile."

Mrs. McGuire pursed her smiling lips together and paused for a moment, before continuing. "Then about halfway through the song, Andre spun Lydia out and started dancing with Elle!"

This time, Dr. McGuire shook his head as he sighed. "And?"

The Mist & the Darkness

Mrs. McGuire pursed her lips, and remonstrated her husband. "Oh come on, Neill, it was *cute!*"

Dr. McGuire nodded, and said he was sure it had been. "But there's more, right?"

Grinning, his wife nodded emphatically. "Andre left before we finished shopping, and went over to the drug store…

"But one of the wheels on Elle's cart locked up as we were leaving, so Lydia and I went ahead to put our bags in your car…

"So Elle was pushing on the cart really hard to get the wheel unlocked – you know, really throwing her hips into it – when Andre walked by again. Anyway, he didn't notice Lydia and me because we were in the shadows about fifty feet away…

"Now are you ready for this?"

Dr. McGuire raised his eyebrows. "Probably not," he said, "But go on…"

Chuckling, his wife stood up and pantomimed Andre. "So he looks over at Elle's, uh…*derriere*, shall we say…"

And then after dropping her voice as far as she could to imitate Andre's, she pretended to be him and said: "*Shake it, Momma!*"

Laughing, Mrs. McGuire walked over and wrapped her arms around her husband's shoulders. "Lydia cracked up, and I couldn't help but laugh too – then Andre heard us, and realized we were standing there in the shadows…

"And Neill – you should have seen the look on that poor boy's face!"

Laughing harder, she told her husband that Andre was so embarrassed his cheeks had turned crimson. "I really wish you had been there – it was *so* funny!"

Chuckling at the story, Dr. McGuire rested his hands on his wife's arms. Then after looking up, he asked her what Elle had done.

Giggling, Mrs. McGuire said she'd called him a "pervert," and whacked him.

Smiling at his daughter's rejoinder, Dr. McGuire pushed himself away from his desk and stood up. Then after wrapping his arms around his wife and pulling her close, he asked her take on the matter. "So what's up with those two?"

"Well," she said, as a huge smile crept across her face. "At 17 it's kind of hard to be sure – but I think it's the real deal"

"They're in love?"

Mrs. McGuire nodded. "Elle won't admit it, and Andre's still wrapped up in the chase – but it's there."

Pulling his wife closer, Dr. McGuire rested his chin atop her head. Then after a long moment, he asked Elizabeth what they were going to do.

After pulling back a bit and looking up into her husband's eyes, Mrs. McGuire smiled. *"Well,"* she said. "I seem to recall a certain other interspecies romance that worked out rather well."

Chuckling, Dr. McGuire looked down at his wife. "But that was different," he said. "You were 26, as I recall…"

Cutting him off in mid-sentence, Mrs. McGuire glared at him in mock anger. *"Was NOT!"* she insisted. "I wasn't a day over 21!"

As Dr. McGuire broke up laughing, Elizabeth McGuire grinned, then retreated a bit. "OK, so maybe I was 22…"

Dr. McGuire grinned. *"Uh huh,"* he said. "And there were other differences as well. "You'd finished your education, and you were a young widow with, shall we say, a bit more experience in love."

Grinning, Mrs. McGuire disputed his account. "I was a virgin!" she huffed.

Suppressing his smile, Dr. McGuire deadpanned. *"Right!"*

Then after pulling her husband close again, Mrs. McGuire turned suddenly serious. "Neill," she asked in a soft voice. "If I hadn't been bitten by that rogue Vampire, would you have changed me?"

After a long moment of silence, Dr. McGuire pulled back a bit to look into her eyes. Then very seriously, he told said it would have been up to her.

Smiling mischievously, Mrs. McGuire looked up again. "Well," she said. "When the time comes – don't you think Andre should have the same choice?"

CHAPTER 35

By the time Andre wheeled his Vette into the student parking lot the next morning, he was reasonably sure he'd managed to get Operation Elspeth back on track. That said, a major complicating factor loomed on the horizon – the Homecoming dance, which was approaching fast. If he didn't show up with a date, there'd be serious consequences.

He'd managed to hold the Cheerleaders and the other socially acceptable girls at bay with his imaginary girlfriend in Montreal, in order to buy time for his plan to seduce Elspeth. Maintaining the deception had been relatively easy so far, especially after Jocks and Cheerleaders had mistaken Tiffany in Burlington for his mythical Canuck. But the Homecoming dance posed a problem – because there wasn't a snowball's chance in hell Dr. and Mrs. McGuire would let Elspeth go out with him until he'd successfully executed Phase IV, which involved gently awakening them to the fact that he knew their secret and could be trusted to keep it.

But since that was still several months downstream – probably late February, if all went well – he was going to have to show up at Homecoming with a girlfriend who didn't actually exist, or find a convincing imposter.

Tricky, he thought as he climbed out of the Vette.

It wasn't that Andre had anything against the girls of the In Crowd. They were nice to other members of Newton's aristocracy, all were pretty and many were gorgeous. But for the most part, they were shallow, frivolous, and none too bright. Puzzled at first, Andre had eventually concluded that was due to peculiar tastes of American men. Suckers for a pretty face and a shapely body, they rarely looked beyond appearances. Having been raised in a culture that had a far more sophisticated approach to love, Andre was a great deal more discriminating. The mere thought of a night with Kathy Norse made him shudder, despite her Olympic-class figure and the amorous skills for which she was justly famous.

Getting along with the Jocks was easier. Most of them were a bit brighter than the girls, and in terms of athletics, at least, Andre could relate. But none of them had any real life experience, and Andre often found it hard not to laugh at their naivety.

Wondering if the general lack of maturity he'd encountered at Newton had anything to do with his infatuation with Elspeth, he paused in front of the school's entry doors to consider the possibility. But since it probably had more to do with her pretty face, quirky personality, and awe-inspiring figure, he shrugged it off.

And then there's that whole Older Woman thing...

Plunging into the throng of students headed for the Student Lounge, he spotted the McGuire girls coming through the doors from the North Wing. Grinning, he pushed his way through a half-dozen students to fall in about ten feet behind them. Both were wearing designer jeans that flattered their hips.

Surprised they hadn't picked up on his scent — he'd smoked one of his trademark Gauloises on the way to school — Andre waited until they'd passed through the double doors into the cafeteria before letting out an earsplitting wolf whistle.

Elspeth pretended she didn't hear it, Lydia grinned over her shoulder and wiggled her butt, and dozens of male students stuck their fists up in the air and started chanting *"Woot! Woot! Woot!"*

All in all, a humorous scene — at least until Headmaster Renfrowe bellowed from behind.

"MARCHAND!"

Wincing, Andre halted in place. Then after forcing a smile on his face, he did an about-face to greet him. "Monsieur le Headmaster!

"How very good to see you!"

Glaring at him as he marched over, Renfrowe stopped six inches short and placed his hands on his hips. After telling Andre to knock off the BS, he demanded to know what the hell he was doing.

Andre pursed his lips and tilted his head back and forth a couple of times before deciding to fess up. "Just hitting on Ms. McGuire, Sir."

As the corners of his mouth began turning up, the Headmaster asked him *which* Ms. McGuire he was referring to.

Realizing Dr. Renfrowe was jerking his chain, Andre suppressed a grin and replied. "That would be Ms. *Elspeth* McGuire, Sir."

The Mist & the Darkness

Grinning, Renfrowe folded his arms across his chest. "Making any progress?"

After pursing his lips together and pondering the question for a moment, Andre nodded tentatively. "Well, she hasn't called me a jerk since Halloween, so I'd say things are looking up."

Chuckling, Dr. Renfrowe shook his head back and forth. "You're an idiot, Marchand…"

Then before Andre could reply, the Headmaster became suddenly stern again. "But be that as it may, this is an *educational* institution…

"So if you want to hustle the coeds – do it off campus, on your own time." Then he pointed a finger at Andre's chest for emphasis. "Got that?"

Andre came to attention and gave the Headmaster a snappy French-style salute. *"Yes, Sir! Mr. Headmaster, Sir!"*

Glaring at him, Dr. Renfrowe told him to knock off the theatrics. Then after glancing down, he asked if Andre's ankle had healed. After Andre nodded and informed him it had, the Headmaster said "Good! You still owe me a thousand pushups – make that 1500 for being a smart-ass today – and two hundred laps."

Since Andre figured jerking the Headmaster's chain was worth at least 1000 extra pushups, he suppressed a grin and promised to report to the gym at the end of 6th period. Then after pausing for just a moment, Andre changed the subject. "But there was something else I wanted to talk to you about, Sir, if you have the time."

Dr. Renfrowe had turned to walk away, but he turned back when Andre spoke. "Yes?"

"Well, it's about sports, Sir. Track and B-Ball are fine, but I'm not really into football or baseball – so I was wondering if we could have a fencing team."

Surprised, Dr. Renfrowe raised his eyebrows and cocked his head. Then after a long pause, he said he liked the idea. "But I don't think the Board of Governors will, for two reasons. First, it will mean a supplemental appropriation for the year. And second, it will give the insurance company an excuse to raise our rates."

Thinking that made sense, Andre nodded. Then after shucking off his backpack, he unzipped it and pulled out a 10x12 envelope. After opening it, he pulled out a sheaf of stapled papers and handed it to the headmaster. "I spent the weekend putting together a proposal for the team." Then after reaching around behind him and pulling his wallet out of his back pocket, he extricated a folded check. "And since my Uncle's a champion swordsman, he offered to help cover the costs."

After taking the check from Andre's outstretched hand and opening it, Dr. Renfrowe's eyes bulged. *"A quarter of a million?"*

Andre grinned. "Uncle Philippe's got more money than God."

After folding the check again and putting it in his vest pocket, Headmaster Renfrowe sighed. "Must be nice." Then after skimming through Andre's proposal, he folded it in two and inserted it in the inside pocket of his suit coat. "With your Uncle's check, I think it might fly," he said. "The next Board of Governors' meeting will be in the first week of December, so I'll pitch the idea then...

"In the meantime, why don't you write up a petition and collect as many student signatures as you can?"

After saying he would, Andre thanked the headmaster before hoisting his backpack and heading into the lounge for his Café au lait. By the time he re-emerged into the cafeteria, Elspeth and Lydia had disappeared and Daniel and Nathan were still nowhere to be seen. But with only five minutes to go before first period kicked off, he downed his coffee and headed for his locker.

English Lit was more boring than usual. By that time they'd finished up with Tristan and Isolde, and moved on to the actual legends of King Arthur. Mrs. Morgan had spent most of the hour explaining that at least a half-dozen distinct versions of the story had grown up between 900 and 1300 AD, and providing the class with a brief overview of each. Then after handing out a 30-page reprint of an article she had published in *The Atlantic Journal of English Literature*, she told the class to read it as their homework assignment and be prepared to discuss it the following day. Since Mrs. Morgan's writing was even more boring than her lectures, Andre was groaning along with the rest of the class when the bell finally rang.

Having spent most of English Lit calculating the possibilities and their various permutations, Andre had come to the conclusion that asking Elspeth to Homecoming was a no-lose proposition. In the unlikely event she said yes – and her parents agreed – then it was simply a matter of adjusting his timetable and modifying his

The Mist & the Darkness

approach for Phase IV. But if she said no, his back was covered – because there was no way in hell she could object to him taking someone else after refusing him.

Piece of pie, he thought, massacring the English-language idiom.

So after congratulating himself for having come up with the perfect plan, he spent most of History class working on his approach. When the bell finally rang, he stuffed his text into his backpack, stood, and waited for Elspeth and Lydia. As the three of them passed through the classroom door into the hallway, he reminded them that they were scheduled to make their class presentation on Wednesday, December 8.

Despite the Ice Princess act, Elspeth hadn't pulled out of the project and they'd been working on both their written paper and their oral presentation by e-mail for the past several weeks. In spite of the frigid tone of Elspeth's electronic messages, she'd worked hard on her part – which was describing the role of noble women in managing large feudal estates – and after combining her half with his, and writing an introductory statement, Andre was convinced they'd nailed it. As far as the written part went, all they had to do was go back over it and polish the language. But they still had to get together for the final fitting of the costumes Lydia had made, and conduct a dress rehearsal of their presentation.

After the McGuire girls checked their daytimers, they agreed to Lydia's suggestion that they meet at his house on Sunday, November 28. By then nearly to Elspeth's locker, Andre glanced over at Lydia before asking Elspeth if he could have a minute in private.

Since it didn't take a rocket scientist to figure out that Andre was about to ask Elle to Homecoming, Lydia gave him a sly grin and an encouraging wink before announcing she was going to fix her makeup. "Catch you in Biology, Elle."

Being nobody's fool, Elspeth had come to that same realization. So after suppressing the bright smile that had attempted to steal across her face, Elspeth opened her locker and deposited her History text before turning back to him. Then looking up expectantly, she said "Yes, Andre?"

Having accidentally looked straight into her milk-chocolate eyes, Andre's train of thought suddenly jumped the tracks. Tumbling into the Valley of Enchantment, the engine dragged the boxcars it had been pulling with it – which, unfortunately, contained the lines he'd so carefully rehearsed in class the hour before. Now at a complete and utter loss, he fumbled. "Well, uhhhhh…

"I was just wondering…"

Shifting uneasily on his feet, Andre realized he was perilously close making a fool out of himself. But after closing his eyes for a moment, he decided to go ahead and roll the dice. "I was just wondering if you have plans for Homecoming."

Flushing, Elspeth hesitated for just a moment before smiling. "Why, are you asking me to the dance?"

Thinking she was jerking his chain, Andre wanted to bang his head against the wall. But since that would make him look like an even bigger fool, he decided to save that for later. Nodding instead, he said yes.

As a huge smile spread across Elspeth's face, he thought for a moment she was going to accept. But after a long pause, she pressed her lips together and apologized instead. "Andre, I'd *love* to go with you," she said in a voice tinged with disappointment. "But my parents won't let us date."

"Not even for Homecoming?"

Elspeth frowned, and shook her head sadly. "Not even for Homecoming."

Andre nodded, and said he understood. "But I wanted to ask you anyway."

Elspeth's eyes suddenly sparkled, and she smiled again. Pressing her books to her chest, she bounced up on her tiptoes and kissed him on the cheek. "Thank you," she said. Then without another word, she slammed her locker shut and took off down the hall.

Having been taken completely off guard by her kiss, Andre stood there against the wall while he worked his way through the decidedly mixed feelings it had evoked. On the one hand, it had definitely been exciting. Her lips had been cool, her breath had been unexpectedly warm, and – as he was forced to admit – the presence of her fangs so close to his neck had been strangely erotic.

But since the human carotid artery was the Vampire equivalent of a Happy Meal, it had also been a bit unsettling. Thinking that was the third time he'd let one of the McGuires get close to his throat, he wondered if he hadn't become a bit too trusting. So after making a mental note to be more careful next time, he pushed off the wall and headed for class.

Caution was all very well and fine, of course, but as he made his way through the throng of students clogging the hallway, Andre suddenly realized that the incident begged an important question: quite specifically, how the hell you do you seduce a Vampire chick without ending up a Midnight Munchie? After mentally rummaging through the *Kama Sutra* and examining the various recommended positions for physical love, he came up blank.

Better ask Uncle Philippe...

Having slipped into yet another erotic fantasy – this one involving a heated waterbed, handcuffs, and a ball gag as a precaution – Andre had been entirely oblivious to the odd looks he'd received as he made his way across the Cafeteria on his way to calculus. But fortunately for him, Wilkinson was coming in the opposite direction just before he reached the South Building. Grinning, he asked Andre what all that red stuff was doing on his cheek. "Kathy finally corner you?"

Rubbing his face, Andre gave him an irritated look and told him to guess again as he passed by. But any hope that Wilkinson would forget about the indiscretion was dashed an hour later in the locker room. While Andre was spinning the combination lock hanging from his locker, Wilkinson started giving him grief about the lipstick. After again denying he had gotten it on with Kathy Norse, Wilkinson cocked his head and stared at him suspiciously as he pulled open his own locker.

Then as a sudden realization spread across his face, his jaw dropped. "Holy shit!" he exclaimed. "You made time with Elspeth McGuire?"

Whipping around to make sure no one had overheard, Andre told Wilkinson to be quiet. Then another furtive glance, he corrected him in a whisper. "And for your information, fool – she kissed me."

With an incredulous look on his face, Wilkinson popped his locker open before leaning over. "Oh man," he whispered. "If the girls find out" – meaning the Cheerleaders – "they're gonna have your butt for breakfast!"

Nodding as he pulled his shirt off, Andre agreed. "Not to mention my hot-tempered honey in Montreal – so keep your damn mouth shut!"

Grinning, Wilkinson told him silence didn't come cheap. "It's gonna cost you a six-pack of Heineken."

After glaring at him, Andre sarcastically thanked him for being such a good friend. "Knew I could count on you, Bro."

After they'd dressed and fallen out on the gym floor, Coach Jordan called roll before announcing the weather forecasters had lucked out and gotten it right when they predicted declining temperatures and heavy fog for The Cove that day. So after fifteen minutes of intense calisthenics, he led them outside for another fifteen minutes of wind sprints. That was fortuitous, from Andre's point of view, because it provided him with a bit more information about Daniel McGuire.

From a technical standpoint, oxygen isn't strictly necessary for a Vampire's survival. Nonetheless, breathing was still important for two reasons. First, they couldn't speak without air in their lungs; and second, breathing was a primary means of exhausting heat from their bodies. So even though Vamps didn't have to breathe to stay alive – or undead, as the case may be – failing to do so could become awfully uncomfortable. And if the temperature were hot enough, there was always the remote but statistically measurable possibility of self-immolation. That being the case, the fact that Daniel McGuire could run the sprints without becoming overheated told Andre that he was in far better shape than he'd imagined.

Having finished the sprints, the Coach took the class back inside and let them blow off the rest of the hour with a murderous game of Dodge Ball. That being one of the few American pastimes Andre actually enjoyed, he was in good spirits when he strolled into the Cafeteria for study hall – especially since the game had given him the chance to exact revenge, by blindsiding Wilkinson with a particularly savage throw.

Grinning at the recollection, Andre picked up a coffee in the Lounge and spent most of the hour sipping the brew and perusing the news on his laptop. Although he wasn't especially hungry, he was bored – so when the bell rang, he stuffed his gear into his backpack and hurried over to the serving line. Then after grabbing a tray and

The Mist & the Darkness

loading up his plate, he made his way over to the Jock table and waited for the rest of Newton's aristocracy to come drifting in.

Surrounded by Jocks and Cheerleaders by the time he finished off the last of his chocolate pudding ten minutes later, Andre worried that news of the hallway kiss had leaked out. He trusted Wilkinson, to be sure – but the hallway had been filled with students when Elspeth had laid it on him, and the odds were better than even that someone had been paying attention. Stealing an uneasy glance at the McGuires' table, he was surprised to see Daniel and Nathan eating alone. After another furtive glance, he spotted Elspeth holding court two tables away from her brothers.

Par for the course, he thought – because resolving disputes and dispensing advice to the lovelorn were part of her duties as Queen of Nerds, Geeks, and Other Outcasts.

But when he spotted Lydia engaged in an intense, whispered conversation with Mary Sue Poindexter in the shadows against the far wall, his blood ran cold.

Uh-oh, he thought. *This can't be good…*

CHAPTER 36

After pulling on his overcoat and locking the door to his office, Headmaster Renfrowe headed for the athletic department in search of Coach Jordan. Unable to find him in his office, the Headmaster made his way through the gym before finally pushing through the double metal doors that opened onto the athletic field. Seeing the Coach standing beside the track, to the right of a mixed group of Cheerleaders and Jocks, he marched across the frozen ground.

Weather in The Cove was unusual at best, and it often bordered on bizarre. Freezing cold accompanied by an unnatural fog had blanketed the town until well after noon. Then the sun had appeared briefly, followed by low-lying clouds. A soft snow had begun falling around four, but by the time classes were dismissed at 5:00 the temperature had warmed a bit. Still dressed in his overcoat as he trod the 500 feet or so to the edge of the track, Dr. Renfrowe was surprisingly comfortable.

He stopped beside the coach as Andre Marchand rounded the east end of the track. Singing the *Do Rae Me* song in French, he was dressed in gym shorts and a sweatshirt. But as he turned into the straightaway on the opposite side, Dr. Renfrowe was surprised to see he was wearing military boots and carrying a pack. Wondering what that was all about, he asked the Coach.

Coach Jordan glanced over and chuckled. "Marchand says he's used to carrying a rucksack and running in boots...

"So he wrapped 40 pounds of weights up in gym towels, and stuffed them in that pack."

Impressed, Dr. Renfrowe nodded. "The kid's hardcore." Then as the Cheerleaders began jumping up and down and waving their pom poms as Andre rounded the west end of the track, he asked how many laps he'd completed.

Glancing to his left, Coach Jordan yelled over to Daniel McGuire. Dressed in a winter parka and standing halfway between the Coach and the Jocks and the Cheerleaders, McGuire looked down at the clipboard he was holding and counted the hash marks he'd made. Then after looking up, he shouted back. "Forty nine, Coach."

Headmaster Renfrowe asked the Coach how many more Marchand was going to run. Chuckling, Coach Jordan said the kid had wanted to go for an even hundred but he'd limited him to 50. "The wife's gonna come unglued if I miss dinner again."

As Headmaster Renfrowe nodded, Andre passed the Cheerleaders and the Jocks. Seeing the Headmaster standing there with the Coach, he did an "eyes right" and flipped them a parade ground perfect, open-palmed French salute. After chuckling, the Coach looked back over his shoulder and grinned. "You know, there's a rumor going around that Marchand was in the military."

Taken aback, Dr. Renfrowe asked Coach Jordan where he'd heard that. After stuffing his hands into the pouch of his hooded sweatshirt, the Coach said he'd overheard the McGuire kids talking about it in the halls. "But I suppose that's just a BS story."

The Headmaster had known that Marchand's secret would leak eventually, but he was irritated nonetheless. So after giving the

The Mist & the Darkness

athletic instructor a stern look, he told him to keep it under his hat. "His parents died when he was about 14, and he had a hard time dealing with it ...

"So he got a hold of a fake ID, and enlisted in the Legion."

Coach Jordan looked at him incredulously. "The *Foreign* Legion? You gotta be kidding!"

Chuckling, Dr. Renfrowe shook his head. "Nope – but like I said, keep it to yourself. I told Marchand I was concerned his background might have a negative influence on the other students, and threatened to throw his ass out of here if the word got out...

"But the real reason I wanted him to keep that quiet was to help him fit in, and readjust to normal life."

Ignoring the Headmaster's explanation, Coach Jordan shook his head and muttered, *"Son-of-a-bitch!"* Then he shrugged, and told the Headmaster he was trying to recruit him for the football team. "Three of my best men are graduating in June."

Dr. Renfrowe nodded, but was interrupted by the Cheerleaders before he could respond. After shouting out one of their cheers and turning cartwheels on the frozen ground, they'd started jumping up and down again, waving their pom poms and yelling *"GO, ANDRE, GO!"*

After they finished, the Coach shouted over to McGuire to confirm the figure. Daniel nodded, and shouted back. "That makes 50, Coach!"

Dr. Renfrowe nodded, before saying he didn't think there was any chance the Coach would snag Marchand for the football team. "Too slow for a European..."

Then he reached into his suit coat pocket and withdrew a photocopy of Andre's proposal. "But he's put together a proposal for a fencing team, and his Uncle offered to pick up the tab." Handing it to the Coach, he told him to look it over and let him know what he thought.

Turning to look at the Headmaster for the first time, Coach Jordan took the proposal from his outstretched hand and grinned "Hey, I like it already – I did a little fencing in college."

Headmaster Renfrowe nodded. "I reviewed your *curriculum vitae* this afternoon. Think you can coach it?"

Coach Jordan thought about it for a moment, then nodded. "I can handle the first-year basics, but we'll need to bring someone in after that." Then after another pause, he told the Headmaster he was pretty sure he could talk the University into lending them an advanced instructor, part-time. "I'm in tight with the Assistant Dean of Athletics."

By that time, the weather had turned suddenly cold again. So having accomplished the task he'd come for, he told Coach Jordan he wanted him to review Andre's proposal with Coach Sommers – otherwise known as Dr. Megan Sommers, the girls' athletic instructor – and put together something he could take to the next Board of Governors' meeting. Coach Jordan nodded and said they'd get right on it.

Coach Sommers was tall, powerfully built, definitely butch and probably a lesbian. But since she was as much of a sports fanatic as he was – and a truly dedicated instructor as well – Coach Jordan had been more than willing to overlook her dubious sexual orientation. In the 18 months or so since she'd arrived at Newton from UCLA, they'd developed a close friendship while watching the sports channel on satellite TV and downing Budweiser tallboys.

Having turned back toward the school, Headmaster Renfrowe had only taken a couple of steps when Coach Jordan called after him. "Hey, Steve!"

After striding over, the Coach glanced over at Daniel McGuire before turning back to the Headmaster. Then after giving Dr. Renfrowe a conspiratorial grin, the Coach lowered his voice to a near whisper and told him there was another rumor floating about. "I heard Marchand's got something going with Elspeth McGuire."

Having seen that one coming, the Headmaster chuckled. So after taking a moment to choose his words carefully, Dr. Renfrowe grinned. "He's sure as hell trying."

After shaking his head in disbelief, Coach Jordan gave the Headmaster a rueful grin. "Oh, Christ!" he said before glancing in the direction of the Cheerleaders. "Let's hope the word doesn't get out on that one – because if it does, the girls are going to kick his ass all the way to Wisconsin!"

Although that was undoubtedly true, Andre's precarious social position would prove to be the least of Headmaster Renfrowe's worries. For at that very moment, in a basement less than half a mile away, the president of the Political Science Club banged her gavel on top of the steamer trunk that served as a makeshift podium, and called the first meeting of Newton's Revolutionary Council to order.

CHAPTER 37

"All right, people – listen up!"

After glaring at the twenty or so assembled club presidents to make sure she had their attention, Mary Sue Poindexter placed her hands behind her back, and began pacing back and forth in a fair imitation of General George S. Patton of World War II fame.

Then turning suddenly to face the crowd, she stopped and glared at them again. "Enough is enough!" she bellowed.

Then after a dramatic pivot, she began pacing back and forth again. "Newton Academy was designed for us – people with brains! People who can appreciate mathematics, science, and technology, people who can appreciate the life of the mind!

"But since Day One, our school – let me repeat that just in case you didn't get it, *OUR SCHOOL* – has been dominated by the Jocks and Cheerleaders and the rest of the so-called "In Crowd."

Then stopping just in front of her makeshift podium, Mary Sue wheeled again to face the assembled students. "Now why is that?" she demanded to know.

Leaning forward and squinting through her thick glasses to stare into the faces of the assorted Nerds and Geeks, she waited for a reply. When none came, she rolled her eyes and inhaled. Then after a moment of complete silence, she bellowed again. "I'll tell you why!

"Because the Jocks are bigger and stronger than everyone else, and none of the other so-called men around here have the nerve to stand up to them!

"And the Cheerleaders are pretty and popular, so the rest of us girls are intimidated because they get all the handsome guys!" Then after drawing another deep breath, she continued.

"That's the reason, people...

Charles S. Viar

"AND WE LET THEM GET AWAY WITH IT!"

Then after glaring at the Nerds and Geeks again, Mary Sue stomped around the makeshift podium, and slammed her fist down on it. "I've had enough of their insults, and I've had enough of their slights! I've had enough of their teasing and their ridicule, and I've had enough of their put downs!"

Then thrusting her finger toward the back, she demanded Jeremy Fenwick stand up. "Take a look at Jeremy! Just this afternoon, the Captain of the Football Team pushed him out of the lunch line – and then to add insult to injury, he made Jeremy pay for his damn dessert!"

Flushing badly, Jeremy took to his feet as ordered. But rather than face his fellow losers, he looked down at the floor through his Coke-bottle glasses as they gasped in shock and horror.

Then reaching behind her, Mary Sue picked up her black, Che Guevara-style beret with the ceramic red star pinned to the front, and placed it on her head. After adjusting it and brushing a wayward strand of mousy hair out of the way, she continued. "Girls, they call us ugly and they call us fat, and they make fun of our hair and our makeup and our clothes…

"And they call our guys wimps and wankers, and they make fun of our glasses and our braces – but when midterms or finals come around, who do they beg for help???"

After waiting for the angry murmur to fade away, Mary Sue thrust her finger at the poster of Vladimir Lenin she'd tacked to the wall. "That's what the Russian In Crowd said about Lenin – and Trotsky, and Stalin!

"And that's what the German In Crowd said about Hitler, and the Chinese In Crowd said about Mao!

"But you know what? They were all smarter than the Jocks and Cheerleaders of their day, and they were tougher too!"

Then after glaring around the basement to make sure she'd built her audience's anger and resentment to a fever pitch, she dropped her voice to a raspy whisper and continued. "They decided they just weren't going to take it any more – and they *revolted* against The Powers That Be…

"And they threw their arrogant butts on the trash heap of history!"

The Mist & the Darkness

Thrusting her balled fist up in the air, Mary Sue began banging it against an imaginary enemy. "Are you with me?" she bellowed.

Then as the Geeks and the Nerds leapt to their feet cheering, she bellowed again. "Come on people, let's hear it...

"REVOLUTION! REVOLUTION! REVOLUTION!"

Now strutting back and forth in front of her makeshift podium as the Nerds and Geeks picked up on the chant, Mary Sue waited until her audience finally exhausted themselves. Then when at last they sank back into their folding chairs, she grinned savagely and dropped her voice again. "The Old Order ends right here, right now...

"Because we're going to take back what's ours!"

Then after basking in a thunderous, three or four minute standing ovation intermixed with the weird noises Nerds make when they're excited, Mary Sue turned her back on the crowd and picked up a stack of stapled papers that had been sitting on a stool by the wall behind her. Striding around the steamer trunk, she began passing them out.

"Here's the game plan, people – and these are all marked and numbered, so if anyone sneaks one out and copies it – we'll know where it came from."

Then she shifted the stack in her arms and slid her index finger across her throat, before warning them of the consequences. "As of this moment, Level One Operational Security is in effect – which means no one breathes a word...

"You talk, you die...

"GOT IT?"

Seeing Randall Johnson and Winston Frederick exchange nervous glances – the two delinquents Andre had banged against the lockers for making fun of Elspeth – Mary Sue pointed at them and glared. "And that goes double for you two perverts – understand?"

Shocked that Mary Sue had somehow found out about their adventures in online pornography, Randall and Winston looked at each other with bulging eyes before flushing and sliding down in their seats. "We got it," they said in unison.

Glaring at the two twerps for added affect, Mary Sue asked if anyone else was getting cold feet. After a long, uncomfortable silence passed, she said "Good!" and resumed handing out the papers. After finishing, she walked back up to her podium

"Homecoming is in 12 days...

"And every year, each of the student clubs has submitted nominees for the King and Queen – and every year, a Jock and a Cheerleader has been elected. So do the math, people...

"Given the near total overlap between teams, we have a grand total of 40 athletes and 12 Cheerleaders out of a school of almost 400!!!

"They're only about 13 per cent of the school's population – maybe a quarter when you add in their flunkies – but they win time and time again!

"So why do you think that is?" she asked rhetorically. "Because we've got almost 20 clubs, and we split our vote 20 separate ways!"

Then after glancing around to make sure that the obvious had sunk in, she continued. "But this year is going to be different – we're gonna sandbag the bastards!"

"Each of the Clubs is going to make their nominations as per usual, just to make sure no one gets suspicious – but this time we're not going to vote for them...

"When we get into the voting booth, we're going to vote for secret write-in candidates – and bury the In Crowd under a landslide!"

Grinning wickedly, Mary Sue waited for the excited murmur to die down. Three seats down in the second row, the President of the Future Accountants of America stuck her hand up in the air and begun waving it back and forth while making funny little grunting sounds. Trying hard to hide her disgust, Mary Sue pointed at her. "Yes, Paula?"

Paula Fenty stood up, and after looking around, lisped through her braces. "But who are we going to vote for?"

After staring at Paula for a long moment, Mary Sue glanced around the room before saying, "Elspeth McGuire for Queen – and Andre Marchand for King."

As the room exploded in weird giggles and gasps, Fenwick Humpherdank started beating on the back of the kid in front of him, making the bizarre honking noise that passed for laughter on his planet. After shaking her head in disbelief, Mary Sue recognized Fawn Mayerhoffer.

After looking around nervously, the president of the Future Quantum Physicists of America stood up hesitantly and cleared her throat before speaking. "But isn't Andre one of the Jocks!"

Turning suddenly serious, Mary Sue nodded. "Technically," she said. "But he's not like the others…

"Andre's always been nice to us – well, except for those two Cyber Twinkies in the back – and he almost got kicked out of school for standing up for Elspeth…

"So we're gonna throw our support behind him."

After pondering Mary Sue's argument for a long moment, Fawn nodded uncertainly. "But what if our people don't vote for Elspeth? I mean…

"We have 15 members in the Future Quantum Physicists – but when all the votes were counted last year, our nominee had only two!"

"Good point!" said Mary Sue as she strolled over to the sidewall.

Then after whipping a sheet off the big wooden box it had covered, she pointed at it. "That's why I had my uncle make us an exact replica of Newton's ballot box…

"We're gonna win this Chicago-style!"

CHAPTER 38

A week later, Andre strolled into History. Having arrived early, he sat down at his desk, and flipped open the book he'd bummed off Susan Jacobs. He'd just finished the third page when Elspeth walked in. Wearing a dark brown sweater dress with her hair up and a strand of pearls with matching earrings, she looked incredibly hot.

Glancing over after she sat down and crossed her legs, she asked him what he was reading. So after closing the cover over his thumb, Andre held it up in his left hand. "*Twilight*," he said.

Thinking that story was way too close for comfort, Elspeth stiffened momentarily. But she recovered quickly, and in an effort to divert his attention, she raised her eyebrows and rolled her head over. Then on the theory that the best defense is a good offense, she teased him. "So you're into Chick Lit, huh?"

Mystified by the expression, Andre knitted his eyebrows together. "You mean the chewing gum?"

Snickering, Elspeth shook her head. "No, dummy – 'Chick Literature' – you know, books for girls."

After looking down at the book he was holding with a puzzled expression, Andre turned it over to glance at the excerpts on the back cover. "I thought it was about Vampires?"

By now less worried than exasperated, Elspeth rolled her eyes. She was about to tell Andre that guys were hopelessly stupid when she heard the sound of the first ambulance far off in the distance. Since the county had been routing trauma cases to the clinic for months, that wasn't entirely out of the ordinary. But the more distant wail of a dozen or more following behind the first was positively ominous.

Oh my God, she thought. *Something terrible has happened...*

She was trying hard to pretend she hadn't heard the sirens when Andre stiffened and looked toward the windows. "Something's up," he said, as he rose from his seat.

Striding across the half-filled room, with Elspeth trailing behind him, he stopped just before the bank of windows and peered out into the dense fog that had hung over The Cove for the past three days. Speaking to no one in particular, he muttered he couldn't see a damn thing. Taking care to conceal the fact that she could, Elspeth nodded silently and waited until she thought Andre would be able to make out the flashing red lights of the first ambulance. Pointing down the slope toward the clinic, she exclaimed: "*LOOK!*"

After peering into the fog for the two or three seconds it took to detect the lights, Andre stiffened. Not wanting to let on to the fact he was fully aware of her enhanced visual abilities, he glanced over at the Vampire beside him, and swore under his breath. "Damn, Elspeth – how the hell did you see that?"

Worried that she'd inadvertently let slip an incriminating clue, Elspeth tried to dodge the question. "Well, I need reading glasses for small print but my distance vision is pretty good."

The Mist & the Darkness

Andre nodded, before suddenly pointing at the elderly woman sprinting across the parking lot. "Isn't that the school nurse?"

Elspeth did a double take. "Yeah, that's Nurse Abercrombie!" Then as a puzzled look spread across her face, she looked up at Andre. "I didn't know someone that old could run that fast!"

That had surprised Andre, too, but by then his attention had returned to the fast moving parade of flashing red lights. "There's at least a dozen emergency vehicles coming in, so it must be serious…"

Then as an afterthought, he hoped Uncle Philippe had made it back from Washington. "They're going to need him."

A mile and a half away, Dr. McGuire was thinking the same thing as he swung his Grand Cherokee onto the Lake Road. It was his day off and he'd been in a meeting with his wife and their architect, discussing the new barn they were going to build when he heard the sirens in the far distance. When the phone rang a moment later, he told Elizabeth to tell the Clinic he was on his way, and made a mad dash for his vehicle. In his hurry, he'd forgotten his wallet – and the driver's license it contained – but as he stood on the accelerator he wasn't worried about getting stopped. Unlike the humans, he could see through the dense fog – and in any event, Chief Beauregard and his deputies knew his Grand Cherokee. Given the circumstances, there was no way they were going to pull him over.

Seeing the Clinic's lot filled with a dozen or so ambulances when he arrived a few minutes later, Dr. McGuire pulled his vehicle up on the half-frozen grass to the right of the building, next to the stone table and benches patients and their relatives enjoyed during the summer months. Then after killing the engine and bounding out of the vehicle, he ran for the main entrance.

After slowing enough to give the sliding glass doors time to open, he raced across the lobby to the receptionist's station. Looking up, she told him that Chief Gomez had just arrived, that Chief Robbins – the other retired Navy Corpsman that split the night shifts with Gomez – was on his way, and that Nurse Abercrombie from the high school was also en route. Nodding hurriedly, Dr. McGuire asked her about Dr. Marchand.

"We got lucky, Doctor – he was a few hundred yards behind the school bus when the lumber truck came across the median and hit it, so he's on the scene doing triage."

"School bus?" he repeated.

The receptionist nodded. "Yeah, a bunch of kids from Burlington on a field trip to Montreal. Dr. Marchand was right behind them."

After thanking God for small favors – or in this case, a rather large one – he asked the receptionist if Dr. Marchand had his bag with him. She shrugged quizzically, and said he'd told her he had a "disaster kit" in his trunk when he called to warn them of the influx. Thinking that must be a European term for an emergency medical pack, Dr. McGuire thanked the girl and headed down the hall to scrub.

The passageway was lined with gurneys holding injured teens, each of whom had a bright orange tag affixed to their wrist with an elastic band. Although they were all soaked in blood, they had already been injected with painkillers; a few were either moaning or crying softly, but most just lay there with their dulled eyes fixed upon the ceiling. Halfway down the hall he encountered Dr. Randall, the dentist they'd just hired, suturing a bloody gash in a young man's arm. Patting him on the shoulder as he wordlessly passed by, Dr. McGuire turned into the scrub room and pulled on a surgical gown. Then after opening the glass cabinet that held the sterile towels, he pushed up his sleeves and began scrubbing his hands.

A moment later Chief Robbins strolled in and repeated the process. Glancing over as he began soaping up, he muttered something about how the hallway reminded him of Fallujah – the bloody battle in Iraq that had claimed the lives of so many Marines. Dr. McGuire nodded, and after finishing with his hands, reached into the cabinet for a towel. Once he'd finished drying, he pulled on a pair of surgical gloves and headed into the tiny operating room they called "Emergency Intake."

He and Dr. Sanders had added the OR and the ten bed overnight ward to the Clinic's design as a precaution. Given The Cove's distant location, they'd assumed circumstances were bound to arise when they'd have to perform emergency surgery there, rather than the hospital in Burlington where they had privileges. But at the time, they'd been thinking along the lines of hunters accidentally shooting themselves or the occasional car wreck. It never occurred to them that they might have to confront an emergency of this magnitude…

Striding over to the second operating table located toward the west wall, he checked in with Dr. Sanders. After receiving his instructions from the senior surgeon, he strode over to the other table and looked over Chief Gomez's shoulder. Unaided, the Chief was in the process of closing up a long incision in the leg of a boy who might have been 15. Glancing up at Dr. McGuire, the Chief gave him a quick briefing. "Broken bone punched through the skin, and it was bleeding like a bitch. I whacked him up with morphine, opened his leg, and reset it." Then after jerking his head toward the IV of whole blood, he told Dr. McGuire the kid had damn near bled to death. "He's on his third pint."

Permitting the Chief to perform surgery was a country mile from legal, but given the circumstances, Dr. McGuire wasn't worried about technicalities. With 28 years of combat medicine under his belt, the Corpsman had probably extracted as many bullets and performed as many emergency procedures as all but the most experienced trauma surgeons. Nodding, he asked the Chief how long their supply of whole blood would hold out.

Glancing up again, the Chief shook his head. "Not long," he said. "We're running through it like water."

After swearing silently in Gaelic, he told the Chief he was going out in the hall to take a look at the others stacked up outside. Then after glancing over at Dr. Stevens – who'd just opened a patient's chest, with Nurse Jackson standing in as an anesthetist – he started to tell Gomez to let him know when he finished up. But before he could speak, he was cut short by Dr. Randall. Still in the hall, the dentist was screaming for a defibrillator. "I'm losing one!"

Wheeling around, he almost collided with Nurse Abercrombie. After skirting her to grab the unit from the open cabinet, he headed out into the hallway where Randall was pumping a boy's heart. Seeing Dr. McGuire approach, he pumped one more time and stepped back. "The kid went into shock and stopped breathing. I can't get a pulse!"

Randall had already ripped the boy's shirt open, so Dr. McGuire pressed the paddles against his cheat and yelled "Clear!" Then he hit the control button, and sent a surge of electricity through him. The kid's body bounced, then fell back on the gurney. After leaning over to listen for a heartbeat, he did it again. The boy gasped, then began breathing.

Looking up over his surgical mask, he told Dr. Randall he'd done a great job. "You just saved that kid's life." Then he handed the dentist the paddles, and told him to stay with him.

As he stepped back, Chief Robbins emerged from the scrub room. Dr. McGuire jerked his head toward the OR, and told him to follow. But after only a few steps, Chief Gomez and Nurse Abercrombie emerged through the double doors, pushing the boy the Chief had just operated on. After waiting until they'd maneuvered the gurney against a wall farther down, Dr. McGuire asked Gomez who was next.

Pointing at a young boy lying face down with his head hanging over the gurney closest to the door, he said, "That one – left side of his face is smashed in, so I fired him up and turned him over so he wouldn't choke on the blood."

Dr. McGuire nodded. "Good thinking." Then after instructing Gomez to take over from Dr. Randall, and Robbins to assist Dr. Sanders, he called for the dentist. "Need a Jawbreaker for this one!"

He was about to grab the gurney and pull it into the OR when a tall, sandy haired figure with a neatly trimmed beard strode into the hallway and called out. "*Monsieur Docteur* – how may I assist?"

Seeing his expensive three-piece suit was covered in blood, Dr. McGuire realized it must be Dr. Marchand. Thinking the Frenchman hadn't arrived a moment too soon, Dr. McGuire pointed at the scrub room. "Join us in the OR when you're prepped, Doctor."

Without breaking his stride, Dr. Marchand nodded, pivoted, and stepped through the door of the scrub room. But as he did, the receptionist came tearing down the hall, screaming. "Dr. McGuire! Dr. McGuire! The Canucks just called – a commuter plane went down just over the border, and the Mounties are routing the survivors here!"

After a moment of stunned silence, Dr. McGuire closed his eyes and whispered a prayer to Saint Cosmas. Then after opening his eyes

The Mist & the Darkness

again, he ordered the receptionist to call the University's hospital in Burlington and tell them they needed a fresh supply of whole blood, dozens of pre-packaged, sterilized surgical instrument kits, and a couple of experienced OR nurses as fast as they could get there. Then after gesturing to Dr. Randall for help, he began pulling the gurney into the OR.

And so it went, for hour after hour, until they'd put the last mangled body back together. Assisted by Nurse Abercrombie, Dr. Marchand had set up a makeshift operating theater in the hallway, where he'd performed a dozen complicated procedures under primitive conditions. But by some miracle, no one had died – the State Police had collected the desperately needed supplies and personnel from the University, and flown them up in helicopters. By the time Dr. McGuire closed the last patient – a victim of the airline crash – it was just after 10:00 pm.

After helping Chief Gomez push the heavily sedated woman into the overnight ward, he gratefully accepted a cup of coffee from Dr. Sander's wife, Marjorie, who'd brought in dozens of homemade doughnuts, and made enough coffee to float the Atlantic Fleet. "Thanks," he said, as he slumped down in one of the folding chairs she'd set up just outside the improvised post-op, next to one of the surgical nurses from the University. "Chief Gomez volunteered to take the overnight shift in the ward."

Glancing over, Chief Robbins said he'd stay too. Then after shaking his head, he muttered it had been Iraq over again. After a dismissive chuckle, the 66-year old Nurse Abercrombie declared the Middle East wars were chump change. "I got off the goddamn plane in Pleiku the day before Victor Charlie launched his Tet Offensive in '68...

"We spent the first three days ankle deep in blood, patching GIs back together, running on cigarettes, coffee, and amphetamines. Then we pulled 12 hours on/12 hours off for the next month, until our guys pushed the bastards back across the Cambodian border...

"You should have seen that goddamn clusterfuck!"

Nodding respectfully, Chief Gomez spoke. "So you were in the Nam, huh?"

Nurse Abercrombie nodded in reply, and drained her coffee cup. "With the Air Force. Three tours and thirty-two months in-country."

Sipping on his coffee, Neill McGuire was wondering if the Tet Offensive had been as hard on Nurse Abercrombie as Gettysburg had been on him, when Dr. Sanders suddenly leaned forward. "So how'd Doc Marchand do, Pat?"

Scoffing at the question, Nurse Abercrombie drained her cup before responding. "You'd think he'd been doing this for centuries, Dale – he's fast, sure, and precise, with an amazing economy of movement...

"You should have seen him pop open that brain trauma case and extract the aluminum shard. He teased that son-of-a-bitch out of the left prefrontal, repaired the damage, and buttoned him back up like it was a walk in the goddamn park."

Then after standing up and announcing she needed another cup of coffee, she added an afterthought. "And you wouldn't believe his stitching – some fancy European technique...

"Elegant, absolutely elegant – and he says it doesn't leave a visible scar."

His curiosity suddenly piqued, Dr. McGuire reached for one of the doughnuts Mrs. Sanders had set on the folding table to his left. "Speaking of Dr. Marchand – where'd he go?"

Still standing, Nurse Abercrombie chuckled. "Same place I'm going after I get another cup of Joe – he's out on the back loading dock, sneaking a smoke...

Then she pointed a warning finger at him. "But you didn't hear that from me!"

Laughing softly, Dr. McGuire promised he wouldn't rat. Then he got up, and announced he was going to take a look at Marchand's handiwork.

Munching on his doughnut as he pushed through the double doors of the Overnight Ward, Neill McGuire was lost in thought. *Sounds like he's using the Padua Technique...*

But that hasn't been taught for centuries...

CHAPTER 39

As the sun dropped beneath the mountains five days later, Elizabeth McGuire lifted the window shade that had been protecting her from the sun. Shifting in her seat, she looked over at her husband beside her in the almost deserted First Class section, and smiled. "A week of night skiing in Vale is an awfully nice gift." Neill McGuire returned her smile, and nodded. "It is indeed – and appreciated all the more with Dr. Marchand covering for me at the Clinic."

Suddenly curious, Mrs. McGuire asked her husband how the Frenchman was doing. Dr. McGuire opened his eyes wide, and cocked his head. "Marchand's amazing," he said. "One year out of his residency and you'd think he's been practicing for decades…

"His surgical skills are world class, and his diagnostic abilities are almost preternatural." Then Dr. McGuire chuckled. "If I didn't know better," he said, "I'd suspect sorcery!"

Encouraged by his sudden responsiveness, Mrs. McGuire decided to see if she could draw him into a conversation. He'd been quiet all day, and she wanted to talk. "Well, having Dr. Marchand volunteer worked out really well, because the kids can afford to give us a vacation. They all did really well last quarter" – a reference to their financial success during the accounting period that ended in September.

Dr. McGuire looked over, and chortled. "So how much did those brigands make this time?"

"A bundle!" said his wife. "Aside from her last CD – which is about to go platinum with downloads from her website – Lydia sold her *entire* spring collection to Bloomingdales!

"And sales from Daniel's online surf and dive shop were way above projections."

As Dr. McGuire nodded, his wife continued. "Then Nathan got that big advance for his next book – you know, the one he's writing about the Revolutionary War in New England."

After smiling approvingly, Neill glanced over again and sighed with feigned exasperation. "So how much did Lydia get for her designs?"

Grinning, Mrs. McGuire told him. *"A quarter of a million!"*

"Good God!" said a genuinely surprised Dr. McGuire. Then after shaking his head ruefully, he muttered something about being in the wrong business.

Laughing, Mrs. McGuire said no. "Don't be silly, Neill…You're a wonderful physician."

After chuckling, Dr. McGuire shrugged. Then dropping his voice to speak in a Vampiric whisper, he said he should be after 500 years of practice. When his wife smiled, he asked how their youngest daughter had made out.

As she shifted in her seat again, Elizabeth smiled back. "Well," she said. "Elle did really well in the stock market, but I think she's going to make a killing with her next novel."

Chuckling, Dr. McGuire asked his wife if she had read it.

Turning in her seat, Mrs. McGuire grinned with excitement. "She has a real gift, Neill – the manuscript was so exciting I couldn't put it down!"

After giving his wife a quizzical glance, he asked her what it was about.

"Well," Elizabeth said. "It's another romance novel – but it's *really* good!

"It's set in the early 1700's, and it's about a young aristocrat who was orphaned at an early age and had to go live with her uncle, the Earl of something or other – who's a dutiful man, but he's completely absorbed with money and status…"

"He was never mean to her or anything, and he gave her everything she wanted and made sure she had fine education. But he was cold and distant, and living with him on his rural estate made the poor girl miserably unhappy. So she grows up dreaming about meeting a handsome young prince, and living happily ever after…

"But on her 17th birthday, he uncle calls her into his study and informs her that he's promised her to an Admiral that's old enough to be her father, and says he's sending her off to the Caribbean the next day to fulfill the marriage contract…"

The Mist & the Darkness

At that point, Dr. McGuire looked over and shook his head sadly. "Sounds familiar," he said. "In my time, the daughters of aristocrats were sold like chattel – and their sons got stuck with whomever their parents arranged for them to marry…

"It was strictly a matter of politics, and money."

Reminded that her husband had only escaped that fate because he had been born out of wedlock and couldn't inherit, Mrs. McGuire scrunched up her nose in distaste. "That must have been awful!"

Dr. McGuire nodded. "My parents really suffered…

"They loved each other passionately, but they weren't allowed to marry because he was an Earl and she was common…

"So he was forced to marry an English Countess for her dowry."

As her eyes began to tear, Mrs. McGuire looked over at her husband. "But at least he was able to spend time with you and your mother."

Dr. McGuire nodded. "Quite a lot, all things considered." Then he smiled softly, and continued. "I think that was the only time he was truly happy."

After an uncomfortably long silence, Mrs. McGuire wiped a tear from the corner of her eye before recounting Elle's story again. "So anyway, the uncle puts the poor girl on a ship bound for some island, and she spends every day standing at the rail crying her eyes out and thinking she should just throw herself into the sea and be done with it…

"But then after a week or so, a pirate ship appears on the horizon just before dawn – and, of course, everyone is scared out of their wits because it's flying the flag of the Dread Pirate Steffan, who has a *really* fearsome reputation…

"So the English captain tries to make a run for it, but Steffan's ship is faster and they're overtaken. And there's a big battle, and the pirates capture the ship. So after robbing all the passengers, they go down in the hold to sort through the cargo they'd captured, and they find the girl hiding in a barrel…

"She's dressed as a boy, but as they drag her out of the barrel her cap falls off and they realize the boy is actually a girl – and since they don't know what to do with her, they take her up on deck and throw her at Steffan's feet. So after staring at her for a minute or two and thinking, he demands to know her name. So after she pulled herself to her feet, she tells him she's the Countess Elaine – niece of the Earl of Whatever.

"But the thing is, Steffan is young and amazingly handsome, and she can tell by the way he talks that he's cultured and well educated – which just doesn't compute with his reputation...

"So Steffan tells his men Elaine will fetch a fine ransom, and they take her and her young maidservant back to the pirate ship and chain them up in separate cabins. But since she knows her uncle will never pay the ransom, she figures they're as good as dead...

"But after a couple of days Steffan comes down to visit her, and she can tell he's really nice – which is, you know, totally confusing. And then he comes back a couple of days later, and then he starts coming back almost every day and they talk and sometimes he even reads poetry to her...

"And little by little, she learns who he really is – the son of a merchant, his father had bought him a commission in the navy as a junior midshipman or something when he was 14, and he'd been rising through the ranks when there was an accident on his ship and a bunch of people were killed. It was all the Captain's fault, but he was able to blame it on Steffan because he was a commoner – so he was court-martialed and sent to this awful prison for 'dereliction of duty.'"

"But he escaped and stowed away on a ship bound for the Islands, where he became a pirate – to get back at the aristocrats who had covered up his captain's negligence and blamed the accident on him."

Smiling sadly, Dr. McGuire remarked that injustices like that happened all the time in those days. Then he looked over again and asked his wife what happened next.

Grinning from ear to ear, Mrs. McGuire said "Well..."

"By this time Elaine is madly in love with Steffan – and even though she knows her uncle won't pay the ransom, she's scared to death the Admiral will...

"So one night while he's reading to her, she blurts it all out and begs him not to turn her over to this old man she's never met. So Steffan – this being a romance novel and all – breaks down and confesses his undying love for her, and says he'll never give her up.

The Mist & the Darkness

Then he says how sorry he is that he'd hidden his heart, but he hadn't been able to tell her how much he loved her because she's a countess and he's a commoner, and a pirate to boot, and then there's this really tender scene where they finally kiss...

"And then, uh...well, things get a bit passionate."

Grinning, Dr. McGuire looked over. "So tell me!"

Embarrassed, Elizabeth shifted around in her seat. "Well," she finally said in a halting voice. "One kiss leads to another, and since she's still chained to the wall...

"Well...he just rips her clothes off, and...

"You know."

Chuckling at his wife's Victorian reticence, Dr. McGuire glanced over again and smiled mischievously. "And she obliges him willingly?"

After folding her hands in her lap and looking down, Mrs. McGuire nodded. "Yeah," she said in a husky whisper.

Thinking Elspeth had outdone herself with this one, Dr. McGuire asked his wife to go on.

So after suppressing an embarrassed smile, Elizabeth looked up again and continued. After endless hours of "physical passion," as she put it, Elaine had come up with a plan. If the Admiral agreed to the ransom – which he already had, even though she didn't know it – they could meet on some secluded beach and trade her maidservant for the money, then make their getaway without the Admiral ever realizing he'd been had...

"No harm, no foul, right?"

"And then she tells Steffan she knows the girl will go along with it, because she's always dreamed of marrying a rich nobleman...

"And, well...because she's a woman of questionable virtue, shall we say."

Chuckling, Dr. McGuire glanced over. "I don't suppose her name is Lydia, by any chance?"

Bursting into laughter, Mrs. McGuire pounded on the seat in front of her. "That was *exactly* what I thought when I read the chapter!"

Then after her merriment finally subsided, Mrs. McGuire continued. "I'm not going to spoil it for you by telling you how it ends, but they enlist the maidservant in the plot – she's the daughter of the local Anglican priest, by the way – and then on the way to the rendezvous with the Admiral there's a really exciting sea battle with another pirate ship, and then an incredibly dramatic scene on the beach where Steffan and his crew square off with the Admiral and his men."

After thinking about it for a moment, Dr. McGuire nodded. "So do the Countess and the Pirate live happily ever after?"

Grinning, Mrs. McGuire abruptly folded her arms across her chest before turning around in her seat to face the front of the cabin. "Not telling!" she said. Then after another moment, she smiled happily. "Let's just say it all works out, and everyone's happy – including the Admiral, and his social-climbing bride."

By now convinced he might actually enjoy reading the tale, Dr. McGuire told his wife he'd pick up a copy when it hit the stands. Then after a moment's pause, he suddenly stiffened in his seat. "You know," he said very slowly. "That Pirate Steffan reminds me of a certain other adventurer we know…"

It took a moment for his words to sink in. But when they did Mrs. McGuire gasped, her mouth fell open and her eyes bulged. "*Oh my God,*" she said in a hushed whisper. "You're right!

"The physical description, everything – he's *just* like Andre!"

Then after throwing herself back against her seat, she took a deep and altogether unnecessary breath. "Neill," she said slowly. "You don't suppose we've been conned, do you – that this incredibly generous, all-expense paid vacation was a trick to get us out of town?"

Dr. McGuire looked over suspiciously. "The Homecoming dance is tonight, isn't it?"

More than a bit irritated, Mrs. McGuire nodded. "*Uh huh.*"

After a long moment, Dr. McGuire turned to his wife again. "Didn't Andre ask Elle to the dance?"

By now seriously concerned, Mrs. McGuire nodded again, but explained Elle had begged off. "And I know she was telling me the truth, Neill, because I can always tell with her."

A long, worried silence followed. Then as the plane banked on its final approach to the airport below, Dr. and Mrs. McGuire suddenly turned to look at one another.

"Lydia!" they exclaimed, in perfect unison.

CHAPTER 40

Dr. McGuire had deliberately left his cell phone behind in The Cove, so it was almost a half hour before he and his wife could disembark from the plane and find a pay phone. But Lydia was nobody's fool – as part of the plan, she'd made sure the Geeks hacked New England's entire communications net. Although outgoing calls were unimpeded, for the next eighteen hours not a single incoming call would make it through the routers, switching stations, cell towers or satellites.

After a half-dozen frustrating attempts to reach the kids by the family's residential landline and each of their cell phones, Dr. McGuire called the operator. Informed that the entire regional network was malfunctioning, he thanked the woman on the other end and hung up. "The whole system's down," he informed his wife.

After sighing and looking down at the floor for a moment, Mrs. McGuire looked up again and gave her husband a worried look. "There's no way that's a coincidence, Neill."

Which, of course was true – because by the time Dr. McGuire had hung up the phone, all the separate plots that swirled around Newton's Homecoming were in motion. And since there wasn't another night flight to the East Coast until 7:00 the next evening, there wasn't a thing Dr. or Mrs. McGuire could do about any of them.

Fully aware of that fact, Lydia had knocked on Elspeth's bedroom door at almost the same instant Dr. McGuire hung up the pay phone in Colorado. Not waiting for her little sister to acknowledge her presence, she pushed the door open a bit and peeked through. "Whatcha doing, girl?"

Elspeth was sitting cross-legged on the floor, sorting through her DVD collection. Without looking up, she informed Lydia she was doing the same thing she did every Homecoming, Prom, and school celebration. "I'm gonna watch *Grease* again."

Grinning, Lydia pushed through the door, and held out the dancing dress she'd made for her little sis. "Not this time, kid – we're going dancing!"

Looking up quizzically, Elspeth gasped when she saw the garment. "Did you make that?"

Lydia smiled, and nodded.

By now up on her feet, Elspeth scurried over. "It's beautiful," she said in an awed whisper. Lydia grinned, and said it should be. "I swiped the design from that Antonio Bandaris movie, *Take the Lead*."

Then after holding it out again, she said she was glad Elle liked it. "Because you're wearing it tonight."

Huh?

Having still not caught Lydia's drift, Elspeth looked up at her older sister quizzically. "I am?"

After sighing and then shaking her head, Lydia told her to get her butt in the shower – and to make sure she washed that mess she'd piled on top of her head. "We're going to Homecoming, girl, and you've got to look pretty."

Elspeth gasped. "Homecoming?"

As her mouth dropped, she took a step back and whispered. *"Oh my God, Lydia – Neill and Elizabeth would stake us both!"*

Grinning wickedly, Lydia denied it. "Nah," she said. "They're in Colorado by now, so there's no way they're going to find out…

"And even if they do, the worst that's gonna happen is we'll get grounded for 15 or 20 years – like that would make any difference…

"So hurry up and get dressed, because we're gonna break some hearts tonight!"

As her eyes bulged, Elspeth clapped her hand over her mouth. "Lydia," she gasped. "You are *sooooooo* naughty!"

Then very hurriedly, she asked if the guys knew.

Lydia nodded triumphantly. "*Uh huh*," she said. "Daniel even helped me plan this scam."

After cupping her face in her hands, Elspeth shook her head in disbelief. Then suddenly incredulous, she looked back up at her sister. "Nathan, too?"

After glancing over at Elle's wall clock, Lydia said he had – carefully omitting the fact that she'd let him in on the con at the last minute, and that he'd only agreed as the lesser of two evils. As far as Nathan was concerned, it was a matter of damage control.

Like his adoptive father, Nathan was very much a person of authority in the McGuire clan. He was a century older than Elizabeth, his nominal mother, and he and Dr. McGuire had been friends since the British overran Washington, D.C., during the War of 1812.

Amazingly calm under even the most stressful circumstances, he wasn't given to rash judgments or precipitous actions – so if Nathan was in, Elspeth figured it had to be OK. So after snatching the hanger that held the dress and the dancing panties Lydia had made for her, she hung it over her closet door and made a run for the shower.

Three or four miles away, Andre was climbing out of his bath as Elspeth stepped into hers. After toweling himself dry, he combed his still damp hair over and strode back into his bedroom to dress. More nervous than excited, he began reviewing his plans. If all went well tonight, he'd have a bit more than two months to go before implementing final phase of Operation Elspeth – which he'd decided to rename "Operation Seduction."

Emphasis on "If all went well..."

One of the first things the Legion had taught him in advanced infantry training was that careful planning and preparation were absolutely essential to victory – and having taken that to heart, Andre had meticulously calculated the Homecoming scam he was about to unfold.

Since Elspeth had turned him down for the dance, he had to show up with someone that could – and would – impersonate his mythical Canuck girlfriend. So naturally, he got on the Internet and began searching for an actress that could fake being his non-existent honey.

It hadn't been easy – most of the so-called "actresses" advertising for work on the Net had turned out to be hookers. Many were good looking, and a few were downright beautiful. But he'd passed on them all, because there was just no way he was going to entrust his social career at Newton to a working girl.

Eventually, he'd stumbled across an aspiring actress who really *was* an aspiring actress. A junior enrolled part-time in Columbia's dramatic arts program, she was drop dead gorgeous. According to her profile, she was 24 – but in the supposedly recent photo she'd posted, she looked much younger. If it had been taken in the last year, Andre was sure she could easily pass the age test.

Her name was Stephanie, and she was looking for a short-term gig that paid – modeling, voice acting, or a part in a local dinner theater. And as icing on the cake, she included an emphatic statement that she was a bona fide acting student – anyone looking for a call girl or an escort should look elsewhere.

After mulling it over, Andre had sent her an e-mail. Identifying himself more or less accurately, he explained his butt was in a sling and he needed a really persuasive actress to help him out. He hadn't gone into any detail, but he'd offered to pay her expenses and the prevailing wage for union actors. Then as an afterthought, he'd attached a picture and clicked "Send."

Not really expecting a reply, he'd gone on checking out profiles. But to his amazement, he'd gotten a cautious and decidedly curious reply the next day. Surprised, he explained his situation in a bit better detail: he had recently moved to the States and enrolled in a new school, where he'd been hanging out with the social aristocracy. But he was interested in a rather shy girl his friends had wrongly labeled a snob, and in order to fend off the other girls and buy time to win her over, he'd made up a story about an older college girlfriend in Montreal. But the Homecoming Dance was fast approaching, and it was crunch time – if he didn't show up with a chick who could fake it, he was gonna be toast.

After receiving a reply demanding to know if he expected her to believe an idiotic story like that, Andre fired back a missive. After swearing to God, the Angels and Archangels of Heaven, and a host of Saints that he was telling the truth – including Saint Martin, the patron saint of French soldiers – he promised he was legit. And if she didn't believe him, she should call him on his uncle's landline in Vermont and he could explain everything from start to finish.

To his complete and utter astonishment, she called a half hour later. Thinking she must be really hard up for work, Andre walked her through his predicament, explaining everything in minute detail – except for the Vamp problem which, in the Grand Scheme of Things, he'd decided was no more than a minor inconvenience. Then

The Mist & the Darkness

he told her he had a big trust fund and promised he'd buy her a first class ticket and put her up in the best room The Cove's one and only hotel had to offer. Then to sweeten the deal, he said he'd double her fee if they managed to pull off the act.

After a long silence, Stephanie finally laughed. "You really like this girl, don't you?"

After flushing, Andre finally 'fessed up. "Yeah," he said. "She's kind of special."

By now convinced that Andre was on the level, Stephanie finally agreed. But since she'd never been to Montreal, she suggested a slight twist. "Tell your friends that you and your girlfriend split up, and say you invited me to the dance as a last minute replacement because we used to hang out when you lived in the City – just friends, nothing special, but we liked to go to plays and art galleries and things like that together."

Having immediately grasped the many advantages of that particular story, Andre quickly agreed. Stephanie told him to e-mail her a detailed description of their supposed relationship in New York, including where and how they supposedly met, events they'd supposedly shared, quirky incidents they could laugh about, and a clear, consistent time-line. Detail was important, she said – she needed to know as much as possible about the character she was going to play, in order to do it well.

Thinking there was no way that scam could go wrong, Andre agreed. So after hanging up, he sat down at his computer and began constructing yet another fantasy relationship.

Having finished reviewing the storyline he and Stephanie had agreed on by the time he knotted his silk tie, Andre was supremely confident. As he slipped on the vest of his elegant and expensively tailored three-piece suit, he grinned into the mirror and congratulated himself on the perfect con.

Genius, he thought. *Pure genius...*

CHAPTER 41

Twenty-five minutes later, Andre wheeled his uncle's new Mercedes into the hotel's parking lot. After turning off the ignition and applying the parking brake, he got out and closed the door. Thinking this was probably his last chance for an hour or more, he pulled a fresh pack of Gauloises out of the pocket of his overcoat and lit one up. Then after smoking it, he strolled into the hotel lobby.

After checking in at the desk to confirm Stephanie's room, he took the elevator to the second floor, and turned left down the hall to the absurdly named "Presidential Suite" he'd booked for her. Coming to a stop in front of the door, he was surprised to find a folded-over piece of paper taped to it with his name written on it in purple ink. Pulling it from the oak, he opened it up. *I'm in the bathroom finishing my makeup*, it said. *The door's unlocked, so come in and make yourself comfortable.*

After pushing the door open and walking in, Andre did a half-turn and closed it behind him. As the lock clicked into place, Stephanie came out of the bathroom. Recognizing him from the pictures he'd emailed her, she smiled and greeted him with a cheery hello. "I'm Stephanie."

As Andre's eyes bulged and his jaw dropped, he whispered *"Holy shit!"*

Seeing the look of consternation on his face, Stephanie stopped at the end of the overly large double bed. Confused and concerned by Andre's unexpected reaction, she tilted her head over. "What's wrong?"

As a worried look spread across her face, she raised a hand to the light brown hair she'd piled on her head. "Is it my hair?" Then still staring at him, she dropped her hand to the side of the stunning black dress she was wearing and grasped the fabric. "My dress?"

Andre swallowed hard, then shook his head. "No, you look beautiful," he said haltingly. "You hair's perfect, and the dress is incredible."

The Mist & the Darkness

By now deeply confused, Stephanie tilted her head over again. "Then what is it?"

"Well," Andre said after swallowing hard. "I was, *uh*...

"Well, I was expecting someone a bit warmer than room temperature."

Stephanie gasped, and threw her hands over her mouth. Then as the look of shock that had swept across her face turned to fear, she took a step back and raised her balled fists. *"Get back!"* she hissed. *"I'm dangerous!"*

This time it was Andre's turn to be confused. So after staring at her for a long moment, he shook his head. "I don't think so."

"Am too!" Stephanie retorted, a bit too quickly. *"I'm a cold blooded killer!"*

After looking her straight in the eye, Andre broke up laughing. "No, you're not."

"Am too!" insisted Stephanie. Then she unballed her fists, and held up the blades of her hands. "And I know karate, so don't come any closer!"

Still chuckling, Andre gave Stephanie an implausible look. "No, you don't."

Exasperated by Andre's repeated denials, Stephanie slammed her foot down on the hotel room's carpet. "Do, too!" she said hotly. "I studied under Master Kwon at the New York Academy of Martial Arts!"

Realizing she'd probably been ripped off by one of the many self-proclaimed "Masters" that run high-priced karate schools in New York, Andre grinned. "Well, in that case," he said, "I think you should ask Master Kwon for a refund…

"Because if he'd taught you karate, you would have dropped into a proper fighting stance – like this." After assuming a combat position, he told her to look down at his feet.

"See? It's called a 'T-stance' – it allows you to punch or kick your opponent without losing your balance."

After a quick glance at Andre's feet, Stephanie retreated another step before defiantly raising her right index finger to the corner of her mouth. "I've got fangs," she said in a voice now tinged with desperation. "And if you try to hurt me, *I'll bite you!*"

Annoyed by the implication, Andre gave her another irritated look. "Now why the hell would I want to hurt you?"

There was a long moment of silence as Stephanie searched his eyes. Then as tears began welling in hers, Stephanie lowered her guard a bit, and looked down. "Because I'm different," she whispered plaintively.

It took a moment for that to sink in. But when it did, Andre cracked up laughing. "Stephanie," he said. "Compared to the Nerds, Geeks, airheads and wannabe Olympians I have to put up with at school – well, you could pass for normal."

Incredulous, Stephanie looked up and scrunched her nose. "Really?"

Andre nodded emphatically. "Really," he said. "You're not going to believe that menagerie."

Stephanie smiled tentatively, and laid her head over on her shoulder. "You're not just saying that, are you?"

Andre shook his head, in a mixture of sadness and lingering disbelief. "No – sadly, I'm not making it up."

Although he could tell Stephanie was still frightened, she tried to smile. "So you're not going to hurt me?"

Andre shook his head. "No – as long as you don't bite anybody, we're good."

Momentarily horrified, Stephanie quickly shook her head back and forth. "Andre, I swear – I've never ever hurt anybody in my whole life!" Then after a moment's reflection, she corrected herself. "Well, except for the low-life that did this to me – but he *deserved* it!"

Suddenly curious, Andre asked her what happened. Then after an embarrassed silence, Stephanie told him. "We'd been dating for like a year, so when he asked me if I wanted to be with him forever, I thought he was proposing…

"So when I said yes – well, the shithead bit me."

After an incredulous look, Andre shook his head in disbelief. "You'd been seeing him for a year, and you didn't know he was a Vampire???"

As a look of troubled embarrassment look crept across her face, Stephanie looked down at her shoes. "I was kinda naive back then."

Thinking "village idiot" might be a better description, Andre laughed. "That's putting it mildly," he said.

The Mist & the Darkness

Looking up, Stephanie frowned at him. "Don't make fun," she said in voice tinged with a mixture of hurt and irritation.

Then she looked down at the floor, and asked him if he still wanted to take her to the dance. "I'll understand if you don't," she said softly.

Responding to the pain in her voice, Andre apologized for hurting her feelings before asking if she was OK with humans. "Someone could get hurt, or cut themselves, or there could be a fight – so if you can't handle blood, let me know and we'll just put in an appearance and then go somewhere else."

Stephanie shook her head, then waved her hand dismissively. "I'm a drama major, Andre – and people get hurt all the time. They trip, they fall, they cut themselves building sets…

"As a matter of fact," she continued. "I was helping make props for a new play just last week, and one of the girls cut herself really bad with a razor knife. Blood was spurting all over the place, but I just put my hands over my mouth, told the guy next to me that blood makes me faint, and ran for the door…"

"Not even tempted," she proudly exaggerated.

Obviously pleased with herself, Stephanie told him not to worry. Then she said she needed just a minute to fix her makeup, and turned back toward the bathroom. Halfway there, she suddenly turned again and gave Andre a puzzled look.

"Andre," she demanded in a voice tinged with irritation. "How did you know I was a Vampire?

"And why aren't you afraid of me?" Then very emphatically, she informed him that he was *supposed* to be afraid of her. "I'm a blood-sucking creature of the night, you know!"

Thinking there was no way in hell he was going to open *that* can of worms, Andre rolled his eyes and sighed. "Long story," he said. "And you wouldn't believe it anyway."

CHAPTER 42

As Andre escorted Stephanie across the hotel's parking lot to the Mercedes five minutes later, he snuck an admiring glance as he steered her around an ice patch the snowplow had missed that afternoon. Standing about 5'7" in her dancing shoes, she had a figure that would make a strong man weep. Exquisitely proportioned, she filled the elegant dress she was wearing to perfection. Black, low cut, and with a side slit that ran high on a magnificent thigh, it was absolutely stunning. With her light brown hair piled on her head, her brilliant green eyes, professionally-perfect makeup, and the pearl necklace with matching earrings, she looked more like a Hollywood *ingénue* than a third year acting student. The *faux fur* wrapped around her shoulders only added to the effect.

As they passed under a light on their way to his uncle's car, Andre couldn't help but notice the nipples of her protruding breasts pressing against the flimsy fabric of her dress. Thinking there was definitely an upside to cold weather, Andre wondered if the Law of Gravity had given Vampire chicks a free pass. Intrigued by the thought, he briefly considered asking Stephanie about that as he opened her door. But as she settled into the seat, and brought up her legs to gracefully pivot into the car, he decided that probably wasn't the best of ideas.

Better ask the Unc, next time I see him...

But Stephanie wasn't just beautiful – she was genuinely nice, as well. So as they chatted during the five-minute drive to the school, Andre decided he liked her. As he wheeled the Mercedes into the student parking lot, he was thinking it was a pity they hadn't actually met when he was living in New York.

It would have been fun...

Fortunately for them both, Andre found a parking spot not far from the sidewalk that led to the main entrance doors. So after turning off the ignition and clambering out, he opened Stephanie's door and extended his hand. Impressed by her graceful exit from the vehicle, he closed the door and offered her his arm – not strictly necessary, given the fact that the parking lot and the walk had been carefully shoveled and salted. But the idea of strolling into Newton with a jaw-dropping beauty clinging to him was more than he could resist.

After one of the hired, uniformed doormen opened the entranceway for them, he led Stephanie across the gigantic foyer to the coat check table. Managed by the Home Economics Club, and manned by a troika of Nerd Girls, Andre ignored their nasty looks and handed Stephanie's wrap and his overcoat across the table. Slipping the claim check into his vest pocket, he placed his hand in the small of his date's back and steered her toward what he thought was the admission table.

Stopping there, Andre pulled their tickets out of his inside coat pocket and handed them across. But the Nerd sitting on the other side demanded to see his right index finger instead – to make sure he'd cast his vote for Homecoming King and Queen. "Can't come in until you vote."

Thinking that was a complete and utter waste of time – because let's face it, the Jocks and Cheerleaders owned the school – Andre shrugged, and told Stephanie he'd be right back. Then he followed the signs and bold red paper arrows to the Administrative Office, where the Political Science Club had set up a row of voting booths behind the receptionist's counter. Thinking the Poly Sci Geeks were taking this election thing way too seriously – they'd actually borrowed the booths from the County Election Commission – Andre presented his school ID and watched as Randall Somebody-or-Another scratched his name off the list. Then he accepted a set of printed election rules from the buck-toothed poll worker sitting beside Randall, before moving down the counter to the next set of Geeks to get his paper ballot. After they handed it to him, along with a set of voting instructions, he stepped through the open divide in the counter that separated the reception area from the work area behind it, strolled into a vacant voting booth, and drew the curtain shut behind him.

Since Andre had never voted in an election before, he paused to glance over the rules and read the instructions. Then after crumpling them up and throwing them in the little trash can underneath the writing surface, he picked up the special pen attached to it by a long chain and began running down the names.

Since Newton didn't have political parties, the candidates were listed by the club or team that nominated them. Finding the captain of the Football team under the Sports Club heading, he took the pen and colored in the circle to the immediate left of his name. Having finished, he was about to color in the circle next to the Kathy Norse's name, when occurred it him that Elspeth might be pleased if someone voted for her. So at the very bottom of the ballot, he carefully printed her name into the write-in box before coloring in the circle beside it.

Chuckling at his little act of mutiny, he folded the paper over as instructed and exited the booth for the ballot box. After depositing it in the slot of the padlocked wooden box, he smiled at the two Poly Sci Geeks guarding it, and dipped his right index finger into the inkpot that sat beside it on the table. Then he followed the red rope out through the side exit of the Admin office.

Turning right into the foyer, he found Stephanie waiting for him by the wall. Holding up his ink-stained finger, he informed her he'd done his democratic duty. Smiling as she turned to walk alongside him, she asked whom he'd voted for. Andre looked over and laughed. "Mussolini for King, and Betty White for Queen."

"Owwwwww," said Stephanie approvingly. "Good choices!"

After showing his finger to the Poly Sci Geek that had stopped them before, and explaining that Stephanie was from out of town, Andre handed their tickets over to the Geek from the Future Accountants of America, who was collecting them at the table set back another ten feet. Then after accepting the stubs, and handing one to his date, Andre extended his arm again as they walked toward the Cafeteria.

Enjoying the stunned looks of envy he was getting from the guys they passed, he dropped his voice to a whisper. "You didn't bite anybody while I was away, did you?"

Chuckling, Stephanie whispered back. "Just the couple of Dweebs who were hitting on me."

"Dweebs?"

Stephanie laughed out loud. *"Uh huh...*

"You know...the people Nerds look down on."

Chuckling, Andre shrugged. "Well in that case, no problem."

CHAPTER 43

After passing through the open double doors, Andre glanced around. The Homecoming Committee had gone all out decorating the cafeteria, and as he guided Stephanie toward the refreshments table he was thinking they must have spent a ton of money on the paper lanterns and bunting, and the signs and faux tapestries hanging from the walls. Equally impressed, Stephanie whispered "Wow!" before asking him if Newton was some sort of rich kids' school.

Not entirely sure how to answer that, Andre shrugged and tried to explain that it was some sort of weird hybrid. "Technically, it's a private school, but it has a contract with the County – so anyone who lives within The Cove is automatically admitted…"

Then he shrugged again, before reaching the refreshments. "There's nothing like this in France, so I really don't know how to explain it."

Still clinging to his arm for effect – Stephanie was clearly enjoying all the looks they were getting – she looked up and asked if he'd gone to high school in France. Chuckling, Andre shook his head. "Nope. My rich uncle insisted that I be homeschooled by private tutors…

"And since he picked up the tab, my Mom and Dad agreed."

Before Stephanie could ask him what that had been like, Andre asked her if she'd like some punch. "The Jocks probably spiked it." Chuckling, Stephanie released his arm so he could reach for cups and the ladle and said, "Sure." So after pouring a generous amount into one of the fake plastic champagne glasses, he handed it to her before pouring one for himself.

Stephanie waited until Andre had finished before raising her glass in a toast. Then with a conspiratorial grin, she clinked her glass against his. "To a successful scam," she said.

Andre smiled, and repeated the toast. Then he raised his glass, and looked up toward the stage, where the band had just finished setting up. As Stephanie followed his eyes, she took a sip. Focused on the band, Andre didn't see her eyes bulge, but he heard her gasp. *"Holy shit!"* she exclaimed. "What the hell did they put in this?"

Not at all sure, Andre took a sip and sloshed it around in his mouth before looking over at his date. "Tastes like punch to me," he said.

"Yeah," Stephanie whispered. "But you're human, so you probably can't pick up on it." Then after taking another delicate sip, she paused for a moment before whispering again. *"Christ almighty,"* she said. "They spiked this stuff with *grain alcohol!*"

Chuckling, Andre looked around. After spotting a half-dozen of the Winter Jocks lounging against the south wall with self-congratulatory grins spread across their faces, he concluded the B-Ball team had probably done it. Turning back to Stephanie, Andre took a larger drink. "Really?" he said.

Stephanie took another sip, and nodded emphatically. "Big time," she said. "And you'd better go easy on this stuff, because it can sneak up on ya."

Then she suddenly changed the subject, and pointed toward the stage. "Who's playing?"

Andre shook his head. "Some band I've never heard of – I think they're called *The Time Machine.*"

Stephanie wheeled around toward him. "Really?" she asked excitedly. "I saw them about a year ago in the Village, and they're incredible!"

Andre cocked an eyebrow. "Yeah?"

Stephanie nodded with extra emphasis. "Definitely! There's like 20 people in the band, with every instrument imaginable…

"And they play everything from Glen Miller all the way up to the present day – and they're *really* good!"

Thinking the opportunity to tease was just too good to pass up, Andre grinned. "So I take it you're a member of The Greatest Generation?"

Stephanie crossed her eyes and huffed. Pretending to be miffed, she denied it. So after laughing at her expression, Andre grinned. "How old are you, really?"

Stephanie glared at him, this time a bit more convincingly. "A gentleman never asks a lady her age, you know."

The Mist & the Darkness

Andre grinned, and teased. "So who says I'm a gentleman?"

But before Stephanie could answer, the speakers first hummed and then screeched. Then after a moment or two of ear splitting noise, the elderly black man who had been adjusting the microphone asked the crowd if they could hear him. When the crowd roared back, he smiled and introduced himself as Paul Hudgens. Then after extending his arm toward the band assembled behind him, he raised his voice. "And this is *The Time Machine* – so hold on to your hats, ladies and gentlemen, because we're going to take you on a trip through the Musical Fourth Dimension!"

Then as a projector mounted high on the opposite wall began clicking through still photographs of young men lined up outside a recruiting station interspersed with newspaper headlines about the Japanese attack on Pearl Harbor, the band began playing the "Boogie Woogie Bugle Boy."

After putting her glass down on the table, Stephanie grabbed Andre's hand and began pulling him toward the still empty space in front of the stage. "Come on," she said excitedly. "Let's dance!"

Having tossed his empty in the overly large trash can at the end of the refreshments table, Andre followed her through the crowd and onto the dance floor. No one was dancing, but that didn't bother Stephanie. After pulling him out into the center, she asked him if he knew how to "Swing." Unfamiliar with the colloquialism, he picked up the rhythm as she grasped both of his hands. "You mean dance?"

Stephanie sort of bit down on her lip, and nodded. Then she looked up and grinned. "Hey, you're pretty good!"

Pulling her towards him, Andre grinned. "You can thank the Unc for that – he claims dancing is an essential part of every aristocrat's education."

Laughing as she danced backward, Stephanie teased. "So you're an aristocrat, huh?"

Ignoring the light-hearted jibe, Andre pulled her back and picked her up off the floor. "Hope you're wearing underwear," he whispered before rolling her over his shoulder.

Landing on her feet laughing, she kept up with Andre's footwork in place. Then for the crowd that was closing in around them, she pushed her arms down along her sides and shimmied a bit before advancing towards him. *"Oh no,"* she said in a naughty whisper. "No undies tonight!"

Seeing Andre's eyes bulge, she wagged a finger at him and laughed. *"Gotcha!"* she said.

By that time, two or three other couples had joined them on the dance floor. But the circling crowd focused on Stephanie, and she was clearly enjoying it. She slowed down as the music faded out, but picked up the slightly slower beat when the band segued into Glen Miller's "In the Mood."

Dancing with Stephanie was fun – especially when the band slowed things down with "Moonlight Serenade." With her breasts pressed against him and her head on his shoulder, his mind began to drift. Caught up in the moment, he forgot about the other couples around them. It was just the two of them, alone in the Universe.

But as the song came to an end, Stephanie pushed him back a few inches. "I think we'd better take a break," she said. Then as an embarrassed look spread across her face, she apologized. "Sorry – I didn't mean to get you all hot and bothered."

After clapping for the band, Andre put his hand in the small of her back and began guiding her off the dance floor. Not entirely sure how she'd picked up on that, he whispered. "So what gave me away?"

Turning in towards him, she tapped her nose. "Pheromones," she whispered.

Thinking about the other day in history class, Andre winced. "You can smell them?"

Chuckling, Stephanie nodded. As they slipped through the crowd, she told him not to feel bad. "This place reeks – and it's not just the guys!"

Thinking that was interesting, Andre cocked his head over and grinned. "Yeah?"

As a knowing smile crept across her face, Stephanie discreetly pointed at a rather conservatively dressed girl a few feet away. "Her date's got it made!"

Halting in place, Andre looked at Stephanie incredulously. *"No way!"* he whispered. "Mary Lou's cold as ice!"

Stephanie chortled. "Maybe so – but not tonight!" Then she tugged on his hand, and told Andre she wanted some more punch.

The Mist & the Darkness

They'd almost made it back to the refreshment table when Wilkinson pushed through the crowd, with Randy Taylor and Rob Fredricks from the baseball team following just behind. After yelling over the music to get Andre's attention, Wilkinson strode over and clapped him on the shoulder. Then after eyeing Stephanie up and down with a look of playfully feigned lechery, he demanded to know who the lovely lady was – and what she was doing hanging out with a loser like him.

CHAPTER 44

As Andre was introducing Stephanie to Wilkinson and the other two Jocks, Nathan pulled off the access road to Newton, and parked behind the long row of cars that spilled from the student parking lot. After turning off the engine and withdrawing the keys from the ignition, he climbed out and adjusted his overcoat before locking the door. Still standing alongside the vehicle, he waited for Daniel to come around from the passenger side, and his sisters to extricate themselves from Elle's VW. Then he waited for them to gather around, before reminding them that he was riding shotgun.
"This is a damned stupid idea, but since I couldn't talk you out of it, I'm going to lay down the law...
"First and foremost, I don't want any problems tonight. I overheard some of the athletes whispering in the halls the other day, and the punch bowl's going to be spiked with grain alcohol. So go easy on the refreshments...
"I know we're not as susceptible to booze as the humans, but that stuff packs a wallop. It's every bit as strong as the rot gut we used to drink on the frontier, and it sneaks up on you – so be careful...
"Second, if you want to dance with a human, that's fine – but we came together, and we're leaving together, so don't even think about sneaking off with someone." Then after giving Lydia a wilting look, he curtly demanded to know if she was paying attention.

After rolling her eyes, Lydia huffed and reminded Nathan that she'd gone out with lots of humans. "And you know I don't bite," she said defensively. "In fact, I don't even take a lick unless they really want me to."

Nathan first glared at her, then turned sarcastic. "Yeah, well I seem to recall an incident with a certain State Trooper – and he was definitely not amused by that little game you played with his handcuffs."

As Lydia chortled and Daniel snickered, Elspeth wondered why nobody had bothered to tell her about that particular scandal – and if it anything to do with their hurried departure from California, some twenty years before. But before she could ask, Lydia interjected. After giving Nathan her most angelic look, she promised to be good. Seeing the skeptical look on her brother's face, she assured him that she had taken into account every contingency. "So what could *possibly* go wrong?"

By then satisfied that Nathan hadn't seen through the unfolding plot – or picked up on the long-running scheme she'd hidden within it – she waved in the direction of the school. "Come on!" she said. "Let's have some fun!"

After seconding her, Daniel took the lead as they made their way through row upon row of parked cars. A good ten feet in front of his adopted siblings, Daniel had just passed by the passenger cab of a van when he suddenly did a double take. Throwing himself back against the side of the vehicle, he hissed a warning to his brother and sisters. "Down! Quick!"

Hearing the fear in his brother's voice, Nathan forced his sisters down behind a Ford station wagon before running toward Daniel in the silent, half-crouch he'd learned while fighting the British. "What's wrong?" he whispered.

Pointing his finger at the side of the van to indicate direction, Daniel whispered back. "Ninjas – seven or eight of them, sneaking across the south clearing."

Incredulous, Nathan slipped past Daniel and raised his head above the engine compartment to look. After staring for a long moment, he shook his head. "Those aren't Ninjas, Bro…

"Take another look."

The Mist & the Darkness

After carefully leaning over to peer through the driver's side window, Daniel stared for an equally long moment before shaking his head in disbelief. "What the hell's going on?"

Nathan said he wasn't sure. "But the chunky one out front with the walkie-talkie is Mary Sue Poindexter...

"And I'm pretty sure the clumsy one with the ropes coiled over his shoulder is Chubby Higanbotham."

By that time Lydia and Elspeth had tiptoed over and crouched down behind them. "So what's up?" Elle whispered.

Nathan shook his head. "Haven't a clue," he said. "Looks like group of students dressed up as Ninjas, carrying an extension ladder and a big box..."

Then as the group stopped at the edge of the South Wing and began extending the ladder, Daniel suddenly realized they were breaking into the building. "Jesus – they must be out of their minds!"

Having missed the feigned look of innocence that passed across Lydia's face, Nathan straightened up and watched as the would-be Ninjas raised the ladder against the side of the building. After it clacked against the stone, someone opened a window from the inside and leaned out to issue a low whistle. "Over here, stupid!"

After studying the bizarre scene for a long moment, he concluded that it was some sort of Homecoming prank. Then after looking over at Daniel, and then at his sisters behind him, he warned them not to say a word to anyone. "Weren't here, didn't see it."

After his siblings nodded, Nathan resumed the march toward the school. Stopping at the sidewalk that led to the main entrance, he held out his hand and asked Lydia for his ticket. Then while he waited for Lydia to retrieve them from her evening bag, Nathan once again admonished the gang to behave. "Neill and I have been friends since 1814, and he's going to go ballistic if he finds out about this...

"So I don't want any problems tonight – *got it???*"

CHAPTER 45

After finally managing to disengage from Wilkinson, Taylor, Fredricks, and the half-dozen or so lechers that turned up after them, Andre placed his hand on Stephanie's lower back and guided her toward the refreshments table. "That went well," he whispered. "They were too busy perving down your top to question our cover story…"

Stephanie laughed wryly, and grinned. "That happens a lot with you youngsters." The she looked up at him again, this time with a lighthearted grin. "But it isn't *just* my amazing figure," she teased. "I'm an actress, you know!"

Then after a moment's pause, she looked around and told Andre he'd been right about Newton. "I really could pass for normal around here!"

Thinking she didn't know the half of it, Andre told her to wait while he got her another glass of punch. He'd just turned away when Stephanie suddenly reached out, and grabbed his arm. *"Andre!"* she hissed. *"We've gotta get out of here!"*

Turning back to find a look of horror spreading across Stephanie's face, Andre asked what was wrong. After a quick, furtive glance around to make sure no one could hear her, she placed her hands on his shoulders and stood up on her tip toes. "Vampires!" she hissed in his ear. "We've gotta run!"

Suddenly alarmed, Andre looked at her intently. "Are you sure?"

As her look of horror morphed into one of sheer terror, she shook her head up and down and said she was positive. "I can sense them – I always know when there's others around." Then she grabbed his hand and tugged on it urgently. "Come on, *let's go…*

"They're going to slaughter everyone – and God only knows what they'll do if they catch me with a human!"

Flashing back to the McGuires' visit to his house, Andre winced and wondered if they could sense the presence of Vampires, too. Because if they'd picked up on his uncle, he was screwed…

The Mist & the Darkness

But since he had more urgent problems at hand, he filed the question under "Later" and asked Stephanie if she could tell which direction they were coming from. After she pointed toward the doors that led to the North Building, Andre jerked his head toward the South. Then after grabbing her hand, he began pulling her through the crowd. As they passed through a knot of students, he whispered over his shoulder, just loud enough for her to hear him over the band. "This way…

"They've probably got the obvious exits covered, so we'll slip out an emergency exit at the far end of the South Building and head for my car. I've got a 9mm in the glove compartment, and a Katana in the trunk…

"I'm going to give you the keys, and I want you to take the car and get the hell out of here – leave it in the long term parking at the airport, and overnight me the stub, OK?"

With another knot of students standing around, off to their right, Stephanie didn't answer. But once they'd passed them, she released his hand and grabbed him by the arm. After jerking it with surprising strength, she told Andre he was nuts. "You can't kill Vampires with guns!"

Glancing down at her as they hurried toward the south doors, Andre nodded in agreement. "But it's loaded with hollow points, so a couple of rounds will lay 'em out flat – long enough to finish them off with the sword."

Scurrying along beside him in her heels, Stephanie objected in a fearful voice. "There's too many, Andre. You'll get killed!"

Andre chuckled. "I doubt it – but how many are there, anyway? Can you tell?"

As they closed in on the double doors that exited into the South Wing, Stephanie said she couldn't be positive. "There's at least three, maybe four coming from the north hall."

Thinking that was no big deal, Andre nodded. "So do they know you're here?"

Stephanie shook her head. "Probably not – after that creep of an ex-boyfriend bit me, I became really sensitive to Vampires. But I'm pretty sure that's just me."

Seriously hoping that Stephanie was right about that, Andre was about to shove the panic bar that opened the doors when he was suddenly overcome by a sinking sensation. Halting abruptly, he turned back toward Stephanie. "How many did you say there were?" he asked intently.

Looking up at him with a still terrified face, Stephanie said, "I told you – three, maybe four." Then in a desperate voice, she warned him that they had to keep moving.

Releasing her hand as he pushed one of the doors open, Andre asked her if she could tell their gender. As she slipped through the half-open door ahead of him, Stephanie nodded. "Two guys, definitely, and at least one girl – maybe two, if they're wearing the same perfume."

As the door closed behind them, Andre winced before lowering his head and shaking it back and forth. Then after muttering an incoherent curse in the half-lit corridor, he looked down at Stephanie and sighed. "There's something I didn't tell you..."

CHAPTER 46

Standing there in the dim light, Andre hoped Stephanie wasn't going to come unglued as he explained about Elspeth, and the McGuires.

No such luck – because as he laid it out, her eyes bulged and her mouth fell open. And then after a long, incredulous moment, she clenched her jaw shut and started whacking him over the head with her evening bag. *"Andre,"* she hissed, *"Are you stupid???"*

"Vampires are dangerous!!!"

Having raised his arms to block the torrent of blows, Andre stepped back and gave her an irritated look as he retreated toward the wall. "You're not."

Fuming, Stephanie lowered her bag, shoved her other index finger in his face, and gave him a dangerous look. *"Don't start on me,"* she growled.

By now backed up against the cinder-block wall, Andre cautiously pushed her finger away and apologized. "But there's nothing to worry about, Stephanie – they're Civilized." Then in an effort to drive his point home, he jerked his head toward the

The Mist & the Darkness

cafeteria doors and asked her just exactly how many screams she was hearing. Frustrated, Stephanie stomped her foot and told him that wasn't the point.

"You just don't get it, Andre – Vampire girls use sex as a lure. They take advantage of teenage hormones to get guys alone in a secluded spot, and then they rip their throats out!"

Without giving Andre a chance to respond, Stephanie continued. "Your girlfriend may seem all safe and cuddly, but how do you know?

"The whole thing could be a con to get you alone someplace…"

Andre shook his head. "Point taken, but I've been around the block a time or two and I know the difference between a Civilized Vamp and a Predator. Trust me on this – the McGuires are Civilized."

Then after pausing for a moment, his irritation overcame his better judgment. "And you're underrating me," he said sharply. "I eat Vamps for *soupe*."

Still angry, but now thoroughly confused as well, Stephanie crossed her eyes and thrust her face forward. "*For what???*"

Andre frowned. "*Soupe* – that's Legion slang for just about anything edible. Breakfast, lunch, dinner, whatever…"

After staring at Andre for another incredulous moment, Stephanie sighed and shook her head. Then after telling him he needed a brain transplant, she asked him what they were going to do.

After thinking about it for a moment, Andre reminded her that Elspeth had blown smoke up his butt about the dance – and that he was more than a little frosted. "So if you think you can pull it off, let's go back inside." Then he gave her a wicked grin, and said Elspeth deserved to get shown up.

After looking up at him and chuckling, Stephanie warned him that the McGuires would recognize her. "They may not be able to pick up on other Vampires the way I do, but believe me – once they see me, they'll know."

Thinking that would really get Elspeth's goat, Andre pushed the Uncle Philippe problem out of mind again, and shrugged. "Well, as long as *THEY* don't know that *I* know – so what?"

Having apparently read Andre's mind, Stephanie chuckled mischievously. So after wagging a finger at him and telling him he was a very naughty boy, she grinned and told him to pay attention — because she was going to put on the performance of a lifetime. "I'm gonna get a Tony for this one!"

Grinning, Andre opened the door for her. "Great!" he said. "But whatever you do, don't let them know I'm onto 'em, OK?"

Smiling as she slipped through the door, Stephanie assured him that her lips were sealed. "Not a word, I promise!"

CHAPTER 47

It turned out that Stephanie had been right when she'd told Andre that other Vamps weren't as sensitive as she was to the presence of others, because the McGuires were still blissfully unaware of her when they strolled into the cafeteria. In fact, it wasn't until they managed to make their way through the crowd to the refreshment table that Daniel spotted her.

When he did, his eyes bulged and his jaw dropped as he froze in place.

"Holy shit!" he whispered. *"Check out Marchand's date!"*

Nathan had been busy supporting Elspeth as she adjusted a shoe, so he hadn't seen her. But when he did, he stiffened and his eyes narrowed. Turning to the girls, he ordered them out of the cafeteria. "Go fix your makeup, or something." Then he turned to Daniel, and instructed him to follow along.

Lydia would have normally ignored her older brother — or at least tried to — but when he slipped into the command mode like that, she instinctively obeyed. Nathan had a sixth sense about danger, and when he tensed up she knew it was time to either run or hide. Grabbing Elle's arm, she told her to come on. "Let's take a powder, girl."

Elspeth hadn't seen Stephanie, and she hadn't really been paying attention when Daniel had sounded the alarm. Looking up as Lydia dragged her toward the door, she demanded to know what was going on. Still pulling on Elle's arm as she pushed through the crowd,

The Mist & the Darkness

Lydia dropped her voice to a Vampiric whisper. "There's another Vamp here…"

"*What???*" Elspeth exclaimed, in a voice that was far too loud. "*Here???*"

Ignoring the leers of the half-dozen or so hockey players who had made a point of expressing their lewd appreciation for the flimsy dress she was wearing, Lydia dragged her little sister through the open doors and into the hallway. Angry and more than a little bit frightened, she hissed. "Why don't you just shout, so everyone can hear!"

Jerking her arm free from Lydia's grasp, Elspeth turned to face her. After glancing around to make sure no one could hear, Elspeth dropped her voice to a low whisper and demanded again to know what was going on.

After rolling her eyes and huffing, Lydia said she'd already told her. "There's another Vamp here, and Nathan wants us out of the way so he can take care of it."

As Elspeth's eyes bulged, she whispered. "*Oh my God – what's he going to do?*"

Lydia jerked her head toward the girls' restroom. "Don't worry about it, Elle – Nathan will deal with it."

Then after casting a worried look over her shoulder at the Cafeteria, she tugged on Elspeth's wrist. "Now come on – we're going to fix our makeup, and lay low for a few minutes…

"And if we don't hear any screaming or police sirens, we'll go back and case the joint – carefully."

Knowing that Lydia had a great deal more experience dealing with tight spots than she did, Elspeth nodded. "Right." Then as they started toward the restroom, she asked Lydia in a worried voice what Nathan would do if the Vamp turned out to be a Predator.

After shuddering, Lydia told Elspeth she didn't want to know. "I've seen him fight, and believe me – you don't want to be around when that happens."

Halting just outside the restroom door, Elspeth looked up fearfully. "You mean all that 'Indian Fighting' stuff he learned on the Frontier?"

Lydia nodded, as she started to push the door open. "The Frontier," she said. "And the Philippines."

Grabbing Lydia's arm, Elspeth gave her sister a shocked look. "The *what???*"

"The Philippines," Lydia whispered. "It was before your time, Elle – he'd gone to Manila to research a book on the Spanish-American War, and the Japs invaded a week or so after he arrived...

"So he spent the next three years leading a guerilla band in the jungle – and I don't think he was dining on Sushi."

"*Oh my God,*" Elspeth gasped. "He *ate* them???"

Still standing in the half-opened door, Lydia shrugged. "Neill said it was his contribution to the war effort..."

Then with a look of smoldering anger, she continued. "And believe me, Elle – after what those bastards did at Pearl Harbor, I would've helped him if I'd had the chance!"

"*Damn!*" Elspeth whispered. "How come I didn't know about this stuff?"

Lydia shuddered again, and shook her head as she pushed through the door. "It must have been really bad, Elle – because Nathan's never said a word about it. Not once, ever..."

CHAPTER 48

That was true, of course. But as the eldest of the McGuire siblings approached Andre and his date, he wasn't thinking about the past – he was thinking about how to handle the presence of an unfamiliar and definitely unwanted Vamp. So after whispering for Daniel to keep his eyes out for others, he pushed through the crowd that had gathered alongside the refreshment table, before stopping just behind Andre. Then after forcing a smile on his face, he clapped him on the shoulder and feigned good humor. "Slumming tonight, Marchand?"

Turning toward the McGuire brother, it was Andre's turn to fake it. Pretending surprise, he eyed Nathan's elegantly tailored three-piece suit before playfully demanding to know who the hell had let him in.

As a feigned smile crept across his face, Nathan shrugged. "The parents went out of town on short notice, so we thought we'd find

The Mist & the Darkness

out how the other half lives." Then he glanced over at Stephanie, and forced another smile. "So who's the lovely lady?"

Pretending he'd forgotten his manners, Andre introduced them. "Stephanie, this is my friend Nathan – and behind him, his brother Daniel." Stephanie smiled convincingly, and extended her hand. "Pleased to meet you, Nathan." The she reached behind him, and shook Daniel's offered hand as well. "And you, too, Daniel."

Turning back to Andre, Nathan asked if Stephanie was his Canuckian girlfriend. Smiling at the jest, Stephanie shook her head and interjected. "No, I'm her last minute replacement – Andre and I are old friends from New York."

Thoroughly impressed by the way Stephanie had carried off that particular lie, Andre interjected. "I split up with the girlfriend a couple of days ago, so Stephanie agreed to come up so I wouldn't have to do the bachelor thing tonight."

Then without missing a beat, he asked Nathan if the McGuire girls had come. Nathan nodded, and said they were in the restroom, fixing their makeup or their hair or whatever it is they do in there.

Seeing the frosty look that had spread across Andre's face, Nathan asked him not to be too hard on Elspeth. "Lydia organized a last minute jailbreak – we didn't even know about it until a few hours ago."

Suppressing a wicked look of disbelief, Andre pursed his lips together and shrugged.

Thinking Marchand had every right to exact a bit of payback, Nathan smiled and changed the subject as the band started up again. "Mind if I borrow your date for a dance?"

After seeing Stephanie nod ever so slightly from the corner of his eye, Andre shrugged and said, "Sure." Then in a light-hearted dig at Stephanie's martial arts pretensions, he warned Nathan to behave himself. "She knows karate!"

After thanking Andre for the warning, Nathan extended his arm and led Stephanie to the dance floor. By that time, *The Time Machine* had worked its way up to the early 1950's and was playing a slow waltz that he vaguely recalled. It had barely broken into the Top 10, but it was perfect for the sort of conversation he had in mind – so after placing one hand on Stephanie's side, and taking her hand with his other, he led to the music.

Stephanie had been desperately hoping to avoid a confrontation, but after the first few steps, Nathan dropped his voice to a Vampiric whisper. "I don't care who you are or where you came from, but Marchand's a friend of ours – so if you bite him, you're dust."

Nathan's dangerous tone made Stephanie's blood run cold – or in the interests of accuracy, colder than usual. So after inhaling sharply, she looked up and anxiously assured him that she was Civilized. "I don't do that, Nathan, I swear…

"I've never hurt anyone in my whole life, and whatever you may think, Andre's my friend." Then after fixing her eyes upon his, she earnestly continued. "I promise."

Nathan nodded calmly. "For your sake, I hope you're telling the truth." Then changing the subject, he asked Stephanie if Andre knew what she was.

Having glimpsed something dark and dangerous lurking behind Nathan's charming disposition and polished manners, Stephanie was by then deathly afraid. "No," she whispered. "He's clueless."

Then after pausing for a moment to recover her wits, she began recounting their agreed-upon cover story. "We lived in the same building in New York, so we used to hang out together – you know, movies, plays, art museums, stuff like that." Then after another moment's pause, she bit her lip and whispered a plea for understanding. "I didn't ask for this life, Nathan…

"It was forced on me."

Nodding thoughtfully, Nathan said he understood. Then he chuckled, and told her it had been the same with his family. "Except for our ostensible father – who deliberately infected himself in a medical experiment."

As she looked up incredulously, Stephanie's eyes crossed involuntarily and she stopped dead in her tracks. *"He what???"*

Still smiling, Nathan nodded. "He was a Magister – that's what they called scientists back in the day – and he was trying to find a cure."

As she resumed the dance, Stephanie chuckled in disbelief. "So how'd that work out for him?"

Nathan laughed softly. "Not very well – but he's still trying. He may never figure out the supernatural aspects of Vampirism, but he's pretty sure he'll eventually find a way to stop the change."

"Wow! So he's a doctor now?"

Nathan nodded again. "He's a surgeon, but he does a lot of private research."

Having a hard time wrapping her head around that one, Stephanie gave Nathan a puzzled look. "Doesn't all that blood get to him?"

Nathan shook his head, then laughed again. "No, it's amazing – I think he's the only Vampire in history who doesn't react to blood."

Then after a thoughtful moment, Nathan continued. "His experimental potion didn't stop the change, but it seems to have blocked the bloodlust..."

Seizing on the opportunity to reassure Nathan, Stephanie smiled. "Well," she said proudly, "I'm pretty good at that myself." Then suddenly focused on his martial bearing, she asked Nathan about his background. "You were a soldier, weren't you?"

Smiling softly as the dance came to an end, Nathan nodded. "South Carolina Militia – I rode with the Swamp Fox during the Revolution."

But he didn't mention the Philippines. He didn't want to talk about the three years he'd spent in Hell.

CHAPTER 49

After the music stopped, Nathan escorted Stephanie through the throng that lined the dance floor, explaining that history was his passion. He'd taken a Ph.D. from the University of Chicago in 1932, and had published 20 some-odd historical works since. Impressed, Stephanie told him she hadn't had the chance to attend college in her human life, but she was working on a degree in drama part time at Columbia. "I don't think there's any way I'll ever be able to do film, but I've got a shot at Broadway."

As Stephanie was explaining her love for the performing arts, Lydia and Elspeth hesitantly emerged from the restroom. Less than five feet from the door, Elspeth was mobbed by a group of late-arriving social outcasts. So while she struggled to find a way to compliment the Nerd Girls on their dresses or their hair, Lydia edged along the wall toward the cafeteria doors and tried to look inconspicuous. Ignoring the half-dozen or so suggestive remarks and the two or three low wolf-whistles from another group of jocks lounging against the opposite wall, she cautiously peeked inside. Seeing nothing amiss, she was about to turn around to gesture for Elspeth when Jonathan Freeman grabbed her rear end. Chuckling at the lewd proposition he whispered in her ear, Lydia turned around slowly before wrapping her arms around his neck and whispering in a sultry voice. "So you want some of that, huh?"

Not waiting for a reply from the surprised Jock, she stood up on her tip toes to kiss him. Then as their lips met, she slammed her knee into his crotch.

Freeman gasped, and his eyes bulged – and as his legs buckled, Lydia reached under his arms and lifted him high up in the air before making a half-turn to deposit him against the wall. As he slowly slid to the floor, she pretended to hold a telephone to her ear. Raising her eyebrows expectantly, she grinned. "Call me!"

Then she laughed, and marched over to Elle – making a special effort to flaunt her stunning hips as she passed by the shocked and disbelieving Jocks. *"Holy shit!"* one of them whispered to the others. *"Did you just see that???"*

Ignoring the fool, Lydia whispered over her diminutive sister's shoulder. "Come on – the coast is clear."

So after Elspeth managed to disengage from her followers, the two strolled back into the cafeteria and headed for the refreshments table. They were almost there when Elle spotted Andre joking around with Daniel, and a couple members of the football team. "Let's go say hi!"

Having by now put two and two together, Lydia placed her hand on Elle's shoulder and suggested that might not be the best of ideas. Still clueless, Elspeth looked up at her and demanded to know why.

"He has a date, Elle."

Puzzled, Elspeth shrugged and said, "So?"

It was at that precise moment that her older brother and Stephanie strolled into view. After turning to thank Nathan for the dance, Stephanie sauntered over to Andre and wrapped her arm around his waist. "Hey, good looking – did ya miss me?"

The Mist & the Darkness

Seeing that, Elspeth's eyes bulged and her jaw dropped. *"Son-of-a-bitch!"* she exclaimed, in a voice much louder than she'd intended.

Hearing her familiar voice behind him, Andre turned around, and looked her over. "Well," he said, in a voice dripping with sarcasm. "This is a surprise."

With her eyes still fixed on Stephanie, Elle muttered – once again, a bit too loudly. *"I don't believe it…"*

Reveling in her discomfort, Andre cocked his head over. "You don't believe what, Elle?"

Now looking at Andre, Elspeth sputtered. "I…

"Well…

"Uh…

"Never mind!"

At that point, Lydia stepped forward and introduced herself to Stephanie. "I'm Lydia," she said politely. Then after glancing back at Elspeth, she continued. "And Little Miss Tongue-tied is my sister, Elspeth."

Smiling, Stephanie said Andre had told her all about them before complimenting Lydia on her dress. "It's gorgeous," she said in honest admiration. Then after praising the elegant simplicity, and the mile-high front slit, which Lydia had offset to the left, she said the look was "Perfect!"

After returning the compliment and remarking on Stephanie's slightly less provocative but equally sexy gown, Lydia explained that she'd designed and sewn her dress – and Elspeth's, too, except that she'd swiped that particular design from an Antonio Banderas film. Impressed by Lydia's excellent taste and obvious skill, Stephanie looked Elspeth up and down before pronouncing her dress "Beautiful." Then as the band started up again, she excused herself and turned to Andre. "Let's dance," she said excitedly.

As the two headed for the dance floor, Stephanie glanced over her shoulder and whispered in a catty voice that only the McGuires could hear. "Don't worry, Elspeth – I'll bring your boyfriend back in a bit!"

Fuming at the put-down, Elspeth watched them disappear into the crowd. "That does it!" she growled. "I'm gonna make that boy's life a living hell!"

Charles S. Viar

After almost choking on the punch Daniel had handed her, Lydia teased. "What's the matter, Elle – you jealous?"

Angry and at the same time incredulous, Elspeth wheeled around and confronted her sister. *"Are you serious?"* she demanded to know. "In case you hadn't noticed, that girl isn't your ordinary, run of the mill co-ed...

"She's a *Vampire*, for God's sake – and that *idiot* brought her to Homecoming!!!"

Then having conveniently forgotten that she was, technically, old enough to Andre's grandmother, Elspeth huffed. "And besides, she's *at least* 23 – and that's *way* too old for him!"

Taken aback by that one, Lydia looked at her little sister skeptically. *"Uh huh,"* she said. "And how old did you say you were???"

After Elspeth hotly informed her that was beside the point, Lydia shrugged. "So he likes older women," she said dismissively. "But in any event, he *did* ask you first."

Then after crossing her arms across her chest and tilting her head back a bit, Lydia looked in the direction Andre and Stephanie had taken. "And you have to admit, that girl's got style – her dress is just amazing!"

After glaring at her sister for an interminable moment, Elspeth marched over to the punch bowl, ladled a glass full, and downed it all. Then after repeating the process, she stormed off swearing in a bewildering variety of languages.

Chuckling, Nathan looked over at Daniel and wondered where Elspeth had learned Chinese.

"Beats me," Daniel whispered back. "But it's about time Marchand gave her some grief. She's got it coming."

CHAPTER 50

Back on the dance floor, Andre and Stephanie were having fun. *The Time Machine* had picked up the pace, playing Carl Perkins' *Blue Suede Shoes* followed by Buddy Holly's *Peggy Sue*. Halfway through the

The Mist & the Darkness

latter, Lydia strolled out on the dance floor with Al Thompson. A junior, he was also the football team's second string halfback.

Although big and colossally stupid, Thompson was good-looking and good natured – and to Andre's surprise, graceful on the dance floor. Following his line of sight as the music came to an end, Stephanie waited until the applause died down before bouncing up on her tip toes to whisper in Andre's ear. "Are you sure that's a good idea?"

Andre chortled, and assured her Lydia wasn't a problem. "The worst she's gonna do is tease him to death."

Stephanie chuckled as she picked up the beat of the next song. Then grinning mischievously, she leaned slightly forward to enhance the view, and shimmied to the drum beat. "You mean tease him like this?"

Playing into the jest, Andre shook his head dismissively. "A bit lower..."

Still moving with the drums, Stephanie balled her fists and pushed her arms down along her torso, before leaning forward a bit more. "Like this?"

Grinning, Andre shook his head. "Lower, baby!"

Laughing, Stephanie straightened up and told him he was dreaming. "Maybe so," Andre said as he jerked his head to the right rear. "But I think you just fried a few minds over there."

Having forgotten about the half-dozen or so jocks who'd been standing up on chairs to watch the dance floor over the heads of the bystanders crowded at the edge, Stephanie's eyes bulged as she threw her left hand up to cover her neckline. *"Oops,"* she said in a laughing voice. "That wasn't meant for them!"

Then as the music faded, Stephanie said she needed a break. "Let's go get some more punch!"

Wondering if that was such a good idea, Andre reminded her it was spiked. "I know," she whispered. "But alcohol doesn't have the same impact on us – and in any event, I know my limit."

Andre grinned as they made their way through the crowd. "Well, I just don't want you trying to take advantage of me – being such a fine, upstanding young man, and all that..."

Laughing, Stephanie turned into him and grasped his lapels. *"Uh huh,"* she said with playful sarcasm. "And I really, *really* believe that!"

Then she bounced up on her tiptoes and kissed him on the cheek. "You're a nut!" she said in a laughing voice. Then she wrapped her arm around his waist and started pulling him toward the refreshments.

They never made it.

Uncertain as to whether Stephanie was "in character" and acting, or whether she was hitting on him, Andre was weighing the odds when the microphone suddenly let forth an ear-splitting, high-pitched squeal. Then after a couple of taps that sounded like a drunken musician trying to make sense of his drums, Heloise Van Dorn asked for everyone's attention. "As Chairman of the Homecoming Committee, I'm pleased to announce that the moment we've all been waiting for has arrived!"

Then after letting out a nervous squeal, she announced the votes for Homecoming King and Queen had been counted, recounted, and certified by the Poly Sci Club's Electoral Commission.

So after pushing her horn-rimmed glasses back up on her nose and smoothing her frilly, fake satin skirt, she asked everyone to gather around the stage before demanding a big round of applause for Mary Sue Poindexter – who as President of the Political Science Club and Chairman of the Electoral Commission, would announce the winners.

As the Nerds, Geeks and other social outcasts went wild for one of their own, a couple of Jocks booed, and the rest provided a smatter of bored applause, as Bob Johnson – the captain of the football team – adjusted his tie in anticipation of victory. Standing next to him, Kathy Norse grasped his arm. Nominated by the Jocks and the Cheerleaders, there was no doubt they'd win by a landslide. The In Crowd always did.

But not this time...

As Andre and Stephanie edged their way up to the front, to take their place alongside Newton's Aristocracy, Mary Sue accepted a sealed envelope from Heloise. After withdrawing a folded sheet of paper, she waited through the melodramatic drum roll provided by the band, before announcing the winners. "And our new Homecoming King is...

"ANDRE MARCHAND!!!"

The Mist & the Darkness

Upon hearing her words, Andre's eyes bulged and his jaw dropped. Then after a moment of stunned disbelief, he raised his hands in protest. "No way!" he shouted. But it was too late, because his protest was drowned out by a roar of approval from the Outcast Alliance.

Andre tried to turn around and protest to the Jocks surrounding him, but by then they were patting him on the back and giving him High Fives. Marchand might not have been their candidate of choice, but he was one of theirs – and there was no way they were going to turn their backs on one of their own.

Andre was still protesting when Mary Sue raised her hands to quiet the din. "And now," she said, "Our new Queen *IS*...

"*ELSPETH MCGUIRE!!!*"

Absolute bedlam broke out, as the Nerds and Geeks went wild again. But having buried his face in his hands as he beseeched the Almighty to explain what he'd done to deserve this punishment, Andre was oblivious to the near riot that had broken out around him. In fact, it wasn't until the Jocks began pushing him toward the band's platform that he snapped back to reality.

Realizing he'd been set up, he was desperately trying to figure out who was behind the plot as he strode over to the dais. Ignoring the stairs off to his right, he placed his left hand on the plywood and mounted it in a graceful leap, before marching over to the microphone. Ordered by Heloise to wait until his Queen arrived, Andre stuffed his hands in his pockets and looked out over the sea of faces, searching for a clue that might unmask the culprit.

This is nuts, he thought – until his eyes fastened on Lydia, who was standing in the front row and grinning like the Cheshire Cat. Suddenly remembering the whispered conversation between Lydia and Mary Sue in the cafeteria a couple of weeks before, he locked his eyes on hers and mouthed a warning. *"You're toast!"*

Lydia laughed before feigning a look of innocence. Pointing her index finger at her chest, she tilted her head over and mouthed back. *"Moi?"*

By that time Elspeth had appeared by his side from somewhere, flushed and radiant with excitement. Still glaring at Lydia, Andre ignored her until Heloise took the mike and announced the Coronation. After a minion stepped forward carrying a crown, she placed it on Andre's head, to deafening applause. Then she repeated the process with Elspeth, taking special care to not to muss the hair piled on her head. Then after another wave of tumultuous applause died down, Heloise announced it was time for their acceptance speeches. Pulling the microphone free from the stand, she handed it to Andre. "Your Majesty?"

Fortunately, Andre had already figured a way out of the trap – one that would not only save face, but keep him in good graces with the Jocks and Cheerleaders. Accepting the mike from Heloise, he thanked the student body for their vote of confidence. He was flattered, but unworthy of the high honor they'd bestowed upon him – and that being the case, he declared he could not accept it personally, but would do so on behalf of Newton's Athletic Department. Then amidst the cheers of Newton's Aristocracy, he went on to thank Coach Jordan and Coach Sommers, the captains of each sports team by name, and the captain of the cheerleading squad. Then after bowing to the applause – while holding his plastic crown in place – he handed the microphone to Elspeth.

Noting the full flush on the Vampire's face, Andre was thinking that was something you don't see every day when Elspeth began stammering out her thanks. She was thrilled, she said, and was trying to explain how she wanted to thank each and every student at Newton personally when she choked up with emotion. "Thank you," she said. "Thank you, thank you, thank you!" Then with tears welling in the corner of her eyes, she handed the microphone back to Heloise.

Heloise turned to Andre, and informed him that it was time for the Royal Dance – and as King, it was his Royal Prerogative to call the tune. Thinking fast, he held up an index finger to signify a pause, before turning on his heel and marching over to the bandleader. Leaning over, he locked his eyes on the elderly musician, and whispered. "Can you do an Argentine tango?"

Inferring Andre's intention, the old man chuckled. "We can play anything, Son..."

"You want the *Asi se Baila El Tango?*"

Realizing the bandleader had intuited his plan, Andre nodded. "The long version – and make sure the spotlights stay on us, OK?"

The Mist & the Darkness

After laughing softly, the old man smiled knowingly. "You trying to even up for something?"

Andre grinned and nodded, and gave him a thumbs up sign. Then after asking the bandleader to wait until they were in the middle of the dance floor, Andre thanked him. "She's been giving me grief since the day we met!"

Andre knew Elspeth had heard him as he turned back to her, but psychological warfare was all part of the plan. But before he could congratulate himself on orchestrating the perfect revenge, the look on Elle's face brought him up short. Serene and confident, with her nose stuck up in the air, she was trying hard to suppress a wicked smile.

Uh oh...

CHAPTER 51

Although Andre had no way of knowing it, Elspeth was no stranger to the dance floor. In addition to her degrees in Elementary Ed and English Lit, she also held a degree in Modern Dance. In fact, she'd owned a studio in Hollywood during the McGuires sojourn in California, and during the 80s she'd taught all the "A-List" stars how to dance – Clint Eastwood, Burt Reynolds, Eddie Murphy and even Tom Cruise. So as Andre led her to the center of the dance floor, she was reveling at the chance to exact revenge for Stephanie.

After marching across the dance area to its very edge, Andre pivoted and glanced over at the bandleader to nod. Then after straightening into an aggressive, forward leaning pose he locked his eyes on Elspeth and nodded to her, the traditional way of signaling the dance had begun. As the band struck the first dramatic chords, he marched toward the center before stopping suddenly, stripping off his coat and – with his eyes still locked on Elspeth's – tossing the garment in Wilkinson's direction.

Shocked to see that Elspeth had imitated his every move, Andre watched in amazement as she stopped halfway to the center point, and thrust her right leg forward to balance on her toes. Then she jerked at her tear-away skirt, and twirled. As it dropped to her side to form a sash, Andre's eyes bulged at the flimsy underskirt it revealed – almost see through, and so short that it barely covered the dancing panties she was wearing underneath.

Then after arching her back and raising first one arm and then the other toward the ceiling, Elspeth slowly lowered them across her shoulders before running her hands down over her breasts and on toward the depths of her abdomen. Then after bringing them back up again in a slow, sensual caress of her nipples, she twirled once more. Ignoring the whistles and catcalls from the Jocks, she locked her eyes on Andre's and gestured for him to come hither with her index finger. Then she slowly advanced across the remaining distance by swinging one foot in front of the other, accentuating the movement of her hips in the erotic, stylized march of the Argentine Tango.

After they met at mid-point, she reached out to grasp his tie as they circled one another, until Andre came to a dramatic, ritualistic pause. Then after drawing himself up, he lunged forward on one knee. As he did so, Elspeth accompanied him, locking her arm in his as they came to a rest. After a moment's pause, they rose slowly in unison for the traditional embrace.

Leaning forward with their backs straight, they pressed their chests together as Andre wrapped his right arm around Elspeth and placed it high on her center back. Then after Elspeth placed her hand low on his hip, they clasped their other hands together and began the dance.

Over the years, the Tango has developed an almost infinite number of variations – so many, in fact, that many consider it a form of freestyle dancing, distinguished only by the eight basic steps and the stylized movements that accompany them. But the Argentine Tango is different from the others by virtue of its unique emphasis upon eroticism – an emphasis so pronounced that it's often referred to as "vertical sex." More than a bit surprised that Elspeth even knew the dance, Andre decided to push her to the limit.

Let's see how far the little liar's gonna go...

Side-stepping to the left, Andre turned her hard, first to the right and then to the left as she performed her *Back Baleos*, bringing first one foot and then the other up high behind her. Impressed by the

The Mist & the Darkness

way she had executed the stylized movement, he was stunned when she leaned back and wrapped her right leg around him. After placing her heel just below his shoulder blades, she ran it down his spine in a slow, sensual caress.

Taken aback by the movement, Andre had frozen as Elspeth's heel traversed his back – because even the amazingly talented dance instructor who had taught him to Tango couldn't have pulled *that* off. Shocked by the fact that Elspeth could, Andre was wondering if he hadn't blundered again. Flashing back to his failed attempt to seduce the stunningly beautiful, 25-year-old teacher back in France, Andre's preference for older and more experienced women suddenly seemed problematical.

Young and stupid might work…

Snapping out of his reverie as Elspeth lowered her foot to the floor, Andre ignored the whistles and catcalls from the crowd that ringed the dance area, and back-stepped before stepping to his left. Then forward with the beat, on the outside of Elspeth, and forward again before bringing his feet together and shifting his weight to "cross" her, as it's called, first to his right and then to his left. Surprised again by the way she executed a *Gancho* with each turn – and relieved she hadn't tripped him out of spite – he stepped forward with the beat on her outside, before performing the *Ocho*, and then a *Salida* before repeating the steps in reverse.

Coming to another *Salida*, Andre crossed her to the left and then to the right before Elspeth twirled and stopped with her back to him. Recognizing the challenge, he stepped up behind her and grasped the left hand she'd held over her shoulder and placed his right hand high on her solar plexus, before leading her sideways through the eight-step march again. Difficult even when executed with a skilled and familiar partner, Andre was sweating bullets that he'd blow it when Elspeth spun at the *Salida*. Then after grasping his tie again, she marched around behind him and wrapped one leg around his waist, before climbing upon his back. She clung to him for a long, teasing moment with her cheek pressed against his shoulder and her hot breath against his skin. Then as she licked his neck in a long, slow motion, Andre's eyes bulged as his life flashed before him…

But she didn't bite. She hopped down instead, and began marching backwards in quick, stylized steps. After taking an instant to recover, Andre wheeled around to race after her. He caught her at the edge of the dance floor, seizing her offered hands as she arched backwards to almost touch the floor with her head.

It was a beautifully executed movement, but a less than auspicious location. Having left nothing to the imagination of the Jocks standing less than five feet away, a stunned Ed Thomas swore under his breath. *"Holy shit,"* he muttered, *"Did you see those..."*

But before he could complete the sentence, a powerful hand seized his neck from behind. Taken by surprise, he turned his head slowly to find Daniel McGuire standing next to him, with a dangerous look in his eyes. "That's my little sister," he hissed.

Mortified by the fact that he'd just violated a Major Guy Rule by making sexual reference to a Little Sis, Thomas was falling all over himself trying to apologize when Andre jerked Elspeth back upright. Then after lifting her high into the air, pivoting, and setting her down in front of him, he began the forward march as she leaned back into his chest. Holding the left hand she'd extended over her shoulder, he cupped the lower portion of her breast with his right as they traversed the dance area.

Although that particular act of eroticism was well within the accepted bounds of the Argentine Tango – in Argentina, anyway – it was way over the top for Newton Academy. So as the Geeks and Nerds gasped, the Jocks went wild.

Ignoring their enthusiastic whistles and catcalls, Elspeth whirled about as they reached the edge, and grasped Andre's right hand with her left before leaning her head against his and locking her eyes upon him. Taking the lead as she pushed him backwards in a series of stylized steps, she whispered in a sarcastically sweet voice. "I hope you enjoyed the touch, Andre...

"Because that's all *you're* ever going to get!"

Then after pushing him away, she whirled and repeated the movement with which she'd begun the dance, before sensually marching from the floor to the fading beat.

Standing alone in the center amidst thunderous applause, catcalls, whistles and a weird assortment of noises from the Nerds, Andre glared at her swaying hips as she disappeared into the crowd.

Show off...

The Mist & the Darkness

Irritated beyond belief that Elspeth had turned his ambush back against him, he was in the process of looking around for the suit coat he'd tossed into the crowd when he spied Wilkinson's frantic gestures. He couldn't make out what the Jock was trying to scream over the still riotous applause – but given the look on his face, it didn't take a rocket scientist to infer his meaning. Hurriedly glancing in the direction Wilkinson was pointing, Andre spotted a furious Dr. Renfrowe pushing his way through the crowd.

Oh shit...

Realizing it was time to make a run for it, Andre bolted in the direction of where he'd last seen Stephanie. As he pushed into the crowd, he heard Bob Johnson scream *"SNAKE DANCE!"* and yell for the band to start playing. As *The Time Machine* struck up Springsteen's *Rosalita*, Andre spotted his date off to the left, clutching Nathan's shoulder in a desperate effort to remain upright. She was laughing hysterically – but Nathan, unfortunately, was far less amused.

Thinking he'd have to deal with the Little Sis issue another time, Andre pushed a group of awestruck Nerds out of the way. Then after shoving their coat checks into Nathan's vest pocket, he grabbed Stephanie and told her they had to get the hell out of Dodge. "The sheriff's hot on my heels!"

Still laughing so hard she could barely remain upright, Stephanie pushed her way through the crowd beside him as they headed for the south exit.

By that time the Jocks and the Cheerleaders had slowed the Headmaster with their snake dance. But they weren't the only one's covering Andre's back, because Mary Sue Poindexter had seen the threat as well. So to force Dr. Renfrowe to give up the chase, she'd hauled off and decked the nearest Geek. As he flew backward onto the refreshment table, she began screaming, *"FIGHT! FIGHT! FIGHT!"*

Having mistakenly concluded the Jocks were beating up on them again, a group of Nerds and Geeks turned upon Newton's Aristocrats in an alcohol-induced fury – which wasn't the best of ideas, all things considered. Because by the time Andre and Stephanie made it to the exit doors, the Jocks were playing the local version of Dwarf Tossing. Turning around just in time to see a Nerd arcing through the air toward what had been the refreshment table just moments before, Stephanie cracked up again.

Then as they pushed through doors to make their escape, she shot a look over her shoulder and grinned. "And you said this was gonna be boring!"

CHAPTER 52

At 9:10 am the following Monday, Andre found himself standing at attention in front of the Headmaster's desk. With shoulders squared and eyes front, he was staring at the wall behind Dr. Renfrowe and wondering how long the Headmaster was going to ignore him. His company commander had played the same mind-game on him after he'd screwed up a night ambush in Afghanistan, and held him at attention for the better part of three hours.

It was an exercise in power and control and Andre had gotten used to it in the Legion. But from the corner of his eye, he could tell the Headmaster's little game was beginning to get to Elspeth. She was standing next to him, scared out of her wits.

At long last Dr. Renfrowe laid the pen he had been writing with down on the legal tablet in front of him, and stood up. Then with barely a glance, he walked around his desk and locked his hands behind him. After pacing back in forth in front of the two miscreants several times, he suddenly whirled around and directed a withering look first at Elspeth, and then at Andre. Then he spoke, in a misleadingly soft voice. "What the *hell* were you two thinking?"

But before Andre could answer, the Headmaster roared at them. *"THE ARGENTINE TANGO?*

"VERTICAL SEX IN MY SCHOOL???"

Resisting the impulse to wince, Andre accepted responsibility. "It was my fault, Sir."

Wheeling around, the Headmaster shoved his face within a half-inch of Andre's and bellowed in his best command voice. *"WELL GOLLY-GODDAMN-JEEPERS, MARCHAND!*

The Mist & the Darkness

"I'M SURE AS HELL GLAD YOU TOLD ME THAT, BECAUSE I WOULDN'T HAVE FIGURED IT OUT IN A MILLION YEARS!!!"
As the Headmaster's words reverberated through the room, he held his pose for a long moment before a tiny, tearful voice spoke in contradiction. "Don't blame Andre, Dr. Renfrowe – it's all my fault."

As a shocked silence fell over the room, the Headmaster slowly turned to look at Elspeth. "Ms. McGuire," he said slowly. "To say that I am shocked by your role in that spectacle is an understatement…

"Since arriving at Newton you've tied your siblings for top scholastic honors, and you have a near perfect attendance record."

Then after jerking his thumb in Andre's direction, Dr. Renfrowe continued. "And until you met *Corporal Knucklehead*, you didn't have a single disciplinary problem!"

Wincing at the reference to his less than Napoleonic rank, Andre was tempted to remind Dr. Renfrowe that he was – technically, at least – a first lieutenant. But he thought better of it as Elspeth looked down at the floor, and whimpered an apology.

Turning on his heel, the Headmaster marched back to his desk, turned around again and crossed his arms across his chest. "OK," he demanded to know. "What's going on with you two?"

Elspeth looked up with tear-stained eyes and apologized again. "It's my fault, Sir…

"I was jealous of Andre's date, and I was mean to him – so he decided to get back at me with the dance…"

The Headmaster looked away, and nodded before turning to look back at Andre. "So is that right, *Corporal Dumbass?*"

Ignoring the affront, Andre nodded. "Yes, Sir, I was trying to embarrass Ms. McGuire."

After glaring at Andre for an interminable moment, Dr. Renfrowe shook his head and sighed before looking over at Elspeth. "You know what your problem is?

"You two are crazy about each other, but you're too damn proud and stubborn to admit it!"

Thinking that was *way* too close for comfort, Andre winced. He was tempted to glance over at Elspeth, but kept his eyes fixed and centered instead. Renfrowe was coming to the punishment part of his calculated drama, and he was worried that any display of emotion would only make it worse.

"All right," the Headmaster said. "Damages came to over $5000, Marchand, and as soon as I get the final tab you're going to be writing me a check...

"And the two of you are on detention for the rest of the term – Ms. McGuire, you will report to the school library immediately after sixth period, where you will help the Library Club re-shelve books, sweep the floors, and perform any other tasks Mrs. Flint assigns you...

"Is that clear?"

Obviously relieved that she wasn't going to get kicked out of school, Elspeth nodded. "Yes, Sir."

"All right," the Headmaster said. "Now get out of here, McGuire, so I can have a little talk with *Corporal Stupid*."

But rather than head for the door as directed, Elspeth turned to the Headmaster and asked in a pleading voice if he was going to tell her parents. Dr. Renfrowe nodded in reply. "Yes, I'll be sending them a letter."

Mortified, Elspeth pleaded with him. *"Oh, please, Sir – don't!"* Then after clasping her hands together and leaning forward to beg for mercy, she told the Headmaster her parents would kill her if they found out she'd gotten in trouble. "They're really strict, and we're not even supposed to attend school functions – and if they find out we defied their orders while they were out of town, we're going to get grounded forever!"

Aware of the fact that Dr. and Mrs. McGuire had a reputation for being excessively severe, Headmaster Renfrowe paused for a moment to think through the implications of his intended letter. A decent man, he instinctively recoiled from the collective punishment that Elspeth said would fall upon her brothers and sister – so after a long moment, he nodded thoughtfully. "All right," he said. "Given your otherwise laudable record, I'll offer you a reasoned compromise: I'll sit on the letter – provided there aren't any other problems for the rest of the term...

"But if I see you in my office again, your parents are going to get that letter *and* another...

"Agreed?"

The Mist & the Darkness

After closing her eyes and letting out a huge sigh of relief, Elspeth thanked him profusely. Then after warning her to stay on her best behavior, the Headmaster ordered her out of his office. "Idiot and I have things to talk about."

Renfrowe waited until Elspeth had closed the door behind her, before looking back at Andre and shaking his head. "Marchand, you are a genuine, first class moron."

Still at attention, Andre nodded. "Yes, Sir, my uncle tells me that all the time."

"All right, before we get down to business, tell me one thing: where the hell did you learn the Argentine Tango?"

Andre shrugged. "My rich uncle insisted I learn how to dance, so he paid for advanced instruction."

"And I suppose that included lessons on grabbing your partner's breasts?"

Andre grinned, and nodded enthusiastically. "Yes, Sir! And let me tell you – they were *FAN*…"

Irritated, the Headmaster cut him off before he could finish the word "fantastic." "I don't want to hear it, Marchand…

"But given how strict Dr. and Mrs. McGuire are, I *would* like to know where Elspeth learned to dance like that…"

Andre shook his head in amazed ignorance. "Beats the hell out of me, Sir – I was planning on making a fool out of her, but she wiped the floor with me…"

Dr. Renfrowe chuckled. "So I heard."

Then without another word, he walked around behind his desk and picked up the military entrenching tool that had been leaning against the wall. Turning around, he tossed it at Andre.

Catching the implement in mid-air, Andre brought the fold-up shovel down along his side in a single, fluid movement. "I'm sure you're familiar with an e-tool," the Headmaster said as he walked back around his desk. After Marchand nodded, he said "Good…

"Because you're going to put this nonsense to rest – in a hole eight feet long, four feet wide, and six feet deep…

"And when you've finished digging, you're going to write 'Andre Marchand's Stupidity' on an eight and a half by eleven sheet of paper, and place it dead center in the bottom of that hole – and then

I'm going to march the entire athletic department out there for a candlelight vigil, while you fill the damn thing back up again."

After a quick calculation told him that digging a hole that size would take him a month or more, Andre winced. "Yes, Sir – but could that wait until Spring? Because the ground's pretty much frozen by now."

Grinning wickedly, the Headmaster nodded. "So it is – which is why I bought you a pickaxe at the hardware store this morning on the way to work. You can pick it up from the Custodian's Office after sixth period – along with a map of where I want that hole."

Thinking he'd really screwed up this time, Andre closed his eyes and nodded dejectedly. "Will there be anything else, Sir?"

The headmaster nodded, and told Andre to stand at ease. "Actually, there is" he said,

"I haven't figured out who did it or how, but somebody managed to switch out the Homecoming ballot box with an exact replica stuffed with fake votes." Then after looking at Andre closely, he asked him if he knew anything about that.

Although momentarily stunned, it didn't take long for Andre to realize that Lydia's con ran a lot deeper than he'd imagined – and that she was going to be in more trouble than he was if the Headmaster figured it out. Desperately hoping the sudden flash of recognition that had run through his mind hadn't played across his face as well, Andre feigned stupidity. *"They stole the ballot box???"*

Renfrowe nodded. "Yeah, and they did a good job of it, too – because I wouldn't have known the difference if Chief Beauregard hadn't pulled the real one out of the Lake yesterday."

Knowing that Lydia was smart enough to weight the damn box, Andre was wondering which dumbass had forgotten the bricks. Realizing that Mary Sue Poindexter – Lydia's apparent partner in crime – was way too savvy to screw that up, Andre figured it must have been one of the Geeks she bossed around. Academically brilliant but terminally stupid when it came to the real world, forgetting to weight the box was precisely the sort of mistake they'd make…

Thinking that might get him off the hook with the Jocks, Andre pretended to be shocked at the skullduggery before looking up hopefully. "So does this mean you're going to void the election?"

The Mist & the Darkness

After uncrossing his arms, Dr. Renfrowe shook his head. "No, the election stands...

"Newton was designed as an elite, science-oriented preparatory academy – and I think it's about time the serious students have a day in the sun.

"But if you should happen to find out who rigged the vote, tell them not to even think about trying it at the Christmas Formal – because they're not going to get away with it twice."

Then suddenly reverting to his taskmaster mode again, the Headmaster ordered Andre to get to his worthless butt out of his office. "I have work to do – but I expect to see you digging tonight."

Andre nodded, turned on his heel and started for the door. But Dr. Renfrowe interrupted his movement as he reached for the handle. "I'm probably wasting my time telling you this, Marchand, because it's not something you're going to understand until you hit 30 or so. But good women are hard to find – and Elspeth McGuire is as good as they get.

"So be nice to her – take the time to get to know her as a person...

"Send her flowers, take her to nice restaurants, art museums and plays...

"And regardless of what they do in Argentina – or France, for that matter – don't go grabbing her breasts on the dance floor..."

Suddenly feeling like a heel for having spent the entire term plotting Elspeth's seduction without having given a single thought to her as a human being – well, figuratively speaking, anyway – Andre wondered if he wasn't becoming a bit too American.

Must be the damn water...

CHAPTER 53

The following Sunday afternoon, Elspeth emerged from Burlington Mall, happy and content. Pleased to have found a blouse to wear with her new winter suit and positively delighted by her successful raid on Victoria's Secret, she pushed through big glass doors that exited onto the parking lot and emerged into the dull light of day. It was overcast again, a fact that had made her shopping expedition all the easier.

That had followed a near-perfect week. Although Nathan had been furious at Lydia for sneaking off with one of the Jocks, he'd either kept his silence or persuaded Neill to let the incident slide. Elspeth was pretty sure the lack of fallout had something to do with the fact that Nathan and Andre's fill-in date had really hit it off. Stephanie had given him her phone number and – after checking with Andre – he'd called her in New York a couple of days later. He still had her wrap, which he'd retrieved after she and Andre had bolted from the Homecoming dance, so they'd made plans to get together in New York for New Year's Eve. And as luck would have it, Stephanie had a single girlfriend – also a Civilized Vamp – so she'd invited Daniel to come down, too.

School had gone even better. True to his word, Headmaster Renfrowe hadn't mailed her parents the threatened disciplinary letter, and she was actually enjoying the sentence he'd meted out. The girls in the Library Club weren't the most exciting people in the world, but they were really nice. Chatting with them as they re-shelved the books and cleaned up after the other students was fun.

But most important of all, Andre seemed to be taking his punishment in stride. As a peace offering, she'd been taking a steaming cup of coffee or hot chocolate out to him every night after leaving the library; and if he was upset with her, he didn't show it. In fact, he was being really nice, and she liked that – a lot.

The mall's parking lot had been packed when she'd arrived four hours before, and most of the cars were still there. But it seemed strangely devoid of life as she cut through the rows towards her VW, which she'd been forced to park near the far edge. After shifting her bags, she picked up the pace – not because she was afraid, but because she didn't want to look out of place: that's what human girls always did when walking alone.

She had almost reached her car when she heard a low wolf-whistle behind her – a whistle so low, in fact, that only a Vampire could have heard it. Startled, she glanced over her shoulder to see an older Vamp trailing a hundred feet or so behind her. He was big and ugly and pot-bellied, and dressed in the country style she'd grown up

The Mist & the Darkness

with in the South. With a blue jean jacket lined with artificial sheep skin, a pair of oversized sunglasses, long, dark sideburns and his slicked-back hair, he looked like a really bad version of an Elvis impersonator.

Knowing that Civilized Vamps don't dress like that, Elspeth's blood ran cold – or in the interest of accuracy, colder than usual. The man following her was a Predator, and they liked to play rough. They killed humans for sustenance, and Civilized Vampires for fun…

Frightened – and by now revolted by the obscene suggestions he was whispering – she picked up her pace again, and tried to ignore him. Shifting her bags once more, she kept her eyes fixed on her car as she blindly searched the bottom of her shoulder bag for her keys.

She'd just found them when she heard the Predator pick up his pace. With less than 30 feet to go, she broke into a run. Throwing her bags to the ground next to her car, she frantically tried to fit her key into the lock to open the door – but by then her hands were shaking so badly that she dropped them. Turning about as the Predator strutted across the lane that separated the last row of cars from hers, she pressed back against her car and slid down its side as she reached for her keys.

Seeing the look of fear on her face, the Predator stopped a few feet from her and leered. "What's the matter, Little Lady – you afraid?"

Then without waiting for her to reply, he continued. "Nuthin to worry about, Baby. I won't hurt you." Then he leered again and added, "Not too much, anyway…"

After reaching down and grabbing Elspeth by the throat, he lifted her up before shoving her back against her car. Then as he dropped his hands to his waist to undo his belt buckle, he continued. "Now let's just do this nice and quiet, Girl – that way, none of your warm-blooded friends have to get hurt."

There was no one else in sight, and even if there had been Elspeth wouldn't have screamed – because if any humans came to her aid, she knew the Predator would slaughter them. But since she also knew he'd kill her after he'd had his way, she was about to make a desperate break and run for it when she heard a familiar voice from behind. *"Back off, fool!"*

Horrified, she whipped around to see Andre. Dressed in a winter camouflage field jacket with his Legion beret perched on his head, he was coming around the back of her car. As he rounded the bumper, she heard herself scream, *"Andre, NO – he'll KILL you!"*

Andre glanced over at her and chortled, before commanding the Vamp to get lost. Sneering back, the Vampire ridiculed him. "*Owwww*... the little soldier-boy come to save the day?"

"That's 'Legionnaire,' fool – and I told you to move on."

After taking off his shades and spitting in Andre's general direction, the Predator swung.

Moving with almost preternatural speed, Andre leaned back and batted the Vamp's fist out of the way, before dropping into a half-crouch and hammering him in the side with three savage blows. As his ribs cracked, the Vamp howled in pain, straightened, and reached for his injured side – and as he did so, Andre stepped back and nailed him with a side-kick. Then another, and another, and yet one more to drive the freak back against the rear end of the van parked across the driving lane.

As the Predator stumbled back against the back doors of the vehicle, Andre caught him with a round kick to the head with his right foot, followed by another with his left. Then as the Vamp began sliding down the rear doors, Andre dropped into a fighting stance and began hammering the freak's face with his fists.

Andre had surprised the Vamp with his speed, his strength and skill – and he'd hurt him, badly. As blood poured down his face, a shocked realization came over the Vamp. Suddenly aware that he was fighting for his life, his eyes changed and his fangs extended. "I'm gonna kill you, boy!"

Launching himself off the back of the van with one arm, the Vamp swung with the other. Andre dodged, but the Predator's fist clipped his lip – nothing serious, he knew, but the tiny trickle of human blood would probably send the freak into a frenzy.

Stopping the follow-on blow by catching the Vamp's fist in his right palm, Andre reached out with his left hand, grabbed his shoulder, and pushed down as he turned. The Vamp howled as his arm popped out of its socket. Holding the screaming Vamp's fist in his hand, Andre pushed forward with his right arm, and down with his left as he made a half-pivot.

The Mist & the Darkness

Still holding the freak's disconnected arm, he grabbed him by the hair with his other hand and pushed him forward towards Elspeth. Then stopping five feet in front of her, he forced the Vamp, still howling with pain, down on his knees and demanded he apologize.

Turning his head over his shoulder, the Vamp hissed a curse through his fangs. After chuckling, Andre twisted his arm farther back. "Apologize, moron!"

With sweat pouring down his forehead and mingling with his blood, and his battered face contorted by pain, the Vamp screamed *"All right, stop - STOP!"* Andre stopped twisting his arm as the freak apologized to Elspeth.

"Not good enough, fool!" As Andre forced the freak's head forward and jerked hard on the disjointed arm, the Vamp arched his back and screamed in agony, before sniveling. *"I'm sorry, Ma'am...*

"I sorry...

"Tell him to stop, please – PLEASE!"

Still holding the Predator in a death grip, Andre looked up at Elspeth. The hand clamped tight over her mouth to mask her fangs partially hid her face, but her eyes betrayed her. They'd morphed into the reddish, cat-like eyes of a frightened Vampire – or one on the verge of attack.

Remembering the tiny trickle of blood at the corner of his mouth, Andre jerked his head at Elspeth's VW Bug and told her to go.

Desperate to escape the horror, Elspeth bent over and snatched her keys up off the ground. Still holding her hand over her mouth, she got the door open and jumped inside. Lowering her head down against the steering wheel so Andre wouldn't see her face or her fangs, she started the car and jammed it into reverse. Then after backing out onto the lane behind her, she threw the Bug into gear and floored it.

CHAPTER 54

With his car carefully hidden in northern Vermont's one and only speed trap, Officer Thornton of the Sanctuary Cove PD watched as Elspeth McGuire's bright pink VW Bug flew past. After checking his radar gun to see if she'd broken the 100 mile per hour mark, he shrugged before stuffing the last of his jelly doughnut in his mouth. Then after swallowing it, he reached for his coffee.
Freaking Vampires...
After taking a swig from the paper cup, he fumbled in his shirt pocket for his cigarettes. He was in the process of lighting one when Andre roared past in his Vette. So after inhaling deeply, he leaned back in his seat and shook his head.
That Marchand kid's playing with fire...

CHAPTER 55

Mrs. McGuire had just lifted the last of the groceries out of the back of her car when she heard the whine of Elspeth's engine from the Lake Road. *Good God*, she thought. *Please tell me she's not drag racing...*
Mrs. McGuire was still standing there in the circular drive when Elspeth came hurtling up the lane. Astonished to see her youngest daughter take the curve of the circular driveway at full throttle, she knew something was desperately wrong. The screech of her brakes and the scent of burning rubber confirmed her fears as the car slid sideways to a stop.
As Elspeth jumped out of her vehicle and ran for the open door, Andre roared up the lane in his Vette. Taking the turn onto the drive a bit more carefully, he came to a stop just behind Elspeth's Bug.

The Mist & the Darkness

Desperately confused – and frightened for her daughter – Mrs. McGuire was struggling to keep her eyes from changing and her fangs from extending as Andre clambered out of his car. "Andre, what's happened???"

Andre approached her calmly, and apologized. "I'm sorry, Mrs. McGuire, but an older man accosted Elspeth at the mall today, and I was forced to intervene."

Dropping the bag of groceries she'd been holding, Elizabeth McGuire gasped. *"Accosted???*

"Oh dear God – was she hurt???"

Andre shook his head. "No, Ma'am – she wasn't harmed."

"But you said you had to intervene? Was there a fight?"

Andre chuckled. "None to speak of, Ma'am. I just had to teach the fool some manners, that's all."

After letting out a deep sigh of relief, Mrs. McGuire suddenly noticed the cut at the edge of Andre's mouth, and the trickle of dried blood that had stained his collar. "Andre, you weren't hurt, were you?"

After dealing with the freak at the Mall, Andre had used the half-empty bottle of water he'd had in his car to wash off his lip and his bloodied fists, and to wipe down the tiny splatter on his collar. But apparently that wasn't enough, because Mrs. McGuire had either seen a spot he missed or smelled the lingering scent. Suddenly concerned that she might succumb to temptation, Andre tried to look nonchalant. "Just a little cut," he said. "It's nothing."

Fighting hard to keep her fangs from extending, Mrs. McGuire reached out with a trembling hand to examine his slightly swollen lip. "Andre, my husband's out back in his lab – please let him take a look at this!"

Andre smiled and shook his head dismissively. "I'll have Uncle Philippe take a look when I get home – but Elspeth's pretty shaken up, and she needs you."

Elizabeth McGuire nodded emphatically, and after Andre promised he'd have his uncle look at his lip again, she made a dash for the door. With her hand cupped over her mouth, she turned as she reached the aperture and called out her thanks before darting inside.

Impressed by Mrs. McGuire's self-control, Andre shrugged before walking back to his car. After retrieving the bags Elspeth had abandoned at the mall – and taking an appreciative glance at the elegant white lace protruding from the Victoria's Secret tote – he placed them by the McGuires' front door with the groceries Mrs. McGuire had dropped, and headed for home.

As he pulled away, a self-congratulatory grin crept across his face. *Slayed the dragon, saved the Princess, did a bit of perving...*

Not bad for a Sunday afternoon.

CHAPTER 56

When Dr. McGuire heard Elspeth's sobs from his laboratory, he'd bolted for the house at a dead run. After racing through the kitchen and the living room, he'd vaulted the banister in the foyer and raced up the stairs after his wife. "Elizabeth, what's happened?"

Stopping just short of the second floor landing, Mrs. McGuire turned to her husband and spoke in a low, Vampiric whisper. "Andre said an older man was harassing Elle at the mall today, and he'd had to intervene..."

"I think there was a fight."

Dr. McGuire winced. "Oh, damn!" he said. "Was Elspeth hurt?"

Mrs. McGuire shook her head. "I don't think so."

After breathing a sigh of relief, Dr. McGuire asked about Andre.

Mrs. McGuire raised a finger to her lips, and whispered again. "He had a cut lip when I saw him, and it had been bleeding a little – but from what he said, I think he gave the other guy a real beating."

Suddenly alarmed, Dr. McGuire asked if the police had been involved. Mrs. McGuire said she didn't think so, and gestured for her husband. "Come on, Neill – Elle needs us."

After rounding the top of the banister, they walked side by side down the hall to their daughter's room. The door was open; she was lying face down on the bed, sobbing hysterically.

The Mist & the Darkness

After Elspeth failed to respond to a gentle knock on her door, Mrs. McGuire tiptoed in and sat down on the side of the bed. "Elle?" she said softly.

Sitting up suddenly, Elspeth threw her arms around her adopted mother and pressed her head against her shoulder. She was still sobbing uncontrollably as Elizabeth pulled her tight. Long minutes passed before she had calmed enough for Mrs. McGuire to speak. "Andre said someone accosted you at the mall."

Hearing his name, Elspeth began wailing again. Nodding, she tried to tell her mother what had happened between sobs. "A Predator...

"He followed me across the parking lot, and whispered all these disgusting things about what he wanted to do to me..."

Alarmed, Mrs. McGuire looked over her shoulder at her husband, who was still standing in the doorway. After sharing a look of consternation, Mrs. McGuire turned back to Elle and asked what happened.

"He followed me to my car, and he was going to hurt me...

"And then Andre came out of nowhere and told the creep to go away, but he wouldn't and they started fighting."

Mrs. McGuire gasped, and closed her eyes. Then after a long, frightened moment, she asked Elle if Andre had been bitten. Elspeth shook her head and began crying again. "No," she sobbed. "After the Vamp swung at him, Andre got all Mediaeval and beat him senseless...

"And then he dragged him over and made him apologize...

"But I was scared to death and there was blood all over everywhere, and I couldn't control myself – and then Andre saw my face..."

Burying her head in her mother's shoulder, she continued to wail. *"And now he's going to hate me..."*

As she stroked Elle's head, Mrs. McGuire looked back at her husband. Fear and sorrow and unimaginable pain were written across her face.

Realizing the time had come for him to get involved, Dr. McGuire crossed the overly large bedroom and knelt down beside his daughter's bed. "I know you must have been terrified, Elle...

"But are you sure he saw you?"

Still crying, Elspeth wailed. "I think so...

"Because after Andre beat up the Predator, he dragged him over and made him kneel down and apologize – and then he looked up at me...

"I had my hand over my mouth, but he must have seen my eyes..."

Mrs. McGuire shook her head, and told Elspeth not to be so sure. "He may have seen your eyes," she said softly. "And maybe he knows – but I promise, he doesn't hate you...

"He followed you home, to make sure you got here safely – and he was worried about you, Elle. He wouldn't have done that if he didn't care about you..."

At that point, a still worried Dr. McGuire intervened. "This may sound off the subject, Elle, but it's important: did Andre kill the Predator?"

Elspeth whispered she didn't know. "After he made him apologize, Andre told me to go – so I did what he said, and drove away as fast as I could."

Dr. McGuire nodded. "So we don't know if Andre killed him or not."

Still crying softly, Elle shook her head and whimpered. "No."

Then after waiting for a minute, Dr. McGuire continued. "So if he didn't kill the Vampire and see him turn to dust, then it's possible he still doesn't know about our kind..."

Elspeth shook her head. "I don't see how – the Vamp's eyes changed and his fangs came out, and he told Andre he was going to rip his throat out or something."

Dr. McGuire nodded. "You'd think Andre would have picked up on that," he said softly. "But adrenalin has a powerful and often overwhelming effect on both the mind and the body – so even if he saw the Predator's eyes and fangs, he may not have made the connection."

Then after another pause, Dr. McGuire reached out to stroke his daughter's hair. "But what really matters is that Andre risked his life to protect you, and that he followed you home to make sure you got here safely..."

Then after a long pause, he looked up at his wife. "We should call Andre, and thank him for that."

CHAPTER 57

Downstairs in his study, Dr. McGuire lifted the handset from the telephone on his desk, and punched in Dr. Marchand's home number. Andre picked it up on the fourth ring.

"Marchand residence," he said in a crisp voice. "Andre Marchand speaking."

After forcing a smile, Dr. McGuire identified himself, and explained why he was calling. "My wife and I would like to thank you for protecting our daughter, Andre – that was very brave and very good of you, and we can't begin to tell you how grateful we are."

Listening in from a few feet away, Mrs. McGuire smiled as Andre tried to shrug it off as "No big deal." Although her husband had the handset pressed to his ear, she could hear him clearly.

"The guy was a creep, and I was happy to help out."

More relaxed now, Dr. McGuire smiled broadly and told him how much they both appreciated it. "And I know Elspeth is grateful as well." Then changing the subject slightly, he asked if Andre had an idea what had led "the creep," as Andre had called him, to harass their daughter.

Andre been expecting that, and had already worked out a cover story. "Well, Sir, I think he must have been strung out on drugs because his skin was pasty white, and his gums had receded way back in his mouth – so far back that it almost looked like he had fangs – and his eyes had this sort of animalistic look about them...

"So I pulled out one of Philippe's medical books on drug addiction, and it described those symptoms as indicative of methamphetamine abuse."

Now both relieved and hopeful, Dr. McGuire nodded gravely. "I've treated a few meth addicts over the years, and I think you're probably right about that."

Thinking he'd foxed the Good Doctor big time, Andre grinned into the phone and congratulated himself for having weaseled his way out of yet another tight spot. If Dr. McGuire bought that particular load of bull, he had it made...

Changing the subject again, Dr. McGuire explained that his wife had told him that Andre's lip had been cut in the fight, and asked if Dr. Marchand had looked at it yet. "Yes, Sir, he did. He told me to duck next time, and charged me 50 bucks for a house call."

Dr. McGuire chuckled at the joke, and Mrs. McGuire giggled. After waiting until she stopped, Dr. McGuire thanked Andre again, and told him if there was anything he or his wife could ever do for him, to just let them know.

Seizing upon the unexpected opportunity, Andre said, "Well, actually, Sir, there is something...

"I know you don't usually permit your kids to date, but I was hoping you'd make an exception and let me take Elspeth to the Christmas Formal."

Realizing that he'd just been ambushed, Dr. McGuire grimaced before silently swearing and looking over at wife – who was nodding emphatically and mouthing the word *"YES!"* So after frowning at his wife and shooting her an irritated look, Dr. McGuire decided a graceful surrender was preferable to spending a month sleeping on the couch. Thinking fast, he offered Andre a compromise. "I'll tell you what – if you're willing to go as a group, Mrs. McGuire and I will spring for a stretch limo."

Thinking that worked for him, Andre quickly agreed. Then in response to his wife's frantic gesturing, Dr. McGuire told Andre to hold on – his wife wanted to say something.

So after taking the phone from her husband, a beaming Mrs. McGuire dropped her voice to conspiratorial whisper and asked if Andre had invited Elspeth to the dance yet. Andre said no, but if it was OK he was going to ask her at school the next day. Smiling from ear to ear, an excited Mrs. McGuire assured him that Elspeth would be thrilled. Then after thanking him again, Mrs. McGuire said goodbye and hung up the phone.

By that time the rest of the McGuire brood had returned from the Sunday matinee in town, and that had apparently given Elspeth's spirits a lift. Because even though the house was heavily sound proofed, Dr. and Mrs. McGuire could faintly hear her as she recounted the Battle of the Mall.

The Mist & the Darkness

"So the creep swung at him, and Andre went all Chuck Norris...
"And punched him in the side a bunch of times – POW! POW! POW!
"And then he started doing all this Karate stuff, kicking him in the head with one foot and then the other – BANG! BANG!
"And then he hit the fool like, ten times, and turned his face into mush...
And then when the creep swung at him again, Andre caught his fist in mid-air, and yanked his arm right out of its socket...

Smiling, Mrs. McGuire looked over at her husband and smiled. "I think Elle's feeling a little better now."

CHAPTER 58

As Andre wheeled his Vette into the student parking lot the next morning, he was still chuckling over the con he put over on Dr. McGuire the night before. He'd not only danced out of a potentially compromising spot, but maneuvered Dr. McGuire into giving him permission to take Elspeth to the Christmas Formal.

After finding a place to park, Andre clambered out of the car before reaching back in to retrieve his backpack. Then he closed the door and locked it, before pulling himself erect and zipping up his parka. As he pulled the zipper into place just below his shoulders, he surveyed the parking lot. Since none of the McGuire cars were in evidence, he hoisted his bag over one shoulder and headed for the cafeteria for his usual pre-class coffee. The Cove was fogged in again, and so bitterly cold that morning that he was looking forward to a steaming brew.

He'd just started up the steps when he heard Nathan calling after him. Turning around, he could see the McGuire brothers trotting after him. He waited until they were within normal hearing range to greet them. "Hey, guys, what's up?"

Nathan was the first to reach him, and after coming to a halt on the stair next to Andre, he reached out with his left hand and clasped him on the shoulder. "I heard what happened at the Mall, and I want to thank you…"

"I know Elle can be a real pain in the butt sometimes – but she's special, and we really appreciate what you did." Then he stuck out his other hand to shake Andre's.

By that time Daniel had caught up, and thanked him as well.

Chuckling, Andre insisted it was no big deal. "The dude was so whacked out on drugs he couldn't see straight – let alone fight."

Daniel chuckled, and shrugged. "Well, he was bothering Elle – so thanks anyway."

Andre grinned, and told them again it was no biggie. Then he jerked his head at the school's entrance doors and suggested they join him for a Café au lait before they froze their butts off. As he turned to head back up the steps, he asked over his shoulder if it always got so cold in Vermont.

Nathan nodded, and warned him about February. "Vermont gets pretty cold, but The Cove is unreal...

"One of the science teachers said something about the unique geography – it generates the fog, and traps the arctic weather coming down from Canada between the lake and the hills."

Pushing through the doors, Andre thought winter in The Cove sounded almost as bad as the French Alps, where he'd done his cold weather training with the Legion. But rather than go into that, he muttered "Oh, joy!" instead.

For some strange reason the serving line wasn't open in the cafeteria, so the three of them trudged into the student lounge instead. After paying for his order of three cake doughnuts and an extra-large brew, he waited for the McGuires at the door. When they finally showed up, Andre suggested they find a table.

Daniel looked at Andre quizzically, and joked about Newton's social hierarchy. "Isn't it illegal to sit with us?"

After putting his stuff down on an empty table, Andre grinned. "Yeah, but it's only a misdemeanor, so don't worry about it." Then he sat down, popped the lid off his coffee, and attacked the first doughnut. He'd skipped breakfast, so he was hungry.

After Nathan sat down, he asked Andre about the fight. "Elle said you're some kind of karate expert."

Not wanting to expose the fact that he had a black belt, Andre shrugged. "I know a bit, but I usually go with *savate-chausson*..."

The Mist & the Darkness

Not familiar with the term, Daniel asked him what it meant. "Well," said Andre, as he leaned over the table, "It's a combination of two French martial arts that were updated in the 19th century as a sport...

"But I learned the old fashioned variety – an especially vicious form of street fighting."

Thinking that sounded like the hand-to-hand combat techniques he'd learned the hard way on the Frontier, Nathan nodded. "So they teach that these days?"

Andre nodded as he put his coffee down and reached for another doughnut. "The cleaned up version is considered a sport. It's taught in martial arts schools, and there are professional and semi-professional matches – especially in the Paris region and northern France." Having satisfied the McGuires' curiosity, he changed the subject and asked where the girls were.

Nathan grinned, and Daniel chuckled. "It seems Lydia suffered a fashion disaster dyeing her hair last night, so they're running a bit behind...

"Elle was helping her get the color right when we left, but they'll turn up eventually." Then he shrugged and gave Andre a knowing look. "You know how girls are about their hair."

The bell rang as Andre was washing down the last of his doughnuts. "Well, gentlemen…It's time to roll." The McGuires stood up with him, and after thanking Andre again for bailing out their Little Sis, the three headed for class.

English Lit was not only more boring than usual, it was also frustrating. By that time they'd made their way up to The Canterbury Tales, and the Middle English that Chaucer had written in was driving him nuts. According to Mrs. Morgan, Middle English was a transitional language that had arisen in Norman England and was, supposedly, mostly Old English – basically, a German dialect – modified first by the Great Vowel Shift and then slightly again by Norman French. That, apparently, accounted for the weirdness of English grammar – which he'd had to copy and memorize from his mother's speech, because it made absolutely no sense. He was wondering if it might also account for the general illogic of English-speakers in general, when the bell rang.

Charles S. Viar

Elspeth and Lydia weren't in history class the next hour. But what was really odd was the fact that Patti – the school's receptionist who had checked him in the first day of class – had come on the intercom, and summoned Daniel and Nathan to the office.

Since the girls hadn't shown up at all, and McGuire brothers had apparently vanished after second period, Andre swung by the school office after sixth period, and sweet-talked *Pah-ti*, as he called her, into spilling the beans. Patti wasn't sure exactly what had come down since the other girl who worked in the admin office had taken Mrs. McGuire's call, but it had something to do with a new addition on the McGuire residence, and Dr. and Mrs. McGuire wanted their kids to come home for some kind of architectural presentation.

Relieved that it wasn't anything serious – like suddenly blowing town – Andre dumped his books in his locker before heading down to the Maintenance Office to change into his "digging clothes." Given the weather, he was going to need the heavily insulated work suit.

Then after checking out the pickaxe and the entrenching tool provided by Headmaster Renfrowe, and two Coleman lanterns that belonged to the Maintenance Department, he headed out back to start digging.

Andre's four-by-eight hole was located beyond the football field, close to the small woods that wrapped around the school. So after reaching the edge and pulling back the orange plastic that covered it, he paused for a moment to admire his work. Knowing the Headmaster would make him do it all over again if he didn't get it right, he'd invested a great deal of effort making sure the corners were perfectly squared and the sides as close to smooth and vertical as possible. Satisfied, he positioned the two lanterns before hopping in the two-foot deep hole to start digging again.

He'd been breaking the ground with the pickaxe for almost half an hour when he noticed a shadowy figure approaching. Since most of the people in The Cove who hung out by the woods weren't actually people, Andre buried the pickaxe in the ground and casually picked up the e-tool. Then after unscrewing the collar that restrained the blade, he extended it and fixed it in place. The e-tool was a savage weapon when properly employed, and Andre knew how to use it.

After tensing, he turned slightly to see a diminutive figure advancing through the darkness. It was Elspeth.

She was wearing fleece-lined boots, which protruded from beneath her dark, three-quarter length down coat, and she had the fur-lined hood pulled up over her head. Due to the absence of frosty breath, he surmised that she was trying to build up her internal body heat by not breathing. Knowing that was a potentially fatal mistake for a Vampire in winter, Andre was thinking she needed to work on her cover – but rather than blow the game by telling her, Andre greeted her with a smile instead. "So what brings you out here?"

Elspeth stopped close to the edge, and held out her hands. She held a thermos in one, and an insulated bag in the other. "I thought you might want some company," she said. Then she set her stuff down, and hopped in the hole. After marching over to him, she wrapped her arms around Andre's neck and laid a kiss on him – which turned out to be a lot more passionate than she'd intended. "And to thank you for protecting me yesterday," she added, in a husky whisper.

Then after pulling Andre tight, she kissed him again, quickly, before pulling away. "I brought a thermos of hot chocolate and a bag of chocolate fudge brownies with nuts – they're straight from the oven, and I think they're still hot!"

Then without another word, she pulled one of those silvery "space blankets" from her coat pocket, and unfolded it part-way before laying it out along the edge of the hole. After sitting down, she patted the ground beside her and asked Andre to join her.

Still savoring the kiss – which had been hot in more ways than one – Andre hesitated for just a moment as he wondered if that was why Elle had been raising her body temperature. Flattered by the possibility, Andre smiled and sat down beside her. "This is really thoughtful," he said, as she pulled two plastic cups from the bag and filled one for him.

Elle had heard him, but she'd become suddenly excited. "They're still hot!" she exclaimed, as she pulled out an overly large brownie wrapped in a paper towel. "Here," she said as she handed it to him. "Eat it before it gets cold!"

After accepting it from her mittened hand and taking a bite, Andre looked over at her incredulously. "Did you make these?"

A beaming Elspeth smiled and nodded. Bending the truth a bit, she said it was kind of a tradition for the McGuire women. "We like to bake," she said. "It's really fun!"

Thinking that had to be a first for Vampires, Andre took a sip of his hot chocolate before thanking Elle again. "This is delicious!" Then suddenly curious, he asked her where she'd been all day.

"Well," she said. "Remember when you rode over with Josephine?

"After you left, we talked Neill and Elizabeth into letting us get horses." Then smiling with anticipation, she explained that their architect had called just before they'd left for school that morning, and asked if he could bring by the plans for the barn Neill was going to build. "So anyway, Elizabeth wanted all of us to be there, to make sure we liked the design."

Andre nodded, and smiled into the darkness. Civilized Vampires have a thing for horses, because they were among the few animals that didn't seem to mind Vampires. They'd been domesticated by Central Asian nomads thousands of years ago, who'd been in the habit of nicking their horses with knives and drinking their blood on long journeys. As far as horses were concerned, it was six of one and a half-dozen of the other with humans and Vamps.

"That'll be great," Andre said. "Maybe we can go trail riding sometime."

Smiling excitedly, Elspeth nodded as she held out the insulated bag, and urged Andre to take another brownie. After pulling the chocolate treat from it, Andre asked Elspeth if she was going to have one.

As an embarrassed half-smile, half-frown passed across her face, Elspeth shook her head. "I better not," she said with feigned sorrow. "I gain ten pounds just looking at those things!"

Knowing that was ridiculous, Andre laughed out loud, but didn't say anything. Instead, he changed the subject again, and told Elspeth that her parents had called him the night before. She nodded, and said they'd told her.

After polishing off the second brownie, Andre asked her if they'd mentioned what they'd talked about. Suddenly quizzical, Elspeth put her hot chocolate down before tilting her head over.

The Mist & the Darkness

"Well," she said. "They wanted to thank you for helping me out – right?"

Andre grinned as he looked over. "That," he said. "And the Christmas Formal."

Confused, Elle crossed her eyes and tilted her head even farther. "The Christmas Formal?"

Andre nodded. "I asked them if it would be OK if I took you to the dance…"

"And they said yes."

Elspeth's eyes bulged and her jaw dropped. Then in an excited whisper, she said "Really?"

After Andre nodded, she clapped her hands together. *"Oh my God!"* she squealed. *"I've never been to a Christmas dance!"*

Then turning toward Andre, she reached out and grabbed his arm with both her hands. "What kind of dress should I wear?" she asked excitedly. Then suddenly aware that she'd queried the wrong person, she laughed and told him to never mind. "Dumb question, huh? Don't worry, I'll have Lydia make me something beautiful…"

Still holding onto his arm, Elspeth scooted closer, and laid her head on Andre's shoulder. "This is *sooooooooo* cool," she whispered.

After waiting a few moments, Andre freed his arm before wrapping it around Elle's shoulder and pulling her against him. Then as he stared off into the woods, he thought about the strangeness of it all…

So here I am sitting in the mist and the darkness, on the edge of a hole that bears an uncanny resemblance to a grave…

With my arm wrapped around a gorgeous, blood-sucking freak – who I just invited to the Christmas Formal…

Then after a moment's contemplation, he smacked his forehead with his free hand. *Way to go, Genius…*

Because aside from Uncle Philippe, there wasn't a man alive who could top that for weirdness…

Charles S. Viar

CHAPTER 59

The following Tuesday was December 8th – the day of their joint presentation for Dr. Marigold's history class. Elspeth and Lydia had spent the previous Sunday at Andre's place, doing the final fit of their costumes and rehearsing their presentations. But since the McGuire girls were still fine-tuning their talks, they'd asked to be excused from their first period classes – which explained why they were sitting in the cafeteria that morning, enjoying a cup of coffee while doing a last minute review of their material.

By the time they'd finished it was almost 9:30, which gave them less than a half hour to change into their Mediaeval costumes. Thinking it was time to get moving, Elspeth was in the process of raising her cup to finish off the last of the brew when she spotted Kathy Norse, sitting at a table across the room. Holding a banana covered with a purple condom between both hands held flat on the table, she was instructing one of the Junior Varsity Cheerleaders in oral sex.

"Oh, *my God!*" a shocked Elspeth exclaimed. "*That girl is disgusting!*"

After following her little sister's line of sight, Lydia raised her eyebrows, leaned back in her chair, and folded her arms across her chest. "You're right," she said slowly, after watching the Cheerleader's head bob up and down on the banana. "Her technique is *terrible!*"

Taken aback by her sister's remarks, Elspeth turned slowly in her chair and stared at her for a long, incredulous moment. "*Good God, Lydia!*" Elspeth sputtered. "*You're as bad as she is!*"

Then as if to distance herself from her sister's salacious observation, Elspeth jumped up and grabbed her dress bag and the gym bag she'd brought for her school clothes, and stomped off to the girls' room to change.

Lydia shrugged, and finished off her coffee. Then after another disdainful glance at Kathy Norse, she gathered up her gear.

The Mist & the Darkness

Amateur...

By the time Lydia caught up with Elspeth in the girls' room, her little sister was struggling with the shelf bra she was going to wear under her dress. She'd thought it made more sense than the bands of linen Mediaeval women had used to support their breasts, but as she struggled with the alien contraption she was beginning to wonder. After finally adjusting it to a point where it felt halfway comfortable, she pulled her dress on over her head.

In the meantime, Lydia had peeled off her top, bra and jeans, and was slipping into her dress. Surprised that Lydia hadn't brought a specialty bra like she had, Elspeth asked her what was up with that. After sniffing to make sure no one else was in the room with them, Lydia whispered. "Well, it's not like we really need the damn things..."

Then after smoothing her dress, Lydia had reached for her *barbette* – the funny, pillbox hats women wore during that era – and was about to tie it in place when Elspeth started swearing.

"Dammit, Lydia!"

"You cut my neckline too low!"

After glancing over to see her little sister trying to stuff her breasts back into her dress, Lydia shook her head and corrected her. "Nope – the low, square cut was the height of fashion for noble women in Provence during the mid-12th Century."

"Yeah, well maybe so," Elspeth retorted. "But if I trip, I'm gonna bounce right out of this thing..."

Lydia chortled as she folded her school clothes into the gym bag she'd brought. "Well, look on the bright side – you'll start another scandal!"

Elspeth rolled her eyes, took a deep breath, and exhaled slowly before glaring at her elder sister. "Well," she said. "Unlike *some* people I know – *I'm* not into showing off!"

Seeing the chance to nail her little sis big time, Lydia fired back. *"NEWS FLASH!!!"*

"You gave the football team a Half Monty at the dance, Girl – and to top it off, one of your little Nerd creeps caught the whole thing with his cell phone cam..."

284

Then she laid her head over, raised her eyebrows, and gave Elspeth a look of sarcastic disapproval. "So for *your* information, Little Miss Puritan..."

"That pic's all over school."

Elspeth winced, kicked her gym bag, and swore. Then after a long uncomfortable moment, she asked Lydia if she'd seen it.

Grinning from ear to ear, Lydia nodded. But then suddenly reminded of the time Big Al Capone had gotten drunk at the Showboat Lounge and demanded she strip while singing on stage, Lydia backed off.

Since saying no to Big Al was a sure-fire way to end up at the bottom of Lake Michigan, she'd done as he'd commanded. But even though the audience had loved the impromptu burlesque show, and Capone had given her a $1000 tip, it had bothered her for years. It wasn't that she minded showing off her wares – given her exhibitionist streak, that was all good fun. But the fact that Big Al hadn't given her a choice in the matter had irritated her to no end.

Thinking Elspeth was in a similar bind with the unsanctioned pic, Lydia became suddenly sympathetic and rushed to reassure her diminutive sister. "But it's a really good pic, Elle..."

"You look great!"

By now deeply chagrined, Elspeth consoled herself by thinking *that* had to count for something. But still, she was hoping Andre wouldn't see it – at least until she'd had a chance to make sure Lydia was telling the truth. Although far from happy that a picture of her breasts was floating around school, Elspeth figured she could live with a good one...

Suddenly hopeful that it was as good as the one the paparazzi snapped when they'd caught her making out with a certain A-List celebrity back in LA, she was about to press her big sister for details. But the bell rang, and Lydia told her to get a move on. "We've got to get set up."

Ignoring the teasing whistles and smatters of applause for their dresses as they strolled down the hall, they turned right into their second period class. After acknowledging an approving smile from Dr. Marigold, they glided over to the side of her desk and asked Andre if he was ready. Having just finished setting up the display for

285

The Mist & the Darkness

Lydia's sketches, Andre turned and nodded. Standing together, they waited as the class filed in.

When the bell rang, Andre glanced over to Dr. Marigold and asked in Mediaeval French if he could begin. Taken aback by his use of the archaic language – and impressed that he'd taken the time to research it – Dr. Marigold smiled and told him to begin.

Striding to the center of the room, Andre explained that their project was intended to present a slice of aristocratic life in the mid-12th Century, by dressing in a regional French garb and reviewing the society and customs that would have been familiar to Lord Montaigne, one of the most famous knights of Christendom.

Then as he strolled over to the opposite wall to pull down a large map of mediaeval Europe, he explained that Montaigne had been born into the feudal society of Europe around 1110 AD. "That society didn't arise by accident," he explained. The Germanic kingdoms that had replaced the Roman Empire had been prototypical democracies, in which every free man sat in local councils and served in the militia – most often, as an infantry soldier. "But all that changed with the Viking attack on Lindisfarne Abbey in 793, which marked the start of 255 years of continuous warfare between the continental Europeans and the Norse invaders."

Since the slow-moving infantry formations of the time were unable to cope with the lightning-fast raids staged by the Vikings, the Carolingian Empire founded by Charlemagne was forced to implement a series of military reforms that had profound social, political, and economic effects. One aspect of their new defense strategy – continued by its successor states after the Empire fragmented – was to fortify towns, ports, and other strategically important positions. But the single most important development was the deliberate decision to de-emphasize their traditional reliance on massed infantry in favor of smaller, rapid-reaction forces composed of heavily armored cavalry.

But in those days, horses and armor were phenomenally expensive – according to one expert, the four horses, armor and weapons required for service in the heavy cavalry cost the equivalent of a furnished, $300,000 home today. So to offset the cost, the best and bravest soldiers were given large land grants in exchange for lifetime, hereditary service as armored knights – and formerly freemen, who had previously made up the militia, were relegated to a support role, and eventually reduced to mere serfs.

Europe's mobilization took more than two and a half centuries to complete, but by the time the Viking raids petered off in the mid-11th Century, the countries of Europe had become the most militarized and heavily armed in the world. The Viking raids had been so devastating that of necessity, everything – and Andre stressed *everything* – had been geared to war.

Seeing that the class was still with him, Andre then called their attention to his dress. Although as a wealthy noble Lord Montaigne doubtless would have owned silk robes, he would have rarely worn them. Having started military training at the age of seven, he would have been far more comfortable in the woolen winter britches Andre was wearing, lined on the inside seam with leather to protect his legs while riding. Then lifting up his rough woolen jersey, to display a heavy linen shirt – and also, to point out how his linen underwear was tied to the outside of his trousers – he directed attention back to his hoodie and the heraldry embroidered on the front. Then he explained that every noble and every knight wore a distinctive herald, so they could be recognized in battle, and went on to explain the symbolism of Lord Montaigne's winged dragon with outstretched talons.

After the class had a chance to view the heraldry, Andre strolled back over to Lydia and Elspeth, pulled his hood over his head and picked up a *faux* chain mail shirt he'd obtained from a costume shop. After pulling that on, he reached down to pick up the sword belt he'd borrowed from his uncle, and the replica hard-rubber dagger beside it. As he buckled the belt to his waist, he explained that only knights, nobles, and a very few free-men-at-arms, were permitted to carry swords in the Middle Ages. Then after drawing the six foot wooden replica from the scabbard to show the class, he hefted the dagger before stuffing it inside his boot. "But everyone carried knives, from the King on down to the lowliest peasant girl, and they all knew how to use them."

Andre went on to explain that while Lord Montaigne would have been superbly well-educated in the castle schools established by Charlemagne, he was first and foremost a soldier. "He certainly would have been able to read and write in Mediaeval French and

The Mist & the Darkness

Latin, and he may well have been fluent in Greek as well. He would have been versed in poetry, literature, logic, mathematics, law, theology, rhetoric, music and dance – but all that was secondary to his fighting skills...

"You have to remember that as an aristocrat, he was born into lifetime military service. He was a warrior, first, last and always." Then after retrieving the shield he'd constructed from where it had lain, Andre demonstrated the basic sword fighting techniques Lord Montaigne would have been trained in.

Having finished, he nodded to Elspeth, and retreated into the background. Elspeth stepped forward and after drawing attention to her dress, she explained that Lydia would be discussing Mediaeval style after she provided an overview of the life of a typical aristocratic lady.

"Women in the Middle Ages worked hard," she said. "And that included the wives of powerful lords." If their husband's job was to manage their fief efficiently, to generate the wealth needed to pay for his war horses, weapons and armor, and the salaries, housing and upkeep of the hundred or so knights and the two or three hundred men-at-arms he was required by law to maintain, the wife's job was to manage their manor house and the fortified redoubt we now call castles. That was no easy feat, Elspeth explained, because with a rich and powerful noble such as Lord Montaigne, that meant managing a staff of at least 100 servants and probably twice that. The lady of the castle, so to speak, was responsible for the kitchens, which would feed 500 or more people twice each day; the laundry, cleaning, sanitation, and interior maintenance; the castle school, which educated her children and those of her husband's knights; and the infirmary which cared for the sick and the wounded. By way of comparison, the duties of Lord Montaigne's wife would have been similar to those of a modern CEO in charge of a mid-sized corporation.

Then Elspeth stepped back, and nodded to Lydia. After stepping forward, Lydia called attention to their dresses. "These are atypical of the times," she explained. "Fashion in Europe was basically functional, and had been for centuries. But in the mid- 12th Century, Provence was an exception – and at that time and place, one could observe for the first time styles that would emerge centuries later in the rest of Europe."

Holding out her skirt, Lydia explained that while the wife of a rich lord would certainly have had several fantastically expensive silk dresses, most of her clothing would be made from finely woven linen, in the summer, or equally high quality wool in the winter. Noting the floor-length hemline and the long, hanging sleeves, and the odd hat she was wearing, she went on to explain that warmth was a major factor in mediaeval dress. In those days a common cold could prove fatal, so men and women alike kept themselves covered, even inside.

The notable exception that had emerged in Provence was the neckline, which wouldn't be copied elsewhere for centuries. Tracing her index fingers along the embroidered edge, she explained that it was cut square and, even by modern standards, daringly low. But there was a reason for that, she said, and it wasn't just sex appeal.

In those days, families were of fundamental importance – and for a lord, a male heir was deemed an absolute necessity. If a lord died without a son, his lands, manor and castle would almost certainly be seized by a rival or – at best – revert to the king. For that reason, female fertility was highly valued.

But fertility is hard to ascertain even with modern science, and in the Middle Ages it was all but impossible. Then after cupping her breasts with her hands and lifting them higher for all to see, she continued. "But since according to the beliefs of the time, a female with prominent breasts was more likely to be fertile than one less endowed, the women of Provence had dropped their necklines to signify their ability and willingness to bear children."

Then after releasing her breasts, she smiled at the class and reminded the guys it wasn't about sex. "It was about fertility and family, Gentlemen – nothing else."

Then as a naughty grin crept across her face, she curtsied and gave the guys the show of a lifetime with an inordinately low bow. Elspeth may have passed her up at the dance – but in the McGuire clan, Lydia was the undisputed Mistress of Tease and she planned on keeping it that way.

Since her back had been to Dr. Marigold, the instructor hadn't seen Lydia's deliberately provocative display – but given her own exhibitionist tendencies, she probably wouldn't have cared one way or another. Thrilled by the superb presentation, Dr. Marigold had leapt to her feet clapping. *"Bravo!"* she exclaimed. *"Bravo!"*

After waiting for the equally enthusiastic guys to quiet down and retake their seats, she told the class that had been the finest presentation she'd seen in her three years at Newton. Then after turning to smile at Andre, Lydia and Elspeth, she told them they'd hit it out of the ball park. "That's an A-Plus for all three of you!"

Then moments before the bell rang, she dismissed the class.

CHAPTER 60

As she closed the glass doors of the family china cabinet, Elspeth turned to her mother. "OK, all the crystal's clean and up – what's next?"

After yelling toward the kitchen to remind Lydia it was almost 3:30 – more or less the time their guests were expected to arrive – Elizabeth McGuire asked Nathan about the fire. After pulling his head out of the cavernous south fireplace, he told her it was good to go. "I'm about to light it now."

After glancing around before turning back toward Elspeth, Mrs. McGuire sighed uncertainly. "Put the vacuum away, and I think that's about it." Then after telling her youngest daughter she was going to check on Lydia, she marched off toward the kitchen. Thinking the guys should do the heavy lifting, Elspeth jerked the vacuum up on its back wheels and dragged it toward the utility closet.

This "women's work" stuff is a crock…

Across the room, Nathan put a long match to the paper he'd shoved between the massive logs he and Daniel had stacked in the fireplace, before standing up and dusting off his hands. Then after pulling the protective, chainmail screen into place, he grinned and whispered to his little sister. "I think Elizabeth takes this hostess thing way too seriously."

Elspeth smiled back. "I know" she said. "But I really like it when the Castiles' visit."

Nathan nodded. Although far less enthusiastic about the McGuire family's closest friends than his parents and siblings, he was nonetheless moderately happy the Castile clan was stopping in on their way back to New York. If nothing else, it would provide a change of pace.

The illegitimate son of a Spanish Cardinal, Julio Ignazio Castile had been born in Rome in 1239 and, as a result of his father's connections, had been apprenticed to a prestigious Venetian accounting house at an early age. Fascinated by numbers, he'd excelled at bookkeeping, and had been well on his way to fame and fortune as the accountant-of-choice for the Venetian mercantile elite when he'd been waylaid on a dark street by a Feral Vampire. Although he'd survived the attack and made it through the subsequent infection, he'd been forced to flee the city for fear of the Holy Inquisition. But despite the Church's less than enthusiastic embrace of Vampires, he'd remained a devout Catholic. Unwilling to take innocent lives, he'd survived off the blood of animals – and the occasional brigand or highwayman who'd tried to rob him – as he wandered about Europe.

But his fascination with numbers never faded, and he eventually settled in Prague where he'd opened a discreet accounting practice. An unsurpassed genius when it came to hiding wealth from tax collectors, he amassed a small fortune before moving on. Over the centuries, he'd lived and prospered in almost every city of Europe, acquiring a wife, Danique, in Amsterdam, and eventually five teenaged children in the various places they'd moved. After landing in the New World in 1761, they'd settled more or less permanently in New York.

Neill had stumbled across him during the American Revolution. Julio – or Jake, as he now preferred to be called – had thrown in his lot with the Rebels. At the time, he was supporting the war effort by counterfeiting Bank of England Notes, and forging shipping invoices and bills of lading for the military contraband the Continentals were smuggling through the British-controlled port. In the process, he'd also managed to obtain desperately needed surgical equipment for Dr. McGuire as well.

The Mist & the Darkness

After the war, he'd become Neill's accountant and chief financial planner – and after the frontier had closed and Nathan had finally settled down, his eldest son's financial guru as well. *A decent guy,* Nathan thought. *But boring as hell...*

Intending to wash his hands off, Nathan had just turned toward the kitchen when he heard an overly large vehicle roar up the drive and screech to a halt out front. Then a moment later, frantic pounding on the front door, and hysterical screams from Danique. *"Neill! Elizabeth!*

"Help! Let us in, let us in!!!"

Alarmed, Nathan ran for the front entrance, with Elizabeth and his two sisters trailing not far behind. As he threw back the bolt that secured it and yanked open the door, he could hear Daniel pounding down the stairs behind him.

Surging past him, the Castile clan almost knocked him over as they screamed for him to bolt the door shut.

Seeing the terrified looks on their faces, Elizabeth McGuire froze in place. *"My God!"* she exclaimed. *"What's wrong?"*

Without even answering, Jake pushed past her to the living room. Inching along the wall to the window, he pulled the curtain back ever so gently. After peering through the glass, he turned to his wife and children and let out an uncertain whisper. "I think we lost him..."

By that time, the other six Castiles had pushed their way past the McGuires and formed a semi-circle in the living room. Frightened and alarmed by their strange behavior – and the ghastly looks upon their faces – Elizabeth had trailed along. Reaching out to put her hand on Danique's trembling shoulder, she softly asked her friend what had happened.

Turing toward Elizabeth with terrified eyes, Danique said it had been terrible. "We'd stopped at the South Overlook first, like you suggested, to take in the view and snap some pictures...

"And we were about to get back in the Winnebago when a Vampire burst out of the woods – and he was *terrified,* Elizabeth, running for his life and screaming...

"And then a moment later, this...

"This...*maniac* came racing out of the tree line, chasing him with a sword...

"Then the Vampire dove into the lake to escape, and the Hunter saw us standing there...

"And he paused for just a second – and then he *charged* us!!!"

As Mrs. McGuire gasped, Danique clutched at her arm and continued. "Elizabeth, I've never been so terrified in my whole life...

"He was dressed head to toe in one of those weird Japanese fighting suits, and he had this maniacal look in his eyes – Elizabeth, I *swear* he was going to *kill* us all!"

Dr. McGuire had heard the commotion from his laboratory out back, and as he raced into the room Jake glanced over at him from his post by the window and shook his head. "It was beyond belief, Neill – one Hunter, attacking *seven* Vampires???

"That Canuk is *insane!*"

At that point, Nathan interjected. "Canuck? How do you know he's Canadian?"

Look over at Nathan, Jake emphatically identified the Hunter as a Quebecer. "Because the lunatic took one look at us, and screamed '*La gloire!*'

"Then he raised his sword and let out this blood-curdling scream, and *charged* ..."

Shaking his head after glancing back through the window, Jake Castile told him they'd been lucky to escape with their lives. "We jumped in the Winnebago and took off, but not before the lunatic took out the rear window with his sword...

"And then he chased us down the road, jumping up and down and screaming at us in French to come back and fight!"

At that point, Lydia chortled. "Well," she said with a huge grin, "I see you met the new sheriff!"

Danique Castile turned to Lydia and gasped. "You *know* him?"

Lydia grinned again, and jerked her thumb at Elspeth. "Elle's boyfriend."

Although momentarily shocked as all eyes turned upon her, Elspeth recovered quickly. "He's *NOT* my boyfriend!"

Lydia rolled her eyes and gave her sister a dismissive look. "*Yeah?*" she retorted. "Then why's he taking you to the Christmas Formal???"

As Elspeth sputtered, Mrs. McGuire gave Lydia a withering look before turning to Mrs. Castile. "That's just speculation, Danique. We

The Mist & the Darkness

don't really know if Elle's friend is the Hunter or not – but I assure you, he's really a very nice young man..."

As Dr. McGuire seconded his wife in a voice of uncertain conviction, a shocked look of disbelief passed across Danique Castile's face. As her knees began to buckle, she threw her arms around Elizabeth McGuire and whimpered. "I need to sit down."

Thinking this was a good time to make herself scarce, Elspeth forced a smile on her face, bounced up on her toes and clapped her hands together. "You must be tired from all that driving today...

"Why don't I go make you all a nice hot cup of coffee?"

Then after a failed attempt to force an expectant smile, she scrunched up her face, covered her eyes with her fists, and fled for the kitchen.

After slamming the slatted doors shut behind her, Elspeth raced to the counter, jerked the carafe from its resting place on the coffee maker and began rinsing it out. Trying hard not to listen to the intense conversation in the living room, she filled the machine with water before pulling a can of coffee and a pack of filters from the right shelf. She'd just started loading the drip basket when Lydia sauntered through the doors. Grinning from ear to ear, she hopped up on the kitchen counter and sat there beside the sink until Elspeth started the machine. "So whatcha gonna do, Elle?"

Irritated beyond belief, Elspeth ignored the taunt as she pulled a large tray from the closet and began assembling saucers and cups. Having noticed that one of them had a tiny spot at the bottom, she was in the process of turning on the water when she caught a sudden flash out of the corner of her eye, from somewhere deep in the woods. Startled, she looked up as the shockwave from the explosion rattled the kitchen windows.

Then as the column of oily black smoke of immolated Vampires began rising from beyond the tree line, she closed her eyes and laid her face in her hands.

Oh dear God, she thought. *This is sooooooo embarrassing...*

CHAPTER 61

Needless to say, the unexpected explosion in the woods – and the stench of incinerated Vampires that drifted over the McGuire property – had persuaded the Castiles to cut short their visit. In an effort to salvage the situation, the McGuires had piled into their cars and escorted them up to the junction; if Andre *was* the Hunter, they reasoned, he'd let their convoy pass. But just in case he *wasn't* the mysterious Ninja, Nathan had climbed into Elspeth's Bug with his new M4 carbine, locked and loaded.

They'd seen the Castiles off at the Interstate, hoping that no lasting harm had been done to the relationship. But the incident had troubled Elspeth all that night, and by the time she turned into the student parking lot the next morning her anxious curiosity had overwhelmed her common sense. She was going to corner Andre, and demand to know if he was the Hunter.

That turned out to be easier decided than done, because halfway through first period the Headmaster had come over the intercom and announced that all gym classes had been cancelled for the day, before summoning Andre, the captains and co-captains of the varsity athletic teams, and the captain and the co-captain of the cheerleading squad to the assembly hall. Thinking that was weird, Elspeth spent the rest of the hour wondering what was up.

It got even weirder when Andre and the rest of the In Crowd leaders failed to show for lunch. Since no one seemed to know where they'd disappeared to, her curiosity had reached epic levels by the time she joined her minions at her Monday table. As Queen of the Outcast Alliance, she held court the first day of each week to resolve disputes, dispense advice to the lovelorn, and – gently – pass along advice on fashion, and tips on hair and makeup.

By the time sixth period French class rolled around, Elspeth was climbing the walls. The fact that Lydia had gone missing at lunchtime had only added to her irritation, especially when she turned up at the start of fifth period with the buttons of her blouse askew and a

The Mist & the Darkness

Cheshire Cat grin on her face. Thinking she and that mentally deficient football player she'd snuck off with should have enough sense to get a room rather than spend the lunch hour fooling around in the back of his van, Elspeth slammed her text shut and headed for her locker when the final bell rang. Still working off her sentence for the Homecoming scandal, she was going to dump her books before heading for the school library.

Thinking her confrontation with Andre was going to have to wait, she'd just finished putting her books away when the now familiar scent of French cigarettes assailed her. Slamming the door of the locker shut, she wheeled about. After thrusting her fists down at her side and glaring at Andre, she demanded to know where he'd been all day.

Resting his palm against the locker beside hers, Andre chortled with mock sarcasm. "Hey, Elle, nice to see you, too...

"And if you must know, the Board of Governors called a special meeting to discuss my proposal for a fencing program – which they unanimously approved, after hearing my brilliant presentation...

"So you, Ms. McGuire, are looking at the captain of our newest varsity squad!"

Taken by surprise, it took Elle a minute to compute. *"Fencing?"* she asked incredulously. *"Captain?"*

"Yes, Ma'am," Andre said with mischievously exaggerated pride. "I'm now the official captain of the Newton Blades!"

Blades, Swords, Knights, Ninjas...

Uh oh...

As the string of associations ran through her mind, Elspeth drew back against the row of metal lockers behind her before quickly glancing around. Thinking some of the other students were way too close for comfort, she grabbed Andre's free hand, and dragged him down the hall toward a more secluded spot. *"We have to talk!"*

Confused and suddenly concerned, Andre followed along until Elspeth was satisfied they were out of hearing range. "What's wrong?"

After glancing up and down the hall again, Elspeth turned and locked her eyes on his. "Andre," she said in a conspiratorial whisper, "Were you out in the woods yesterday?"

Having been caught completely off guard by that one, Andre suddenly realized the game was up – and if he didn't think fast, his meticulously planned Operation Seduction was going to crash and burn. So after forcing a look of fear and consternation upon his face, he slipped into the absurdly exaggerated French accent he used when he wanted to jerk Elspeth's chain. Forcing his eyes open and dropping his jaw, Andre denied it with all the melodrama he could muster. "*Oh, no, Mademoiselle – zee woods are dangerous!*"

"*Zey are feeled with zee lions and zee tigers and zee bears!*"

Then after raising his index finger to his lips, he looked around furtively before dropping his voice to a barely audible whisper. "*And zee Vham-piers...*"

As Elspeth's eyes bulged and her jaw dropped, Andre took another furtive look around and whispered again. "*But you must tell no one, Mademoiselle...*"

"*Eet eez zee see-cret!*"

Under any other circumstances, Elspeth would have been power-freaked. But Andre's denial had been so hilariously absurd that she broke up laughing instead. Throwing one hand against the wall for support, and pressing the other against her side to keep it from splitting, she tried to look up at him through teary eyed hysterics.

But she just couldn't pull it off – after catching Andre's ear-to-ear grin out of the corner of her eye, she lost it completely. Laughing uncontrollably, she turned into the row of lockers and began banging her fist against one.

Thoroughly pleased with himself for having danced out of yet *another* tight spot, Andre grinned as Elspeth accidentally bashed in the locker she'd been pounding on. Deciding to play the farce for all it was worth, he leaned over Elspeth's shoulder and grinned, before playfully threatening to call Buffy.

"Now get outta here, you little monster!"

Then after chuckling, he whacked her rear end with his notebook and sauntered down the hall.

CHAPTER 62

Aside from the Predators that liked to kill them for sport, having their identities uncovered by a human was a Civilized Vampire's worst nightmare. When that happened, as it did from time to time, some would kill to protect their secret; others would flee.

Andre's hallway antics had left no doubt in Elspeth's mind that he'd somehow discovered that she and her family were Vampires, but his theater of the absurd had gone a long way toward reassuring her. He'd obviously been out in the woods hunting Vampires the day before – but it was equally obvious that he wasn't going to expose them.

So rather than hit the panic button, she'd reported to the Library instead. But as she pushed the cart of books she'd been ordered to re-shelve into the forest of six foot high shelves, she whipsawed back and forth – desperately trying to not to laugh at his absurdity one moment, and crazed by curiosity the next.

How did he find out??? And when???
And what about Stephanie – the girl he brought to Homecoming? Did he know she was a Vampire, too???
Did she tell him about us??? Or did he already know???
What about that creep at the Mall??? Did Andre know what he was???
And he was just teasing with that "little monster" thing – right???

Thinking that better have been a joke, Elspeth was determined to find Andre as soon as she finished her assigned tasks. Lucky for her – and her sanity – re-shelving the books took less than half an hour. So after informing Mrs. Flint, the librarian, that she'd finished, Elspeth headed back upstairs to her locker to retrieve her long winter coat. Having foolishly believed the weather forecast, she'd worn a mini-skirt rather than jeans that day. Almost warm when she'd started out for school, the temperature had dropped a good 30 degrees during the ten minute drive to Newton.

But it had changed again by the time she pushed through the rear doors of the cafeteria, and as she made her way down the steps it seemed almost warm again. So after reaching the bottom, she'd stopped for a moment to unbutton the top two or three buttons of her coat, before starting across the frozen ground toward Andre's excavation project. But after taking only a few steps into the gloomy darkness, she could see he wasn't there. Being a Vampire has its advantages, after all, and the ability to see in the dark is a definite plus.

After halting in mid-stride, Elspeth paused for a moment as she wondered about his absence. Disappointed – and not quite sure what to do next – she turned around to retrace her steps. She had Andre's cell phone and residential numbers from their History project, but interrogating him over the phone didn't seem like a good idea. Given his uncanny ability to wiggle out of tight spots, that was something she was going to have to do face-to-face.

He makes the Artful Dodger look lame...

After she transited the Cafeteria and pushed her way through the Foyer's exit doors, she was trying to work up the nerve to swing by his house as she trod down the front steps of the school. Most of the female students at Newton wouldn't have given it a second thought, but Elspeth had grown up in the South during the 1950's – and turning up at a boy's home unannounced was something no self-respecting girl would have dreamt of.

Trying hard to convince herself that the times had changed as she picked her way across the still-icy student parking lot, she didn't notice Andre lounging against her car until she reached a clear patch of pavement. As a huge smile spread across her face, she lifted up the hem of her coat and scurried across the ten feet or so that separated them. Then throwing propriety to the wind, she grabbed the lapels of his half-open parka before bouncing up on her toes to kiss him.

Chuckling at the shocked look that had swept across his face, she playfully shoved him back against the door of her car. "OK, Mr. Funny Man – *start* talking!"

His wits momentarily scattered by both the kiss and her unexpected strength, Andre looked down at Elspeth as one surprise mingled with the other. "Talk? About what?"

Mistaking genuine confusion for yet another dodge, Elspeth forced her lips together in an unsuccessful effort to look stern. Having failed at that, she looked up and informed him in the most imperious tone she could muster that he knew what she meant.

"*Oh!*" said Andre, after a making the connection. "You mean that Vampire thing?"

But before Elspeth could say, "Yeah – that Vampire thing!" Andre had slipped back into his farcical mode and feigned a look of abject terror. "*But Mademoiselle – we must not speak of eet!*"

Then after an exaggerated, furtive look first to the left then to the right, he raised his index finger to his lips and warned her, "*Eet eez zee see-cret!*"

Even more ridiculous than before, Andre's facial expression made Elspeth to crack up again. Holding onto the lapels of his parka for support, she buried her head in his shoulder and laughed uncontrollably. But after a minute or so, she managed to pull herself together. Looking up again, she demanded to know how long he'd known.

Andre grinned, and shrugged evasively. Then after a frustrating pause, he looked down at her with a triumphant smile. "I tagged you guys the first day of school…"

Incredulous, Elspeth looked up in shocked disbelief. "*The first day???*"

After Andre nodded, she looked down at the pavement and shook her head in amazement, before looking back up again. "But how?" she demanded to know. "We *really* try to fit in!"

Andre shrugged again, and gave her a playful grin. "Well, let's just say I've been around the block once or twice…"

After chortling at the suggestive boast, Elspeth looked at him suspiciously. "It was Stephanie, right – she told you about our kind?"

After wrapping his arms around Elspeth's waist, Andre shook his head. "Nope – the Unc clued me in."

Surprised, Elspeth leaned back and looked up at Andre. "Really?" she asked. "So how did he find out?"

Throwing his head back, Andre laughed. "The hard way – an overpriced hooker bit him during the Crusades."

Elspeth's eyes bulged, and her jaw dropped. "Your uncle's a Vampire???"

Andre nodded. "For the past 900-years or so."

"From the Crusades? Good Lord – how *old* is he?" But before Andre could answer, Elspeth giggled. "Turned by a hooker? Now that's *got* to be embarrassing!"

Andre laughed, and said that's the story his Uncle liked to tell when he was joking around. "But he was actually saved by a Civilized Vamp after being mortally wounded in battle..."

"He was escorting a caravan north from Jerusalem to Antioch when they were attacked by a huge force of Saracens – so after ordering the civilians to make a run for it, he fell back on a narrow pass and fought a rear-guard action to cover their escape...

"Long story short, he held them off for almost an entire day, but he and his knights were eventually overwhelmed – and he ended up taking a lance just before sunset. But a one-time Roman Legionnaire had been watching the battle from a cave above the pass, and admired his skill and his courage...

"So after the Saracens withdrew, the Vamp came down to give Uncle Philippe a decent burial – but since Philippe was still barely alive, he turned him instead."

Elspeth knitted her eyebrows together, looked down for a moment and nodded thoughtfully. Then after making a connection of her own, she suddenly looked up again. "All those swords, and shields and armor, and the books and the flags..."

Andre nodded. "Yeah – mementos from a life, long passed..."

Then after a long pause, she asked about Lord Montaigne.

Andre nodded again. "His best friend – they fell together, but Lord Montaigne died before the Vamp reached them..."

After a subdued pause, Elspeth finally looked up. "But how is this possible? When I met your uncle he smelled human, his hands were warm, and he had a heartbeat...

"And then there was that wreck up at the Junction – he must have spent at least an hour out in the sun, helping all those kids who'd been hurt..."

Andre grinned, and shook his head back and forth. "Philippe's a sly one, Elle – he's got more tricks than Houdini!"

After trying hard to suppress teasing a grin, Elspeth chortled. "So *that's* where you get it from!"

CHAPTER 63

Forty-five minutes later, Elspeth roared up the lane to her house. Taking the circular drive a bit too fast, she screeched to a halt in front of the main entrance. After turning off the ignition and hopping out, she slammed the door shut. Then after forcing her hands down at her side and doing a little Snoopy Dance, she raced around the car and yanked the passenger door open.

After pulling out the case of wine and the two big boxes Andre had given her, she skipped up to the front door. Then after pushing it open and leaning her head inside, she stuck her index fingers in her mouth and let out an ear-splitting whistle. Raising her voice unnecessarily, she called for Nathan and Daniel. "I need a couple of strong backs and weak minds down here!" And then as an afterthought she yelled, *"Chop, chop!"* for emphasis.

It took a minute, but the two came bounding down the stairs in response to her summons. Puzzled, they asked her what was up. So after grinning, she pointed at the boxes stacked by her car and told them it was their turn to do the heavy lifting. Then almost as an afterthought, she asked if their father was out back in his lab.

Shaking his head, Nathan informed her that he was in his study reading some medical journals. So after yelling through the still open doorway, "Family meeting in Dad's office!" she led her brothers outside. "I'll get the smaller box on top – you guys bring the rest into Neill's office…"

After the guys hoisted their assigned loads, a euphoric Elspeth led them through the foyer, then right through the TV room and back to their father's office. Pushing open the half-closed door, she marched in and set her box down on the side of Neill's desk. Surprised by his daughter's unusual behavior, Dr. McGuire looked up quizzically as Daniel and Nathan filed in, followed first by Lydia and then by his rather confused wife. "What's all this?" her father asked.

Grinning from ear to ear as she pulled off her coat, Elspeth informed her dad that they were "Gifts from that big faker, Dr. Marchand."

Taken aback by her characterization of the French physician, and far from pleased, Dr. McGuire hastily corrected his daughter. "Dr. Marchand is a respected colleague, Elspeth – so I would appreciate it if you would refer to him as such…"

Having tossed her coat over one of her father's leather-bound chairs, Elspeth grinned again. "Well," she said in a voice so sweet that it bordered on sarcasm, "Your *respected colleague* – formerly known as His Grace, the Duke of Gascony – is *also* a 900-hundred-and-some-odd-year-old Knight Templar!"

Then grinning even more, Elspeth continued. "Who, by the way, is a Vampire – just like us!"

Stunned, it took Dr. McGuire a moment to recover. "Elspeth," he finally said. "I don't know where you got that idea, but I can assure you that Dr. Marchand is human…

"He looks human, he smells human, his hands are warm to the touch, he has a normal heartbeat and reflection…

"He's completely indifferent to human blood and he has no problems with sunlight…"

"Right!" said Elspeth. Then she held up her left hand and began ticking off her father's objections by pointing with her right index finger. "First, he looks human – well, so do we…

"Second, he smells human." Pointing to the top box, Elspeth explained "That's because of the body wash and shampoo he uses – it's specially scented to make him smell like a normal person…"

"Third, his hands are warm – well, his whole body's that way because he's figured out a drug that raises his skin temperature…

"Samples of which are in the same box as the body wash and shampoo, by the way…

"And fourth, he has a human heartbeat – that's because he implanted some sort of gizmo in his chest that thumps like a normal heart…

Then starting over with her fingers, Elspeth continued. "Fifth, he has a reflection – well, so do we when we make the effort…"

"Sixth, he's indifferent to human blood – *News Flash!* – so are you…

The Mist & the Darkness

"And according to Andre, that synthetic blood of his – in the bottom box – really takes the edge off...

"Start drinking that stuff, and the rest of us will stop reacting to human blood, too...

Then Elspeth paused, momentarily confused. "Where was I?"

Suddenly remembering, she said "Oh, right – sunlight!"

"Well, Dr. Marchand had been fighting in the Holy Land for six or seven years when he was infected, so he'd developed a high tolerance for sunlight to start with...

"And that body wash of his comes with a nice little side benefit, as well – Andre said if we use that stuff for five or ten years, we'll be able to go sunbathing at the beach!"

Less certain, but still unconvinced, Neill McGuire rose out of his chair and pried open the box Nathan had carried in. Then after retrieving the papers that had been clipped together and lain on top of the contents it held, he scanned Dr. Marchand's handwritten note before turning the page to study the molecular structure of the capsules that filled a large, brown tinted bottle, and then the data describing the composition of the body wash and the shampoo. Looking up at Elspeth as he lay the papers back down on the box, he shook his head. *"Son-of-a-bitch,"* he said softly. "Marchand should get a Nobel Prize for this..."

Then he started around his desk to examine the box that held his synthetic blood.

Grinning from ear to ear back by the door, Lydia elbowed Daniel before holding out the palm of her hand. "Told ya, Sucker!"

After frowning and muttering an incoherent curse, Daniel reached into his back pocket and pulled out his wallet. Then as Lydia chuckled, he began counting out the hundred dollars he'd bet against her claim that Dr. Marchand was a Vamp.

After shooting a darkly suspicious look in their direction, Elizabeth McGuire interjected. "But what about Andre, Elle? Is he a Vampire, too?"

Elspeth's smile was radiant. "Well, sort of," she said excitedly. "He'd been out bar hopping with a fake ID before they moved here, and three Predators jumped him in an alley on the way home..."

Then she giggled. "And he said one of the 'sissies' bit him before he dusted the lot – so he told his uncle what happened when he got home, and Dr. Marchand pumped him full of antiviral meds...

"So that arrested the infection and Andre says his uncle thinks he can stall the change until he's 30 or maybe even 35."

Chuckling wickedly, Lydia looked over at Daniel and held out the palm of her hand again. "Pay up, Fool!"

After glaring at his gloating sibling, Daniel refused. "No way!" he said in a dismissive voice. "He hasn't turned yet."

Lydia rolled her eyes before giving him a nasty look. "But he's *gonna,*" she huffed. "So that's worth *half?*" Then she pointed at her open palm, and demanded to see some more green. "That'll be 50 bucks, Mister!"

Realizing they'd been sandbagged by Daniel and Lydia, Mrs. McGuire and Elspeth turned to look at one another, before giving the two a look of outraged disbelief.

"You knew???" Elspeth sputtered.

Ignoring his fuming sister, Nathan chortled at Daniel. "You lose, Bro."

So after giving his older brother a disgusted look, Daniel reached for his wallet again. Muttering yet another curse, he counted out two twenties and a ten and slapped them in Lydia's outstretched hand. "Just wait till Superbowl," he growled.

While all that was going on, Dr. McGuire had been completely engrossed in the technical details Dr. Marchand had included with the four gallons of synthetic blood. Sensing the perfect time to ambush her father, Elspeth turned to her mother. "So all things considered – I can go out with Andre, right???"

After throwing her arms around her, Elizabeth McGuire hugged her. Then without waiting for her husband's input, she smiled and said, *"YES!"* in an emphatic voice.

Being nobody's fool, Dr. McGuire knew defeat when he saw it. So rather than object to his wife's preemptory approval, he closed his eyes and shook his head in silence. Then suddenly remembering the premonition that had seized him so many months before, he realized that this was all, somehow, a part of God's Grand Design.

But why the Almighty had seen fit to inject Andre Marchand into his previously stable and happy existence was a complete mystery.

Why me, Lord? Why me...

CHAPTER 64

Sitting on the floor in front of the family Christmas tree, Elspeth pulled her legs up and wrapped her arms around her knees as she reflected on the past week. The Christmas Dance had been wonderful beyond description – and it wasn't just the fact that she'd *finally* had a real date. It was Andre's easy acceptance – he knew who she was, and what she was, and he liked her anyway...

And the fact that Newton's Aristocracy had stopped being mean to her was an unexpected bonus. After Homecoming, they had, however reluctantly, come to the inescapable conclusion that she and Andre were an item – and since there was no way they were going to make fun of a Varsity Captain's girlfriend, the hurtful whispers about "Weird Elspeth" faded into the past. They'd even started saying "Hi" to her in the hallways, and some of the girls had actually talked to her at the Christmas Formal. And with the exception of Kathy Norse and Janice What's-Her-Face, they'd seemed sincere.

That had made her feel good, too – but the icing on the cake was the beautiful dress Lydia had sewn for her. *It was almost like Cinderella*, she thought. Because true or not, the gorgeous, full length velvet gown had made her feel like the Belle of the Ball...

And Andre, of course, had been the most handsome of men.

Still smiling at the reverie, she turned to look over her shoulder at Daniel, who was stoking the flames in the fireplace. "This is going to be a great Christmas," she whispered.

Glancing over, Daniel grinned, and nodded in agreement. "The best we've had in years."

Then he smiled wickedly, before continuing. "And with any luck, Nathan and I are going to finish off Merciless Ming tomorrow and conquer our cyber galaxy!"

Elspeth chortled. "You mean that 12-year old girl in China who's been kicking your butts in that online game?"

Daniel grinned, a bit sheepishly. "Hey, she's tough!"

Then to change the subject, he asked Elspeth when Andre was coming by. She'd given him his Christmas present at school just before the holiday break – a gorgeous, chocolate brown ski sweater with leather elbow patches – but the gift he'd ordered for her had become snarled in the Christmas rush. UPS hadn't delivered it to his house until late that afternoon, so he'd called to see if he could drop it by around 9:00 that evening. Excited, she glanced down at her watch. "Any minute now!"

Suddenly drawn to a distant sound, Daniel cocked his head over to listen more carefully. "That's not Andre's Vette…

"Busses???"

Unable to imagine why busses would be pulling up on the Lake Road, he pulled the chainmail screen shut across the fireplace and stood up, before striding over to the front door. After pulling it open and stepping outside, he paused for a moment before whirling around and slamming the door shut. *"Bug out time!"* he shouted. *"There's a mob with torches coming up the lane!"*

Shocked – and now stricken with fear – Elspeth hesitated for just a moment. Then she jumped up and followed Daniel in a mad dash for the rear closet, where the McGuires kept their escape gear. After jerking the door open, her brother pulled out Lydia's pack and extra cold weather parka and tossed them in the general direction of the pounding feet behind him, then tossed Elspeth hers. Then after grabbing his own, he stepped back to allow Nathan to grab his gear, and his M4 carbine and a bandolier with extra magazines. Stepping out of the way as he slammed a magazine into his rifle and cycled the action, Nathan told the rest of the family to get it in gear. "Come on, people – we've practiced this a thousand times."

By then his parents and siblings had their jackets on, and their Alice-packs up on their shoulders and strapped – but with the exception of Neill, they were frightened and fumbling. Reminded of raw recruits on the battle line, he began barking orders to focus their attention. "All right people, we're going with Plan A…

"Neill, you take the lead and I'll cover the rear…

"Out the back, keep low and quiet and don't bunch up…

"We'll split into our pre-assigned teams at the edge of the woods, and rendezvous at the Lake House as planned…

"Details are in your packs, including Plan B if this goes bad."

The Mist & the Darkness

Then after shoving Lydia toward the door, he ordered everyone to move. *"Go! Go! Go!"*

After his family raced out the door and into the darkness, he jogged along behind them, but more slowly. If the humans had guns, his plan was to draw their fire and keep them busy while the rest escaped. After they'd made the tree line, he'd slip away, too. It wasn't the first time he'd covered a withdrawal under fire – and he didn't think it would be the last.

His family had almost reached the woods when they heard a trumpet blast, and then the sound of hundreds of voices raised to song:

> *Oh come, all ye faithful*
> *Joyful and triumphant*
> *Oh come ye, oh come ye*
> *To Beth-eth-lehem…*

Careening to a halt, Elizabeth McGuire turned to her shocked husband. "That's not a mob, Neill – they're carolers!"

"We have to greet them!"

Then after turning to Elspeth, she asked how much hot chocolate they had on hand.

After looking at her mother as if she was crazy, Elspeth told her, "Not even close, Elizabeth! There must be hundreds of 'em – and besides, we don't have time!" Then she turned and began running back to the house with Lydia and Daniel.

Nathan, who'd reversed direction and was now in the lead, ordered them to drop their gear in the kitchen, grab their regular coats, and get out front as fast as possible. "Act surprised, act pleased – and for God's sake, *ACT NORMAL!*"

Thinking the surprised part just wasn't going to be a problem, Elspeth followed Lydia through the back door and tossed her pack behind the prep island in the kitchen before struggling out of her parka. Then the two of them raced for the coat tree by the front door and donned their regular coats. After brushing her tousled hair back with her hands, Lydia opened the door and stepped out on the front porch. As her eyes bulged, she whispered. *"Holy shit!"*

Thinking that expletive didn't even begin to cover it, Elspeth's jaw dropped as hundreds of carolers marched into view, four abreast and carrying large candles. Out front was a young girl, dressed in choir robes, and holding aloft a cross. Following behind her was a swarthy priest, a gold crucifix dangling from his neck, with Dr. Marchand and Andre a step behind on either side.

Wincing in pain after looking at the cross, Elspeth swore under her breath and looked away. From behind, her father put his hand on her shoulder and whispered. "Just don't look straight at it, Elle – you'll be fine."

Turning to his father, Daniel told him to forget the damn cross. "Check out the priest!"

After turning to look at the cleric, Neill's jaw dropped, his wife gasped, and Lydia swore under her breath. "No way in hell," she said.

Nodding to no one in particular, Nathan slipped into his native drawl and whispered his agreement. "I've fought two wars, crossed a continent alone on foot, been to three world fairs and more rodeos than I can remember – but this here takes the cake..."

Struck mute, Elspeth watched in disbelief as the priest and the Marchands stopped on the circle in front of them, while the cross bearer led the hundreds of carolers around the circular drive to the other side. Still singing as they formed up on the distant asphalt, the choir was almost deafening.

By now they'd finished singing *Oh Come, All ye Faithful!* and had begun *Hark the Herald Angels Sing*. Supported by trumpets and drums, it was magnificent. Staring across the way into the sea of candles, tears welled in Elspeth's eyes. *This is wonderful*, she thought in amazement. *But how can it be?*

As the choir came to the end of the song, the priest took one step forward and threw his arms toward the heavens. *"REJOICE!"* he cried in heavily accented English. *"REJOICE!"*

And then after lowering his voice ever so slightly, he continued. "For on this night, shepherds were abiding in the field, watching their flock, when suddenly the Angel of the Lord appeared unto them...

"And the glory of the Lord shone round them, and they were afraid..."

The Mist & the Darkness

Then as a huge smile spread across his face, the priest continued. "But the Angel said to them, Fear not: for, behold, I bring you good tidings of great joy, which shall be to all people...

"For unto you is born this day in the city of David a *Savior*, which is Christ the Lord...

"And this shall be a sign unto you; you shall find the babe wrapped in swaddling clothes, lying in a manger."

Still beaming, the priest continued in an excited voice. "And do you know what? The shepherds went to Bethlehem, the City of David, and they found the baby Jesus, the Christ, just as the Angel had foretold, given to us by God for our salvation!"

Then after a dramatic pause, the priest said, "Isn't it wonderful?"

Then without waiting for them to reply, he strode forward, stopping just before the McGuires. And then in a whisper, he said he would tell them a story. "You see I know this to be true, because I met our Lord, so many years ago..."

Then as his eyes danced, he smiled and looked into each of the McGuires' faces one by one. "Today I am a priest, but in those times I was Quintinius Severus, military tribune to the Tenth Legion – and as it happened, my commander had sent me to Jerusalem with a report for the governor, Pontius Pilate...

"As I arrived, the Lord was brought before him for interrogation. And since Pilate spoke only a little Greek and no Aramaic at all, he ordered me to translate. I was so impressed by this humble man, who claimed to be the Son of God, that I took food and wine and salves to His cell after Pilate had condemned Him, and washed and bound the wounds the soldiers had inflicted upon Him...

"And he told me of many wonders, and foretold to me all that would happen and all that has happened, in the times that would come...

"And then as the sun rose, and I had to leave Him, He told me that a terrible misfortune would soon befall me – but he promised that if I kept faith, and believed in Him, I too would inherit the Kingdom of God!"

Then the priest grinned, and arched his eyebrows. "Can you imagine? A miserable sinner like me – in the Heavenly Kingdom???

"As the young people would say, that's 'over the top' – no ?

"But he promised me, and gave me many signs, and all have come to pass…"

Then after another dramatic pause, Father Severus' face lit up again as he looked from one McGuire to another. "And do you know what else?

"He has promised me yet another sign tonight, so that you may take heart and know that you, too, are loved by our Father in Heaven." Then after pointing up over his shoulder, the priest continued. "You see?"

The McGuires looked up, and for a moment saw nothing. Then they gasped as a cross of soft light formed slowly in the distant sky. "That is just for us – the humans can't see it, you know…

"It is a gift, a proof of God's love and His promise of salvation…"

Then he chuckled. "Lucky for us, the Lord has very low standards!"

Before the McGuires could respond, Father Severus leaned forward again, and said he would bless them. "You are Catholic, no?"

Dr. McGuire acknowledged that he'd been raised in the Church, but the rest of his family were Protestant. Still smiling, Severus laughed softly and winked at him. "We can't all be perfect, you know – and if our Lord can love a sinner like me, I'm sure he can find a bit of love for the Protestants, too!"

Then he bowed his head as he clasped his hands together, and prayed in Latin, switching to English only to mention their names. "For Neill, physician and healer. For Elizabeth, artist, bringer of beauty. For Nathan, soldier and protector. For Lydia, whose voice uplifts our spirits. For Elspeth, the writer, whose heart overflows with love. For Daniel, athlete, child of the sea…"

Then after he'd finished the prayer, Father Severus stepped back, and held up his crucifix. "You see? It stings only a bit now, to remind us of our unnatural resurrection." Then he smiled and laughed again, and assured them that God's love surpassed all understanding.

"Now let us celebrate the birth of our Lord with song," he said, before turning around and raising his arms to the choir.

CHAPTER 65

Still stunned, Elspeth watched in silence as Father Severus returned to his place on the circular drive. But it wasn't until she saw Andre trying to suppress a grin that her senses began to return.

By that time, the choir was singing *The First Noel*. Standing beside her, Lydia was singing along softly as tears rolled down her cheeks. Wiping away her own tears, Elspeth caught Andre's eye and silently mouthed *"Thank you..."*

After smiling an acknowledgement, Andre winked before unzipping his field jacket a bit, to show her he was wearing the sweater she'd given him. Then he reached in a pocket, and pulled a small, gift-wrapped box out just enough so that she could see it. Excited again, Elspeth was wondering what it was when the choir began singing *What Child is This?*

One by one, they worked their way through all of Elspeth's favorite carols until they suddenly fell silent after *The Little Drummer Boy*. Then suddenly, the trumpets blared and the drums began pounding out *Joy to the World* to a fast reggae beat, as a half-dozen girls dressed as Angels raced across the snow toward them, stopping just short of the drive to turn cartwheels before breaking into a joyous, contemporary dance. Following just behind was a slightly older girl with a fiddle, playing it as she danced and leapt to the music.

Following the lead of the heavyset girl in the center, the Angels danced up and down to the beat with almost professional precision. Standing just behind Lydia with his eyes fixed on the plus-sized Angel in the center, Nathan chuckled and whispered. *"Shake it, Momma!"*

Lydia chortled, Elspeth grinned and Daniel whispered back. *"I didn't think a fat girl could dance like that!"* Irritated by his gratuitous remark, Elspeth glared over her shoulder before slamming her elbow into his solar plexus. *"She's not fat – she's got big bones!"*

After straightening up and inhaling to force some air into his lungs, Daniel whispered back. "Do that again, and yours are gonna get broken!" Cut short by her mother's disapproving glare, Elspeth huffed rather than return fire. She was thinking she'd even up with him later when the dancers suddenly raced together, formed a circle, and began tossing one of the smaller girls towards the heavens, first once, then twice, and then a third time. Amazed, Elspeth's jaw dropped. *"Wow!"*

Then as the song came to an end, the Angels raced back to the choir on the other side of the circle, turning cartwheels and leaping into the air as they went. So even though it was probably a bit out of place, the performance had been so incredible that the McGuires clapped in appreciation.

As a soft silence descended, Elspeth was thinking there was no way they could top that one when Dr. Marchand stepped forward and began singing *Silent Night* in a language only vaguely familiar. His voice was deep, and rich.

Turning to Neill, Nathan asked in a whisper what language it was. "*Mittledeutsch*, I think – the German dialect it was first written in." Then after completing the third verse, Dr. Marchand stepped back and Andre stepped forward and sang the carol in his native tongue. His voice wasn't as deep as his uncle's, but it was as rich and melodic, and *Silent Night* was unbelievably beautiful in French. Then after he'd completed the third verse, the choir sang softly, in English. When they finished, someone far off in the distance rang a bell, slowly, three times.

By that time, tears were pouring down the faces of Elizabeth, Elspeth, and Lydia, and even the McGuire men had become misty-eyed. Stepping forward, Andre strode across the short distance of the drive, and handed Elle her Christmas gift. "Merry Christmas, Elspeth."

By now crying so hard she could barely talk, Elspeth threw her arms around him and thanked him for everything. After hugging her, Andre kissed her on the top of her head and whispered. "Everyone's invited – pool party, my house, New Year's Eve." Then he stepped back, smiled graciously, and wished the McGuires a Merry Christmas before turning to rejoin his uncle and the priest. Stepping forward once again, Father Severus lowered his head and recited a brief

313

The Mist & the Darkness

prayer, before throwing up his arms and bellowing, *"MERRY CHRISTMAS TO ALL!"*

At that point, the entire choir echoed him. Then they turned, burst into *Jingle Bells* and raced down the lane to their busses. Standing huddled together on their porch, the McGuires waved and yelled back, thanking them for their wonderful performance and wishing them all a Merry Christmas as well.

Then after Andre, Dr. Marchand and Father Severus had hugged them or shaken their hands, the McGuires stood on their porch and watched until the three disappeared into the darkness.

Smiling from ear-to-ear and still holding the little gift-wrapped box Andre had given her, Elspeth bounced up on her toes. *"Best Christmas EVER!"* she exclaimed.

EPILOGUE:
THE SECOND SEMESTER

Still playing with the Majorica pearl necklace Andre had given her Christmas Eve, Elspeth worked her way down the corridor toward the Assembly Hall. They were the creamy, rose-colored variety, perfect for her complexion.

But on this first day of the second semester, the beautiful necklace and matching earrings weren't the only things on her mind. She was enjoying the attention being lavished upon her – and not just by the Geeks and the Nerds. The Aristocrats were fawning on her, as well...

She'd been a big hit with the Jocks and Cheerleaders at Andre's New Year's Eve pool party. Lydia was taller than she was, and a bit curvier, but Elspeth's figure bordered on perfection – and the tiny little bikini she'd worn under the Plexiglas dome had set tongues wagging and lips drooling. Making a great night even better, Lydia had snuck off with her mentally deficient football player again, leaving her as the center of attention...

Elspeth was still reveling in the memory when she heard a low wolf-whistle from behind her. After discreetly sniffing the air for the scent of French cigarettes, she chortled as she turned around. "See something you like, Cowboy?"

Grinning, Andre corrected her. "That's *Legionnaire*, Darlin...

"And yes, as a matter of fact, I did." Then after telling her he'd enjoy the view even more if she was wearing four inch stilettos, he put his arm around her shoulders as they walked along, and asked what was up with the assembly.

After first chuckling and telling Andre that Hell would freeze over before she'd put on four-inch heels, Elspeth answered his question. "Well, Winston DePew – you know, the guy who owns Infinity Entertainment? – he built Newton, and when he's not in rehab he's head of the school's Board of Governors...

"Anyway, he's going to give a speech or something."

Thinking that had to beat his new second period class, Andre shrugged as they pushed through the double doors into the dimly lit Auditorium. Nathan and Daniel were already there, in the second to the last row, and they'd saved seats for them. Curious that Lydia was nowhere in sight, Elspeth asked about her as she sat down next to Nathan. Jerking his head toward the far corner of the last row across the aisle, he said she was back in the shadows, making out with the Incredible Hulk.

Exasperated, Elspeth shook her head. "I don't get it. She's got an IQ of 160, and he's dumb as a post – so what's she see in that oversized moron?" Then after Nathan gave her his "Village Idiot" look, Elspeth slapped her fingers over her mouth and flushed. *"Oh!"* she said in response to a sudden insight.

At that point, the lights flickered to signal the start of the assembly, and Headmaster Renfrowe got up from his chair and strode over to the podium in the center of the elevated stage. After adjusting the height and volume of the attached microphone, he welcomed one and all back from Christmas break, before launching into an abbreviated history of The Cove's redevelopment by the esteemed Chairman of Newton Preparatory Academy's Board of Governors – who had generously taken time out of his busy schedule to address the student body. "So please give a warm welcome to our Founder, Mr. Winston DePew!"

After a moment or two of desultory applause from the bored students, Winston stepped up to the podium, and began speaking.

The Mist & the Darkness

The usual stuff about the critical importance of a quality education and the ever-increasing need for the scientific and engineering leadership that Newton's graduates would one day provide.

Just about the time most of the students and staff were about to nod off, Winston came to a sudden halt. After picking up the sheaf of papers in front of him, he pitched them off to the side. "This is all BS!" he said.

Then after leaning over the podium, he pointed a finger at the audience, and said he was going to tell it like it really was. "When I was a kid growing up here in The Cove, I was fat and I wore glasses and I had a stammer – and everyone picked on me!

"So I developed a burning ambition: one day, I promised myself, I'd become rich and famous and powerful, and I'd make 'em all pay!"

Then after pausing for dramatic effect, he continued. "And I did – after I made my first billion, I went after the bastards who'd made my life miserable, and I got 'em back – including that tramp of an ex-wife, who was screwing every Tom, Dick and Harry that came along...

"But now I have a new ambition – I'm going to be the greatest *CRIMINAL MASTERMIND* the world has ever known, the *GREATEST VILLAIN* in human history...

"And you know what?

"*I CAN DO IT, BECAUSE I'VE BEEN TRANSFORMED...*

"*I'M A VAMPIRE NOW, AND I CAN DO ANYTHING I WANT!!!*"

Then he ripped his shirt open and starting banging on his chest, yelling like Tarzan. After finishing with that particular weirdness, he extended his fangs and held up his fingers like claws, before leaping off the stage and running out the side doors, screaming incoherently about his plan for Global Domination.

Chaos...

Complete, absolute chaos...

As pandemonium broke out, Andre slumped in his chair and swore in disbelief. "*Son-of-a-bitch!*" he whispered. "*More freaking Vampires...*

After whipping around in her seat and glaring at him, Elspeth slammed her elbow into his side. Gasping, Andre doubled over and clutched his ribs before looking up at her and grunting. "Present company excepted..."

"*Better be!*" she huffed.

By that time, a shocked Dr. Renfrowe had recovered enough of his wit to dismiss the assembly, and order the students back to class. Still holding his side as he pushed himself up from his seat, Andre saw Lydia's head pop up from wherever it had been. After taking a quizzical look around, she shrugged, pulled her coat over her head, and disappeared again.

After giving Al Thompson a sly grin and a discreet thumbs-up, Andre feigned injury to divert Elle's attention. "I think you broke my ribs," he said as he hobbled into the aisle.

Elspeth pursed her lips together, and shook her head as she brushed past him. "Nope," she whispered. "I would have heard 'em crack if I had."

Thinking that was probably true, Andre shrugged and followed her through the auditorium's double doors and out into the hallway. Suddenly thoughtful as the crowd of bemused students began spreading out in the corridor, he asked Elspeth if she'd read *Twilight.*

Nodding, she asked what had brought that to mind. "DePew's idiot act?"

"No, I was just hoping you could see the future like that Alice chick."

"Nope, sorry." Elspeth said. "No superpowers here."

Andre shrugged, before wrapping his arm around her shoulders. "Too bad," he said. "Because I was wondering if there's any lovin' in my future."

After chortling, Elspeth looked up with a teasing smile. "Well, maybe," she said in a sultry voice.

"If you play your cards right..."

Charles S. Viar

ABOUT THE AUTHOR

Charles S. Viar is Chairman of the Center for Intelligence Studies in Washington, DC.

Just Before Midnight: A Tale of Love, Romance, Treachery and Treason was Mr. Viar's first work of fiction; *The Mist and the Darkness* is his second. Both are available on Amazon.com.

A third, presently untitled book is in progress.

Readers are invited to e-mail their comments on *The Mist and the Darkness* to Mr. Viar at CFISPress@aol.com.

MUSICAL ACKNOWLEGEMENTS

Several popular songs provide backdrops for the story told in *The Mist and the Darkness*.

In order to comply with my best understanding of the "Fair Use" provision of U.S. copyright laws, no more than two lines from each have been quoted.

Charles S. Viar

Made in the USA
Charleston, SC
07 June 2015